ROALD DAHL

THE BFG · MATILDA
GEORGE'S MARVELLOUS MEDICINE

ROALD DAHL

THE BFG · MATILDA
GEORGE'S MARVELLOUS MEDICINE
Illustrated by Quentin Blake

WH SMITH
EXCLUSIVE
· BOOKS ·

This edition produced in 1992
exclusively for
W H Smith Limited
Greenbridge Road
Swindon
Wiltshire
SN3 3LD
by Jonathan Cape Ltd
an imprint of Random House UK Limited

ISBN 0-224-03715-3

Printed and bound in Great Britain by
Mackays of Chatham PLC, Chatham, Kent

Contents

Roald Dahl
THE BFG

Illustrated by Quentin Blake

For Olivia

20th April, 1955 – 17th November, 1962

Contents

THE CHARACTERS IN THIS STORY ARE:

HUMANS

THE QUEEN OF ENGLAND
MARY, the Queen's maid
MR TIBBS, the Palace butler
THE HEAD OF THE ARMY
THE HEAD OF THE AIR FORCE
And of course SOPHIE, *an orphan*

GIANTS

THE FLESHLUMPEATER
THE BONECRUNCHER
THE MANHUGGER
THE CHILDCHEWER
THE MEATDRIPPER
THE GIZZARDGULPER
THE MAIDMASHER
THE BLOODBOTTLER
THE BUTCHER BOY
And of course THE BFG

The Witching Hour

Sophie couldn't sleep.

A brilliant moonbeam was slanting through a gap in the curtains. It was shining right on to her pillow.

The other children in the dormitory had been asleep for hours.

Sophie closed her eyes and lay quite still. She tried very hard to doze off.

It was no good. The moonbeam was like a silver blade slicing through the room on to her face.

The house was absolutely silent. No voices came up from downstairs. There were no footsteps on the floor above either.

The window behind the curtain was wide open, but nobody was walking on the pavement outside. No cars went by on the street. Not the tiniest sound could be heard anywhere. Sophie had never known such a silence.

Perhaps, she told herself, this was what they called the witching hour.

The witching hour, somebody had once whispered to her, was a special moment in the middle of the night when every child and every grown-up was in a deep deep sleep, and all the dark things came out from hiding and had the world to themselves.

The moonbeam was brighter than ever on Sophie's pillow. She decided to get out of bed and close the gap in the curtains.

You got punished if you were caught out of bed after lights-out. Even if you said you had to go to the lavatory, that was not accepted as an excuse and they punished you just the same. But there was no one about now, Sophie was sure of that.

She reached out for her glasses that lay on the chair beside her bed. They had steel rims and very thick lenses, and she could hardly see a thing without them. She put them on, then she slipped out of bed and tip-toed over to the window.

When she reached the curtains, Sophie hesitated. She longed to duck underneath them and lean out of the window to see what the world looked like now that the witching hour was at hand.

She listened again. Everywhere it was deathly still.

The longing to look out became so strong she couldn't resist it. Quickly, she ducked under the curtains and leaned out of the window.

12

In the silvery moonlight, the village street she knew so well seemed completely different. The houses looked bent and crooked, like houses in a fairy tale. Everything was pale and ghostly and milky-white.

Across the road, she could see Mrs Rance's shop, where you bought buttons and wool and bits of elastic. It didn't look real. There was something dim and misty about that too.

Sophie allowed her eye to travel further and further down the street.

Suddenly she froze. *There was something coming up the street on the opposite side.*

It was something black . . .

Something tall and black . . .

Something very tall and very black and very thin.

Who?

It wasn't a human. It couldn't be. It was four times as tall as the tallest human. It was so tall its head was higher than the upstairs windows of the houses. Sophie opened her mouth to scream, but no sound came out. Her throat, like her whole body, was frozen with fright.

This was the witching hour all right.

The tall black figure was coming her way. It was keeping very close to the houses across the street, hiding in the shadowy places where there was no moonlight.

On and on it came, nearer and nearer. But it was moving in spurts. It would stop, then it would move on, then it would stop again.

But what on earth was it doing?

Ah-ha! Sophie could see now what it was up to. It was stopping in front of each house. It would stop and peer into the upstairs window of each house in the street. It actually had to bend down to peer into the upstairs windows. That's how tall it was.

It would stop and peer in. Then it would slide on to the next house and stop again, and peer in, and so on all along the street.

It was much closer now and Sophie could see it more clearly.

14

Looking at it carefully, she decided it *had* to be some kind of PERSON. Obviously it was not a human. But it was definitely a PERSON.

A GIANT PERSON, perhaps.

Sophie stared hard across the misty moonlit street. The Giant (if that was what he was) was wearing a long BLACK CLOAK.

In one hand he was holding what looked like a VERY LONG, THIN TRUMPET.

In the other hand, he held a LARGE SUITCASE.

The Giant had stopped now right in front of Mr and Mrs Goochey's house. The Goocheys had a greengrocers shop in the middle of the High Street, and the family lived above the shop. The two Goochey children slept in the upstairs front room, Sophie knew that.

The Giant was peering through the window into the room where Michael and Jane Goochey were sleeping. From across the street, Sophie watched and held her breath.

She saw the Giant step back a pace and put the suitcase down on the pavement. He bent over and opened the suitcase. He took something out of it. It looked like a glass jar, one of those square ones with a screw top. He unscrewed the top of the jar and poured what was in it into the end of the long trumpet thing.

Sophie watched, trembling.

She saw the Giant straighten up again and she saw him poke the trumpet in through the open upstairs window of the room where the Goochey children were sleeping. She saw the Giant take a

15

deep breath and *whoof*, he blew through the trumpet.

No noise came out, but it was obvious to Sophie that whatever had been in the jar had now been blown through the trumpet into the Goochey children's bedroom.

What could it be?

As the Giant withdrew the trumpet from the window and bent down to pick up the suitcase he happened to turn his head and glance across the street.

In the moonlight, Sophie caught a glimpse of an enormous long pale wrinkly face with the most enormous ears. The nose was as sharp as a knife, and above the nose there were two bright flashing eyes, and the eyes were staring straight at Sophie. There was a fierce and devilish look about them.

Sophie gave a yelp and pulled back from the window. She flew across the dormitory and jumped into her bed and hid under the blanket.

And there she crouched, still as a mouse, and tingling all over.

The Snatch

Under the blanket, Sophie waited.

After a minute or so, she lifted a corner of the blanket and peeped out.

For the second time that night her blood froze to ice and she wanted to scream, but no sound came out. There at the window, with the curtains pushed aside, was the enormous long pale wrinkly face of the Giant Person, staring in. The flashing black eyes were fixed on Sophie's bed.

The next moment, a huge hand with pale fingers came snaking in through the window. This was followed by an arm, an arm as thick as a tree-trunk, and the arm, the hand, the fingers were reaching out across the room toward Sophie's bed.

This time Sophie really did scream, but only for a second because very quickly the huge hand clamped down over her blanket and the scream was smothered by the bedclothes.

Sophie, crouching underneath the blanket, felt strong fingers grasping hold of her, and then she was lifted up from her bed, blanket and all, and whisked out of the window.

If you can think of anything more terrifying than that happening to you in the middle of the night, then let's hear about it.

The awful thing was that Sophie knew exactly what was going on although she couldn't see it happening. She knew that a Monster (or Giant) with an enormous long pale wrinkly face and dangerous eyes had plucked her from her bed in the middle of the witching hour and was now carrying her out through the window smothered in a blanket.

What actually happened next was this. When the Giant had got Sophie outside, he arranged the blanket so that he could grasp all the four corners of it at once in one of his huge hands, with Sophie imprisoned inside. In the other hand he seized the suitcase and the long trumpet thing and off he ran.

Sophie, by squirming around inside the blanket, managed to push the top of her head out through a little gap just below the Giant's hand. She stared around her.

She saw the village houses rushing by on both sides. The Giant was sprinting down the High

Street. He was running so fast his black cloak was streaming out behind him like the wings of a bird. Each stride he took was as long as a tennis court. Out of the village he ran, and soon they were racing across the moonlit fields. The hedges dividing the fields were no problem to the Giant. He simply strode over them. A wide river appeared in his path. He crossed it in one flying stride.

Sophie crouched in the blanket, peering out. She was being bumped against the Giant's leg like a sack of potatoes. Over the fields and hedges and rivers they went, and after a while a frightening thought came into Sophie's head. *The Giant is running fast,* she told herself, *because he is hungry and he wants to get home as quickly as possible, and then he'll have me for breakfast.*

The Cave

The Giant ran on and on. But now a curious change took place in his way of running. He seemed suddenly to go into a higher gear. Faster and faster he went and soon he was travelling at such a speed that the landscape became blurred. The wind stung Sophie's cheeks. It made her eyes water. It whipped her head back and whistled in her ears. She could no longer feel the Giant's feet touching the ground. She had a weird sensation they were flying. It was impossible to tell whether they were over land or sea. This Giant had some sort of magic in his legs. The wind rushing against Sophie's face became so strong that she had to duck down again into the blanket to prevent her head from being blown away.

Was it really possible that they were crossing oceans? It certainly felt that way to Sophie. She crouched in the blanket and listened to the howling of the wind. It went on for what seemed like hours.

Then all at once the wind stopped its howling. The pace began to slow down. Sophie could feel the Giant's feet pounding once again over the earth. She poked her head up out of the blanket to have a look. They were in a country of thick forests and rushing rivers. The Giant had definitely slowed down and was now running more normally, although normal was a silly word to use to describe a galloping giant. He leaped over a dozen rivers. He went rattling through a great forest, then down into a valley and up over a range of hills as bare as concrete, and soon he was galloping over a desolate wasteland that was not

quite of this earth. The ground was flat and pale yellow. Great lumps of blue rock were scattered around, and dead trees stood everywhere like skeletons. The moon had long since disappeared and now the dawn was breaking.

Sophie, still peering out from the blanket, saw suddenly ahead of her a great craggy mountain. The mountain was dark blue and all around it the sky was gushing and glistening with light. Bits of pale gold were flying among delicate frosty-white flakes of cloud, and over to one side the rim of the morning sun was coming up red as blood.

Right beneath the mountain, the Giant stopped. He was puffing mightily. His great chest was heaving in and out. He paused to catch his breath.

Directly in front of them, lying against the side of the mountain, Sophie could see a massive round stone. It was as big as a house. The Giant reached out and rolled the stone to one side as easily as if it had been a football, and now, where the stone had been, there appeared a vast black hole. The hole was so large the Giant didn't even have to duck his head as he went in. He strode into the black hole still carrying Sophie in one hand, the trumpet and the suitcase in the other.

As soon as he was inside, he stopped and turned and rolled the great stone back into place so that the entrance to his secret cave was completely hidden from outside.

Now that the entrance had been sealed up, there was not a glint of light inside the cave. All was black.

24

Sophie felt herself being lowered to the ground.
Then the Giant let go the blanket completely. His
footsteps moved away. Sophie sat there in the
dark, shivering with fear.

He is getting ready to eat me, she told herself.
He will probably eat me raw, just as I am.

Or perhaps he will boil me first.

Or he will have me fried. He will drop me like a

rasher of bacon into some gigantic frying-pan sizzling with fat.

A blaze of light suddenly lit up the whole place. Sophie blinked and stared.

She saw an enormous cavern with a high rocky roof.

The walls on either side were lined with shelves, and on the shelves there stood row upon row of glass jars. There were jars everywhere. They were piled up in the corners. They filled every nook and cranny of the cave.

In the middle of the floor there was a table twelve feet high and a chair to match.

The Giant took off his black cloak and hung it against the wall. Sophie saw that under the cloak he was wearing a sort of collarless shirt and a dirty old leather waistcoat that didn't seem to have any buttons. His trousers were faded green and were far too short in the legs. On his bare feet he was wearing a pair of ridiculous sandals that for some reason had holes cut along each side, with a large hole at the end where his toes stuck out. Sophie, crouching on the floor of the cave in her nightie, gazed back at him through thick steel-rimmed glasses. She was trembling like a leaf in the wind, and a finger of ice was running up and down the length of her spine.

"Ha!" shouted the Giant, walking forward and rubbing his hands together. "What has us got here?" His booming voice rolled around the walls of the cave like a burst of thunder.

The BFG

The Giant picked up the trembling Sophie with one hand and carried her across the cave and put her on the table.

Now he really is going to eat me, Sophie thought.

The Giant sat down and stared hard at Sophie. He had truly enormous ears. Each one was as big as the wheel of a truck and he seemed to be able to move them inwards and outwards from his head as he wished.

"I is hungry!" the Giant boomed. He grinned, showing massive square teeth. The teeth were very white and very square and they sat in his mouth like huge slices of white bread.

"P . . . please don't eat me," Sophie stammered.

The Giant let out a bellow of laughter. "Just because I is a giant, you think I is a man-gobbling cannybull!" he shouted. "You is about right! Giants is all cannybully and murderful! And they *does* gobble up human beans! We is in Giant Country now! Giants is everywhere around! Out there us has the famous Bonecrunching Giant! Bonecrunching Giant crunches up two wopsey whiffling human beans for supper every night! Noise is earbursting! Noise of crunching bones goes crackety-crack for miles around!"

"Owch!" Sophie said.

"Bonecrunching Giant only gobbles human beans from Turkey," the Giant said. "Every night Bonecruncher is galloping off to Turkey to gobble Turks."

Sophie's sense of patriotism was suddenly so bruised by this remark that she became quite angry. "Why Turks?" she blurted out. "What's wrong with the English?"

"Bonecrunching Giant says Turks is tasting oh ever so much juicier and more scrumdiddlyumptious! Bonecruncher says Turkish human beans has a glamourly flavour. He says Turks from Turkey is tasting of turkey."

"I suppose they would," Sophie said.

"Of course they would!" the Giant shouted. "Every human bean is diddly and different. Some is scrumdiddlyumptious and some is uckyslush. Greeks is all full of uckyslush. No giant is eating Greeks, ever."

"Why not?" Sophie asked.

"Greeks from Greece is all tasting greasy," the Giant said.

"I imagine that's possible too," Sophie said. She was wondering with a bit of a tremble what all this talk about eating people was leading up to. Whatever happened, she simply *must* play along with this peculiar giant and smile at his jokes.

But were they jokes? Perhaps the great brute was just working up an appetite by talking about food.

"As I am saying," the Giant went on, "all human beans is having different flavours. Human

beans from Panama is tasting very strong of hats."

"Why hats?" Sophie said.

"You is not very clever," the Giant said, moving his great ears in and out. "I thought all human beans is full of brains, but your head is emptier than a bundongle."

"Do you like vegetables?" Sophie asked, hoping to steer the conversation towards a slightly less dangerous kind of food.

"You is trying to change the subject," the Giant said sternly. "We is having an interesting babblement about the taste of the human bean. The human bean is not a vegetable."

"Oh, but the bean *is* a vegetable," Sophie said.

"Not the *human* bean," the Giant said. "The human bean has two legs and a vegetable has no legs at all."

Sophie didn't argue any more. The last thing she wanted to do was to make the Giant cross.

"The human bean," the Giant went on, "is coming in dillions of different flavours. For instance, human beans from Wales is tasting very whooshey of fish. There is something very fishy about Wales."

"You mean *whales*," Sophie said. "Wales is something quite different."

"Wales is whales," the Giant said. "Don't gobblefunk around with words. I will now give you another example. Human beans from Jersey has a most disgustable woolly tickle on the tongue," the Giant said. "Human beans from Jersey is tasting of cardigans."

30

"You mean jerseys," Sophie said.

"You are once again gobblefunking!" the Giant shouted. "Don't do it! This is a serious and snitching subject. May I continue?"

"Please do," Sophie said.

"Danes from Denmark is tasting ever so much of dogs," the Giant went on.

"Of course," Sophie said. "They taste of great danes."

"Wrong!" cried the Giant, slapping his thigh. "Danes from Denmark is tasting doggy because they is tasting of *labradors!*"

"Then what do the people of Labrador taste of?" Sophie asked.

"Danes," the Giant cried, triumphantly. "Great danes!"

"Aren't you getting a bit mixed up?" Sophie said.

"I is a very mixed up Giant," the Giant said. "But I does do my best. And I is not nearly as mixed up as the other giants. I know one who gallops all the way to Wellington for his supper."

"Wellington?" Sophie said. "Where is Wellington?"

"Your head is full of squashed flies," the Giant said. "Wellington is in New Zealand. The human beans in Wellington has an especially scrumdiddlyumptious taste, so says the Welly-eating Giant."

"What do the people of Wellington taste of?" Sophie asked.

"Boots," the Giant said.

"Of course," Sophie said. "I should have known."

Sophie decided that this conversation had now gone on long enough. If she was going to be eaten, she'd rather get it over and done with right away than be kept hanging around any more. "What sort of human beings do *you* eat?" she asked, trembling.

"*Me!*" shouted the Giant, his mighty voice

making the glass jars rattle on their shelves. "Me gobbling up human beans! This I never! The others, yes! All the others is gobbling them up every night, but not me! I is a freaky Giant! I is a nice and jumbly Giant! I is the only nice and jumbly Giant in Giant Country! I is THE BIG FRIENDLY GIANT! I is the BFG. What is *your* name?"

"My name is Sophie," Sophie said, hardly daring to believe the good news she had just heard.

The Giants

"But if you are so nice and friendly," Sophie said, "then why did you snatch me from my bed and run away with me?"

"Because you SAW me," the Big Friendly Giant answered. "If anyone is ever SEEING a giant, he or she must be taken away hipswitch."

"Why?" asked Sophie.

"Well, first of all," said the BFG, "human beans is not really *believing* in giants, is they? Human beans is not *thinking* we exist."

"I do," Sophie said.

"Ah, but that is only because you has SEEN me!" cried the BFG. "I cannot possibly allow *anyone*, even little girls, to be SEEING me and staying at home. The first thing you would be doing, you would be scuddling around yodelling the news that you were actually SEEING a giant, and then a great giant-hunt, a mighty giant look-see, would be starting up all over the world, with the human beans all rummaging for the great giant you saw and getting wildly excited. People would be coming rushing and bushing after me with goodness knows what and they would be catching me and locking me into a cage to be stared at. They would be putting me into the zoo or the bunkumhouse with all those squiggling hippodumplings and

34

crocadowndillies."

Sophie knew that what the Giant said was true. If any person ever reported actually having seen a giant haunting the streets of a town at night, there would most certainly be a terrific hullabaloo across the world.

"I will bet you," the BFG went on, "that *you* would have been splashing the news all over the wonky world, wouldn't you, if I hadn't wiggled you away?"

"I suppose I would," Sophie said.

"And that would never do," said the BFG.

"So what will happen to me now?" Sophie asked.

"If you do go back, you will be telling the world," said the BFG, "most likely on the telly-telly bunkum box and the radio squeaker. So you will just have to be staying here with me for the rest of your life."

"Oh no!" cried Sophie.

"Oh yes!" said the BFG. "But I am warning you not ever to go whiffling about out of this cave without I is with you or you will be coming to an ucky-mucky end! I is showing you now who is going to eat you up if they is ever catching even one tiny little glimp of you."

The Big Friendly Giant picked Sophie off the table and carried her to the cave entrance. He rolled the huge stone to one side and said, "Peep out over there, little girl, and tell me what you is seeing."

Sophie, sitting on the BFG's hand, peeped out of

the cave.

The sun was up now and shining fiery-hot over the great yellow wasteland with its blue rocks and dead trees.

"Is you seeing them?" the BFG asked.

Sophie, squinting through the glare of the sun, saw several tremendous tall figures moving among the rocks about five hundred yards away. Three or four others were sitting quite motionless on the rocks themselves.

"This is Giant Country," the BFG said. "Those is all giants, every one."

It was a brain-boggling sight. The giants were all naked except for a sort of short skirt around their waists, and their skins were burnt brown by the sun. But it was the sheer size of each one of them that boggled Sophie's brain most of all. They were

simply colossal, far taller and wider than the Big Friendly Giant upon whose hand she was now sitting. And oh how ugly they were! Many of them had large bellies. All of them had long arms and big feet. They were too far away for their faces to be seen clearly, and perhaps that was a good thing.

"What on earth are they doing?" Sophie asked.

"Nothing," said the BFG. "They is just moocheling and footcheling around and waiting for the night to come. Then they will all be galloping off to places where *people* is living to find their suppers."

"You mean to Turkey," Sophie said.

"Bonecrunching Giant will be galloping to Turkey, of course," said the BFG. "But the others will be whiffling off to all sorts of flungaway places like Wellington for the booty flavour and Panama for the hatty taste. Every giant is having his own favourite hunting ground."

"Do they ever go to England?" Sophie asked.

"Often," said the BFG. "They say the English is tasting ever so wonderfully of crodscollop."

"I'm not sure I quite know what that means," Sophie said.

"Meanings is not important," said the BFG. "I cannot be right all the time. Quite often I is left instead of right."

"And are all those beastly giants over there really going off again tonight to eat people?" Sophie asked.

"All of them is guzzling human beans every night," the BFG answered. "All of them excepting me. That is why you will be coming to an ucky-mucky end if any of them should ever be getting his gogglers upon you. You would be swalloped up like a piece of frumpkin pie, all in one dollop!"

"But eating people is horrible!" Sophie cried. "It's frightful! Why doesn't someone stop them?"

"And who please is going to be stopping them?" asked the BFG.

"Couldn't you?" said Sophie.

"Never in a pig's whistle!" cried the BFG. "All of those man-eating giants is enormous and very fierce! They is all at least two times my wideness and double my royal highness!"

"Twice as high as you!" cried Sophie.

"Easily that," said the BFG. "You is seeing them in the distance but just you wait till you get them

close up. Those giants is all at least fifty feet tall
with huge muscles and cockles alive alive-o. I is
the titchy one. I is the runt. Twenty-four feet is
puddlenuts in Giant Country."

"You mustn't feel bad about it," Sophie said. "I
think you are just great. Why even your toes must
be as big as sausages."

"Bigger," said the BFG, looking pleased. "They
is as big as bumplehammers."

39

"How many giants are there out there?" Sophie asked.

"Nine altogether," answered the BFG.

"That means," said Sophie, "that somewhere in the world, every single night, nine wretched people get carried away and eaten alive."

"More," said the BFG. "It is all depending, you see, on how big the human beans is. Japanese beans is very small, so a giant will need to gobble up about six Japanese before he is feeling full up. Others like the Norway people and the Yankee-Doodles is ever so much bigger and usually two or three of those makes a good tuck-in."

"But do these disgusting giants go to every single country in the world?" Sophie asked.

"All countries excepting Greece is getting visited some time or another," the BFG answered. "The country which a giant visits is depending on how he is feeling. If it is very warm weather and a giant is feeling as hot as a sizzlepan, he will probably go galloping far up to the frisby north to get himself an Esquimo or two to cool him down. A nice fat Esquimo to a giant is like a lovely ice-cream lolly to you."

"I'll take your word for it," Sophie said.

"And then again, if it is a frotsy night and the giant is fridging with cold, he will probably point his nose toward the swultering hotlands to guzzle a few Hottentots to warm him up."

"How perfectly horrible," Sophie said.

"Nothing hots a cold giant up like a hot Hottentot," the BFG said.

40

"And if you were to put me down on the ground and I was to walk out among them now," Sophie said, "would they really eat me up?"

"Like a whiffswiddle!" cried the BFG. "And what is more, you is so small they wouldn't even have to chew you. The first one to be seeing you would pick you up in his fingers and down you'd go like a drop of drain-water!"

"Let's go back inside," Sophie said. "I hate even watching them."

The Marvellous Ears

Back in the cave, the Big Friendly Giant sat Sophie down once again on the enormous table. "Is you quite snuggly there in your nightie?" he asked. "You isn't fridgy cold?"

"I'm fine," Sophie said.

"I cannot help thinking," said the BFG, "about your poor mother and father. By now they must be jipping and skumping all over the house shouting 'Hello hello where is Sophie gone?' "

"I don't have a mother and father," Sophie said. "They both died when I was a baby."

"Oh, you poor little scrumplet!" cried the BFG. "Is you not missing them very badly?"

"Not really," Sophie said, "because I never knew them."

"You is making me sad," the BFG said, rubbing his eyes.

"Don't be sad," Sophie said. "No one is going to be worrying too much about me. That place you took me from was the village orphanage. We are all orphans in there."

"You is a norphan?"

"Yes."

"How many is there in there?"

"Ten of us," Sophie said. "All little girls."

"Was you happy there?" the BFG asked.

42

"I hated it," Sophie said. "The woman who ran it was called Mrs Clonkers and if she caught you breaking any of the rules, like getting out of bed at night or not folding up your clothes, you got punished."

"How is you getting punished?"

"She locked us in the dark cellar for a day and a night without anything to eat or drink."

"The rotten old rotrasper!" cried the BFG.

"It was horrid," Sophie said. "We used to dread it. There were rats down there. We could hear them creeping about."

"The filthy old fizzwiggler!" shouted the BFG. "That is the horridest thing I is hearing for years! You is making me sadder than ever!" All at once, a huge tear that would have filled a bucket rolled down one of the BFG's cheeks and fell with a splash on the floor. It made quite a puddle.

Sophie watched with astonishment. What a strange and moody creature this is, she thought. One moment he is telling me my head is full of squashed flies and the next moment his heart is melting for me because Mrs Clonkers locks us in the cellar.

"The thing that worries *me*," Sophie said, "is having to stay in this dreadful place for the rest of my life. The orphanage was pretty awful, but I wouldn't have been there for ever, would I?"

"All is my fault," the BFG said. "I is the one who kidsnatched you." Yet another enormous tear welled from his eye and splashed on to the floor.

"Now I come to think of it, I won't actually be

43

here all that long," Sophie said.

"I is afraid you will," the BFG said.

"No, I won't," Sophie said. "Those brutes out there are bound to catch me sooner or later and have me for tea."

"I is *never* letting that happen," the BFG said.

For a few moments the cave was silent. Then Sophie said, "May I ask you a question?"

The BFG wiped the tears from his eyes with the back of his hand and gave Sophie a long thoughtful stare. "Shoot away," he said.

"Would you please tell me what you were doing in our village last night? Why were you poking that long trumpet thing into the Goochey children's bedroom and then blowing through it?"

"Ah-ha!" cried the BFG, sitting up suddenly in his chair. "Now we is getting nosier than a parker!"

"And the suitcase you were carrying," Sophie said. "What on earth was *that* all about?"

The BFG stared suspiciously at the small girl sitting cross-legged on the table.

"You is asking me to tell you whoppsy big secrets," he said. "Secrets that nobody is ever hearing before."

"I won't tell a soul," Sophie said. "I swear it. How could I anyway? I am stuck here for the rest of my life."

"You could be telling the other giants."

"No, I couldn't," Sophie said. "You told me they would eat me up the moment they saw me."

"And so they would," said the BFG. "You is a

44

human bean and human beans is like strawbunkles and cream to those giants."

"If they are going to eat me the moment they see me, then I wouldn't have time to tell them anything, would I?" Sophie said.

"You wouldn't," said the BFG.

"Then why did you say I might?"

"Because I is brimful of buzzburgers," the BFG said. "If you listen to everything I am saying you will be getting earache."

"Please tell me what you were doing in our village," Sophie said. "I promise you can trust me."

"Would you teach me how to make an elefunt?" the BFG asked.

"What *do* you mean?" Sophie said.

"I would dearly love to have an elefunt to ride on," the BFG said dreamily. "I would so much love to have a jumbly big elefunt and go riding through green forests picking peachy fruits off the trees all day long. This is a sizzling-hot muckfrumping country we is living in. Nothing grows in it except snozzcumbers. I would love to go somewhere else and pick peachy fruits in the early morning from the back of an elefunt."

Sophie was quite moved by this curious statement.

"Perhaps one day we will get you an elephant," she said. "And peachy fruits as well. Now tell me what you were doing in our village."

"If you is really wanting to know what I am doing in your village," the BFG said, "I is blowing

45

a dream into the bedroom of those children."

"*Blowing a dream?*" Sophie said. "What *do* you mean?"

"I is a dream-blowing giant," the BFG said. "When all the other giants is galloping off every what way and which to swollop human beans, I is scuddling away to other places to blow dreams into the bedrooms of sleeping children. Nice dreams. Lovely golden dreams. Dreams that is giving the dreamers a happy time."

"Now hang on a minute," Sophie said. "Where do you get these dreams?"

"I collect them," the BFG said, waving an arm toward all the rows and rows of bottles on the shelves. "I has billions of them."

"You can't *collect* a dream," Sophie said. "A dream isn't something you can catch hold of."

"You is never going to understand about it," the BFG said. "That is why I is not wishing to tell you."

"Oh, please tell me!" Sophie said. "I *will* understand! Go on! Tell me how you collect dreams! Tell me everything!"

The BFG settled himself comfortably in his chair and crossed his legs. "Dreams," he said, "is very mysterious things. They is floating around in the air like little wispy-misty bubbles. And all the time they is searching for sleeping people."

"Can you see them?" Sophie asked.

"Never at first."

"Then how do you catch them if you can't see them?" Sophie asked.

"Ah-ha," said the BFG. "Now we is getting on to the dark and dusky secrets."

"I won't tell a soul."

"I is trusting you," the BFG said. He closed his eyes and sat quite still for a moment, while Sophie waited.

"A dream," he said, "as it goes whiffling through the night air, is making a tiny little buzzing-humming noise. But this little buzzy-hum is so silvery soft, it is impossible for a human bean to be hearing it."

"Can *you* hear it?" Sophie asked.

The BFG pointed up at his enormous truck-wheel ears which he now began to move in and out. He performed this exercise proudly, with a little proud smile on his face. "Is you seeing these?" he asked.

"How could I miss them?" Sophie said.

"They maybe is looking a bit propsposterous to you," the BFG said, "but you must believe me when I say they is very extra-usual ears indeed. They is not to be coughed at."

"I'm quite sure they're not," Sophie said.

"They is allowing me to hear absolutely every single twiddly little thing."

"You mean you can hear things I can't hear?" Sophie said.

"You is *deaf as a dumpling* compared with me!" cried the BFG. "You is hearing only thumping loud noises with those little earwigs of yours. But I am hearing *all the secret whisperings of the world!*"

"Such as what?" Sophie asked.

"In your country," he said, "I is hearing the footsteps of a ladybird as she goes walking across a leaf."

"*Honestly?*" Sophie said, beginning to be impressed.

"What's more, I is hearing those footsteps *very loud,*" the BFG said. "When a ladybird is walking across a leaf, I is hearing her feet going *clumpety-clumpety-clump* like giants' footsteps."

"Good gracious me!" Sophie said. "What else can you hear?"

"I is hearing the little ants chittering to each other as they scuddle around in the soil."

"You mean you can hear ants talking?"

"Every single word," the BFG said. "Although I is not exactly understanding their langwitch."

"Go on," Sophie said.

"Sometimes, on a very clear night," the BFG said, "and if I is swiggling my ears in the right direction," – and here he swivelled his great ears upwards so they were facing the ceiling – "if I is swiggling them like this and the night is very clear, I is sometimes hearing faraway music coming from the stars in the sky."

A queer little shiver passed through Sophie's body. She sat very quiet, waiting for more.

"My ears is what told me you was watching me out of your window last night," the BFG said.

"But I didn't make a sound," Sophie said.

"I was hearing your heart beating across the road," the BFG said. "Loud as a drum."

"Go on," Sophie said. "Please."

"I can hear plants and trees."

"Do *they* talk?" Sophie asked.

"They is not exactly talking," the BFG said. "But they is making noises. For instance, if I come along and I is picking a lovely flower, if I is twisting the stem of the flower till it breaks, then the plant is screaming. I can hear it screaming and screaming very clear."

"You don't mean it!" Sophie cried. "How awful!"

"It is screaming just like you would be screaming if someone was twisting *your* arm right off."

"Is that really true?" Sophie asked.

"You think I is swizzfiggling you?"

"It *is* rather hard to believe."

"Then I is stopping right here," said the BFG

sharply. "I is not wishing to be called a fibster."

"Oh no! I'm not calling you anything!" Sophie cried. "I believe you! I do really! Please go on!"

The BFG gave her a long hard stare. Sophie looked right back at him, her face open to his. "I believe you," she said softly.

She had offended him, she could see that.

"I wouldn't ever be fibbling to you," he said.

"I know you wouldn't," Sophie said. "But you must understand that it isn't easy to believe such amazing things straightaway."

"I understand that," the BFG said.

"So do please forgive me and go on," she said.

He waited a while longer, and then he said, "It is the same with trees as it is with flowers. If I is chopping an axe into the trunk of a big tree, I is hearing a terrible sound coming from inside the heart of the tree."

"What sort of sound?" Sophie asked.

"A soft moaning sound," the BFG said. "It is like the sound an old man is making when he is dying slowly."

He paused. The cave was very silent.

"Trees is living and growing just like you and me," he said. "They is alive. So is plants."

He was sitting very straight in his chair now, his hands clasped tightly together in front of him. His face was bright, his eyes round and bright as two stars.

"Such wonderful and terrible sounds I is hearing!" he said. "Some of them you would never wish to be hearing yourself! But some is like glorious music!"

He seemed almost to be transfigured by the excitement of his thoughts. His face was beautiful in its blaze of emotions.

"Tell me some more about them," Sophie said quietly.

"You just ought to be hearing the little micies talking!" he said. "Little micies is always talking to each other and I is hearing them as loud as my own voice."

"What do they say?" Sophie asked.

"Only the micies know that," he said. "Spiders is also talking a great deal. You might not be thinking it but spiders is the most tremendous natterboxes. And when they is spinning their webs, they is singing all the time. They is singing sweeter than a nightingull."

"Who else do you hear?" Sophie asked.

"One of the biggest chatbags is the cattlepiddlers," the BFG said.

"What do they say?"

"They is argying all the time about who is going to be the prettiest butteryfly. That is all they is ever talking about."

"Is there a dream floating around in here now?" Sophie asked.

The BFG moved his great ears this way and that, listening intently. He shook his head. "There is no dream in here," he said, "except in the bottles. I has a special place to go for catching dreams. They is not often coming to Giant Country."

"How do you catch them?"

"The same way you is catching butteryflies,"
the BFG answered. "With a net." He stood up and
crossed over to a corner of the cave where a pole
was leaning against the wall. The pole was about
thirty feet long and there was a net on the end of it.
"Here is the dream-catcher," he said, grasping the
pole in one hand. "Every morning I is going out
and snitching new dreams to put in my bottles."

Suddenly, he seemed to lose interest in the
conversation. "I is getting hungry," he said. "It is
time for eats."

Snozzcumbers

"But if you don't eat people like all the others," Sophie said, "then what *do* you live on?"

"That is a squelching tricky problem around here," the BFG answered. "In this sloshflunking Giant Country, happy eats like pineapples and pigwinkles is simply not growing. Nothing is growing except for one extremely icky-poo vegetable. It is called the snozzcumber."

"The snozzcumber!" cried Sophie. "There's no such thing!"

The BFG looked at Sophie and smiled, showing about twenty of his square white teeth. "Yesterday," he said "we was not believing in giants, was we? Today we is not believing in snozzcumbers. Just because we happen not to have actually *seen* something with our own two little winkles, we think it is not existing. What about for instance the great squizzly scotch-hopper?"

"I beg your pardon?" Sophie said.

"And the humplecrimp?"

"What's that?" Sophie said.

"And the wraprascal?"

"The what?" Sophie said.

"And the crumpscoddle?"

"Are they animals?" Sophie asked.

"They is *common* animals," said the BFG

contemptuously. "I is not a very know-all giant myself, but it seems to me that you is an absolutely know-nothing human bean. Your brain is full of rotten-wool."

"You mean cotton-wool," Sophie said.

"What I mean and what I say is two different things," the BFG announced rather grandly. "I will now show you a snozzcumber."

The BFG flung open a massive cupboard and took out the weirdest-looking thing Sophie had ever seen. It was about half as long again as an ordinary man but was much thicker. It was as thick around its girth as a perambulator. It was black with white stripes along its length. And it was covered all over with coarse knobbles.

"Here is the repulsant snozzcumber!" cried the BFG, waving it about. "I squoggle it! I mispise it! I dispunge it! But because I is refusing to gobble up human beans like the other giants, I must spend my life guzzling up icky-poo snozzcumbers instead. If I don't, I will be nothing but skin and groans."

"You mean skin and *bones*," Sophie said.

"I *know* it is bones," the BFG said. "But please understand that I cannot be helping it if I sometimes is saying things a little squiggly. I is trying my very best all the time." The Big Friendly Giant looked suddenly so forlorn that Sophie got quite upset.

"I'm sorry," she said. "I didn't mean to be rude."

"There never was any schools to teach me talking in Giant Country," the BFG said sadly.

"But couldn't your mother have taught you?" Sophie asked.

"My *mother!*" cried the BFG. "Giants don't have mothers! Surely you is knowing *that*."

"I did *not* know that," Sophie said.

"Whoever heard of a *woman* giant!" shouted the BFG, waving the snozzcumber around his head like a lasso. "There never was a woman giant! And there never will be one. Giants is always men!"

Sophie felt herself getting a little muddled. "In that case," she said, "how were you born?"

"Giants isn't born," the BFG answered. "Giants *appears* and that's all there is to it. They simply *appears*, the same way as the sun and the stars."

"And when did you appear?" Sophie asked.

55

"Now how on earth could I be knowing a thing like that?" said the BFG. "It was so long ago I couldn't count."

"You mean you don't even know how *old* you are?"

"No giant is knowing that," the BFG said. "All I is knowing about myself is that I is very old, very very old and crumply. Perhaps as old as the earth."

"What happens when a giant dies?" Sophie asked.

"Giants is never dying," the BFG answered. "Sometimes and quite suddenly, a giant is disappearing and nobody is ever knowing where he goes to. But mostly us giants is simply going on and on like whiffsy timetwiddlers."

The BFG was still holding the awesome snozzcumber in his right hand, and now he put one end into his mouth and bit off a huge hunk of it. He started crunching it up and the noise he made was like the crunching of lumps of ice.

"It's filthing!" he spluttered, speaking with his mouth full and spraying large pieces of snozzcumber like bullets in Sophie's direction. Sophie hopped around on the table-top, ducking out of the way.

"It's disgusterous!" the BFG gurgled. "It's sickable! It's rotsome! It's maggotwise! Try it yourself, this foulsome snozzcumber!"

"No, thank you," Sophie said, backing away.

"It's all you're going to be guzzling around here from now on so you might as well get used to it," said the BFG. "Go on, you snipsy little winkle,

have a go!"

Sophie took a small nibble "Ugggggggh!" she spluttered. "Oh no! Oh gosh! Oh help!" She spat it out quickly. "It tastes of frogskins!" she gasped. "And rotten fish!"

"Worse than that!" cried the BFG, roaring with laughter. "To me it is tasting of clockcoaches and slimewanglers!"

"Do we really have to eat it?" Sophie said.

"You do unless you is wanting to become so thin you will be disappearing into a thick ear."

"Into *thin air*," Sophie said. "A thick ear is something quite different."

Once again that sad winsome look came into the BFG's eyes. "Words," he said, "is oh such a twitch-tickling problem to me all my life. So you must simply try to be patient and stop squibbling. As I am telling you before, I know exactly what words I am wanting to say, but somehow or other they is always getting squiff-squiddled around."

"That happens to everyone," Sophie said.

"Not like it happens to me," the BFG said. "I is speaking the most terrible wigglish."

"I think you speak beautifully," Sophie said.

"You do?" cried the BFG, suddenly brightening. "You really do?"

"Simply beautifully," Sophie repeated.

"Well, that is the nicest present anybody is ever giving me in my whole life!" cried the BFG. "Are you sure you is not twiddling my leg?"

"Of course not," Sophie said. "I just love the way you talk."

"How wondercrump!" cried the BFG, still beaming. "How whoopsey-splunkers! How absolutely squiffling! I is all of a stutter."

"Listen," Sophie said. "We don't *have* to eat snozzcumbers. In the fields around our village there are all sorts of lovely vegetables like cauliflowers and carrots. Why don't you get some of those next time you go visiting?"

The BFG raised his great head proudly in the air. "I is a very honourable giant," he said. "I would rather be chewing up rotsome snozzcumbers than snitching things from other people."

"You stole *me*," Sophie said.

"I did not steal you very much," said the BFG, smiling gently. "After all, you is only a tiny little girl."

The Bloodbottler

Suddenly, a tremendous thumping noise came from outside the cave entrance and a voice like thunder shouted, "Runt! Is you there, Runt! I is hearing you jabbeling! Who is you jabbeling to, Runt?"

"Look out!" cried the BFG. "It's the Bloodbottler!" But before he had finished speaking, the stone was rolled aside and a fifty-foot giant, more than twice as tall and wide as the BFG, came striding into the cave. He was naked except for a dirty little piece of cloth around his bottom.

Sophie was on the table-top. The enormous partly-eaten snozzcumber was lying near her. She ducked behind it.

The creature came clumping into the cave and stood towering over the BFG. "Who was you jabbeling to in here just now?" he boomed.

"I is jabbeling to myself," the BFG answered.

"Pilfflefizz!" shouted the Bloodbottler. "Bugswallop!" he boomed. "You is talking to a human bean, that's what I is thinking!"

"No no!" cried the BFG.

"Yus yus!" boomed the Bloodbottler. "I is guessing you has snitched away a human bean and brought it back to your bunghole as a pet! So now I is winkling it out and guzzling it as extra snacks

before my supper!"

The poor BFG was very nervous. "There's n-no one in here," he stammered. "W-hy don't you l-leave me alone?"

The Bloodbottler pointed a finger as large as a tree-trunk at the BFG. "Runty little scumscrewer!" he shouted. "Piffling little swishfiggler! Squimpy little bottlewart! Prunty little pogswizzler! I is now going to search the primroses!" He grabbed the BFG by the arm. "And you is going to help me do it. Us together is going to winkle out this tasteful little human bean!" he shouted.

The BFG had intended to whisk Sophie off the table as soon as he got the chance and hide her behind his back, but now there was no hope of doing this. Sophie peered around the chewed-off end of the enormous snozzcumber, watching the two giants as they moved away down the cave. The Bloodbottler was a gruesome sight. His skin was reddish-brown. There was black hair sprouting on his chest and arms and on his stomach. The hair on his head was long and dark and tangled. His foul face was round and squashy-looking. The eyes were tiny black holes. The nose was small and flat. But the mouth was huge. It spread right across the face almost ear to ear, and it had lips that were like two gigantic purple frankfurters lying one on top of the other. Craggy yellow teeth stuck out between the two purple frankfurter lips, and rivers of spit ran down over the chin.

It was not in the least difficult to believe that this ghastly brute ate men, women and children every night.

The Bloodbottler, still holding the BFG by the arm, was examining the rows and rows of bottles. "You and your pibbling bottles!" he shouted. "What is you putting in them?"

"Nothing that would interest you," the BFG answered. "You is only interested in guzzling human beans."

"And you is dotty as a dogswoggler!" cried the Bloodbottler.

Soon the Bloodbottler would be coming back, Sophie told herself, and he was bound to search the table-top. But she couldn't possibly jump off the table. It was twelve feet high. She'd break a leg. The snozzcumber, although it was as thick as a perambulator, was not going to hide her if the Bloodbottler picked it up. She examined the chewed-off end. It had large seeds in the middle, each one as big as a melon. They were embedded in soft slimy stuff. Taking care to stay out of sight, Sophie reached forward and scooped away half a dozen of these seeds. This left a hole in the middle of the snozzcumber large enough for her to crouch in so long as she rolled herself up into a ball. She crawled into it. It was a wet and slimy hiding-place, but what did that matter if it was going to save her from being eaten.

The Bloodbottler and the BFG were coming back towards the table now. The BFG was nearly fainting with fear. Any moment, he was telling himself, Sophie would be discovered and eaten.

Suddenly, the Bloodbottler grabbed the half-eaten snozzcumber. The BFG stared at the bare table. Sophie, where is you? he thought desperately. You cannot possibly be jumpelling off that high table, so where is you hiding, Sophie?

"So this is the filthing rotsome glubbage you is eating!" boomed the Bloodbottler, holding up the partly-eaten snozzcumber. "You must be cockles to be guzzling such rubbsquash!"

For a moment, the Bloodbottler seemed to have forgotten about his search for Sophie. The BFG decided to lead him further off the track. "That is the scrumdiddlyumptious snozzcumber," he said. "I is guzzling it gleefully every night and day. Is you never trying a snozzcumber, Bloodbottler?"

"Human beans is juicier," the Bloodbottler said.

"You is talking rommytot," the BFG said, growing braver by the second. He was thinking that if only he could get the Bloodbottler to take one bite of the repulsive vegetable, the sheer foulness of its flavour would send him bellowing out of the cave. "I is happy to let you sample it," the BFG went on. "But please, when you see how truly glumptious it is, do not be guzzling the whole thing. Leave me a little snitchet for my supper."

The Bloodbottler stared suspiciously with small piggy eyes at the snozzcumber.

Sophie, crouching inside the chewed-off end, began to tremble all over.

"You is not switchfiddling me, is you?" said the Bloodbottler.

"Never!" cried the BFG passionately. "Take a

bite and I am positive you will be shouting out oh how scrumdiddlyumptious this wonderveg is!"

The BFG could see the greedy Bloodbottler's mouth beginning to water more than ever at the prospect of extra food. "Vegitibbles is very good for you," he went on. "It is not healthsome always to be eating meaty things."

"Just this once," the Bloodbottler said, "I is going to taste these rotsome eats of yours. But I is warning you that if it is filthsome, I is smashing it over your sludgy little head!"

He picked up the snozzcumber.

He began raising it on its long journey to his mouth, some fifty feet up in the air.

Sophie wanted to scream *Don't!* But that would have been an even more certain death. Crouching among the slimy seeds, she felt herself being lifted up and up and up.

Suddenly, there was a *crunch* as the Bloodbottler bit a huge hunk off the end. Sophie saw his yellow teeth clamping together, a few inches from her head. Then there was utter darkness. She was in his mouth. She caught a whiff of his evil-smelling breath. It stank of bad meat. She waited for the teeth to go *crunch* once more. She prayed that she would be killed quickly.

"*Eeeeeowtch!*" roared the Bloodbottler. "Ugh-bwelch! Ieeeech!" And then he spat.

All the great lumps of snozzcumber that were in his mouth, as well as Sophie herself, went shooting out across the cave.

If Sophie had struck the stony wall of the cave,

she would most certainly have been killed. Instead, she hit the soft folds of the BFG's black cloak hanging against the wall. She dropped to the ground, half-stunned. She crawled under the hem of the cloak and there she crouched.

"You little swinebuggler!" roared the Bloodbottler. "You little pigswiller!" He rushed at the BFG and smashed what was left of the snozzcumber over his head. Fragments of the filthy vegetable splashed all over the cave.

"You is not loving it?" the BFG asked innocently, rubbing his head.

"Loving it!" yelled the Bloodbottler. "That is the most disgusterous taste that is ever touching my teeth! You must be buggles to be swalloping slutch like that! Every night you could be galloping off happy as a hamburger and gobbling juicy human beans!"

"Eating human beans is wrong and evil," the BFG said.

"It is guzzly and glumptious!" shouted the Bloodbottler. "And tonight I is galloping off to Chile to swobble a few human Chile beans. Is you wishing to know why I is choosing Chile?"

"I is not wishing to know anything," the BFG said, very dignified.

"I is choosing Chile," the Bloodbottler said, "because I is fed up with the taste of Esquimos. It is important I has plenty of cold eats in this scuddling hot weather, and the next coldest thing to an Esquimo is a Chile bean. Human beans from Chile is very chilly."

"Horrible," the BFG said. "You ought to be ashamed."

"Other giants is all saying they is wanting to gallop off to England tonight to guzzle school-chiddlers," the Bloodbottler said. "I is very fond indeed of English school-chiddlers. They has a nice inky-booky flavour. Perhaps I will change my mind and go to England with them."

"You is disgusting," the BFG said.

"And you is an insult to the giant peoples!" shouted the Bloodbottler. "You is not fit to be a giant! You is a squinky little squiddler! You is a pibbling little pitsqueak! You is a ... cream puffnut!"

With that, the horrible Bloodbottling Giant strode out of the cave. The BFG ran to the cave

67

entrance and quickly rolled the stone back into place.

"Sophie," he whispered. "Sophie, where is you, Sophie?"

Sophie emerged from under the hem of the black cloak. "I'm here," she said.

The BFG picked her up and held her tenderly in the palm of his hand. "Oh, I is so happy to be finding you all in one lump!" he said.

"I was in his mouth," Sophie said.

"You was *what!*" cried the BFG.

Sophie told him what had happened.

"And there I was telling him to eat the filthsome snozzcumber and you was all the time inside it!" the BFG cried.

"Not much fun," Sophie said.

"Just look at you, you poor little chiddler!" cried the BFG. "You is all covered in snozzcumber and giant spit." He set about cleaning her up as best he could. "I is hating those other giants more than ever now," he said. "You know what I should like?"

"What?" Sophie said.

"I should like to find a way of disappearing them, every single one."

"I'd be glad to help you," Sophie said. "Let me see if I can't think up a way of doing it."

Frobscottle and Whizzpoppers

By now Sophie was beginning to feel not only extremely hungry, but very thirsty as well. Had she been at home she would have finished her breakfast long ago.

"Are you sure there's nothing else to eat around here except those disgusting smelly snozzcumbers?" she asked.

"Not even a fizzwinkle," answered the Big Friendly Giant.

"In that case, may I please have a little water?" she said.

"Water?" said the BFG, frowning mightily. "What is water?"

"We drink it," Sophie said. "What do you drink?"

"Frobscottle," announced the BFG. "All giants is drinking frobscottle."

"Is it as nasty as your snozzcumbers?" Sophie asked.

"Nasty!" cried the BFG. "Never is it nasty! Frobscottle is sweet and jumbley!" He got up from his chair and went to a second huge cupboard. He opened it and took out a glass bottle that must have been six feet tall. The liquid inside it was pale green, and the bottle was half full.

"Here is frobscottle!" he cried, holding the

bottle up proud and high, as though it contained
some rare wine. "Delumptious fizzy frobscottle!"
he shouted. He gave it a shake and the green stuff
began to fizz like mad.

"But look! It's fizzing the *wrong way!*" Sophie
cried. And indeed it was. The bubbles, instead of
travelling upwards and bursting on the surface,
were shooting downwards and bursting at the
bottom. A pale green frothy fizz was forming at
the bottom of the bottle.

"What on earth is you meaning *the wrong
way?*" asked the BFG.

"In our fizzy drinks," Sophie said, "the bubbles
always go up and burst at the top."

"*Upwards* is the *wrong way!*" cried the BFG.

"You mustn't ever be having the bubbles going upwards! That's the most flushbunking rubbish I ever is hearing!"

"Why do you say that?" Sophie asked.

"You is asking me *why?*" cried the BFG, waving the enormous bottle around as though he were conducting an orchestra. "You is actually meaning to tell me you cannot see *why* it is a scrotty mistake to have the bubbles flying up instead of down?"

"You said it was flushbunking. Now you say it's scrotty. Which is it?" Sophie asked politely.

"Both!" cried the BFG. "It is a flushbunking *and* a scrotty mistake to let the bubbles go upwards! If you can't see why, you must be as quacky as a duckhound! By ringo, your head must be so full of frogsquinkers and buzzwangles, I is frittered if I know how you can think at all!"

"Why shouldn't the bubbles go upward?" Sophie asked.

"I will explain," said the BFG. "But tell me first what name is you calling *your* frobscottle by?"

"One is Coke," Sophie said. "Another is Pepsi. There are lots of them."

"And the bubbles is *all* going up?"

"They all go up," Sophie said.

"Catasterous!" cried the BFG. "Upgoing bubbles is a catasterous disastrophe!"

"Will you *please* tell me why" Sophie said.

"If you will listen carefully I will try to explain," said the BFG. "But your brain is so full of bugwhiffles, I doubt you will ever understand."

"I'll do my best," Sophie said patiently.

"Very well, then. When you is drinking this cokey drink of yours," said the BFG, "it is going straight down into your tummy. Is that right? Or is it left?"

"It's right," Sophie said.

"And the *bubbles* is going also into your tummy. Right or left?"

"Right again," Sophie said.

"And the bubbles is fizzing upwards?"

"Of course," Sophie said.

"Which means," said the BFG, "that they will all come swishwiffling up your throat and out of your mouth and make a foulsome belchy burp!"

"That is often true," Sophie said. "But what's wrong with a little burp now and again? It's sort of fun."

"Burping is filthsome," the BFG said. "Us giants is never doing it."

"But with *your* drink," Sophie said, "what was it you called it?"

"Frobscottle," said the BFG.

"With frobscottle," Sophie said, "the bubbles in your tummy will be going *downwards* and that could have a far nastier result."

"Why nasty?" asked the BFG, frowning.

"Because," Sophie said, blushing a little, "if they go down instead of up, they'll be coming out somewhere else with an even louder and ruder noise."

"A whizzpopper!" cried the BFG, beaming at her. "Us giants is making whizzpoppers all the time! Whizzpopping is a sign of happiness. It is music in our ears! You surely is not telling me that a little whizzpopping is forbidden among human beans?"

"It is considered extremely rude," Sophie said.

"But you is whizzpopping, is you not, now and again?" asked the BFG.

"Everyone is whizzpopping, if that's what you call it," Sophie said. "Kings and Queens are whizzpopping. Presidents are whizzpopping. Glamorous film stars are whizzpopping. Little babies are whizzpopping. But where I come from, it is not polite to talk about it."

"Redunculous!" said the BFG. "If everyone is making whizzpoppers, then why not talk about it? We is now having a swiggle of this delicious frobscottle and you will see the happy result." The BFG shook the bottle vigorously. The pale green stuff fizzed and bubbled. He removed the cork and took a tremendous gurgling swig.

"It's glummy!" he cried. "I love it!"

For a few moments, the Big Friendly Giant stood quite still, and a look of absolute ecstasy began to spread over his long wrinkly face. Then suddenly the heavens opened and he let fly with a series of the loudest and rudest noises Sophie had ever heard in her life. They reverberated around the walls of the cave like thunder and the glass jars rattled on their shelves. But most astonishing of all, the force of the explosions actually lifted the enormous giant clear off his feet, like a rocket.

"*Whoopee!*" he cried, when he came down to

earth again. "Now *that* is whizzpopping for you!"

Sophie burst out laughing. She couldn't help it.

"Have some yourself!" cried the BFG, tipping the neck of the enormous bottle towards her.

"Don't you have a cup?" Sophie said.

"No cups. Only bottle."

Sophie opened her mouth, and very gently the BFG tipped the bottle forward and poured some of the fabulous frobscottle down her throat.

And oh gosh, how delicious it was! It was sweet and refreshing. It tasted of vanilla and cream, with just the faintest trace of raspberries on the edge of the flavour. And the bubbles were wonderful. Sophie could actually feel them bouncing and bursting all around her tummy. It was an amazing sensation. It felt as though hundreds of tiny people were dancing a jig inside her and tickling her with their toes. It was lovely.

"It's lovely!" she cried.

"Just wait," said the BFG, flapping his ears.

Sophie could feel the bubbles travelling lower and lower down her tummy, and then suddenly, inevitably . . . the explosion came. The trumpets sounded and she too made the walls of the cavern ring with the sound of music and thunder.

"Bravo!" shouted the BFG, waving the bottle. "You is very good for a beginner! Let's have some more!"

Journey to Dream Country

After the mad frobscottle party was over, Sophie settled herself again on top of the enormous table.

"You is feeling better now?" asked the Big Friendly Giant.

"Much better, thank you," Sophie said.

"Whenever I is feeling a bit scrotty," the BFG said, "a few gollops of frobscottle is always making me hopscotchy again."

"I must say it's quite an experience," Sophie said.

"It's a razztwizzler," the BFG said. "It's glor-iumptious." He turned away and strode across the cave and picked up his dream-catching net. "I is galloping off now," he said, "to catch some more whoppsy-whiffling dreams for my collection. I is doing this every day without missing. Is you wishing to come with me?"

"Not me, thank you very much!" Sophie said. "Not with those other giants lurking outside!"

"I is snuggling you very cosy into the pocket of my waistcoat," the BFG said. "Then no one is seeing you."

Before Sophie could protest, he had picked her up off the table and popped her into the waistcoat pocket. There was plenty of room in there. "Is you wishing for a little hole to peep out from?" he asked her.

"There's one here already," she said. She had found a small hole in the pocket, and when she put one eye close to it, she could see out very well indeed. She watched the BFG as he bent down and filled his suitcase with empty glass jars. He closed the lid, picked up the suitcase in one hand, took the pole with the net on the end in the other hand, and marched toward the entrance of the cave.

As soon as he was outside, the BFG set off across the great hot yellow wasteland where the blue rocks lay and the dead trees stood and where all the other giants were skulking about.

Sophie, squatting low on her heels in the pocket of the leather waistcoat, had one eye glued to the little hole. She saw the group of enormous giants about three hundred yards ahead.

"Hold your breaths!" the BFG whispered down to her. "Cross your figglers! Here we go! We is going right past all these other giants! Is you seeing that whopping great one, the one nearest to us?"

"I see him," Sophie whispered back, quivering.

"That is the horriblest of them all. And the biggest of them all. He is called the Fleshlumpeating Giant."

"I don't want to hear about him," Sophie said.

"He is fifty-four feet high," the BFG said softly as he jogged along. "And he is swolloping human beans like they is sugar-lumps, two or three at a time."

"You're making me nervous," Sophie said.

"I is nervous myself," the BFG whispered. "I always gets as jumpsy as a joghopper when the Fleshlumpeating Giant is around."

"Keep away from him," Sophie pleaded.

"Not possible," the BFG answered. "He is galloping easily two times as quicksy as me."

"Shall we turn back?" Sophie said.

"Turning back is worse," the BFG said. "If they is seeing me running away, they is all giving chase and throwing rocks."

"They would never *eat* you though would they?" Sophie asked.

"Giants is never guzzling other giants," the BFG said. "They is fighting and squarreling a lot with each other, but never guzzling. Human beans is more tasty to them."

The giants had already spotted the BFG and all heads were turned, watching him as he jogged forward. He was aiming to pass well to the right of the group.

Through her little peep-hole, Sophie saw the Fleshlumpeating Giant moving over to intercept them. He didn't hurry. He just loped over casually to a point where the BFG would have to pass. The others loped after him. Sophie counted nine of them altogether and she recognised the Bloodbottler in the middle of them. They were bored. They had nothing to do until nightfall. There was an air of menace about them as they loped slowly across the plain with long lolloping strides, heading for the BFG.

"Here comes the runty one!" boomed the

79

Fleshlumpeater. "Ho-ho there, runty one! Where is you splatchwinkling away to in such a hefty hurry?" He shot out an enormous arm and grabbed the BFG by the hair. The BFG didn't struggle. He simply stopped and stood quite still and said, "Be so kind as to be letting go of my hair, Fleshlumpeater."

The Fleshlumpeater released him and stepped back a pace. The other giants stood around, waiting for the fun to start.

"Now then, you little grobsquiffler!" boomed the Fleshlumpeater. "We is all of us wanting to know where you is galloping off to every day in the daytime. Nobody ought to be galloping off to anywhere until it is getting dark. The human beans could easily be spotting you and starting a giant hunt and we is not wanting that to happen, is we not?"

"We is not!" shouted the other giants. "Go back to your cave, runty one!"

"I is not galloping to any human bean country," the BFG said. "I is going to other places."

"I is thinking," said the Fleshlumpeater, "that you is catching human beans and keeping them as pets!"

"Right you is!" cried the Bloodbottler. "Just now I is hearing him chittering away to one of them in his cave!"

"You is welcome to go and search my cave from frack to bunt," the BFG answered. "You can go looking into every crook and nanny. There is no human beans or stringy beans or runner beans or jelly beans or any other beans in there."

Sophie crouched still as a mouse inside the BFG's pocket. She hardly dared breathe. She was terrified she might sneeze. The slightest sound or movement would give her away. Through the tiny peep-hole she watched the giants clustering around the poor BFG. How revolting they were! All of them had piggy little eyes and enormous mouths with thick sausage lips. When the Fleshlumpeater was speaking, she got a glimpse of his tongue. It was jet black, like a slab of black steak. Every one of them was more than twice as tall as the BFG.

Suddenly, the Fleshlumpeater shot out two enormous hands and grabbed the BFG around the waist. He tossed him high in the air and shouted, "Catch him, Manhugger!"

The Manhugger caught him. The other giants spread out quickly in a large circle, each giant about twenty yards from his neighbour, preparing for the game they were going to play. Now the Manhugger threw the BFG high and far, shouting "Catch him, Bonecruncher!"

The Bonecruncher ran forward and caught the tumbling BFG and immediately swung him up again. "Catch him, Childchewer!" he shouted.

And so it went on. The giants were playing ball with the BFG, vying with each other to see who could throw him the highest. Sophie dug her nails into the sides of the pocket, trying to prevent herself from tumbling out when she was upside down. She felt as though she were in a barrel going

81

over the Niagara Falls. And all the time there was
the fearful danger that one of the giants would fail
to catch the BFG and he would go crashing to the
ground.

"Catch him, Meatdripper!" . . .

"Catch him, Gizzardgulper!" . . .

"Catch him, Maidmasher!" . . .

"Catch him, Bloodbottler!" . . .

"Catch him! . . . Catch him! . . . Catch him!
. . ."

In the end, they got bored with this game. They
dumped the poor BFG on the ground. He was
dazed and shattered. They gave him a few kicks
and shouted, "Run, you little runt! Let us be
seeing how fast you is galloping!" The BFG ran.
What else could he do? The giants picked up rocks
and hurled them after him. He managed to dodge
them. "Ruddy little runt!" they shouted. "Troggy
little twit! Shrivelly little shrimp! Mucky little
midget! Squaggy little squib! Grobby little grub!"

83

At last the BFG got clear of them all and in another couple of minutes the pack of giants was out of sight over the horizon. Sophie popped her head up from the pocket. "I didn't like that," she said.

"Phew!" said the BFG. "Phew and far between! They was in a nasty crotching mood today, was they not! I is sorry you was having such a whirlgig time."

"No worse than you," Sophie said. "Would they ever *really* hurt you?"

"I isn't ever trusting them," the BFG said.

"How do they actually catch the humans they eat?" Sophie asked.

"They is usually just sticking an arm in through the bedroom window and snitching them from their beds," the BFG said.

"Like you did to me."

"Ah, but I isn't eating you," the BFG said.

"How else do they catch them?" Sophie asked.

"Sometimes," the BFG said, "they is swimmeling in from the sea like fishies with only their heads showing above the water, and then out comes a big hairy hand and grabbles someone off the beach."

"Children as well?"

"Often chiddlers," the BFG said. "Little chiddlers who is building sandcastles on the beach. That is who the swimmeling ones are after. Little chiddlers is not so tough to eat as old grandmamma, so says the Childchewing Giant."

As they talked, the BFG was galloping fast over

84

the land. Sophie was standing right up in his waistcoat pocket now and holding on to the edge with both hands. Her head and shoulders were in the open and the wind was blowing in her hair.

"How else do they catch people?" she asked.

"All of them is having their own special ways of catching the human bean," the BFG said. "The Meatdripping Giant is preferring to pretend he is a big tree growing in the park. He is standing in the park in the dusky evening and he is holding great big branches over his head, and there he is waiting until some happy families is coming to have a picnic under the spreading tree. The Meatdripping Giant is watching them as they lay out their little picnic. But in the end it is the Meatdripper who is having the picnic."

"It's too awful!" Sophie cried.

"The Gizzardgulping Giant is a city lover," the BFG went on. "The Gizzardgulper is lying high up between the roofs of houses in the big cities. He is lying there snuggy as a sniggler and watching the human beans walking on the street below, and when he sees one that looks like it has a whoppsy-good flavour, he grabs it. He is simply reaching down and snitching it off the street like a monkey taking a nut. He says it is nice to be able to pick and choose what you is having for your supper. He says it is like choosing from a menu."

"Don't people *see* him doing it?" Sophie asked.

"Never is they seeing him. Do not forget it is dusky-dark at this time. Also, the Gizzardgulper has a very fast arm. His arm is going up and down quicker than squinkers."

"But if all these people are disappearing every night, surely there's some sort of an outcry?" Sophie said.

"The world is a whopping big place," the BFG said. "It has a hundred different countries. The giants is clever. They is careful not to be skididdling off to the same country too often. They is always switchfiddling around."

"Even so . . . " Sophie said.

"Do not forget," the BFG said, "that human beans is disappearing everywhere all the time even *without* the giants is guzzling them up. Human beans is killing each other much quicker than the giants is doing it."

"But they don't *eat* each other," Sophie said.

"Giants isn't eating each other either," the BFG said. "Nor is giants *killing* each other. Giants is not very lovely, but they is not killing each other. Nor is crockadowndillies killing other crockadowndillies. Nor is pussy-cats killing pussy-cats."

"They kill mice," Sophie said.

"Ah, but they is not killing their own kind," the BFG said. "Human beans is the only animals that is killing their own kind."

"Don't poisonous snakes kill each other?" Sophie asked. She was searching desperately for another creature that behaved as badly as the human.

"Even poisnowse snakes is never killing each other," the BFG said. "Nor is the most fearsome creatures like tigers and rhinostossterisses. None of them is ever killing their own kind. Has you ever thought about that?"

Sophie kept silent.

"I is not understanding human beans at all," the BFG said. "*You* is a human bean and you is saying it is grizzling and horrigust for giants to be eating human beans. Right or left?"

"Right," Sophie said.

"But human beans is squishing *each other* all the time," the BFG said. "They is shootling guns and going up in aerioplanes to drop their bombs on each other's heads every week. Human beans is always killing other human beans."

He was right. Of course he was right and Sophie knew it. She was beginning to wonder whether humans were actually any better than giants. "Even so," she said, defending her own race, "I think it's rotten that those foul giants should go off every night to eat humans. Humans have never done *them* any harm."

"That is what the little piggy-wig is saying every day," the BFG answered. "He is saying, 'I has never done any harm to the human bean so why should he be eating me?' "

"Oh dear," Sophie said.

"The human beans is making rules to suit themselves," the BFG went on. "But the rules they is making do not suit the little piggy-wiggies. Am I right or left?"

"Right," Sophie said.

"Giants is also making rules. Their rules is not

suiting the human beans. Everybody is making his own rules to suit himself."

"But you don't like it that those beastly giants are eating humans every night, do you?" Sophie asked.

"I do not," the BFG answered firmly. "One right is not making two lefts. Is you quite cosy down there in my pocket?"

"I'm fine," Sophie said.

Then suddenly, once again, the BFG went into that magical top gear of his. He began hurtling forward with phenomenal leaps. His speed was unbelievable. The landscape became blurred and again Sophie had to duck down out of the whistling gale to save her head from being blown off her shoulders. She crouched in the pocket and listened to the wind screaming past. It came knifing in through the tiny peep-hole in the pocket and whooshed around her like a hurricane.

But this time the BFG didn't stay in top gear long. It seemed as though he had had some barrier to cross, a vast mountain perhaps or an ocean or a great desert, but having crossed it, he once again slowed down to his normal gallop and Sophie was able to pop her head up and look out once more at the view.

She noticed immediately that they were now in an altogether paler country. The sun had disappeared above a film of vapour. The air was becoming cooler every minute. The land was flat and treeless and there seemed to be no colour in it at all.

Every minute, the mist became thicker. The air became colder still and everything became paler and paler until soon there was nothing but grey and white all around them. They were in a country of swirling mists and ghostly vapours. There was some sort of grass underfoot but it was not green. It was ashy grey. There was no sign of a living creature and no sound at all except for the soft thud of the BFG's footsteps as he hurtled on through the fog.

Suddenly he stopped. "We is here at last!" he announced. He bent down and lifted Sophie from his pocket and put her on the ground. She was still in her nightie and her feet were bare. She shivered and stared around her at the swirling mists and ghostly vapours.

"Where are we?" she asked.

"We is in Dream Country," the BFG said. "This is where all dreams is beginning."

Dream-Catching

The Big Friendly Giant put the suitcase on the ground. He bent down low so that his enormous face was close to Sophie's. "From now on, we is keeping as still as winky little micies," he whispered.

Sophie nodded. The misty vapour swirled around her. It made her cheeks damp and left dewdrops in her hair.

The BFG opened the suitcase and took out several empty glass jars. He set them ready on the ground, with their screw tops removed. Then he stood up very straight. His head was now high up in the swirling mist and it kept disappearing, then appearing again. He was holding the long net in his right hand.

Sophie, staring upwards, saw through the mist that his colossal ears were beginning to swivel out from his head. They began waving gently to and fro.

Suddenly the BFG pounced. He leaped high in the air and swung the net through the mist with a great swishing sweep of his arm. "Got him!" he cried. "A jar! A jar! Quick quick quick!" Sophie picked up a jar and held it up to him. He grabbed hold of it. He lowered the net. Very carefully he tipped something absolutely invisible from the net into the jar. He dropped the net and swiftly clapped one hand over the jar. "The top!" he whispered. "The jar top quick!" Sophie picked up the screw top and handed it to him. He screwed it on tight and the jar was closed. The BFG was very excited. He held the jar close to one ear and listened intently.

"It's a winksquiffler!" he whispered with a thrill in his voice. "It's...it's...it's...it's even better. It's a phizzwizard! It's a golden phizzwizard!"

Sophie stared at him.

"Oh my, oh my!" he said, holding the jar in front of him. "This will be giving some little tottler a very happy night when I is blowing it in!"

"Is it really a good one?" Sophie asked.

"A *good one?*" he cried. "It's a golden phizz-wizard! It is not often I is getting one of these!" He handed the jar to Sophie and said "Please be still as a starfish now. I is thinking there may be a whole swarm of phizzwizards up there today. And do kindly stop breathing. You is terribly noisy down there."

"I haven't moved a muscle," Sophie said.

"Then don't," the BFG answered sharply. Once again he stood up tall in the mist, holding his net at the ready. Then came the long silence, the waiting, the listening, and at last, with surprising suddenness came the leap and the swish of the net.

"Another jar!" he cried. "Quick quick quick!"

When the second dream was safely in the jar and the top was screwed down, the BFG held it to his ear.

"Oh *no!*" he cried. "Oh mince my maggots! Oh swipe my swoggles!"

"What's the matter?" Sophie asked.

"It's a trogglehumper!" he shouted. His voice was filled with fury and anguish. "Oh, save our solos!" he cried. "Deliver us from weasels! The devil is dancing on my dibbler!"

"What *are* you talking about?" Sophie said. The BFG was getting more distressed every moment.

"Oh, bash my eyebones!" he cried, waving the jar in the air. "I come all this way to get lovely golden dreams and what is I catching?"

"What *are* you catching?" Sophie said.

"I is catching a frightsome trogglehumper!" he cried. "This is a *bad bad dream!* It is worse than a bad dream! It is a *nightmare!*"

"Oh dear," Sophie said. "What will you do with that?"

"I is never never letting it go!" the BFG cried. "If I do, then some poor little tottler will be having the most curdbloodling time! This one is a real kicksy bogthumper! I is exploding it as soon as I get home!"

"Nightmares are horrible," Sophie said. "I had one once and I woke up sweating all over."

"With this one you would be waking up *scream-ing* all over!" the BFG said. "This one would make your teeth stand on end! If this one got into you, your blood would be freezing to icicles and your skin would go creeping across the floor!"

"Is it as bad as that?"

"It's worse!" cried the BFG. "This is a real

whoppsy grobswitcher!"

"You said it was a trogglehumper," Sophie told him.

"It *is* a trogglehumper!" cried the exasperated BFG. "But it is also a *bogthumper* and a *grobswitcher!* It is all three riddled into one! Oh, I is so glad I is clutching it tight. Ah, you wicked beastie, you!" he cried, holding up the jar and staring into it. "Never more is you going to be bunkdoodling the poor little human-beaney tottlers!"

Sophie, who was also staring into the glass jar, cried out, "I can see it! There's something in there!"

"Of course there is something in there," the BFG said. "You is looking at a frightsome trogglehumper."

"But you told me dreams were invisible."

"They is always invisible until they is *captured,*" the BFG told her. "After that they is losing a little of their invisibility. We is seeing this one very clearly."

Inside the jar Sophie could see the faint scarlet outline of something that looked like a mixture between a blob of gas and a bubble of jelly. It was moving violently, thrashing against the sides of the jar and forever changing shape.

"It's wiggling all over the place!" Sophie cried. "It's fighting to get out! It'll bash itself to bits!"

"The nastier the dream, the angrier it is getting when it is in prison," the BFG said. "It is the same as with wild animals. If an animal is very fierce and you is putting it in a cage, it will make a

94

tremendous rumpledumpus. If it is a nice animal like a cockatootloo or a fogglefrump, it will sit quietly. Dreams is exactly the same. This one is a nasty fierce bogrotting nightmare. Just look at him splashing himself against the glass!"

"It's quite frightening!" Sophie cried.

"I would be hating to get this one inside me on a darksome night," the BFG said.

"So would I!" Sophie said.

The BFG started putting the bottles back into the suitcase.

"Is that all?" Sophie asked. "Are we going?"

"I is so upset by this trogglehumping bog-thumping grobswitcher," the BFG said, "that I is not wishing to go on. Dream-catching is finished for today."

Soon Sophie was back in the waistcoat pocket and the BFG was racing home as fast as he could go. When, at last, they emerged out of the mist and came again on to the hot yellow wasteland, all the other giants were sprawled out on the ground, fast asleep.

A Trogglehumper for the Fleshlumpeater

"They is always having fifty winks before they goes scumpering off to hunt human beans in the evening," the BFG said. He stopped for a few moments to let Sophie have a better look. "Giants is only sleeping every then and now," he said. "Not nearly as much as human beans. Human beans is crazy for sleeping. Is it ever occurring to you that a human bean who is fifty is spending about *twenty* years sleeping fast?"

"I must admit that never occurred to me," Sophie said.

"You should *allow* it to occur to you," the BFG said. "Imagine it please. This human bean who says he is fifty has been fast asleep for twenty years and is not even knowing where he is! Not even *doing* anything! Not even thinking!"

"It's a funny thought," Sophie said.

"Exunckly," the BFG said. "So what I is trying to explain to you is that a human bean who says he is fifty is not fifty, he is only thirty."

"What about me?" Sophie said. "I am eight."

"You is not eight at all," the BFG said. "Human bean babies and little chiddlers is spending half their time sleeping, so you is only four."

"I'm eight," Sophie said.

"You may *think* you is eight," the BFG said,

"but you has only spent four years of your life with your little eyes open. You is only four and please stop higgling me. Titchy little snapperwhippers like you should not be higgling around with an old sage and onions who is hundreds of years more than you."

"How much do giants sleep?" Sophie asked.

"They is never wasting much time snozzling," the BFG said. "Two or three hours is enough."

"When do *you* sleep?" Sophie asked.

"Even less," the BFG answered. "I is sleeping only once in a blue baboon."

Sophie, peeping out from her pocket, examined the nine sleeping giants. They looked even more grotesque now than when they were awake. Sprawled out across the yellow plain, they covered an area about the size of a football field. Most of them were lying on their backs with their enormous mouths wide open, and they were snoring like foghorns. The noise was awful.

Suddenly the BFG gave a jump in the air. "By gumfrog!" he cried. "I is just having the most whoppsy-whiffling idea!"

"What?" Sophie said.

"Wait!" he cried. "Hold your horsefeathers! Keep your skirt on! Just you wait to see what I is going to bring about!" He galloped off fast to his cave with Sophie hanging on tight to the rim of the pocket. He rolled back the stone. He entered the cave. He was very excited. He was moving quickly. "You stay where you is in my pocket, huggybee," he said. "We is doing this lovely bit of

97

buckswashling both together." He laid aside the dream-catching net but hung on to the suitcase. He ran across to the other side of the cave and grabbed the long trumpet thing, the one he had been carrying when Sophie had first seen him in the village. With the suitcase in one hand and the trumpet in the other, he dashed out of the cave.

What *is* he up to now, Sophie wondered.

"Peep your head up good," the BFG said, "then you will get a fine winkle of what is going on."

When the BFG came near to the sleeping giants, he slowed his pace. He began moving softly. He crept on his toes toward the ugly brutes. They were still snoring loudly. They looked repulsive, filthy, diabolical. The BFG tip-toed around them. He went past the Gizzardgulper, the Bloodbottler, the Meatdripper, the Childchewer. Then he stop-

ped. He had reached the Fleshlumpeater. He pointed at him, then he looked down at Sophie and gave her a big wink.

He knelt on the ground and very quietly he opened the suitcase. He took out of it the glass jar containing the terrible nightmarish troggle-humper.

At that point, Sophie guessed what was going to happen next.

Owtch, she thought. This could be rather dangerous. She crouched lower in the pocket so that only the top of her head and her eyes were showing. She wanted to be ready to duck out of sight very fast should anything go wrong.

They were about ten feet away from the Fleshlumpeater's face. The snoring-snorting noise he was making was disgusting. Every now and again a

big bubble of spit formed between his two open lips and then it would burst with a splash and cover his face with saliva.

Taking infinite care, the BFG unscrewed the top of the glass jar and tipped the squiggling squirming faintly scarlet trogglehumper into the wide end of his long trumpet. He put the other end of the trumpet to his lips. He aimed the instrument directly at the Fleshlumpeater's face. He took a deep breath, puffed out his cheeks and then *whoof!* He blew!

Sophie saw a flash of pale red go darting towards the giant's face. For a split second it hovered above the face. Then it was gone. It seemed to have been sucked up the giant's nose, but it had all happened so quickly, Sophie couldn't be sure.

"We had better be skiddling away quick to where it is safe," the BFG whispered. He trotted off for about a hundred yards, then he stopped. He crouched low to the earth. "Now," he said, "we is waiting for the gun and flames to begin."

They didn't have long to wait.

The air was suddenly pierced by the most fearful roar Sophie had ever heard, and she saw the Fleshlumpeater's body, all fifty-four feet of it, rise up off the ground and fall back again with a thump. Then it began to wriggle and twist and bounce about in the most violent fashion. It was quite frightening to watch.

"Eeeow!" roared the Fleshlumpeater. "Ayeee! Oooow!"

"He's still asleep," the BFG whispered. "The

terrible trogglehumping nightmare is beginning to hit him."

"Serves him right," Sophie said. She could feel no sympathy for this great brute who ate children as though they were sugar-lumps.

"Save us!" screamed the Fleshlumpeater, thrashing about madly. "He is after me! He is getting me!"

The thrashing of limbs and the waving of arms became more violent by the second. It was an awesome thing to watch such a massive creature having such mighty convulsions.

"It's Jack!" bellowed the Fleshlumpeater. "It's the grueful gruncious Jack! Jack is after me! Jack is wackcrackling me! Jack is spikesticking me! Jack

is splashplunking me! It is the terrible frightswiping Jack!" The Fleshlumpeater was writhing about over the ground like some colossal tortured snake. "Oh, spare me, Jack!" he yelled. "Don't hurt me, Jack!"

"Who is this Jack he's on about?" Sophie whispered.

"Jack is the only human bean all giants is frightened of," the BFG told her. "They is all absolutely terrified of Jack. They is all hearing that Jack is a famous giant-killer."

"Save me!" screamed the Fleshlumpeater. "Have mercy on this poor little giant! The beanstalk! He is coming at me with his terrible spikesticking beanstalk! Take it away! I is begging you, Jack, I is praying you not to touch me with your terrible spikesticking beanstalk!"

"Us giants," the BFG whispered, "is not knowing very much about this dreaded human bean called Jack. We is knowing only that he is a famous giant-killer and that he is owning something called a beanstalk. We is knowing also that the beanstalk is a fearsome thing and Jack is using it to kill giants."

Sophie couldn't stop smiling.

"What is you griggling at?" the BFG asked her, slightly nettled.

"I'll tell you later," Sophie said.

The awful nightmare had now gripped the great brute to such an extent that he was tying his whole body into knots. "Do not do it, Jack!" he screeched. "I was not eating you, Jack! I is never

102

eating human beans! I swear I has never gobbled a single human bean in all my wholesome life!"

"Liar," said the BFG.

Just then, one of the Fleshlumpeater's flailing fists caught the still-fast-asleep Meatdripping Giant smack in the mouth. At the same time, one of his furiously thrashing legs kicked the snoring Gizzardgulping Giant right in the guts. Both the injured giants woke up and leaped to their feet.

"He is swiping me right in the mouth!" yelled the Meatdripper.

"He is bungswoggling me smack in the guts!" shouted the Gizzardgulper.

The two of them rushed at the Fleshlumpeater and began pounding him with their fists and feet. The wretched Fleshlumpeater woke up with a bang. He awoke straight from one nightmare into

another. He roared into battle, and in the bellowing thumping rough and tumble that followed, one
sleeping giant after another either got stepped
upon or kicked. Soon, all nine of them were on
their feet having the most almighty free-for-all.
They punched and kicked and scratched and bit
and butted each other as hard as they could. Blood
flowed. Noses went crunch. Teeth fell out like
hailstones. The giants roared and screamed and
cursed, and for many minutes the noise of battle
rolled across the yellow plain.

The BFG smiled a big wide smile of absolute
pleasure. "I is loving it when they is all having a

good tough and rumble," he said.

"They'll kill each other," Sophie said.

"Never," the BFG answered. "Those beasts is always bishing and walloping at one another. Soon it will be getting dusky and they will be galloping off to fill their tummies."

"They're coarse and foul and filthy," Sophie said. "I hate them!"

As the BFG headed back to the cave, he said quietly, "We certainly was putting that nightmare to good use though, wasn't we?"

"Excellent use," Sophie said. "Well done you."

Dreams

The Big Friendly Giant was seated at the great table in his cave and he was doing his homework.

Sophie sat cross-legged on the table-top near by, watching him at work.

The glass jar containing the one and only good dream they had caught that day stood between them.

The BFG, with great care and patience, was printing something on a piece of paper with an enormous pencil.

"What are you writing?" Sophie asked him.

"Every dream is having its special label on the bottle," the BFG said. "How else could I be finding the one I am wanting in a hurry?"

"But can you really and truly tell what sort of a dream it's going to be simply by listening to it?" Sophie asked.

"I can," the BFG said, not looking up.

"But *how?* Is it by the way it hums and buzzes?"

"You is less or more right," the BFG said. "Every dream in the world is making a different sort of buzzy-hum music. And these grand swashboggling ears of mine is able to read that music."

"By music, do you mean tunes?"

"I is not meaning tunes."

"Then what *do* you mean?"

106

"Human beans is having their own music, right or left?"

"Right," Sophie said. "Lots of music."

"And sometimes human beans is very overcome when they is hearing wonderous music. They is getting shivers down their spindels. Right or left?"

"Right," Sophie said.

"So the music is saying something to them. It is sending a message. I do not think the human beans is knowing what that message is, but they is loving it just the same."

"That's about right," Sophie said.

"But because of these jumpsquiffling ears of

mine," the BFG said, "I is not only able to *hear* the music that dreams is making but I is *understanding* it also."

"What do you mean *understanding* it?" Sophie said.

"I can read it," the BFG said. "It talks to me. It is like a langwitch."

"I find that just a little hard to believe," Sophie said.

"I'll bet you is also finding it hard to believe in quogwinkles," the BFG said, "and how they is visiting us from the stars."

"Of course I don't believe that," Sophie said.

The BFG regarded her gravely with those huge eyes of his. "I hope you will forgive me," he said, "if I tell you that human beans is thinking they is very clever, but they is not. They is nearly all of them notmuchers and squeakpips."

"I *beg* your pardon," Sophie said.

"The matter with human beans," the BFG went on, "is that they is absolutely refusing to believe in anything unless they is actually seeing it right in front of their own schnozzles. Of course quogwinkles is existing. I is meeting them oftenly. I is even chittering to them." He turned away contemptuously from Sophie and resumed his writing. Sophie moved over to read what he had written so far. The letters were printed big and bold, but were not very well formed. Here is what it said:

THIS DREAM IS ABOUT HOW I IS SAVING MY TEECHER

108

FROM DROWNING. I IS DIVING INTO THE RIVER FROM
A HIGH BRIDGE AND I IS DRAGGING MY TEECHER TO
THE BANK AND THEN I IS GIVING HIM THE KISS OF
DEATH...

"The kiss of *what?*" Sophie asked.

The BFG stopped writing and raised his head
slowly. His eyes rested on Sophie's face. "I is
telling you once before," he said quietly, "that I is
never having a chance to go to school. I is full of
mistakes. They is not my fault. I do my best. You
is a lovely little girl, but please remember that *you*
is not exactly Miss Knoweverything yourself."

"I'm sorry," Sophie said. "I really am. It is very
rude of me to keep correcting you."

The BFG gazed at her for a while longer, then he
bent his head again to his slow laborious writing.

"Tell me honestly," Sophie said. "If you blew
this dream into my bedroom when I was asleep,
would I really and truly start dreaming about how
I saved my teacher from drowning by diving off the
bridge?"

"More," the BFG said. "A lot more. But I cannot be squibbling the whole gropefluncking dream on a titchy bit of paper. Of course there is more."

The BFG laid down his pencil and placed one massive ear close to the jar. For about thirty seconds he listened intently. "Yes," he said, nodding his great head solemnly up and down. "This dream is continuing very nice. It has a very dory-hunky ending."

"How does it end?" Sophie said. *"Please* tell me."

"You would be dreaming," the BFG said, "that the morning after you is saving the teacher from the river, you is arriving at school and you is seeing all the five hundred pupils sitting in the assembly hall, and all the teachers as well, and the head teacher is then standing up and saying, 'I is wanting the whole school to give three cheers for Sophie because she is so brave and is saving the life of our fine arithmetic teacher, Mr Figgins, who was unfortunately pushed off the bridge into the river by our gym-teacher, Miss Amelia Up-scotch. So three cheers for Sophie!' And the whole school is then cheering like mad and shouting bravo well done, and, for ever after that, even when you is getting your sums all gungswizzled and muggled up, Mr Figgins is always giving you ten out of ten and writing *Good Work Sophie* in your exercise book. Then you is waking up."

"I like that dream," Sophie said.

"Of course you like it," the BFG said. "It is a phizzwizard." He licked the back of the label and stuck it on the jar. "I is usually writing a bit more than this on the labels," he said. "But you is watching me and making me jumpsy."

"I'll go and sit somewhere else," Sophie said.

"Don't go," he said. "Look in the jar carefully and I think you will be seeing this dream."

Sophie peered into the jar and there, sure enough, she saw the faint translucent outline of something about the size of a hen's egg. There was just a touch of colour in it, a pale sea-green, soft and shimmering and very beautiful. There it lay, this small oblong sea-green jellyish thing, at the bottom of the jar, quite peaceful, but pulsing gently, the whole of it moving in and out ever so slightly, as though it were breathing.

"It's moving!" Sophie cried. "It's alive!"

"Of course it is alive."

"What will you feed it on?" Sophie asked.

"It is not needing any food," the BFG told her.

"That's cruel," Sophie said. "Everything alive needs food of some sort. Even trees and plants."

"The north wind is alive," the BFG said. "It is moving. It touches you on the cheek and on the hands. But nobody is feeding it."

Sophie was silent. This extraordinary giant was disturbing her ideas. He seemed to be leading her toward mysteries that were beyond her understanding.

"A dream is not needing anything," the BFG went on. "If it is a good one, it is waiting peaceably for ever until it is released and allowed to do its job. If it is a bad one, it is always fighting to get

111

out."

The BFG stood up and walked over to one of the many shelves and placed the latest jar among the thousands of others.

"Please can I see some of the other dreams?" Sophie asked him.

The BFG hesitated. "Nobody is ever seeing them before," he said. "But perhaps after all I is letting you have a little peep." He picked her up off the table and stood her on the palm of one of his huge hands. He carried her toward the shelves. "Over here is some of the good dreams," he said. "The phizzwizards."

"Would you hold me closer so I can read the labels," Sophie said.

"My labels is only telling bits of it," the BFG said. "The dreams is usually much longer. The labels is just to remind me."

Sophie started to read the labels. The first one seemed long enough to her. It went right round the jar, and as she read it, she had to keep turning the jar. This is what it said:

TODAY I IS SITTING IN CLASS AND I DISCOVER THAT IF I IS STARING VERY HARD AT MY TEECHER IN A SPESHAL WAY, I IS ABLE TO PUT HER TO SLEEP. SO I KEEP STARING AT HER AND IN THE END HER HEAD DROPS ON TO HER DESK AND SHE GOES FAST TO SLEEP AND SNORKLES LOUDLY. THEN IN MARCHES THE HEAD TEACHER AND HE SHOUTS "WAKE UP MISS PLUMRIDGE! HOW DARE YOU GO TO SLEEP IN CLASS! GO FETCH YOUR HAT AND COTE AND LEAVE THIS

SCHOOL FOR EVER! YOU IS SACKED!" BUT IN A JIFFY I
IS PUTTING THE HEAD TEECHER TO SLEEP AS WELL,
AND HE JUST CRUMPLES SLOWLY TO THE FLOOR LIKE
A LUMP OF JELLY AND THERE HE LIES ALL IN A HEAP
AND STARTS SNORKELLING EVEN LOWDER THAN MISS
PLUMRIDGE. AND THEN I IS HEARING MY MUMMY'S
VOICE SAYING WAKE UP YOUR BREKFUST IS REDDY.

"What a funny dream," Sophie said.

"It's a ringbeller," the BFG said. "It's whoppsy."

Inside the jar, just below the edge of the label,
Sophie could see the putting-to-sleep dream lying
peacefully on the bottom, pulsing gently, sea-
green like the other one, but perhaps a trifle larger.

"Do you have separate dreams for boys and for
girls?" Sophie asked.

"Of course," the BFG said. "If I is giving a girl's
dream to a boy, even if it was a really whoppsy
girl's dream, the boy would be waking up and
thinking what a rotbungling grinksludging old
dream that was."

"Boys would," Sophie said.

"These here is all girls' dreams on this shelf,"
the BFG said.

"Can I read a boy's dream?"

113

"You can," the BFG said, and he lifted her to a higher shelf. The label on the nearest boy's-dream jar read as follows:

I IS MAKING MYSELF A MARVELUS PAIR OF SUCTION BOOTS AND WHEN I PUT THEM ON I IS ABEL TO WALK STRATE UP THE KITSHUN WALL AND ACROSS THE CEILING. WELL, I IS WALKING UPSIDE DOWN ON THE CEILING WEN MY BIG SISTER COMES IN AND SHE IS STARTING TO YELL AT ME AS SHE ALWAYS DOES, YELLING WOT ON EARTH IS YOU DOING UP THERE WALKING ON THE CEILING AND I LOOKS DOWN AT HER AND I SMILES AND I SAYS I *TOLD* YOU YOU WAS DRIVING ME UP THE WALL AND NOW YOU HAS DONE IT.

"I find that one rather silly," Sophie said.

"Boys wouldn't," the BFG said, grinning. "It's another ringbeller. Perhaps you has seen enough now."

"Let me read another boy's one," Sophie said. The next label said:

THE TELLYFONE RINGS IN OUR HOUSE AND MY FATHER PICKS IT UP AND SAYS IN HIS VERY IMPORTANT TELLYFONE VOICE "SIMPKINS SPEAKING." THEN HIS FACE GOES WHITE AND HIS VOICE GOES ALL FUNNY AND HE SAYS *"WHAT! WHO?"* AND THEN HE SAYS "YES SIR I UNDERSTAND SIR BUT SURELY IT IS *ME* YOU IS WISHING TO SPEKE TO SIR NOT MY LITTLE SON?" MY FATHER'S FACE IS GOING FROM WHITE TO DARK PURPEL AND HE IS GULPING LIKE HE HAS A LOBSTER STUCK IN HIS THROTE AND THEN AT LAST HE IS SAYING "YES SIR VERY WELL SIR I WILL GET HIM SIR" AND HE TURNS TO ME AND HE SAYS IN A RATHER RESPECKFUL VOICE "IS YOU KNOWING THE PRESIDENT OF THE UNITED STATES?" AND I SAYS "NO BUT I EXPECT HE IS HEARING ABOUT ME." THEN I IS HAVING A LONG TALK ON THE FONE AND SAYING THINGS LIKE "LET ME TAKE CARE OF IT, MR PRESIDENT. YOU'LL BUNGLE IT ALL UP IF YOU DO IT YOUR WAY." AND MY FATHER'S EYES IS GOGGLING RIGHT OUT OF HIS HEAD AND THAT IS WHEN I IS HEARING MY FATHER'S REAL VOICE SAYING GET UP YOU LAZY SLOB OR YOU WILL BE LATE FOR SKOOL.

"Boys are crazy," Sophie said. "Let me read this next one." Sophie started reading the next label:

I IS HAVING A BATH AND I IS DISCOVERING THAT IF I PRESS QUITE HARD ON MY TUMMY BUTTON A FUNNY FEELING COMES OVER ME AND SUDDENLEY MY LEGS

IS NOT THERE NOR IS MY ARMS. IN FACT I HAS
BECOME ABSOLOOTLY INVISIBLE ALL OVER. I IS STILL
THERE BUT NO ONE CAN SEE ME NOT EVEN MYSELF.
SO MY MUMMY COMES IN AND SAYS "WHERE IS THAT
CHILD! HE WAS IN THE BATH A MINIT AGO AND HE
CAN'T POSSIBLY HAVE WASHED HIMSELF PROPERLY!"
SO I SAYS "HERE I IS" AND SHE SAYS "WHERE?" AND I
SAYS "HERE" AND SHE SAYS "WHERE?" AND I SAYS
"HERE!" AND SHE YELLS "HENRY! COME UP QUICK!"
AND WHEN MY DADDY RUSHES IN I IS WASHING
MYSELF AND MY DADDY SEES THE SOAP FLOATING
AROUND IN THE AIR BUT OF CORSE HE IS NOT SEEING
ME AND HE SHOUTS "WHERE ARE YOU BOY?" AND I
SAYS "HERE" AND HE SAYS "WHERE?" AND I SAYS
"HERE" AND HE SAYS "*WHERE*" AND I SAYS "*HERE!*"
AND HE SAYS "THE SOAP, BOY! THE SOAP! IT'S FLYING
IN THE AIR!" THEN I PRESS MY TUMMY BUTTON
AGAIN AND NOW I IS VISIBLE. MY DADDY IS SQUIFFY

116

WITH EXCITEMENT AND HE SAYS "YOU IS THE INVISIBLE BOY !" AND I SAYS "NOW I IS GOING TO HAVE SOME FUN," SO WHEN I IS OUT OF THE BATH AND I HAVE DRIED MYSELF I PUT ON MY DRESSING-GOWN AND SLIPPERS AND I PRESS MY TUMMY BUTTON AGAIN TO BECOME INVISIBLE AND I GO DOWN INTO THE TOWN AND WALK IN THE STREETS . OF CORSE ONLY ME IS INVISIBLE BUT NOT THE THINGS I IS WEARING SO WHEN PEEPLE IS SEEING A DRESSING GOWN AND SLIPPERS FLOATING ALONG THE STREET WITH NOBODY IN IT THERE IS A PANIC WITH EVERYBODY YELLING "A GHOST! A GHOST!" AND PEEPLE IS SCREAMING LEFT AND RIGHT AND BIG STRONG POLICEMEN IS RUNNING FOR THEIR LIVES AND BEST OF ALL I SEE MR GRUMMIT MY ALGEBRA TEECHER COMING OUT OF A PUB AND I FLOAT UP TO HIM AND SAY "BOO!" AND HE LETS OUT A FRIGHT-SOME HOWL AND DASHES BACK INTO THE PUB AND THEN I IS WAKING UP AND FEELING HAPPY AS A WHIFFSQUIDDLER.

"Pretty ridiculous," Sophie said. All the same, she couldn't resist reaching down and pressing her own tummy button to see if it worked. Nothing happened.

"Dreams is very mystical things," the BFG said. "Human beans is not understanding them at all. Not even their brainiest prossefors is understanding them. Has you seen enough?"

"Just this last one," Sophie said. "This one here."

She started reading:

I HAS RITTEN A BOOK AND IT IS SO EXCITING NOBODY CAN PUT IT DOWN. AS SOON AS YOU HAS RED THE FIRST LINE YOU IS SO HOOKED ON IT YOU CANNOT STOP UNTIL THE LAST PAGE. IN ALL THE CITIES PEEPLE IS WALKING IN THE STREETS BUMPING INTO EACH OTHER BECAUSE THEIR FACES IS BURIED IN MY BOOK AND DENTISTS IS READING IT AND TRYING TO FILL TEETHS AT THE SAME TIME BUT NOBODY MINDS BECAUSE THEY IS ALL READING IT TOO IN THE DENTIST'S CHAIR. DRIVERS IS READING IT WHILE DRIVING AND CARS IS CRASHING ALL OVER THE COUNTRY. BRAIN SURGEONS IS READING IT WHILE THEY IS OPERATING ON BRAINS AND AIRLINE PILOTS IS READING IT AND GOING TO TIMBUCTOO INSTEAD OF LONDON. FOOTBALL PLAYERS IS READING IT ON THE FIELD BECAUSE THEY CAN'T PUT IT DOWN AND SO IS OLIMPICK RUNNERS WHILE THEY IS RUNNING. EVERYBODY HAS TO SEE WHAT IS GOING TO HAPPEN NEXT IN MY BOOK AND WHEN I WAKE UP I IS STILL TINGLING WITH EXCITEMENT AT BEING

THE GREATEST RITER THE WORLD HAS EVER KNOWN
UNTIL MY MUMMY COMES IN AND SAYS I WAS
LOOKING AT YOUR ENGLISH EXERCISE BOOK LAST
NITE AND REALLY YOUR SPELLING IS ATROSHUS SO IS
YOUR PUNTULASHON.

"That's enough for now," the BFG said. "There is
dillions more but my arm is getting tired holding
you up."

"What are all those over there?" Sophie said.
"Why have they got such tiny labels?"

"That," the BFG said, "is because one day I is
catching so many dreams I is not having the
time or energy to write out long labels. But there
is enough to remind me."

"Can I look?" Sophie said.

The long-suffering BFG carried her across to the jars she was pointing to. Sophie read them rapidly, one after the other:

I IS CLIMBING MOUNT EVERAST WITH JUST MY PUSSY-CAT FOR CUMPANY.

I IS INVENTING A CAR THAT RUNS ON TOOTHPASTE.

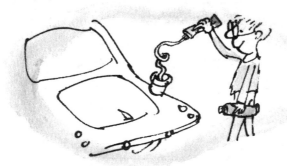

I IS ABLE TO MAKE THE ELEKTRIK LITES GO ON AND OFF JUST BY WISHING IT.

I IS ONLY AN EIGHT YEAR OLD LITTLE BOY BUT I IS
GROWING A SPLENDID BUSHY BEARD AND ALL THE
OTHER BOYS IS JALOUS.

I IS ABEL TO JUMP OUT OF ANY HIGH WINDOW AND
FLOTE DOWN SAFELY.

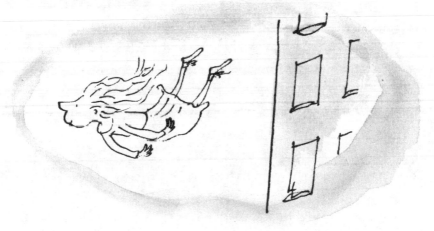

I HAS A PET BEE THAT MAKES ROCK AND ROLL MUSIK
WHEN IT FLIES.

"What amazes me," Sophie said, "is how you ever learned to write in the first place."

"Ah," said the BFG. "I has been wondering how long it is before you is asking me that."

"Considering you never went to school, I think it's quite marvellous," Sophie said. "How *did* you learn?"

The BFG crossed the cave and opened a tiny secret door in the wall. He took out a book, very old and tattered. By human standards, it was an ordinary sized book, but it looked like a postage stamp in his huge hand.

"One night," he said, "I is blowing a dream through a window and I sees this book lying on the little boy's bedroom table. I wanted it so very badly, you understand. But I is refusing to steal it. I would never do that."

"So how did you get it?" Sophie asked.

"I *borrowed* it," the BFG said, smiling a little. "Just for a short time I borrowed it."

"How long have you had it?" Sophie asked.

"Perhaps only about eighty years," the BFG said. "Soon I shall be putting it back."

"And that's how you taught yourself to write?" Sophie asked him.

"I is reading it hundreds of times," the BFG said. "And I is still reading it and teaching new words to myself and how to write them. It is the most scrumdiddliumptious story."

Sophie took the book out of his hand. "*Nicholas Nickleby*," she read aloud.

"By Dahl's Chickens," the BFG said.

"By *who*?" Sophie said.

Just then, there came a tremendous noise of galloping feet from outside the cave. "What's that?" Sophie cried.

"That is all the giants zippfizzing off to another country to guzzle human beans," the BFG said. He quickly popped Sophie into his waistcoat pocket, then hurried to the cave entrance and rolled back the stone.

Sophie, peeping out of her spy-hole, saw all nine of the fearsome giants coming past at full gallop.

"Where is you off to tonight?" shouted the BFG.

"We is all of us flushbunking off to England tonight," answered the Fleshlumpeater as they went galloping past. "England is a luctuous land and we is fancying a few nice little English chiddlers."

"I," shouted the Maidmasher, "is knowing where there is a gigglehouse for girls and I is guzzling myself full as a frothblower!"

"And I knows where there is a bogglebox for boys!" shouted the Gizzardgulper. "All I has to do is reach in and grab myself a handful! English boys is tasting extra lickswishy!"

In a few seconds, the nine galloping giants were out of sight.

"What *did* he mean?" Sophie said, poking her head out of the pocket. "What is a gigglehouse for girls?"

"He is meaning a girls' school," the BFG said. "He will be eating them by the bundle."

"Oh no!" cried Sophie.

"And boys from a boys' school," said the BFG.

"It mustn't happen!" Sophie cried out. "We've got to stop them! We can't just sit here and do nothing!"

"There's not a thing we can do," the BFG said. "We is helpless as horsefeathers." He sat down on a large craggy blue rock near the entrance to his cave. He took Sophie from his pocket and put her beside him on the rock. "It is now quite safe for you to be outside until they is coming back," he said.

The sun had dipped below the horizon and it was getting dark.

The Great Plan

"We've absolutely *got* to stop them!" Sophie cried. "Put me back in your pocket quick and we'll chase after them and warn everyone in England they're coming."

"Redunculus and *um*-possiple," the BFG said. "They is going two times as fast as me and they is finishing their guzzle before we is halfway."

"But we can't just sit here doing nothing!" Sophie cried. "How many girls and boys are they going to eat tonight?"

"Many," the BFG said. "The Fleshlumpeating Giant alone has a most squackling whoppsy appetite."

"Will he snatch them out of their beds while they're sleeping?"

"Like peas out of a poddle," the BFG said.

"I can't bear to think of it!" Sophie cried.

"Then don't," the BFG said. "For years and years I is sitting here on this very rock every night after night when they is galloping away, and I is feeling so sad for all the human beans they is going to gobble up. But I has had to get used to it. There is nothing I can do. If I wasn't a titchy little runty giant only twenty-four feet high then I would be stopping them. But that is absolutely out of the window."

"Do you always know where they're going?" Sophie asked.

"Always," the BFG said. "Every night they is yelling it at me as they go bootling past. The other day they was yelling 'We is off to Mrs Sippi and Miss Souri to guzzle them both!' "

"Disgusting," Sophie said. "I hate them."

She and the Big Friendly Giant sat quietly side by side on the blue rock in the gathering dusk. Sophie had never felt so helpless in her life. After a while, she stood up and cried out, "I can't stand it! Just think of those poor girls and boys who are going to be eaten alive in a few hours time! We can't just sit here and do nothing! We've got to go after those brutes!"

"No," the BFG said.

"We must!" Sophie cried. "Why won't you go?"

The BFG sighed and shook his head firmly. "I has told you five or six times," he said, "and the third will be the last. I is *never* showing myself to human beans."

"Why ever not?"

"If I do, they will be putting me in the zoo with all the jiggyraffes and cattypiddlers."

"Nonsense," Sophie said.

"And they will be sending *you* straight back to a norphanage," the BFG went on. "Grown-up human beans is not famous for their kindnesses. They is all squifflerotters and grinksludgers."

"That simply isn't true!" Sophie cried angrily. "Some of them are very kind indeed."

"Who?" the BFG said. "Name one."

126

"The Queen of England," Sophie said. "You can't call her a squifflerotter or a grinksludger."

"Well..." the BFG said.

"You can't call her a squeakpip or a notmucher either," Sophie said, getting angrier and angrier.

"The Fleshlumpeater is longing dearly to guzzle her up," the BFG said, smiling a little now.

"Who, the *Queen?*" Sophie cried, aghast.

"Yes," the BFG answered. "Fleshlumpeater says he is never eating a queen and he thinks perhaps she has an especially scrumdiddlyumptious flavour."

"How dare he!" Sophie cried.

"But Fleshlumpeater says there is too many soldiers around her palace and he dursent try it."

"He'd better not!" Sophie said.

"He is also saying he would like very much to guzzle one of the soldiers in his pretty red suit but he is worried about those big black furry hats they is wearing. He thinks they might be sticking in his throat."

"I hope he chokes," Sophie said.

"Fleshlumpeater is a very careful giant," the BFG said.

Sophie was silent for a few moments. Then suddenly, in a voice filled with excitement, she cried out, "I've got it! By golly, I think I've got it!"

"Got what?" asked the BFG.

"The answer!" cried Sophie. "We'll go to the Queen! It's a terrific idea! If I went and told the Queen about these disgusting man-eating giants, I'm sure she'd do something about it!"

The BFG looked down at her sadly and shook his head. "She is never believing you," he said. "Never in a month of Mondays."

"I think she would."

"Never," the BFG said. "It is sounding such a wonky tall story, the Queen will be laughing and saying 'What awful rubbsquash!'"

"She would not!"

"Of course she would," the BFG said. "I has told you before that human beans is simply not *believing* in giants."

"Then it's up to us to find a way of *making* her believe in them," Sophie said.

"And how is you getting in to see the Queen anyway?" the BFG asked.

"Now hold on a sec," Sophie said. "Just you hold on a sec because I've got another idea."

"Your ideas is full of crodswoggle," the BFG said.

"Not this one," Sophie said. "You say that if we tell the Queen, she would never believe us?"

"I is certain she wouldn't," the BFG said.

"But we aren't *going* to tell her!" Sophie said excitedly. "We don't *have* to tell her! We'll make her *dream* it!"

"That is an even more frothbungling suggestion," the BFG said. "Dreams is lots of fun but nobody is believing in dreams either. You is only believing in a dream while you is actually dreaming it. But as soon as you is waking up you is saying 'Oh thank goodness it was only a dream.'"

"Don't you worry about that part of it," Sophie said. "I can fix that."

"Never can you fix it," the BFG said.

"I can! I swear I can! But first of all, let me ask

129

you a very important question. Here it is. Can you make a person dream absolutely anything in the world?"

"Anything you like," the BFG said proudly.

"If I said I wanted to dream that I was in a flying bathtub with silver wings, could you make me dream it?"

"I could," the BFG said.

"But how?" Sophie said. "You obviously don't have exactly that dream in your collection."

"I do not," the BFG said. "But I could soon be mixing it up."

"How could you mix it up?"

"It is a little bit like mixing a cake," the BFG said. "If you is putting the right amounts of all the different things into it, you is making the cake come out any way you want, sugary, splongy, curranty, Christmassy or grobswitchy. It is the same with dreams."

"Go on," Sophie said.

"I has dillions of dreams on my shelfs, right or left?"

"Right," Sophie said.

"I has dreams about bathtubs, lots of them. I has dreams about silver wings. I has dreams about flying. So all I has to do is mix those dreams together in the proper way and I is very quickly making a dream where you is flying in a bathtub with silver wings."

"I see what you mean," Sophie said. "But I didn't know you could mix one dream with another."

"Dreams *like* being mixed," the BFG answered. "They is getting very lonesome all by themselves in those glassy bottles."

"Right," Sophie said. "Now then, do you have dreams about the Queen of England?"

"Lots of them," the BFG said.

"And about giants?"

"Of course," the BFG said.

"And about giants eating people?"

"Swiggles of them," the BFG said.

"And about little girls like me?"

"Those is commonest of all," the BFG said. "I has bottles and bottles of dreams about little girls."

"And you could mix them all up just as I want you to?" Sophie asked, getting more and more excited.

"Of course," the BFG said. "But how is this helping us? I think you is barking up the wrong dog."

"Now hold on," Sophie said. "Listen carefully. I want you to mix a dream which you will blow into the Queen of England's bedroom when she is asleep. And this is how it will go."

"Now hang on a mintick," the BFG said. "How is I possibly going to get near enough to the Queen of England's bedroom to blow in my dream? You is talking dumbsilly."

"I'll tell you that later," Sophie said. "For the moment please listen carefully. Here is the dream I want you to mix. Are you paying attention?"

"Very close," the BFG said.

131

"I want the Queen to dream that nine disgusting giants, each one about fifty feet tall are galloping to England in the night. She must dream their names as well. What are their names again?"

"Fleshlumpeater," the BFG said. "Manhugger. Bonecruncher. Childchewer. Meatdripper. Gizzardgulper. Maidmasher. Bloodbottler. And the Butcher Boy."

"Let her dream all those names," Sophie said. "And let her dream that they will be creeping into England in the depths of the witching hour and snatching little boys and girls from their beds. Let her dream that they will be reaching into the bedroom windows and pulling the little boys and girls out of their beds and then..." Sophie paused. "Do they eat them on the spot or do they carry them away first?" she asked.

"They is usually just popping them straight into their mouths like popcorn," the BFG said.

"Put that in the dream," Sophie said. "And then...then the dream must say that when their tummies are full, they will go galloping back to Giant Country where no one can find them."

"Is that all?" The BFG said.

"Certainly not," Sophie said. "You must then explain to the Queen in her dream that there is a Big Friendly Giant who can tell her where all those beasts are living, so that she can send her soldiers and her armies to capture them once and for all. And now let her dream one last and very important thing. Let her dream that there is a little girl called Sophie sitting on her window-sill who will tell her where the Big Friendly Giant is hiding."

"Where is he hiding?" asked the BFG.

"We'll come to that later," Sophie said. "So the Queen dreams her dream, right?"

"Right," the BFG said.

"Then she wakes up and the first thing she thinks is oh what a horrid dream. I'm so glad it *was* only a dream. And then she looks up from her pillow and what does she see?"

"What *does* she see?" the BFG asked.

"She sees a little girl called Sophie sitting on her window-sill, right there in real life before her very eyes."

"How is you going to be sitting on the Queen's window-sill, may I beg?" the BFG said.

"*You* are going to put me there," Sophie said. "And that's the lovely part about it. If someone *dreams* that there is a little girl sitting on her window-sill and then she wakes up and sees that the little girl *really is* sitting there, that is a dream come true, is it not?"

"I is beginning to see where you is driving to," the BFG said. "If the Queen is knowing that part of her dream is true, then perhaps she is believing the rest of it is true as well."

"That's about it," Sophie said. "But I shall have to convince her of that myself."

"You said you is wanting the dream to say there is a Big Friendly Giant who is also going to talk to the Queen?"

"Absolutely," Sophie said. "You must. You are the only one who can tell her where to find the other giants."

"How is I meeting the Queen?" asked the BFG. "I is not wanting to be shooted at by her soldiers."

"The soldiers are only in the front of the Palace," Sophie said. "At the back there is a huge garden and there are no soldiers in there at all. There is a very high wall with spikes on it around the garden to stop people climbing in. But you could simply walk over that."

"How is you knowing all this about the Queen's Palace?" the BFG asked.

"Last year I was in a different orphanage," Sophie said. "It was in London and we used to go for walks all around there."

"Is you helping me to find this Palace?" the BFG asked. "I has never dared to go hide and sneaking around London in my life."

"I'll show you the way," Sophie said confidently.

"I is frightened of London," the BFG said.

"Don't be," Sophie said. "It's full of tiny dark streets and there are very few people about in the witching hour."

The BFG picked Sophie up between one finger and a thumb and placed her gently in the palm of the other hand. "Is the Queen's Palace very big?" he asked.

"Huge," Sophie said.

"Then how is we finding the right bedroom?"

"That's up to you," Sophie said. "You're supposed to be an expert at that sort of thing."

"And you is absolutely sure the Queen will not

put me in a zoo with all the cattypiddlers?"

"Of course she won't," Sophie said. "You'll be a hero. And you'll never have to eat snozzcumbers again."

Sophie saw the BFG's eyes widen. He licked his lips.

"You mean it?" he said. "You really mean it? No more disgustive snozzcumbers?"

"You couldn't get one if you wanted to," Sophie said. "Humans don't grow them."

That did it. The BFG got to his feet. "When is you wanting me to mix this special dream?" he asked.

"Now," Sophie said. "At once."

"When is we going to see the Queen?" he said.

"Tonight," Sophie said. "As soon as you've mixed the dream."

"Tonight?" the BFG cried. "Why such a flushbunking flurry?"

"If we can't save tonight's children, we can anyway save tomorrow's," Sophie said. "What is more, I'm getting famished. I haven't had a thing to eat for twenty-four hours."

"Then we had better get crackling," the BFG said, moving back toward the cave.

Sophie kissed him on the tip of his thumb. "I knew you'd do it!" she said. "Come on! Let's hurry!"

Mixing the Dream

It was dark now. The night had already begun. The BFG, with Sophie sitting on his hand, hurried into the cave and put on those brilliant blinding lights that seemed to come from nowhere. He placed Sophie on the table. "Stay there please," he said, "and no chittering. I is needing to listen only to silence when I is mixing up such a knotty plexicated dream as this."

He hurried away from her. He got out an enormous empty glass jar that was the size of a washing machine. He clutched it to his chest and hurried toward the shelves on which stood the thousands and thousands of smaller jars containing the captured dreams.

"Dreams about giants," he muttered to himself as he searched the labels. "The giants is guzzling human beans ... no, not that one ... nor that one ... here's one! ... And here's another! ... " He grabbed the jars and unscrewed the tops. He tipped the dreams into the enormous jar he was clutching and as each one went in, Sophie caught a glimpse of a small sea-green blob tumbling from one jar into the other.

The BFG hurried towards another shelf. "Now," he muttered, "I is wanting dreams about giggle-houses for girls ... and about boggleboxes for

boys." He was becoming very tense now. Sophie could almost see the excitement bubbling inside him as he scurried back and forth among his beloved jars. There must have been fifty thousand dreams altogether up there on the shelves, but he seemed to know almost exactly where every one of them was. "Dreams about a little girl," he muttered. "And dreams about me . . . about the BFG . . . come on, come on, hurry up, get on with it . . . now where in the wonky world is I keeping those? . . ."

And so it went on. In about half an hour the BFG had found all the dreams he wanted and had tipped them into the one huge jar. He put the jar on the table. Sophie sat watching him but said nothing. Inside the big jar, lying on the bottom of it, she could clearly see about fifty of those oval sea-green jellyish shapes, all pulsing gently in and out, some lying on top of others, but each one still a quite separate individual dream.

"Now we is mixing them," the BFG announced. He went to the cupboard where he kept his bottles of frobscottle, and from it he took out a gigantic egg-beater. It was one of those that has a handle which you turn, and down below there are a lot of overlapping blades that go whizzing round. He inserted the bottom end of this contraption into the big jar where the dreams were lying. "Watch," he said. He started turning the handle very fast.

Flashes of green and blue exploded inside the jar. The dreams were being whisked into a sea-green froth.

"The poor things!" Sophie cried.

"They is not feeling it," the BFG said as he turned the handle. "Dreams is not like human beans or animals. They has no brains. They is made of zozimus."

After about a minute, the BFG stopped whisk-

ing. The whole bottle was now full to the brim
with large bubbles. They were almost exactly like
the bubbles we ourselves blow from soapy water,
except that these had even brighter and more
beautiful colours swimming on their surfaces.

"Keep watching," the BFG said.

Quite slowly, the topmost bubble rose up
through the neck of the jar and floated away. A
second one followed. Then a third and a fourth.
Soon the cave was filled with hundreds of beautifully coloured bubbles, all drifting gently through
the air. It was truly a wonderful sight. As Sophie
watched them, they all started floating towards

the cave entrance, which was still open.

"They're going out," Sophie whispered.

"Of course," the BFG said.

"Where to?"

"Those is all little tiny dream-bits that I isn't using," the BFG said. "They is going back to the misty country to join up with proper dreams."

"It's all a bit beyond me," Sophie said.

"Dreams is full of mystery and magic," the BFG said. "Do not try to understand them. Look in the big bottle and you will now see the dream you is wanting for the Queen."

Sophie turned and stared into the great jar. On the bottom of it, something was thrashing around wildly, bouncing up and down and flinging itself against the walls of the jar. "Good heavens!" she cried. "Is that it?"

"That's it," the BFG said proudly.

"But it's . . . it's horrible!" Sophie cried. "It's jumping about! It wants to get out!"

"That's because it's a trogglehumper," the BFG said. "It's a nightmare."

"Oh, but I don't want you to give the Queen a nightmare!" Sophie cried.

"If she is dreaming about giants guzzling up little boys and girls, then what is you expecting it to be except a nightmare?" the BFG said.

"Oh, no!" Sophie cried.

"Oh, yes," the BFG said. "A dream where you is seeing little chiddlers being eaten is about the most frightsome trogglehumping dream you can get. It's a kicksy bogthumper. It's a whoppsy

141

grobswitcher. It is all of them riddled into one. It is as bad as that dream I blew into the Fleshlumpeater this afternoon. It is worse."

Sophie stared down at the fearful nightmare dream that was still thrashing away in the huge glass jar. It was much larger than the others. It was about the size and shape of, shall we say, a turkey's egg. It was jellyish. It had tinges of bright scarlet deep inside it. There was something terrible about the way it was throwing itself against the sides of the jar.

"I don't want to give the Queen a nightmare," Sophie said.

"I is thinking," the BFG said, "that your Queen will be happy to have a nightmare if having a nightmare is going to save a lot of human beans from being gobbled up by filthsome giants. Is I right or is I left?"

"I suppose you're right," Sophie said. "It's got to be done."

"She will soon be getting over it," the BFG said.

"Have you put all the other important things

into it?" Sophie asked.

"When I is blowing that dream into the Queen's bedroom," the BFG said, "she will be dreaming every single little thingalingaling you is asking me to make her dream."

"About me sitting on the window-sill?"

"That part is very strong."

"And about a Big Friendly Giant?"

"I is putting in a nice long gobbit about him," the BFG said. As he spoke, he picked up one of his smaller jars and very quickly tipped the struggling thrashing trogglehumper out of the large jar into the small one. Then he screwed the lid tightly on to the small jar.

"That's it," he announced. "We is now ready." He fetched his suitcase and put the small jar into it.

"Why bother to take a great big suitcase when you've only got one jar?" Sophie said. "You could put the jar in your pocket."

The BFG looked down at her and smiled. "By goggles," he said, taking the jar out of the suitcase, "your head is not quite so full of grimesludge after all! I can see you is not born last week."

"Thank you, kind sir," Sophie said, making a little curtsey from the table-top.

"Is you ready to leave?" the BFG asked.

"I'm ready!" Sophie cried. Her heart was beginning to thump at the thought of what they were about to do. It really was a wild and crazy thing. Perhaps they would both be thrown into prison.

The BFG was putting on his great black cloak.

He tucked the jar into a pocket in his cloak. He picked up his long trumpet-like dream-blower. Then he turned and looked at Sophie who was still on the table-top. "The dream-bottle is in my pocket," he said. "Is you going to sit in there with it during the travel?"

"Never!" cried Sophie. "I refuse to sit next to that beastly thing!"

"Then where is you going to sit?" the BFG asked her.

Sophie looked him over for a few moments. Then she said, "If you would be kind enough to swivel one of your lovely big ears so that it is lying flat like a dish, that would make a very cosy place for me to sit."

"By gumbo, that is a squackling good idea!" the BFG said.

Slowly, he swivelled his huge right ear until it was like a great shell facing the heavens. He lifted Sophie up and placed her into it. The ear itself, which was about the size of a large tea-tray, was full of the same channels and crinkles as a human ear. It was extremely comfortable.

"I hope I don't fall down your earhole," Sophie said, edging away from the large hole just beside her.

"Be very careful not to do that," the BFG said. "You would be giving me a cronking earache."

The nice thing about being there was that she could whisper directly into his ear.

"You is tickling me a bit," the BFG said. "Please do not jiggle about."

"I'll try not to," Sophie said. "Are we ready?"

"Oweeee!" yelled the BFG. "Don't *do* that!"

"I didn't do anything," Sophie said.

"You is talking too *loud!* You is forgetting that I is hearing every little thingalingaling fifty times louder than usual and there you is shouting away right inside my ear!"

"Oh gosh," Sophie murmured. "I forgot that."

"Your voice is sounding like tunder and thrumpets!"

"I'm so sorry," Sophie whispered. "Is that better?"

"No!" cried the BFG. "It sounds as though you is shootling off a bunderbluss!"

"Then how can I talk to you?" Sophie whispered.

"Don't!" cried the poor BFG. "Please don't! Each word is like you is dropping buzzbombs in my earhole!"

Sophie tried speaking right under her breath. "Is this better?" she said. She spoke so softly she couldn't even hear her own voice.

"That's better," the BFG said. "Now I is hearing you very nicely. What is it you is trying to say to me just now?"

"I was saying are we ready?"

"We is off!" cried the BFG, heading for the cave entrance. "We is off to meet Her Majester the Queen!"

Outside the cave, he rolled the large round stone back into place and set off at a tremendous gallop.

145

Journey to London

The great yellow wasteland lay dim and milky in the moonlight as the Big Friendly Giant went galloping across it.

Sophie, still wearing only her nightie, was reclining comfortably in a crevice of the BFG's right ear. She was actually in the outer rim of the ear, near the top, where the edge of the ear folds over, and this folding-over bit made a sort of roof for her and gave her wonderful protection against the rushing wind. What is more, she was lying on skin that was soft and warm and almost velvety. Nobody, she told herself, had ever travelled in greater comfort.

Sophie peeped over the rim of the ear and watched the desolate landscape of Giant Country go whizzing by. They were certainly moving fast. The BFG went bouncing off the ground as though there were rockets in his toes and each stride he took lifted him about a hundred feet into the air. But he had not yet gone into that whizzing top gear of his, when the ground became blurred by speed and the wind howled and his feet didn't seem to be touching anything but air. That would come later.

Sophie had not slept for a long time. She was very tired. She was also warm and comfortable. She dozed off.

She didn't know how long she slept, but when she woke up again and looked out over the edge of the ear, the landscape had changed completely. They were in a green country now, with mountains and forests. It was still dark but the moon was shining as brightly as ever.

Suddenly and without slowing his pace, the BFG turned his head sharply to the left. For the first time during the entire journey he spoke a few words. "Look quick-quick over there," he said, pointing his long trumpet.

Sophie looked in the direction he was pointing. Through the murky darkness all she saw at first was a great cloud of dust about three hundred yards away.

"Those is the other giants all galloping back home after their guzzle," the BFG said.

Then Sophie saw them. In the light of the moon, she saw all nine of those monstrous half-naked brutes thundering across the landscape together.

They were galloping in a pack, their necks craned forward, their arms bent at the elbows, and worst of all, their stomachs bulging. The strides they took were incredible. Their speed was unbelievable. Their feet pounded and thundered on the ground and left a great sheet of dust behind them. But in ten seconds they were gone.

"A lot of little girlsies and boysies is no longer sleeping in their beds tonight," the BFG said.

Sophie felt quite ill.

But this grim encounter made her more than ever determined to go through with her mission.

It must have been about an hour or so later that the BFG began to slow his pace. "We is in England now," he said suddenly.

Dark though it was, Sophie could see that they were in a country of green fields with neat hedges in between the fields. There were hills with trees all over them and occasionally there were roads

with the lights of cars moving along. Each time they came to a road, the BFG was over it and away, and no motorist could possibly have seen anything except a quick black shadow flashing overhead.

All at once, a curious orange-coloured glow appeared in the night sky ahead of them.

"We is coming close to London," the BFG said.

He slowed to a trot. He began looking about cautiously.

Groups of houses were now appearing on all sides. But there were still no lights in their windows. It was too early for anyone to be getting up yet.

"Someone's bound to see us," Sophie said.

"Never is they seeing me," the BFG said confidently. "You is forgetting that I is doing this sort of thing for years and years and years. No human bean is ever catching even the smallest wink of me."

"I did," Sophie whispered.

"Ah," he said. "Yes. But you was the very first."

During the next half-hour, things moved so swiftly and so silently that Sophie, crouching in the giant's ear, was unable to understand exactly what was going on. They were in streets. There were houses everywhere. Sometimes there were shops. There were bright lamps in the streets. There were quite a few people about and there were cars with their lights on. But nobody ever noticed the BFG. It was impossible to understand quite how he did it. There was a kind of magic in his movements. He seemed to melt into the

149

shadows. He would glide — that was the only word to describe his way of moving — he would glide noiselessly from one dark place to another, always moving, always gliding forward through the streets of London, his black cloak blending with the shadows of the night.

It is quite possible that one or two late-night wanderers might have thought they saw a tall black shadow skimming swiftly down a murky sidestreet, but even if they had, they would never have believed their own eyes. They would have dismissed it as an illusion and blamed themselves for seeing things that weren't there.

Sophie and the BFG came at last to a large place full of trees. There was a road running through it, and a lake. There were no people in this place and the BFG stopped for the first time since they had set out from his cave many hours before.

"What's the matter?" Sophie whispered in her under-the-breath voice.

"I is in a bit of a puddle," he said.

"You're doing marvellously," Sophie whispered.

"No, I isn't," he said. "I is now completely boggled. I is lost."

"But why?"

"Because we is meant to be in the middle of London and suddenly we is in green pastures."

"Don't be silly," Sophie whispered. "This *is* the middle of London. It's called Hyde Park. I know exactly where we are."

"You is joking."

"I'm not. I swear I'm not. We're almost there."

"You mean we is nearly at the Queen's Palace?" cried the BFG.

"It's just across the road," Sophie whispered. "This is where *I* take over."

"Which way?" the BFG asked.

"Straight ahead."

151

The BFG trotted forward through the deserted park.

"Now stop."

The BFG stopped.

"You see that huge roundabout ahead of us just outside the Park?" Sophie whispered.

"I see it."

"That is Hyde Park Corner."

Even now, when it was still an hour before dawn, there was quite a lot of traffic moving around Hyde Park Corner.

Then Sophie whispered, "In the middle of the roundabout there is an enormous stone arch with a statue of a horse and rider on top of it. Can you see that?"

The BFG peered through the trees. "I is seeing it," he said.

"Do you think that if you took a very fast run at it, you could jump clear over Hyde Park Corner, over the arch and over the horse and rider and land on the pavement the other side?"

"Easy," the BFG said.

"You're sure? You're absolutely sure?"

"I promise," the BFG said.

"Whatever you do, you mustn't land in the middle of Hyde Park Corner."

"Don't get so flussed," the BFG said. "To me that is a snitchy little jump. There's not a thingalingaling to it."

"Then go!" Sophie whispered.

The BFG broke into a full gallop. He went scorching across the Park and just before he

reached the railings that divided it from the street, he took off. It was a gigantic leap. He flew high over Hyde Park Corner and landed as softly as a cat on the pavement the other side.

"Well *done!*" Sophie whispered. "Now quick! Over that wall!"

Directly in front of them, bordering the pavement, there was a brick wall with fearsome-looking spikes all along the top of it. A swift crouch, a little leap and the BFG was over it.

"We're there!" Sophie whispered excitedly. "We're in the Queen's back garden!"

The Palace

"By gumdrops!" whispered the Big Friendly Giant. "Is this really it?"

"There's the Palace," Sophie whispered back.

Not more than a hundred yards away, through the tall trees in the garden, across the mown lawns and the tidy flower-beds, the massive shape of the Palace itself loomed through the darkness. It was made of whitish stone. The sheer size of it staggered the BFG.

"But this place is having a hundred bedrooms at least!" he said.

"Easily, I should think," Sophie whispered.

"Then I is boggled," the BFG said. "How is I possibly finding the one where the Queen is sleeping?"

"Let's go a bit closer and have a look," Sophie whispered.

The BFG glided forward among the trees. Suddenly he stopped dead. The great ear in which Sophie was sitting began to swivel round. "Hey!" Sophie whispered. "You're going to tip me out!"

"Ssshh!" the BFG whispered back. "I is hearing something!" He stopped behind a clump of bushes. He waited. The ear was still swinging this way and that. Sophie had to hang on tight to the side of it to save herself from tumbling out. The

BFG pointed through a gap in the bushes, and there, not more than fifty yards away, she saw a man padding softly across the lawn. He had a guard-dog with him on a leash.

The BFG stayed as still as a stone. So did Sophie. The man and the dog walked on and disappeared into the darkness.

"You was telling me they has no soldiers in the back garden," the BFG whispered.

"He wasn't a soldier," Sophie whispered. "He was some sort of a watchman. We'll have to be careful."

"I is not too worried," the BFG said. "These wacksey big ears of mine is picking up even the noise of a man *breathing* the other side of this garden."

"How much longer before it begins to get light?" Sophie whispered.

"Very short," the BFG said. "We must go pell-mell for leather now!"

He glided forward through the vast garden, and once again Sophie noticed how he seemed to melt into the shadows wherever he went. His feet made no sound at all, even when he was walking on gravel.

Suddenly, they were right up close against the back wall of the great Palace. The BFG's head was level with the upper windows one flight up, and Sophie, sitting in his ear, had the same view. In all the windows on that floor the curtains seemed to be drawn. There were no lights showing anywhere. In the distance they could hear the muted

155

sound of traffic going round Hyde Park Corner.

The BFG stopped and put his other ear, the one Sophie wasn't sitting in, close to the first window.

"No," he whispered.

"What are you listening for?" Sophie whispered back.

"For breathing," the BFG whispered. "I is able to tell if it is a man human bean or a lady by the breathing-voice. We has a man in there. Snortling a little bit, too."

He glided on, flattening his tall, thin, black-cloaked body against the side of the building. He came to the next window. He listened.

"No," he whispered.

He moved on.

"This room is empty," he whispered.

He listened in at several more windows, but at each one he shook his head and moved on.

When he came to the window in the very centre of the Palace, he listened but did not move on. "Ho-ho," he whispered. "We has a lady sleeping in there."

Sophie felt a little quiver go running down her spine. "But who?" she whispered back.

The BFG put a finger to his lips for silence. He reached up through the open window and parted the curtains ever so slightly.

The orange glow from the night-sky over London crept into the room and cast a glimmer of light on to its walls. It was a large room. A lovely room. A rich carpet. Gilded chairs. A dressing-table. A bed. And on the pillow of the bed lay the head of a sleeping woman.

Sophie suddenly found herself looking at a face she had seen on stamps and coins and in the newspapers all her life.

For a few seconds she was speechless.

"Is that her?" the BFG whispered.

"Yes," Sophie whispered back.

The BFG wasted no time. First, and very carefully, he started to raise the lower half of the large window. The BFG was an expert on windows. He had opened thousands of them over the years to blow his dreams into children's bedrooms. Some windows got stuck. Some were wobbly. Some creaked. He was pleased to find that the Queen's window slid upward like silk. He pushed up the lower half as far as it would go so as to leave a place on the sill for Sophie to sit.

Next, he closed the crack in the curtains.

Then, with finger and thumb, he lifted Sophie out of his ear and placed her on the window-ledge with her legs dangling just inside the room, but behind the curtains.

"Now don't you go tip-toppling backwards," the BFG whispered. "You must always be holding on tight with both hands to the inside of the window-sill."

Sophie did as he said.

It was summertime in London and the night was not cold, but don't forget that Sophie was wearing only her thin nightie. She would have given anything for a dressing-gown, not just to keep her warm but to hide the whiteness of her nightie

157

from watchful eyes in the garden below.

The BFG was taking the glass jar from the pocket of his cloak. He unscrewed the lid. Now, very cautiously, he poured the precious dream into the wide end of his trumpet. He steered the trumpet through the curtains, far into the room, aiming it at the place where he knew the bed to be. He took a deep breath. He puffed out his cheeks and *pooff*, he blew.

Now he was withdrawing the trumpet, sliding it out very very carefully, like a thermometer.

"Is you all right sitting there?" he whispered.

"Yes," Sophie murmured. She was quite terrified, but determined not to show it. She looked down over her shoulder. The ground seemed miles away. It was a nasty drop.

"How long will the dream take to work?" Sophie whispered.

"Some takes an hour," the BFG whispered back. "Some is quicker. Some is slower still. But it is sure to find her in the end."

Sophie said nothing.

"I is going off to wait in the garden," the BFG whispered. "When you is wanting me, just call out my name and I is coming very quick."

"Will you hear me?" Sophie whispered.

"You is forgetting these," the BFG whispered, smiling and pointing to his great ears.

"Goodbye," Sophie whispered.

Suddenly, unexpectedly, the BFG leaned forward and kissed her gently on the cheek.

Sophie felt like crying.

When she turned to look at him, he was already gone. He had simply melted away into the dark garden.

The Queen

Dawn came at last, and the rim of a lemon-coloured sun rose up behind the roof-tops somewhere behind Victoria Station.

A while later, Sophie felt a little of its warmth on her back and was grateful.

In the distance, she heard a church clock striking. She counted the strikes. There were seven.

She found it almost impossible to believe that she, Sophie, a little orphan of no real importance in the world, was at this moment actually sitting high above the ground on the window-sill of the Queen of England's bedroom, with the Queen herself asleep in there behind the curtain not more than five yards away.

The very idea of it was absurd.

No one had ever done such a thing before.

It was a terrifying thing to be doing.

What would happen if the dream didn't work?

No one, least of all the Queen, would believe a word of her story.

It seemed possible that nobody had ever woken up to find a small child sitting behind the curtains on his or her window-sill.

The Queen was bound to get a shock.

Who wouldn't?

With all the patience of a small girl who has something important to wait for, Sophie sat motionless on the window-sill.

How much longer? she wondered.

What time do Queens wake up?

Faint stirrings and distant sounds came to her from deep inside the belly of the Palace.

Then, all at once, beyond the curtains, she heard the voice of the sleeper in the bedroom. It was a slightly blurred sleep-talker's voice. "Oh no!" it cried out. "No! Don't — Someone stop them! — Don't let them do it! — I can't bear it! — Oh please stop them! — It's horrible! — Oh, it's ghastly! — No! No! No! . . . "

She is having the dream, Sophie told herself. It must be really horrid. I feel so sorry for her. But it has to be done.

After that, there were a few moans. Then there was a long silence.

Sophie waited. She looked over her shoulder. She was terrified that she would see the man with the dog down in the garden staring up at her. But the garden was deserted. A pale summer mist hung over it like smoke. It was an enormous garden, very beautiful, with a large funny-shaped lake at the far end. There was an island in the lake and there were ducks swimming on the water.

Inside the room, beyond the curtains, Sophie suddenly heard what was obviously a knock on the door. She heard the doorknob being turned. She heard someone entering the room.

"Good morning, Your Majesty," a woman was

161

saying. It was the voice of an oldish person.

There was a pause and then a slight rattle of china and silver.

"Will you have your tray on the bed, ma'am, or on the table?"

"Oh Mary! Something awful has just happened!" This was a voice Sophie had heard many times on radio and television, especially on Christmas Day. It was a very well-known voice.

"Whatever is it, ma'am?"

"I've just had the most frightful dream! It was a nightmare! It was awful!"

"Oh, I am sorry, ma'am. But don't be distressed. You're awake now and it will all go away. It *was* only a dream, ma'am."

"Do you know what I dreamt, Mary? I dreamt that girls and boys were being snatched out of their beds at boarding-school and were being eaten by the most ghastly giants! The giants were putting their arms in through the dormitory windows and plucking the children out with their fingers! One lot from a girls' school and another from a boys' school! It was all so . . . so *vivid*, Mary! It was so *real!*"

There was a silence. Sophie waited. She was quivering with excitement. But why the silence? Why didn't the other one, the maid, why didn't she say something?

"What on earth's the matter, Mary?" the famous voice was saying.

There was another silence.

"Mary! You've gone as white as a sheet! Are you

feeling ill?"

There was suddenly a crash and a clatter of crockery which could only have meant that the tray the maid was carrying had fallen out of her hands.

"Mary!" the famous voice was saying rather sharply. "I think you'd better sit down at once! You look as though you're going to faint! You really mustn't take it so hard just because I've had an awful dream."

"That . . . that . . . that isn't the reason, ma'am." The maid's voice was quivering terribly.

"Then for heaven's sake what *is* the reason?"

"I'm very sorry about the tray, ma'am."

"Oh, don't worry about the *tray*. But what on earth was it that made you drop it? Why did you go white as a ghost all of a sudden?"

"You haven't seen the papers yet, have you, ma'am?"

"No, what do they say?"

Sophie heard the rustling of a newspaper as it was being handed over.

"It's like the very dream you had in the night, ma'am."

"Rubbish, Mary. Where is it?"

"On the front page, ma'am. It's the big head-lines."

"Great Scott!" cried the famous voice. "Eighteen girls vanish mysteriously from their beds at Roedean School! Fourteen boys disappear from Eton! Bones are found underneath dormitory windows!"

163

Then there was a pause punctuated by gasps from the famous voice as the newspaper article was clearly being read and digested.

"Oh, how ghastly!" the famous voice cried out. "It's *absolutely* frightful! Bones under the windows! What *can* have happened? Oh, those *poor* children!"

"But ma'am . . . don't you see, ma'am . . . "

"See what, Mary?"

"Those children were taken away almost exactly as you dreamt it, ma'am!"

"Not by giants, Mary."

"No, ma'am. But the bit about the girls and boys disappearing from their dormitories, you dreamt it so clearly and then it actually happened. That's why I came over all queer, ma'am."

"I'm coming over a bit queer myself, Mary."

"It gives me the shakes, ma'am, when something like that happens, it really does."

"I don't blame you, Mary."

"I shall get you some more breakfast, ma'am, and have this mess cleared up."

"No! Don't go, Mary! Stay here a moment!"

Sophie wished she could see into the room, but she didn't dare touch the curtains. The famous voice began speaking again. "I really *did* dream about those children, Mary. It was clear as crystal."

"I know you did, ma'am."

"I don't know how *giants* got into it. That was rubbish."

"Shall I draw the curtains, ma'am, then we shall

all feel better. It's a lovely day."

"Please do."

With a swish, the great curtains were pulled aside.

The maid screamed.

Sophie froze to the window-ledge.

165

The Queen, sitting up in her bed with *The Times* on her lap, glanced up sharply. Now it was *her* turn to freeze. She didn't scream as the maid had done. Queens are too self-controlled for that. She simply sat there staring wide-eyed and white-faced at the small girl who was perched on her window-sill in a nightie.

Sophie was petrified.

Curiously enough, the Queen looked petrified, too. One would have expected her to look surprised, as you or I would have done had we discovered a small girl sitting on our window-sill first thing in the morning. But the Queen didn't look surprised. She looked genuinely frightened.

The maid, a middle-aged woman with a funny cap on the top of her head, was the first to recover. "What in the name of heaven do you think you're doing in here?" she shouted angrily to Sophie.

Sophie looked beseechingly toward the Queen for help.

The Queen was still staring at Sophie. Gaping at her would be more accurate. Her mouth was slightly open, her eyes were round and wide as two saucers, and the whole of that famous rather lovely face was filled with disbelief.

"Now listen here, young lady, how on earth did you get into this room?" the maid shouted furiously.

"I don't believe it," the Queen was murmuring. "I simply don't believe it."

"I'll take her out, ma'am, at once," the maid was saying.

"No, Mary! No, don't do that!" The Queen spoke so sharply that the maid was quite taken aback. She turned and stared at the Queen. What on earth had come over her? It looked as though she was in a state of shock.

"Are you all right, ma'am?" the maid was saying.

When the Queen spoke again, it was in a strange strangled sort of whisper. "Tell me, Mary," she said, "tell me quite truthfully, is there *really* a little girl sitting on my window-sill, or am I still dreaming?"

"She is sitting there all right, ma'am, as clear as daylight, but heaven only knows how she got there! Your Majesty is certainly not dreaming it this time!"

"But that's exactly what I *did* dream!" the Queen cried out. "I dreamt that *as well!* I dreamt there would be a little girl sitting on my window-sill in her nightie and she would talk to me!"

The maid, with her hands clasped across her starched white bosom, was staring at her mistress with a look of absolute disbelief on her face. The situation was getting beyond her. She was lost. She had not been trained to cope with this kind of madness.

"Are you real?" the Queen said to Sophie.

"Y-y-yes, Your Majesty," Sophie murmured.

"What is your name?"

"Sophie, Your Majesty."

"And how did you get up on to my window-sill? No, don't answer that! Hang on a moment! I dreamed that part of it, too! I dreamed that a giant put you there!"

"He did, Your Majesty," Sophie said.

The maid gave a howl of anguish and clasped her hands over her face.

"Control yourself, Mary," the Queen said sharply. Then to Sophie she said, "You are not serious about the giant, are you?"

"Oh yes, Your Majesty. He's out there in the garden now."

"Is he indeed," the Queen said. The sheer absurdity of it all was helping her to regain her composure. "So he's in the garden, is he?" she said, smiling a little.

"He is a *good* giant, Your Majesty," Sophie said.

"You need not be frightened of him."

"I'm delighted to hear it," said the Queen, still smiling.

"He is my best friend, Your Majesty."

"How nice," the Queen said.

"He's a lovely giant, Your Majesty."

"I'm quite sure he is," the Queen said. "But why have you and this giant come to see me?"

"I think you have dreamed that part of it, too, Your Majesty," Sophie said calmly.

That pulled the Queen up short.

It took the smile right off her face.

She certainly *had* dreamed that part of it. She was remembering now how, at the end of her dream, it had said that a little girl and a big friendly giant would come and show her how to find the nine horrible man-eating giants.

But be careful, the Queen told herself. Keep very calm. Because this is surely not very far from the place where madness begins.

169

"You *did* dream that, didn't you, Your Majesty?" Sophie said.

The maid was out of it now. She just stood there goggling.

"Yes," the Queen murmured. "Yes, now you come to mention it, I did. But how do *you* know what I dreamed?"

"Oh, that's a long story, Your Majesty," Sophie said. "Would you like me to call the Big Friendly Giant?"

The Queen looked at the child. The child looked straight back at the Queen, her face open and quite serious. The Queen simply didn't know what to make of it. Was someone pulling her leg, she wondered.

"Shall I call him for you?" Sophie went on. "You'll like him very much."

The Queen took a deep breath. She was glad no one except her faithful old Mary was here to see what was going on. "Very well," she said. "You may call your giant. No, wait a moment. Mary, pull yourself together and give me my dressing-gown and slippers."

The maid did as she was told. The Queen got out of bed and put on a pale pink dressing-gown and slippers.

"You may call him now," the Queen said.

Sophie turned her head toward the garden and called out, "BFG! Her Majesty The Queen would like to see you!"

The Queen crossed over to the window and stood beside Sophie.

"Come down off that ledge," she said. "You're going to fall backwards any moment."

Sophie jumped down into the room and stood beside the Queen at the open window. Mary, the maid, stood behind them. Her hands were now planted firmly on her hips and there was a look on her face which seemed to say, 'I want no part of this fiasco.'

"I don't see any giant," the Queen said.

"Please wait," Sophie said.

"Shall I take her away now, ma'am?" the maid said.

"Take her downstairs and give her some break-fast," the Queen said.

Just then, there was a rustle in the bushes beside the lake.

Then out he came!

Twenty-four feet tall, wearing his black cloak with the grace of a nobleman, still carrying his long trumpet in one hand, he strode magnificently across the Palace lawn toward the window.

The maid screamed.

The Queen gasped.

Sophie waved.

The BFG took his time. He was very dignified in his approach. When he was close to the window where the three of them were standing, he stopped and made a slow graceful bow. His head, after he had straightened up again, was almost exactly level with the watchers at the window.

"Your Majester," he said. "I is your humbug servant." He bowed again.

171

Considering she was meeting a giant for the first time in her life, the Queen remained astonishingly self-composed. "We are very pleased to meet you," she said.

Down below, a gardener was coming across the lawn with a wheelbarrow. He caught sight of the BFG's legs over to his left. His gaze travelled slowly upwards along the entire height of the enormous body. He gripped the handles of the wheelbarrow. He swayed. He tottered. Then he keeled over on the grass in a dead faint. Nobody noticed him.

"Oh, Majester!" cried the BFG. "Oh, Queen! Oh Monacher! Oh, Golden Sovereign! Oh, Ruler! Oh, Ruler of Straight Lines! Oh, Sultana! I is come here with my little friend Sophie . . . to give you a . . . " The BFG hesitated, searching for the word.

"To give me *what?*" the Queen said.

"A *sistance,*" the BFG said, beaming.

The Queen looked puzzled.

"He sometimes speaks a bit funny, Your Majesty," Sophie said. "He never went to school."

"Then we must send him to school," the Queen

173

said. "We have some very good schools in this country."

"I has great secrets to tell Your Majester," the BFG said.

"I should be delighted to hear them," the Queen said. "But not in my dressing-gown."

"Shall you wish to get dressed, ma'am?" the maid said.

"Have either of you had breakfast?" the Queen said.

"Oh, *could we?*" Sophie cried. "Oh, *please!* I

haven't eaten a thing since yesterday!"

"I was about to have mine," the Queen said, "but Mary dropped it."

The maid gulped.

"I imagine we have more food in the Palace," the Queen said, speaking to the BFG. "Perhaps you and your little friend would care to join me."

"Will it be repulsant snozzcumbers, Majester?" the BFG asked.

"Will it be *what?*" the Queen said.

"Stinky snozzcumbers," the BFG said.

"What *is* he talking about?" the Queen said. "It sounds like a rude word to me." She turned to the maid and said, "Mary, ask them to serve breakfast for three in the . . . I think it had better be in the Ballroom. That has the highest ceiling." To the BFG, she said, "I'm afraid you will have to go through the door on your hands and knees. I shall send someone to show you the way."

The BFG reached up and lifted Sophie out of the window. "You and I is leaving Her Majester alone to get dressed," he said.

"No, leave the little girl here with me," the Queen said. "We'll have to find something for her to put on. She can't have breakfast in her nightie."

The BFG returned Sophie to the bedroom.

"Can we have sausages, Your Majesty?" Sophie said. "And bacon and fried eggs?"

"I think that might be managed," the Queen answered, smiling.

"Just you wait till you taste it!" Sophie said to the BFG. "No more snozzcumbers from now on!"

The Royal Breakfast

There was a frantic scurry among the Palace servants when orders were received from the Queen that a twenty-four-foot giant must be seated at breakfast with Her Majesty in the Great Ballroom within the next half-hour.

The butler, an imposing personage named Mr Tibbs, was in supreme command of all the palace servants and he did the best he could in the short time available. A man does not rise to become the Queen's butler unless he is gifted with extraordinary ingenuity, adaptability, versatility, dexterity, cunning, sophistication, sagacity, discretion and a host of other talents that neither you nor I possess. Mr Tibbs had them all. He was in the butler's pantry sipping an early morning glass of light ale when the order reached him. In a split second he had made the following calculations in his head: if a normal six-foot man requires a three-foot-high table to eat off, a twenty-four-foot giant will require a twelve-foot-high table.

And if a six foot man requires a chair with a two-foot-high seat, a twenty-four-foot giant will require a chair with an eight-foot-high seat.

Everything, Mr Tibbs told himself, must be multiplied by four. Two breakfast eggs must become eight. Four rashers of bacon must become sixteen. Three pieces of toast must become twelve, and so on. These calculations about food were immediately passed on to Monsieur Papillion, the royal chef.

Mr Tibbs skimmed into the ballroom (butlers don't walk, they skim over the ground) followed by a whole army of footmen. The footmen all wore knee-breeches and every one of them displayed beautifully-rounded calves and ankles. There is no way you can become a royal footman unless you have a well-turned ankle. It is the first thing they look at when you are interviewed.

"Push the grand piano into the centre of the room," Mr Tibbs whispered. Butlers never raise their voices above the softest whisper.

Four footmen moved the piano.

"Now fetch a large chest-of-drawers and put it on top of the piano," Mr Tibbs whispered.

Three other footmen fetched a very fine Chippendale mahogany chest-of-drawers and placed it on top of the piano.

"That will be his chair," Mr Tibbs whispered. "It is exactly eight feet off the ground. Now we shall make a table upon which this gentleman may eat his breakfast in comfort. Fetch me four very tall grandfather clocks. There are plenty of them around the Palace. Let each clock be twelve feet high."

Sixteen footmen spread out around the Palace to find the clocks. They were not easy to carry and required four footmen to each one.

"Place the four clocks in a rectangle eight feet

by four alongside the grand piano," Mr Tibbs whispered.

The footmen did so.

"Now fetch me the young Prince's ping-pong table," Mr Tibbs whispered.

The ping-pong table was carried in.

"Unscrew its legs and take them away," Mr Tibbs whispered. This was done.

"Now place the ping-pong table on top of the four grandfather clocks," Mr Tibbs whispered. To manage this, the footmen had to stand on step-ladders.

Mr Tibbs stood back to survey the new furniture. "None of it is in the classic style," he whispered, "but it will have to do." He gave orders that a damask table-cloth should be draped over the ping-pong table, and in the end it looked really quite elegant after all.

At this point, Mr Tibbs was seen to hesitate. The footmen all stared at him, aghast. Butlers never hesitate, not even when they are faced with the most impossible problems. It is their job to be totally decisive at all times.

"Knives and forks and spoons," Mr Tibbs was heard to mutter. "Our cutlery will be like little pins in his hands."

But Mr Tibbs didn't hesitate for long. "Tell the head gardener," he whispered, "that I require immediately a brand new unused garden fork and also a spade. And for a knife we shall use the great sword hanging on the wall in the morning-room. But clean the sword well first. It was last used to cut off the head of King Charles the First and there may still be a little dried blood on the blade."

When all this had been accomplished, Mr Tibbs stood near the centre of the Ballroom casting his expert butler's eye over the scene. Had he forgotten anything? He certainly had. What about a coffee cup for the large gentleman?

"Fetch me," he whispered, "the biggest jug you can find in the kitchen."

A splendid one gallon porcelain water-jug was brought in and placed on the giant's table beside the garden fork and the garden spade and the great sword.

So much for the giant.

Mr Tibbs then had the footmen move a small delicate table and two chairs alongside the giant's table. This was for the Queen and for Sophie. The fact that the giant's table and chair towered far above the smaller table simply could not be helped.

All these arrangements were only just completed when the Queen, now fully dressed in a trim skirt and cashmere cardigan, entered the Ballroom holding Sophie by the hand. A pretty blue dress that had once belonged to one of the Princesses had been found for Sophie, and to make her look prettier still, the Queen had picked up a superb sapphire brooch from her dressing-table and had pinned it on the left side of Sophie's chest. The Big Friendly Giant followed behind them, but he had an awful job getting through the door. He had to squeeze himself through on his hands and knees, with two footmen pushing him from behind and two pulling from the front. But he got through in the end. He had removed his black cloak and got rid of his trumpet, and was now wearing his ordinary simple clothes.

As he walked across the Ballroom he had to stoop quite a lot to avoid hitting the ceiling. Because of this he failed to notice an enormous crystal chandelier. *Crash* went his head right into the chandelier. A shower of glass fell upon the poor BFG. "Gunghummers and bogswinkles!" he cried. "What was that?"

"It *was* Louis the Fifteenth," the Queen said, looking slightly put out.

"He's never been in a house before," Sophie said.

181

Mr Tibbs scowled. He directed four footmen to clear up the mess, then, with a disdainful little wave of the hand, he indicated to the giant that he should seat himself on top of the chest-of-drawers on top of the grand piano.

"What a phizz-whizzing flushbunking seat!" cried the BFG. "I is going to be bug as a snug in a rug up here."

"Does he always speak like that?" the Queen asked.

"Quite often," Sophie said. "He gets tangled up with his words."

The BFG sat down on the chest-of-drawers-piano and gazed in wonder around the Great Ballroom. "By gumdrops!" he cried. "What a spliffling whoppsy room we is in! It is so gigantuous I is needing bicirculers and telescoops to see what is going on at the other end!"

Footmen arrived carrying silver trays with fried eggs, bacon, sausages and fried potatoes.

At this point, Mr Tibbs suddenly realised that in order to serve the BFG at his twelve-foot-high-grandfather-clock table, he would have to climb to the top of one of the tall step-ladders. What's more, he must do it balancing a huge warm plate on the palm of one hand and holding a gigantic silver coffee-pot in the other. A normal man would have flinched at the thought of it. But good butlers never flinch. Up he went, up and up and up, while the Queen and Sophie watched him with great interest. It is possible they were both secretly hoping he would lose his balance and go crashing to the floor. But good butlers never crash.

At the top of the ladder, Mr Tibbs, balancing like an acrobat, poured the BFG's coffee and placed the enormous plate before him. On the plate there were eight eggs, twelve sausages, sixteen rashers of bacon and a heap of fried potatoes.

"What is this please, Your Majester?" the BFG asked, peering down at the Queen.

"He has never eaten anything except snozzcumbers before in his life," Sophie explained. "They taste revolting."

"They don't seem to have stunted his growth," the Queen said.

The BFG grabbed the garden spade and scooped up all the eggs, sausages, bacon and potatoes in one go and shovelled them into his enormous mouth.

"By goggles!" he cried. "This stuff is making snozzcumbers taste like swatchwallop!"

The Queen glanced up, frowning. Mr Tibbs looked down at his toes and his lips moved in silent prayer.

"That was only one titchy little bite," the BFG said. "Is you having any more of this delunctious grubble in your cupboard, Majester?"

"Tibbs," the Queen said, showing true regal hospitality, "fetch the gentleman another dozen fried eggs and a dozen sausages."

Mr Tibbs swam out of the room muttering unspeakable words to himself and wiping his brow with a white handkerchief.

The BFG lifted the huge jug and took a swallow.

"Owch!" he cried, blowing a mouthful across the ballroom. "Please, what is this horrible swigpill I is drinking, Majester?"

"It's coffee," the Queen told him. "Freshly roasted."

"It's filthsome!" the BFG cried out. "Where is the frobscottle?"

"The *what?*" the Queen asked.

"Delumptious fizzy frobscottle," the BFG answered. "Everyone must be drinking frobscottle with breakfast, Majester. Then we can all be whizzpopping happily together afterwards."

"What *does* he mean?" the Queen said, frowning at Sophie. "What is whizzpopping?"

Sophie kept a very straight face. "BFG," she said, "there is no frobscottle here and whizzpopping is strictly forbidden! "

"What!" cried the BFG. "No frobscottle? No whizzpopping? No glumptious music? No boom-

184

boom-boom?''

"Absolutely not," Sophie told him firmly.

"If he wants to sing, please don't stop him," the Queen said.

"He doesn't want to sing," Sophie said.

"He said he wants to make music," the Queen went on. "Shall I send for a violin?"

"No, Your Majesty," Sophie said. "He's only joking."

A sly little smile crossed the BFG's face. "Listen," he said, peering down at Sophie, "if they isn't having any frobscottle here in the Palace, I can still go whizzpopping perfectly well without it if I is trying hard enough."

"No!" cried Sophie. "Don't! You're not to! I beg you!"

"Music is very good for the digestion," the Queen said. "When I'm up in Scotland, they play the bagpipes outside the window while I'm eating. Do play something."

"I has Her Majester's permission!" cried the BFG, and all at once he let fly with a whizzpopper that sounded as though a bomb had exploded in the room.

The Queen jumped.

"Whoopee!" shouted the BFG. "That is better than bagglepipes, is it not, Majester?"

It took the Queen a few seconds to get over the shock. "I prefer the bagpipes," she said. But she couldn't stop herself smiling.

During the next twenty minutes, a whole relay of footmen were kept busy hurrying to and from the kitchen carrying third helpings and fourth helpings and fifth helpings of fried eggs and sausages for the ravenous and delighted BFG.

When the BFG had consumed his seventy-second fried egg, Mr Tibbs sidled up to the Queen. He bent low from the waist and whispered in her ear, "Chef sends his apologies, Your Majesty, and he says he has no more eggs in the kitchen."

"What's wrong with the hens?" the Queen said.

"Nothing's wrong with the hens, Your Majesty," Mr Tibbs whispered.

"Then tell them to lay more," the Queen said. She looked up at the BFG. "Have some toast and marmalade while you're waiting," she said to him.

"The toast is finished," Mr Tibbs whispered, "and chef says there is no more bread."

"Tell him to bake more," the Queen said.

While all this was going on, Sophie had been telling the Queen everything, absolutely everything about her visit to Giant Country. The Queen listened, appalled. When Sophie had finished, the Queen looked up at the BFG who was sitting high above her. He was now eating a sponge-cake.

"Big Friendly Giant," she said, "last night those man-eating brutes came to England. Can you remember where they went the night before?"

The BFG put a whole round sponge-cake into his mouth and chewed it slowly while he thought about this question. "Yes, Majester," he said. "I do think I is remembering where they said they was going the night before last. They was galloping off to Sweden for the Sweden sour taste."

187

"Fetch me a telephone," the Queen commanded.

Mr Tibbs placed the instrument on the table. The Queen lifted the receiver. "Get me the King of Sweden," she said.

"Good morning," the Queen said. "Is everything all right in Sweden?"

"Everything is terrible!" the King of Sweden answered. "There is panic in the capital! Two nights ago, twenty-six of my loyal subjects disappeared! My whole country is in a panic!"

"Your twenty-six loyal subjects were all eaten by giants," the Queen said. "Apparently they like the taste of Swedes."

"Why do they like the taste of Swedes?" the King asked.

"Because the Swedes of Sweden have a sweet and sour taste. So says the BFG," the Queen said.

"I don't know *what* you're talking about," the King said, growing testy. "It's hardly a joking matter when one's loyal subjects are being eaten like popcorn."

"They've eaten mine as well," the Queen said.

"Who's *they*, for heaven's sake?" the King asked.

"Giants," the Queen said.

"Look here," the King said, "are you feeling all right?"

"It's been a rough morning," the Queen said. "First I had a horrid nightmare, then the maid dropped my breakfast and now I've got a giant on the piano."

"You need a doctor quick!" cried the King.

"I'll be all right," the Queen said. "I must go now. Thanks for your help." She replaced the receiver.

"Your BFG is right," the Queen said to Sophie. "Those nine man-eating brutes *did* go to Sweden."

"It's horrible," Sophie said. "Please stop them. Your Majesty."

"I'd like to make one more check before I call out the troops," the Queen said. Once more, she looked up at the BFG. He was eating doughnuts now, popping them into his mouth ten at a time, like peas. "Think hard, BFG," she said. "Where did those horrid giants say they were galloping off to *three* nights ago?"

The BFG thought long and hard.

"Ho-ho!" he cried at last. "Yes, I is remembering!"

"Where?" asked the Queen.

"One was off to Baghdad," the BFG said. "As they is galloping past my cave, Fleshlumpeater is waving his arms and shouting at me, 'I is off to Baghdad and I is going to Baghdad and mum and every one of their ten children as well!' "

Once more, the Queen lifted the receiver. "Get me the Lord Mayor of Baghdad," she said. "If they don't have a Lord Mayor, get me the next best thing."

In five seconds, a voice was on the line. "Here is the Sultan of Baghdad speaking," the voice said.

"Listen, Sultan," the Queen said. "Did anything unpleasant happen in your city three nights ago?"

189

"Every night unpleasant things are happening in Baghdad," the Sultan said. "We are chopping off people's heads like you are chopping parsley."

"I've never chopped parsley in my life," the Queen said. "I want to know if anyone has *disappeared* recently in Baghdad?"

"Only my uncle, Caliph Haroun al Rashid," the Sultan said. "He disappeared from his bed three nights ago together with his wife and ten children."

"There you is!" cried the BFG, whose wonderful ears enabled him to hear what the Sultan was saying to the Queen on the telephone. "Fleshlumpeater did that one! He went off to Baghdad to bag dad and mum and all the little kiddles!"

The Queen replaced the receiver. "That proves it," she said, looking up at the BFG. "Your story is apparently quite true. Summon the Head of the Army and the Head of the Air Force immediately!"

The Plan

The Head of the Army and the Head of the Air Force stood at attention beside the Queen's breakfast table. Sophie was still in her seat and the BFG was still high up on his crazy perch.

It took the Queen only five minutes to explain the situation to the military men.

"I *knew* there was something like this going on, Your Majesty," the Head of the Army said. "For the last ten years we have been getting reports from nearly every country in the world about people disappearing mysteriously in the night. We had one only the other day from Panama..."

"For the hatty taste!" cried the BFG.

"And one from Wellington, in New Zealand," said the Head of the Army.

"For the booty flavour!" cried the BFG.

"What *is* he talking about?" said the Head of the Air Force.

"Work it out for yourself," the Queen said. "What time is it? Ten a.m. In eight hours those nine blood-thirsty brutes will be galloping off to gobble up another couple of dozen unfortunate wretches. They have to be stopped. We must act fast."

"We'll bomb the blighters!" shouted the Head of the Air Force.

"We'll mow them down with machine-guns!" cried the Head of the Army.

"I do not approve of murder," the Queen said.

"But they are murderers themselves!" cried the Head of the Army.

"That is no reason why we should follow their example," the Queen said. "Two wrongs don't make a right."

"And two rights don't make a left!" cried the BFG.

"We must bring them back alive," the Queen said.

"How?" the two military men said together. "They are all fifty feet high. They'd knock us down like ninepins!"

"Wait!" cried the BFG. "Hold your horseflies! Keep your skirts on! I think I has the answer to the maiden's hair!"

"Let him speak," the Queen said.

"Every afternoon," the BFG said, "all these giants is in the Land of Noddy."

"I can't understand a word this feller says," the Head of the Army snapped. "Why doesn't he speak clearly?"

"He means the Land of Nod," Sophie said. "It's pretty obvious."

"Exunckly!" cried the BFG. "Every afternoon all these nine giants is lying on the ground snoozling away in a very deep sleep. They is always resting like that before they is galloping off to guzzle another helping of human beans."

"Go on," they said. "So what?"

"So what your soldiers has to do is to creep up to the giants while they is still in the Land of Noddy and tie their arms and legs with mighty ropes and whunking chains."

"Brilliant," the Queen said.

"That's all very well," said the Head of the Army. "But how do we get the brutes back here? We can't load fifty-foot giants on to trucks! Shoot 'em on the spot, that's what I say!"

The BFG looked down from his lofty perch and said, this time to the Head of the Air Force, "You is having bellypoppers, is you not?"

"Is he being rude?" the Head of the Air Force said.

"He means helicopters," Sophie told him.

"Then why doesn't he say so? Of course we have helicopters."

"Whoppsy big bellypoppers?" asked the BFG.

"Very big ones," the Head of the Air Force said proudly. "But no helicopter is big enough to get a giant like that inside it."

"You do not put him inside," the BFG said. "You sling him underneath the belly of your bellypopper and carry him like a porteedo."

"Like a *what*?" said the Head of the Air Force.

"Like a torpedo," Sophie said.

"Could you do that, Air Marshal?" the Queen asked.

"Well, I suppose we *could*," the Head of the Air Force admitted grudgingly.

"Then get cracking!" the Queen said, "You'll need nine helicopters, one for each Giant."

193

"Where is this place?" the Air Force man said to the BFG. "I presume you can pinpoint it on the map?"

"*Pinpoint!*" said the BFG. "*Map!* I is never hearing these words before. Is this Air Force bean talking slushbungle?"

The Air Marshal's face turned the colour of a ripe plum. He was not used to being told he was talking slushbungle. The Queen, with her usual admirable tact and good sense, came to the rescue. "BFG," she said, "can you tell us *more or less* where this Giant Country is?"

"No, Majester," the BFG said. "Not on my nelly."

"Then we're jiggered!" cried the Army General.

"This is ridiculous!" cried the Air Marshal.

"You must not be giving up so easy," the BFG said calmly. "The first titchy bobsticle you meet

and you begin shouting you is biffsquiggled."

The Army General was no more used to being insulted that the Air Marshal. His face began to swell with fury and his cheeks blew out until they looked like two huge ripe tomatoes. "Your Majesty!" he cried. "We are dealing with a lunatic! I want nothing more to do with this ridiculous operation!"

The Queen, who was used to the tantrums of her senior officials, ignored him completely. "BFG," she said, "Would you please tell these rather dim-witted characters exactly what to do."

"A pleasure, Majester," said the BFG. "Now listen to me carefully, you two bootbogglers."

The military men began to twitch, but they stayed put.

"I is not having the foggiest idea where Giant Country is in the world," the BFG said, "but I is always able to gallop there. I is galloping forthwards and backwards from Giant Country every night to blow my dreams into little chiddlers bedrooms. I is knowing the way very well. So all you is having to do is this. Put your nine big bellyhoppers up in the air and let them follow me as I is galloping along."

"How long will the journey take?" the Queen asked.

"If we is leaving now," the BFG said, "we will be arriving just as the giants is having their afternoon snozzle."

"Splendid," said the Queen. Then turning to the two military men, she said, "Prepare to leave immediately."

The Head of the Army, who was feeling pretty miffed by the whole business, said. "That's all very well, Your Majesty, but what are we going to do with the blighters once we've got them back?"

"Don't you worry about that," the Queen told him. "We'll be ready for them. Hurry up, now! Off you go!"

"If it pleases Your Majesty," Sophie said, "I should like to ride with the BFG, to keep him company."

"Where will you sit?" asked the Queen.

"In his ear," Sophie said. "Show them, BFG."

The BFG got down from his high chair. He picked Sophie up in his fingers. He swivelled his huge right ear until it was parallel with the gound, then he placed Sophie gently inside it.

The Heads of the Army and the Air Force stood there goggling. The Queen smiled. "You really are rather a wonderful giant," she said.

"Majester," the BFG said, "I is wishing to ask a very special thing from you."

"What is it?" the Queen said.

"Could I please bring back here in the bellypoppers all my collection of dreams? They is taking me years and years to collect and I is not wanting to lose them."

"Why of course," the Queen said. "I wish you a safe journey."

Capture!

The BFG had made thousands of journeys to and from Giant Country over the years, but he had never in his life made one quite like this, with nine huge helicopters roaring along just over his head. He had never before travelled in broad

198

daylight either. He hadn't dared to. But this was
different. Now he was doing it for the Queen of
England herself and he was frightened of nobody.

As he galloped across the British Isles with the

helicopters thundering above him, people stood and gaped and wondered what on earth was going on. They had never seen the likes of it before. And they never would again.

Every now and then, the pilots of the helicopters would catch a glimpse of a small girl wearing glasses crouching in the giant's right ear and waving to them. They always waved back. The pilots marvelled at the giant's speed and at the way he leapt across wide rivers and over huge houses.

But they hadn't seen anything yet.

"Be careful to hang on tight!" the BFG said. "We is going fast as a fizzlecrump!" The BFG changed into his famous top gear and all at once he began to fly forward as though there were springs in his legs and rockets in his toes. He went skimming over the earth like some magical hop-skip-and-jumper with his feet hardly ever touching the ground. As usual, Sophie had to crouch low in the crevice of his ear to save herself from being swept clean away.

The nine pilots in their helicopters suddenly realised they were being left behind. The giant was streaking ahead. They opened their throttles to full speed, and even then they were only just able to keep up.

In the leading machine, the Head of the Air Force was sitting beside the pilot. He had a world atlas on his knees and he kept staring first at the atlas, then at the ground below, trying to figure out where they were going. Frantically he turned the pages of the atlas. "Where the devil *are* we going?" he cried.

"I haven't the foggiest idea," the pilot answered. "The Queen's orders were to follow the giant and that's exactly what I'm doing."

The pilot was a young Air Force officer with a bushy moustache. He was very proud of his moustache. He was also quite fearless and he loved adventure. He thought this was a super adventure. "It's fun going to new places," he said.

"New places!" shouted the Head of the Air Force. "What the blazes d'you mean *new places?"*

"This place we're flying over now isn't in the atlas, is it?" the pilot said, grinning.

"You're darn right it isn't in the atlas!" cried the Head of the Air Force. "We've flown clear off the last page!"

"I expect that old giant knows where he's going," the young pilot said.

"He's leading us to disaster!" cried the Head of the Air Force. He was shaking with fear. In the seat behind him sat the Head of the Army who was even more terrified.

"You don't mean to tell me we've gone right out of the atlas?" he cried, leaning forward to look.

"That's exactly what I *am* telling you!" cried the Air Force man. "Look for yourself. Here's the very last map in the whole flaming atlas! We went off that over an hour ago!" He turned the page. As in all atlases, there were two completely blank pages at the very end. "So now we must be somewhere here," he said, putting a finger on one of the blank pages.

"Where's here?" cried the Head of the Army.

The young pilot was still grinning broadly. He said to them, "That's why they always put two blank pages at the back of the atlas. They're for new countries. You're meant to fill them in yourself."

The Head of the Air Force glanced down at the ground below. "Just look at this godforsaken desert!" he cried. "All the trees are dead and all the rocks are blue!"

"The giant has stopped," the young pilot said.

"He's waving us down."

The pilots throttled back the engines and all nine helicopters landed safely on the great yellow wasteland. Then each of them lowered a ramp from its belly. Nine jeeps, one from each helicopter, were driven down the ramps. Each jeep contained six soldiers and a vast quantity of thick rope and heavy chains.

"I don't see any giants," the Head of the Army said.

"The giants is all just out of sight over there," the BFG told him. "But if you is taking these sloshbuckling noisy bellypoppers any closer, all the giants is waking up at once and then pop goes the weasel."

"So you want us to proceed by jeep?" the Head of the Army said.

"Yes," the BFG said. "But you must all be very very hushy quiet. No roaring of motors. No shouting. No mucking about. No piggery-jokery."

The BFG, with Sophie still in his ear, trotted forward and the jeeps followed close behind.

Suddenly the most dreadful rumbling noise was heard by everyone. The Head of the Army went pea-green in the face. "Those are guns!" he cried. "There is a battle raging somewhere up ahead of us! Turn back, the lot of you! Let's get out of here!"

"Pigspiffle!" the BFG said. "Those noises is not guns."

"Of course they're guns!" shouted the Head of the Army. "I am a military man and I know a gun

when I hear one! Turn back!"

"Those is just the giants snortling in their sleep," the BFG said. "I is a giant myself and I know a giant's snortle when I is hearing one."

"Are you quite sure?" the Army man said anxiously.

"Positive," the BFG said.

"Proceed cautiously," the Army man ordered.

They all moved on.

Then they saw them!

Even at a distance, they were enough to scare the daylights out of the soldiers. But when they got close and saw what the giants really looked like, they began to sweat with fear. Nine fearsome, ugly, half-naked, fifty-feet-long brutes lay sprawled over the ground in various grotesque attitudes of sleep, and the sound of their snoring was indeed like gunfire in a battle.

The BFG raised a hand. The jeeps all stopped. The soldiers got out.

"What happens if one of them wakes up?" whispered the Head of the Army, his knees knocking together from fear.

"If any one of them is waking up, he will gobble you down before you can say knack jife," the BFG answered, grinning hugely. "Me is the only one what won't be gobbled up because giants is never eating giants. Me and Sophie is the only safe ones because I is hiding her if that happens."

The Head of the Army took several paces to the rear. So did the Head of the Air Force. They climbed rather quickly back into their jeep, ready to make a fast getaway if necessary. "Go forward, men!" the Head of the Army said. "Go forward and do your duty bravely!"

The soldiers crept forward with their ropes and chains. All of them were trembling mightily. None dared speak a word.

The BFG, with Sophie now sitting on the palm of his hand, stood near by watching the operation.

To give the soldiers their due, they were extremely courageous. There were six well-trained efficient men working on each giant and within ten minutes eight out of the nine giants had been trussed up like chickens and were still snoring contentedly. The ninth, who happened to be the Fleshlumpeater, was causing trouble for the soldiers because he was lying with his right arm tucked underneath his enormous body. It was impossible to tie his wrists and arms together

206

without first getting that arm out from underneath him.

Very very cautiously, the six soldiers who were working on the Fleshlumpeater began to pull at the huge arm, trying to release it. The Fleshlumpeater opened his tiny piggy black eyes.

"Which of you foulpesters is wiggling my arm?" he bellowed. "Is that you, you rotsome Manhugger?"

Suddenly he saw the soldiers. In a flash, he was sitting up. He looked around him. He saw more soldiers. With a roar, he leapt to his feet. The soldiers, petrified with fear, froze where they were. They had no weapons with them. The Head of the Army put his jeep into reverse.

"Human beans!" the Fleshlumpeater yelled. "What is all you flushbunking rotsome half-baked beans doing in our country?" He made a grab at a soldier and swept him up in his hand.

"I is having early suppers today!" he shouted, holding the poor squirming soldier at arm's length and roaring with laughter.

Sophie, standing on the palm of the BFG's hand, was watching horrorstruck. "Do something!" she cried. "Quick, before he eats him!"

"Put that human bean down!" the BFG shouted.

The Fleshlumpeater turned and stared at the BFG. "What is *you* doing here with all these grotty twiglets?" he bellowed. "You is making me very suspichy!"

The BFG made a rush at the Fleshlumpeater, but the colossal fifty-four-foot-high giant simply knocked him over with a flick of his free arm. At the same time, Sophie fell off the BFG's palm on to the ground. Her mind was racing. She *must* do something! She *must!* She *must!* She remembered the sapphire brooch the Queen had pinned on to her chest. Quickly, she undid it.

"I is guzzling you nice and slow!" the Fleshlumpeater was saying to the soldier in his hand. "Then I is guzzling ten or twenty more of you midgy little maggots down there! You is not getting away from me ever because I is galloping fifty times faster than you!"

Sophie ran up behind the Fleshlumpeater. She was holding the brooch between her fingers. When she was right up close to the great naked hairy legs, she rammed the three-inch long pin of the brooch as hard as she could into the Fleshlumpeater's right ankle. It went deep into the flesh and stayed there.

The giant gave a roar of pain and jumped high in the air. He dropped the soldier and made a grab for his ankle.

The BFG, knowing what a coward the Fleshlumpeater was, saw his chance. "You is bitten by a snake!" he shouted. "I seed it biting you! It was a frightsome poisnowse viper! It was a dreadly dungerous vindscreen viper!"

"Save our souls!" bellowed the Fleshlumpeater. "Sound the crumpets! I is bitten by a septicous venomsome vindscreen viper!" He flopped to the ground and sat there howling his head off and clutching his ankle with both hands. His fingers

209

felt the brooch. "The teeth of the dreadly viper is
still sticking into me!" he yelled. "I is feeling the
teeth sticking into my anklet!"

The BFG saw his second chance. "We must be
getting those viper's teeth out at once!" he cried.
"Otherwise you is deader than duck-soup! I is
helping you!"

The BFG knelt down beside the Fleshlumpeater.
"You must grab your anklet very tight with both
hands!" he ordered. "That will stop the poisnowse
juices from the venomsome viper going up your
leg and into your heart!"

The Fleshlumpeater grabbed his ankle with both
his hands.

"Now close your eyes and grittle your teeth and
look up to heaven and say your prayers while I is
taking out the teeth of the venomsome viper," the

BFG said.

The terrified Fleshlumpeater did exactly as he was told.

The BFG signalled for some rope. A soldier rushed it over to him. With both the Fleshlumpeater's hands gripping his ankle, it was a simple matter for the BFG to tie the ankles and hands together with a tight knot.

"I is pulling out the frightsome viper's teeth!" the BFG said as he pulled the knot tight.

"Do it quickly!" shouted the Fleshlumpeater, "before I is pizzened to death!"

"There we is," said the BFG, standing up. "You can look now."

When the Fleshlumpeater saw that he was trussed up like a turkey, he gave a yell so loud that the heavens trembled. He rolled and he wriggled, he fought and he figgled, he squirmed and he squiggled. But there was not a thing he could do.

"Well done you!" Sophie cried.

"Well done *you!*" said the BFG, smiling down at the little girl. "You is saving all of our lives!"

"Will you please get that brooch back for me," Sophie said. "It belongs to the Queen."

The BFG pulled the beautiful brooch out of the Fleshlumpeater's ankle. The Fleshlumpeater howled. The BFG wiped the pin and handed it back to Sophie.

Curiously, not one of the other eight snoring giants had woken up during this shimozzle. "When you is only sleeping one or two hours a day, you is sleeping extra doubly deep," the BFG

explained.

The Heads of the Army and the Air Force drove forward once again in their jeep. "Her Majesty will be very pleased with me," the Head of the Army said. "I shall probably get a medal. What's the next move?"

"Now you is all driving over to my cave to load up my bottles of dreams," the BFG said.

"We can't waste time with that rubbish," the Army General said.

"It is the Queen's order," Sophie said. She was now back on the BFG's hand.

So the nine jeeps drove across to the BFG's cave and the great dream-loading operation began. There were fifty-thousand jars in all to be loaded up, more than five thousand to each jeep, and it took over an hour to finish the job.

While the soldiers were loading the dreams, the BFG and Sophie disappeared over the mountains on a mysterious errand. When they came back, the BFG had a sack the size of a small house slung over his shoulder.

"What's that you've got in there?" the Head of the Army demanded to know.

"Curiosity is killing the rat," the BFG said, and he turned away from the silly man.

When he was sure that all his precious dreams had been safely loaded on to the jeeps, the BFG said, "Now we is driving back to the bellypoppers and picking up the frightsome giants."

The jeeps drove back to the helicopters. The fifty thousand dreams were carried carefully, jar by jar, on to the helicopters. The soldiers climbed back on board, but the BFG and Sophie stayed on the ground. Then they all returned to where the nine giants were lying.

It was a fine sight to see them, these great air machines hovering over the trussed-up giants. It was an even finer sight to see the giants being woken up by the terrific thundering of the engines overhead, and the finest sight of all was to observe those nine hideous brutes squirming and twisting about on the ground like a mass of mighty snakes as they tried to free themselves from their ropes and chains.

"I is flushbunkled!" roared the Fleshlumpeater.

"I is splitzwiggled!" yelled the Childchewer.

"I is swogswalloped!" bellowed the Bonecruncher.

213

"I is goosegruggled!" howled the Manhugger.

"I is gunzleswiped!" shouted the Meatdripper.

"I is fluckgungled!" screamed the Maidmasher.

"I is slopgroggled!" squawked the Gizzard-gulper.

"I is crodsquinkled!" yowled the Bloodbottler.

"I is bopmuggered!" screeched the Butcher Boy.

The nine giant-carrying helicopters each chose a separate giant and hovered directly over him. Very

strong steel hawsers with hooks on the ends of them were lowered from the front and rear of each helicopter. The BFG quickly secured the hooks to the giants' chains, one hook near the legs and the other near the arms. Then very slowly, the giants were winched up into the air, parallel with the ground. The giants roared and bellowed, but there was nothing they could do.

The BFG, with Sophie once more resting comfortably in his ear, set off at a gallop for England. The helicopters all banked around and followed after him.

It was an amazing spectacle, those nine helicopters winging through the sky, each with a trussed-up fifty-foot-long giant slung underneath it. The giants themselves must have found it an interesting experience. They never stopped bellowing, but their howls were drowned by the noise of the engines.

When it began to get dark, the helicopters switched on powerful searchlights and trained them on to the galloping giant so as to keep him in sight. They flew right through the night and arrived in England just as dawn was breaking.

Feeding Time

While the giants were being captured, a tremendous bustle and hustle was going on back home in England. Every earth-digger and mechanical contrivance in the country had been mobilised to dig the colossal hole in which the nine giants were to be permanently imprisoned.

Ten thousand men and ten thousand machines worked ceaselessly through the night under powerful arc-lights, and the massive task was completed only just in time.

The hole itself was about twice the size of a football field and five hundred feet deep. The walls were perpendicular and engineers had calculated that there was no way a giant could escape once he was put in. Even if all nine giants were to stand on each other's shoulders, the topmost giant would still be some fifty feet from the top of the hole.

The nine giant-carrying helicopters hovered over the massive pit. The giants, one by one, were lowered to the floor. But they were still trussed up and now came the tricky business of releasing them from their bonds. Nobody wanted to go down and do this because the moment a giant was freed, he would be sure to turn on the wretched person who had freed him and gobble him up.

As usual, the BFG had the answer. "I has told

you before," he said, "giants is never eating giants, so I is going down and I shall untie them myself before you can say rack jobinson."

With thousands of fascinated spectators, including the Queen, peering down into the pit, the BFG was lowered on a rope. One by one, he released the giants. They stood up, stretched their stiffened limbs and started leaping about in fury.

"Why is they putting us down here in this grobsludging hole?" they shouted at the BFG.

"Because you is guzzling human beans," the BFG answered. "I is always warning you not to do it and you is never taking the titchiest bit of notice."

"In that case," the Fleshlumpeater bellowed, "I think we is guzzling *you* instead!"

The BFG grabbed the dangling rope and was hoisted out of the pit just in time.

The great bulging sack he had brought back with him from Giant Country lay at the top of the pit.

"What's in there?" the Queen asked him.

The BFG put an arm into the sack and pulled out a gigantic black and white striped object the size of a man.

"Snozzcumbers!" he cried. "This is the repulsant snozzcumber, Majester, and that is all we is going to give these disgustive giants from now on!"

"May I taste it?" the Queen asked.

"Don't, Majester, don't!" cried the BFG. "It is tasting of trogfilth and pigsquibble!" With that he tossed the snozzcumber down to the giants below.

"There's your supper!" he shouted. "Have a munch on that!" He fished out more snozzcumbers from the sack and threw them down. The giants below howled and cursed. The BFG laughed. "It serves them right left and centre!" he said.

"What will we feed them on when the snozzcumbers are all used up?" the Queen asked him.

"They is never being used up, Majester," the BFG answered, smiling. "I is also bringing in this sack a whole bungle of snozzcumber plants which I is giving, with your permission, to the royal gardener to put in the soil. Then we is having an everlasting supply of this repulsant food to feed these thirstbloody giants on."

"What a clever fellow you are," the Queen said. "You are not very well educated but you are really nobody's fool, I can see that."

The Author

Every country in the world that had in the past been visited by the foul man-eating giants sent telegrams of congratulations and thanks to the BFG and to Sophie. Kings and Presidents and Prime Ministers and Rulers of every kind showered the enormous giant and the little girl with compliments and thank-yous, as well as all sorts of medals and presents.

The Ruler of India sent the BFG a magnificent elephant, the very thing he had been wishing for all his life.

The King of Arabia sent them a camel each.

The Lama of Tibet sent them a llama each.

Wellington sent them one hundred pairs of wellies each.

Panama sent them beautiful hats.

The King of Sweden sent them a barrelful of sweet and sour pork.

Jersey sent them pullovers.

There was no end to the gratitude of the world.

The Queen herself gave orders that a special house with tremendous high ceilings and enormous doors should immediately be built in Windsor Great Park, next to her own castle, for the BFG to live in. And a pretty little cottage was put up next door for Sophie. The BFG's house was to have a special dream-storing room with hundreds of shelves in it where he could put his beloved bottles. What is more, he was given the title of The Royal Dream-Blower. He was allowed to go galloping off to any place in England on any night of the year to blow his splendid phizzwizards in through the windows to sleeping children. And letters poured into his house by the million from children begging him to pay them a visit.

Meanwhile, tourists from all over the globe came flocking to gaze down in wonder at the nine horrendous man-eating giants in the great pit. They came especially at feeding-time, when the

snozzcumbers were being thrown down to them by the keeper, and it was a pleasure to listen to the howls and growls of horror coming up from the pit as the giants began to chew upon the filthiest-tasting vegetable on earth.

There was only one disaster. Three silly men who had drunk too much beer for lunch decided to climb over the high fence surrounding the pit, and of course they fell in. There were yells of delight from the giants below, followed by the crunching of bones. The head keeper immediately put up a big notice on the fence saying, IT IS FORBIDDEN TO FEED THE GIANTS. And after that, there were no more disasters.

The BFG expressed a wish to learn how to speak properly, and Sophie herself, who loved him as she would a father, volunteered to give him lessons every day. She even taught him how to spell and to write sentences, and he turned out to be a splendid intelligent pupil. In his spare time, he read books. He became a tremendous reader. He read all of Charles Dickens (whom he no longer called Dahl's Chickens), and all of Shakespeare and literally thousands of other books. He also started to write essays about his own past life. When Sophie read some of them, she said, "These are very good. I think perhaps one day you could become a real writer."

"Oh, I would love that!" cried the BFG. "Do you think I could?"

"I know you could," Sophie said. "Why don't you start by writing a book about you and me?"

"Very well," the BFG said. "I'll give it a try."

So he did. He worked hard on it and in the end he completed it. Rather shyly, he showed it to the Queen. The Queen read it aloud to her grandchildren. Then the Queen said, "I think we ought to

225

get this book printed properly and published so that other children can read it.'' This was arranged, but because the BFG was a very modest giant, he wouldn't put his own name on it. He used somebody else's name instead.

But where, you might ask, is this book that the BFG wrote?

It's right here. You've just finished reading it.

Roald Dahl

MATILDA

Illustrated by Quentin Blake

For
Michael and Lucy

Contents

The Reader of Books

It's a funny thing about mothers and fathers. Even when their own child is the most disgusting little blister you could ever imagine, they still think that he or she is wonderful.

Some parents go further. They become so blinded by adoration they manage to convince themselves their child has qualities of genius.

Well, there is nothing very wrong with all this. It's the way of the world. It is only when the parents begin telling *us* about the brilliance of their own revolting offspring, that we start shouting, "Bring us a basin! We're going to be sick!"

School teachers suffer a good deal from having
to listen to this sort of twaddle from proud parents,
but they usually get their own back when the time
comes to write the end-of-term reports. If I were a
teacher I would cook up some real scorchers for
the children of doting parents. "Your son Maximil-
ian", I would write, "is a total wash-out. I hope
you have a family business you can push him into
when he leaves school because he sure as heck
won't get a job anywhere else." Or if I were feeling
lyrical that day, I might write, "It is a curious truth
that grasshoppers have their hearing-organs in the
sides of the abdomen. Your daughter Vanessa, judg-
ing by what she's learnt this term, has no hearing-
organs at all."

I might even delve deeper into natural history and say, "The periodical cicada spends six years as a grub underground, and no more than six *days* as a free creature of sunlight and air. Your son Wilfred has spent six years as a grub in this school and we are still waiting for him to emerge from the chrysalis." A particularly poisonous little girl might sting me into saying, "Fiona has the same glacial beauty as an iceberg, but unlike the iceberg she has absolutely nothing below the surface." I

think I might enjoy writing end-of-term reports for the stinkers in my class. But enough of that. We have to get on.

233

Occasionally one comes across parents who take the opposite line, who show no interest at all in their children, and these of course are far worse than the doting ones. Mr and Mrs Wormwood were two such parents. They had a son called Michael and a daughter called Matilda, and the parents looked upon Matilda in particular as nothing more than a scab. A scab is something you have to put up with until the time comes when you can pick it off and flick it away. Mr and Mrs Wormwood looked forward enormously to the time when they could pick their little daughter off and flick her away, preferably into the next county or even further than that.

It is bad enough when parents treat *ordinary* children as though they were scabs and bunions, but it becomes somehow a lot worse when the child in question is *extra-ordinary*, and by that I mean sensitive and brilliant. Matilda was both of these things, but above all she was brilliant. Her mind was so nimble and she was so quick to learn that her ability should have been obvious even to the most half-witted of parents. But Mr and Mrs Wormwood were both so gormless and so wrapped up in their own silly little lives that they failed to notice anything unusual about their daughter. To tell the truth, I doubt they would have noticed had she crawled into the house with a broken leg.

Matilda's brother Michael was a perfectly normal boy, but the sister, as I said, was something to make your eyes pop. By the age of *one and a half* her speech was perfect and she knew as many words as most grown-ups. The parents, instead of applauding her, called her a noisy chatterbox and told her sharply that small girls should be seen and not heard.

By the time she was *three*, Matilda had taught herself to read by studying newspapers and magazines that lay around the house. At the age of *four*, she could read fast and well and she naturally began hankering after books. The only book in the whole of this enlightened household was something called *Easy Cooking* belonging to her mother, and when she had read this from cover to cover and had learnt all the recipes by heart, she decided she wanted something more interesting.

"Daddy," she said, "do you think you could buy me a book?"

"A *book*?" he said. "What d'you want a flaming book for?"

"To read, Daddy."

"What's wrong with the telly, for heaven's sake? We've got a lovely telly with a twelve-inch screen and now you come asking for a book! You're getting spoiled, my girl!"

Nearly every weekday afternoon Matilda was left alone in the house. Her brother (five years older than her) went to school. Her father went to work and her mother went out playing bingo in a town eight miles away. Mrs Wormwood was hooked on bingo and played it five afternoons a week. On the afternoon of the day when her father had refused to buy her a book, Matilda set out all by herself to walk to the public library in the village. When she arrived, she introduced herself to the librarian, Mrs Phelps. She asked if she might sit awhile and read a book. Mrs Phelps, slightly taken aback at the arrival of such a tiny girl unaccompanied by a parent, nevertheless told her she was very welcome.

"Where are the children's books please?" Matilda asked.

"They're over there on those lower shelves," Mrs Phelps told her. "Would you like me to help you find a nice one with lots of pictures in it?"

"No, thank you," Matilda said. "I'm sure I can manage."

From then on, every afternoon, as soon as her mother had left for bingo, Matilda would toddle down to the library. The walk took only ten minutes and this allowed her two glorious hours sitting quietly by herself in a cosy corner devouring one book after another. When she had read every single children's book in the place, she started wandering round in search of something else.

Mrs Phelps, who had been watching her with fascination for the past few weeks, now got up from her desk and went over to her. "Can I help you, Matilda?" she asked.

"I'm wondering what to read next," Matilda said. "I've finished all the children's books."

"You mean you've looked at the pictures?"

"Yes, but I've read the books as well."

Mrs Phelps looked down at Matilda from her great height and Matilda looked right back up at her.

"I thought some were very poor," Matilda said, "but others were lovely. I liked *The Secret Garden* best of all. It was full of mystery. The mystery of

the room behind the closed door and the mystery of the garden behind the big wall."

Mrs Phelps was stunned. "Exactly how old are you, Matilda?" she asked.

"Four years and three months," Matilda said.

Mrs Phelps was more stunned than ever, but she had the sense not to show it. "What sort of a book would you like to read next?" she asked.

Matilda said, "I would like a really good one that grown-ups read. A famous one. I don't know any names."

Mrs Phelps looked along the shelves, taking her time. She didn't quite know what to bring out. How, she asked herself, does one choose a famous grown-up book for a four-year-old girl? Her first thought was to pick a young teenager's romance of the kind that is written for fifteen-year-old school-girls, but for some reason she found herself instinctively walking past that particular shelf.

"Try this," she said at last. "It's very famous and very good. If it's too long for you, just let me know and I'll find something shorter and a bit easier."

"*Great Expectations*," Matilda read, "by Charles Dickens. I'd love to try it."

I must be mad, Mrs Phelps told herself, but to Matilda she said, "Of course you may try it."

Over the next few afternoons Mrs Phelps could hardly take her eyes from the small girl sitting for hour after hour in the big armchair at the far end of the room with the book on her lap. It was necessary to rest it on the lap because it was too heavy for her to hold up, which meant she had to sit leaning forward in order to read. And a strange sight it was, this tiny dark-haired person sitting there with her feet nowhere near touching the floor, totally absorbed in the wonderful adventures of Pip and old Miss Havisham and her cobwebbed house and by the spell of magic that Dickens the great story-teller had woven with his words. The only movement from the reader was the lifting of the hand every now and then to turn over a page, and Mrs Phelps always felt sad when the time came for her to cross the floor and say, "It's ten to five, Matilda."

During the first week of Matilda's visits Mrs Phelps had said to her, "Does your mother walk you down here every day and then take you home?"

"My mother goes to Aylesbury every afternoon to play bingo," Matilda had said. "She doesn't know I come here."

"But that's surely not right," Mrs Phelps said. "I think you'd better ask her."

"I'd rather not," Matilda said. "She doesn't encourage reading books. Nor does my father."

"But what do they expect you to do every afternoon in an empty house?"

"Just mooch around and watch the telly."

"I see."

"She doesn't really care what I do," Matilda said a little sadly.

Mrs Phelps was concerned about the child's safety on the walk through the fairly busy village High Street and the crossing of the road, but she decided not to interfere.

240

Within a week, Matilda had finished *Great Expectations* which in that edition contained four hundred and eleven pages. "I loved it," she said to Mrs Phelps. "Has Mr Dickens written any others?"

"A great number," said the astounded Mrs Phelps. "Shall I choose you another?"

Over the next six months, under Mrs Phelps's

watchful and compassionate eye, Matilda read the following books:

Nicholas Nickleby by Charles Dickens
Oliver Twist by Charles Dickens
Jane Eyre by Charlotte Brontë
Pride and Prejudice by Jane Austen
Tess of the D'Urbervilles by Thomas Hardy
Gone to Earth by Mary Webb
Kim by Rudyard Kipling
The Invisible Man by H. G. Wells
The Old Man and the Sea by Ernest Hemingway
The Sound and the Fury by William Faulkner
The Grapes of Wrath by John Steinbeck
The Good Companions by J. B. Priestley
Brighton Rock by Graham Greene
Animal Farm by George Orwell

It was a formidable list and by now Mrs Phelps was filled with wonder and excitement, but it was probably a good thing that she did not allow herself to be completely carried away by it all. Almost anyone else witnessing the achievements of this small child would have been tempted to make a great fuss and shout the news all over the village and beyond, but not so Mrs Phelps. She was someone who minded her own business and had long since discovered it was seldom worth while to interfere with other people's children.

"Mr Hemingway says a lot of things I don't understand," Matilda said to her. "Especially about men and women. But I loved it all the same. The

242

way he tells it I feel I am right there on the spot watching it all happen."

"A fine writer will always make you feel that," Mrs Phelps said. "And don't worry about the bits you can't understand. Sit back and allow the words to wash around you, like music."

"I will, I will."

"Did you know", Mrs Phelps said, "that public libraries like this allow you to borrow books and take them home?"

"I didn't know that," Matilda said. "Could *I* do it?"

"Of course," Mrs Phelps said. "When you have chosen the book you want, bring it to me so I can make a note of it and it's yours for two weeks. You can take more than one if you wish."

From then on, Matilda would visit the library only once a week in order to take out new books and return the old ones. Her own small bedroom now became her reading-room and there she would sit and read most afternoons, often with a mug of hot chocolate beside her. She was not quite tall enough to reach things around the kitchen, but she kept a small box in the outhouse which she brought in and stood on in order to get whatever she wanted. Mostly it was hot chocolate she made, warming the milk in a saucepan on the stove before mixing it. Occasionally she made Bovril or Ovaltine. It was pleasant to take a hot drink up to her room and have it beside her as she sat in her silent room reading in the empty house in the afternoons. The books transported her into new worlds and intro-duced her to amazing people who lived exciting lives. She went on olden-day sailing ships with Joseph Conrad. She went to Africa with Ernest Hemingway and to India with Rudyard Kipling. She travelled all over the world while sitting in her little room in an English village.

Mr Wormwood,
the Great Car Dealer

Matilda's parents owned quite a nice house with three bedrooms upstairs, while on the ground floor there was a dining-room and a living-room and a kitchen. Her father was a dealer in second-hand cars and it seemed he did pretty well at it.

"Sawdust", he would say proudly, "is one of the great secrets of my success. And it costs me nothing. I get it free from the sawmill."

"What do you use it for?" Matilda asked him.

"Ha!" the father said. "Wouldn't you like to know."

"I don't see how sawdust can help you to sell second-hand cars, daddy."

"That's because you're an ignorant little twit," the father said. His speech was never very delicate but Matilda was used to it. She also knew that he liked to boast and she would egg him on shamelessly.

"You must be very clever to find a use for something that costs nothing," she said. "I wish I could do it."

"You couldn't," the father said. "You're too stupid. But I don't mind telling young Mike here about it seeing he'll be joining me in the business one day." Ignoring Matilda, he turned to his son and said, "I'm always glad to buy a car when some fool

246

has been crashing the gears so badly they're all worn out and rattle like mad. I get it cheap. Then all I do is mix a lot of sawdust with the oil in the gear-box and it runs as sweet as a nut."

"How long will it run like that before it starts rattling again?" Matilda asked him.

"Long enough for the buyer to get a good distance away," the father said, grinning. "About a hundred miles."

"But that's dishonest, daddy," Matilda said. "It's cheating."

"No one ever got rich being honest," the father said. "Customers are there to be diddled."

Mr Wormwood was a small ratty-looking man whose front teeth stuck out underneath a thin ratty moustache. He liked to wear jackets with large brightly-coloured checks and he sported ties that were usually yellow or pale green. "Now take mileage for instance," he went on. "Anyone who's buying a second-hand car, the first thing he wants to know is how many miles it's done. Right?"

"Right," the son said.

"So I buy an old dump that's got about a hundred and fifty thousand miles on the clock. I get it cheap. But no one's going to buy it with a mileage like that, are they? And these days you can't just take the speedometer out and fiddle the numbers back like you used to ten years ago. They've fixed it so it's impossible to tamper with it unless you're a ruddy watchmaker or something. So what do I do? I use my brains, laddie, that's what I do."

"How?" young Michael asked, fascinated. He

seemed to have inherited his father's love of crookery.

"I sit down and say to myself, how can I convert a mileage reading of one hundred and fifty thousand into only ten thousand without taking the speedometer to pieces? Well, if I were to run the car backwards for long enough then obviously that would do it. The numbers would click backwards, wouldn't they? But who's going to drive a flaming car in reverse for thousands and thousands of miles? You couldn't do it!"

"Of course you couldn't," young Michael said.

"So I scratch my head," the father said. "I use my brains. When you've been given a fine brain like I have, you've got to use it. And all of a sudden, the answer hits me. I tell you, I felt exactly like that other brilliant fellow must have felt when he discovered penicillin. 'Eureka!' I cried. 'I've got it!'"

"What did you do, dad?" the son asked him.

"The speedometer", Mr Wormwood said, "is run off a cable that is coupled up to one of the front wheels. So first I disconnect the cable where it joins the front wheel. Next, I get one of those high-speed electric drills and I couple that up to the end of the cable in such a way that when the drill turns, it turns the cable *backwards*. You got me so far? You following me?"

"Yes, daddy," young Michael said.

"These drills run at a tremendous speed," the father said, "so when I switch on the drill the mileage numbers on the speedo spin backwards at

248

a fantastic rate. I can knock fifty thousand miles off the clock in a few minutes with my high-speed electric drill. And by the time I've finished, the car's only done ten thousand and it's ready for sale. 'She's almost new,' I say to the customer. 'She's hardly done ten thou. Belonged to an old lady who only used it once a week for shopping.'"

"Can you really turn the mileage back with an electric drill?" young Michael asked.

"I'm telling you trade secrets," the father said. "So don't you go talking about this to anyone else. You don't want me put in jug, do you?"

"I won't tell a soul," the boy said. "Do you do this to many cars, dad?"

"Every single car that comes through my hands gets the treatment," the father said. "They all have their mileage cut to under under ten thou before they're offered for sale. And to think I invented that all by myself," he added proudly. "It's made me a mint."

Matilda, who had been listening closely, said, "But daddy, that's even more dishonest than the sawdust. It's disgusting. You're cheating people who trust you."

"If you don't like it then don't eat the food in this house," the father said. "It's bought with the profits."

"It's dirty money," Matilda said. "I hate it."

Two red spots appears on the father's cheeks. "Who the heck do you think you are," he shouted, "The Archbishop of Canterbury or something, preaching to me about honesty? You're just an ignorant little squirt who hasn't the foggiest idea what you're talking about!"

"Quite right, Harry," the mother said. And to Matilda she said, "You've got a nerve talking to your father like that. Now keep your nasty mouth shut so we can all watch this programme in peace."

They were in the living-room eating their suppers on their knees in front of the telly. The suppers were TV dinners in floppy aluminium containers with separate compartments for the stewed meat,

the boiled potatoes and the peas. Mrs Wormwood sat munching her meal with her eyes glued to the American soap-opera on the screen. She was a large woman whose hair was dyed platinum blonde except where you could see the mousy-brown bits growing out from the roots. She wore heavy make-up and she had one of those unfortunate bulging figures where the flesh appears to be strapped in all around the body to prevent it from falling out.

"Mummy," Matilda said, "would you mind if I ate my supper in the dining-room so I could read my book?"

The father glanced up sharply. "*I* would mind!" he snapped. "Supper is a family gathering and no one leaves the table till it's over!"

"But we're not at the table," Matilda said. "We never are. We're always eating off our knees and watching the telly."

"What's wrong with watching the telly, may I ask?" the father said. His voice had suddenly become soft and dangerous.

Matilda didn't trust herself to answer him, so she kept quiet. She could feel the anger boiling up inside her. She knew it was wrong to hate her parents like this, but she was finding it very hard not to do so. All the reading she had done had given her a view of life that they had never seen. If only they would read a little Dickens or Kipling they would soon discover there was more to life than cheating people and watching television.

Another thing. She resented being told constantly that she was ignorant and stupid when she knew she wasn't. The anger inside her went on boiling and boiling, and as she lay in bed that night she made a decision. She decided that every time her father or her mother was beastly to her, she would get her own back in some way or another. A small victory or two would help her to tolerate their idiocies and would stop her from going crazy. You must remember that she was still hardly five years old and it is not easy for somebody as small as that to score points against an all-powerful grown-up. Even so, she was determined to have a go. Her father, after what had happened in front of the telly that evening, was first on her list.

The Hat
and the Superglue

The following morning, just before the father left for his beastly second-hand car garage, Matilda slipped into the cloakroom and got hold of the hat he wore each day to work. She had to stand on her toes and reach up as high as she could with a walking-stick in order to hook the hat off the peg, and even then she only just made it. The hat itself was one of those flat-topped pork-pie jobs with a jay's feather stuck in the hat-band and Mr Wormwood was very proud of it. He thought it gave him a rakish daring look, especially when he wore it at an angle with his loud checked jacket and green tie.

Matilda, holding the hat in one hand and a thin tube of Superglue in the other, proceeded to squeeze a line of glue very neatly all round the inside rim of the hat. Then she carefully hooked the hat back on to the peg with the walking-stick. She timed this operation very carefully, applying the glue just as her father was getting up from the breakfast table.

Mr Wormwood didn't notice anything when he put the hat on, but when he arrived at the garage he couldn't get it off. Superglue is very powerful stuff, so powerful it will take your skin off if you pull too hard. Mr Wormwood didn't want to be

scalped so he had to keep the hat on his head the whole day long, even when putting sawdust in gear-boxes and fiddling the mileages of cars with his electric drill. In an effort to save face, he adopted a casual attitude hoping that his staff would think that he actually *meant* to keep his hat on all day long just for the heck of it, like gangsters do in the films.

When he got home that evening he still couldn't get the hat off. "Don't be silly," his wife said. "Come here. I'll take it off for you."

She gave the hat a sharp yank. Mr Wormwood let out a yell that rattled the window-panes. "Ow-w-w!" he screamed. "Don't do that! Let go! You'll take half the skin off my forehead!"

Matilda, nestling in her usual chair, was watching this performance over the rim of her book with some interest.

"What's the matter, daddy?" she said. "Has your head suddenly swollen or something?"

The father glared at his daughter with deep suspicion, but said nothing. How could he? Mrs Wormwood said to him, "It *must* be Superglue. It couldn't be anything else. That'll teach you to go playing round with nasty stuff like that. I expect you were trying to stick another feather in your hat."

"I haven't touched the flaming stuff!" Mr Wormwood shouted. He turned and looked again at Matilda who looked back at him with large innocent brown eyes.

Mrs Wormwood said to him, "You should read the label on the tube before you start messing with dangerous products. Always follow the instructions on the label."

"What in heaven's name are you talking about, you stupid witch?" Mr Wormwood shouted, clutching the brim of his hat to stop anyone trying to pull it off again. "D'you think I'm so stupid I'd glue this thing to my head on purpose?"

Matilda said, "There's a boy down the road who got some Superglue on his finger without knowing it and then he put his finger to his nose."

Mr Wormwood jumped. "What happened to him?" he spluttered.

"The finger got stuck inside his nose," Matilda said, "and he had to go around like that for a week. People kept saying to him, 'Stop picking your nose,' and he couldn't do anything about it. He looked an awful fool."

"Serve him right," Mrs Wormwood said. "He shouldn't have put his finger up there in the first place. It's a nasty habit. If all children had Superglue put on their fingers they'd soon stop doing it."

Matilda said, "Grown-ups do it too, mummy. I saw you doing it yesterday in the kitchen."

"That's quite enough from you," Mrs Wormwood said, turning pink.

258

Mr Wormwood had to keep his hat on all through supper in front of the television. He looked ridiculous and he stayed very silent.

When he went up to bed he tried again to get the thing off, and so did his wife, but it wouldn't budge. "How am I going to have my shower?" he demanded.

"You'll just have to do without it, won't you," his wife told him. And later on, as she watched her skinny little husband skulking around the bedroom in his purple-striped pyjamas with a pork-pie hat on his head, she thought how stupid he looked. Hardly the kind of man a wife dreams about, she told herself.

Mr Wormwood discovered that the worst thing about having a permanent hat on his head was having to sleep in it. It was impossible to lie comfortably on the pillow. "Now do stop fussing around," his wife said to him after he had been tossing and turning for about an hour. "I expect it will be loose by the morning and then it'll slip off easily."

But it wasn't loose by the morning and it wouldn't slip off. So Mrs Wormwood took a pair of scissors and cut the thing off his head, bit by bit, first the top and then the brim. Where the inner band had stuck to the hair all around the sides and back, she had to chop the hair off right to the skin so that he finished up with a bald white ring round his head, like some sort of a monk. And in the front, where the band had stuck directly to the bare skin, there remained a whole lot of small patches of brown leathery stuff that no amount of washing would get off.

At breakfast Matilda said to him, "You *must* try to get those bits off your forehead, daddy. It looks as though you've got little brown insects crawling about all over you. People will think you've got lice."

"Be quiet!" the father snapped. "Just keep your nasty mouth shut, will you!"

All in all it was a most satisfactory exercise. But it was surely too much to hope that it had taught the father a permanent lesson.

The Ghost

There was comparative calm in the Wormwood household for about a week after the Superglue episode. The experience had clearly chastened Mr Wormwood and he seemed temporarily to have lost his taste for boasting and bullying.

Then suddenly he struck again. Perhaps he had had a bad day at the garage and had not sold enough crummy second-hand cars. There are many things that make a man irritable when he arrives home from work in the evening and a sensible wife will usually notice the storm-signals and will leave him alone until he simmers down.

When Mr Wormwood arrived back from the garage that evening his face was as dark as a thundercloud and somebody was clearly for the high-jump pretty soon. His wife recognised the signs immediately and made herself scarce. He then strode into the living-room. Matilda happened to be curled up in an arm-chair in the corner, totally absorbed in a book. Mr Wormwood switched on the television. The screen lit up. The programme blared. Mr Wormwood glared at Matilda. She hadn't moved. She had somehow trained herself by now to block her ears to the ghastly sound of the dreaded box. She kept right on reading, and for some reason this infuriated the father. Perhaps his anger was

intensified because he saw her getting pleasure from something that was beyond his reach.

"Don't you *ever* stop reading?" he snapped at her.

"Oh, hello daddy," she said pleasantly. "Did you have a good day?"

"What is this trash?" he said, snatching the book from her hands.

"It isn't trash, daddy, it's lovely. It's called *The Red Pony*. It's by John Steinbeck, an American writer. Why don't you try it? You'll love it."

"Filth," Mr Wormwood said. "If it's by an American it's certain to be filth. That's all they write about."

"No daddy, it's beautiful, honestly it is. It's about . . . "

"I don't want to know what it's about," Mr Wormwood barked. "I'm fed up with your reading anyway. Go and find yourself something useful to

do." With frightening suddenness he now began ripping the pages out of the book in handfuls and throwing them in the waste-paper basket.

Matilda froze in horror. The father kept going. There seemed little doubt that the man felt some kind of jealousy. How dare she, he seemed to be saying with each rip of a page, how dare she enjoy reading books when he couldn't? How dare she?

"That's a *library* book!" Matilda cried. "It doesn't belong to me! I have to return it to Mrs Phelps!"

"Then you'll have to buy another one, won't you?" the father said, still tearing out pages. "You'll have to save your pocket-money until there's enough in the kitty to buy a new one for your precious Mrs Phelps, won't you?" With that he dropped the now empty covers of the book into the basket and marched out of the room, leaving the telly blaring.

Most children in Matilda's place would have burst into floods of tears. She didn't do this. She sat there very still and white and thoughtful. She seemed to know that neither crying nor sulking ever got anyone anywhere. The only sensible thing to do when you are attacked is, as Napoleon once said, to counter-attack. Matilda's wonderfully subtle mind was already at work devising yet another suitable punishment for the poisonous parent. The plan that was now beginning to hatch in her mind depended, however, upon whether or not Fred's parrot was really as good a talker as Fred made out.

Fred was a friend of Matilda's. He was a small
boy of six who lived just around the corner from
her, and for days he had been going on about this
great talking parrot his father had given him.

So the following afternoon, as soon as Mrs
Wormwood had departed in her car for another
session of bingo, Matilda set out for Fred's house
to investigate. She knocked on his door and asked
if he would be kind enough to show her the famous

bird. Fred was delighted and led her up to his bedroom where a truly magnificent blue and yellow parrot sat in a tall cage.

"There it is," Fred said. "It's name is Chopper."

"Make it talk," Matilda said.

"You can't *make* it talk," Fred said. "You have to be patient. It'll talk when it feels like it."

They hung around, waiting. Suddenly the parrot said, "Hullo, hullo, hullo." It was exactly like a human voice. Matilda said, "That's amazing! What else can it say?"

"Rattle my bones!" the parrot said, giving a wonderful imitation of a spooky voice. "Rattle my bones!"

"He's always saying that," Fred told her .

"What else can he say?" Matilda asked.

"That's about it," Fred said. "But it is pretty marvellous don't you think?"

"It's fabulous," Matilda said. "Will you lend him to me just for one night?"

"No," Fred said. "Certainly not."

"I'll give you all my next week's pocket-money," Matilda said.

That was different. Fred thought about it for a few seconds. "All right, then," he said, "If you promise to return him tomorrow."

Matilda staggered back to her own empty house carrying the tall cage in both hands. There was a large fireplace in the dining-room and she now set about wedging the cage up the chimney and out of sight. This wasn't so easy, but she managed it in the end.

267

"Hullo, hullo, hullo!" the bird called down to her. "Hullo, hullo!"

"Shut up, you nut!" Matilda said, and she went out to wash the soot off her hands.

That evening while the mother, the father, the brother and Matilda were having supper as usual in the living-room in front of the television, a voice came loud and clear from the dining-room across the hall. "Hullo, hullo, hullo," it said.

"Harry!" cried the mother, turning white. "There's someone in the house! I heard a voice!"

"So did I!" the brother said. Matilda jumped up and switched off the telly. "Ssshh!" she said. "Listen!"

They all stopped eating and sat there very tense, listening.

"Hullo, hullo, hullo!" came the voice again.

"There it is!" cried the brother.

"It's burglars!" hissed the mother. "They're in the dining-room!"

"I think they are," the father said, sitting tight.

"Then go and catch them, Harry!" hissed the mother. "Go out and collar them red-handed!"

The father didn't move. He seemed in no hurry to dash off and be a hero. His face had turned grey.

"Get on with it!" hissed the mother. "They're probably after the silver!"

The husband wiped his lips nervously with his napkin. "Why don't we all go and look together?" he said.

"Come on, then," the brother said. "Come on, mum."

"They're definitely in the dining-room," Matilda whispered. "I'm sure they are."

The mother grabbed a poker from the fireplace. The father took a golf-club that was standing in the corner. The brother seized a table-lamp, ripping the plug out of its socket. Matilda took the knife she had been eating with, and all four of them crept towards the dining-room door, the father keeping well behind the others.

"Hullo, hullo, hullo," came the voice again.

"Come on!" Matilda cried and she burst into the room, brandishing her knife. "Stick 'em up!" she yelled. "We've caught you!" The others followed

her, waving their weapons. Then they stopped.
They stared around the room. There was no one
there.

"There's no one here," the father said, greatly
relieved.

"I heard him, Harry!" the mother shrieked, still
quaking. "I distinctly heard his voice! So did you!"

"I'm certain I heard him!" Matilda cried. "He's
in here somewhere!" She began searching behind
the sofa and behind the curtains.

Then came the voice once again, soft and spooky
this time, "Rattle my bones," it said. "Rattle my
bones."

They all jumped, including Matilda who was a pretty good actress. They stared round the room. There was still no one there.

"It's a ghost," Matilda said.

"Heaven help us!" cried the mother, clutching her husband round the neck.

"I know it's a ghost!" Matilda said. "I've heard it here before! This room is haunted! I thought you knew that."

"Save us!" the mother screamed, almost throttling her husband.

"I'm getting out of here," the father said, greyer than ever now. They all fled, slamming the door behind them.

The next afternoon, Matilda managed to get a rather sooty and grumpy parrot down from the chimney and out of the house without being seen. She carried it through the back-door and ran with it all the way to Fred's house.

"Did it behave itself?" Fred asked her.

"We had a lovely time with it," Matilda said. "My parents adored it."

Arithmetic

Matilda longed for her parents to be good and loving and understanding and honourable and intelligent. The fact that they were none of these things was something she had to put up with. It was not easy to do so. But the new game she had invented of punishing one or both of them each time they were beastly to her made her life more or less bearable.

Being very small and very young, the only power Matilda had over anyone in her family was brain-power. For sheer cleverness she could run rings around them all. But the fact remained that any five-year-old girl in any family was always obliged to do as she was told, however asinine the orders might be. Thus she was always forced to eat her evening meals out of TV-dinner-trays in front of the dreaded box. She always had to stay alone on weekday afternoons, and whenever she was told to shut up, she had to shut up.

Her safety-valve, the thing that prevented her from going round the bend, was the fun of devising and dishing out these splendid punishments, and the lovely thing was that they seemed to work, at any rate for short periods. The father in particular became less cocky and unbearable for several days after receiving a dose of Matilda's magic medicine.

The parrot-in-the-chimney affair quite definitely

cooled both parents down a lot and for over a week they were comparatively civil to their small daughter. But alas, this couldn't last. The next flare-up came one evening in the sitting-room. Mr Wormwood had just returned from work. Matilda and her brother were sitting quietly on the sofa waiting for their mother to bring in the TV dinners on a tray. The television had not yet been switched on.

In came Mr Wormwood in a loud check suit and a yellow tie. The appalling broad orange-and-green check of the jacket and trousers almost blinded the onlooker. He looked like a low-grade bookmaker dressed up for his daughter's wedding, and he was clearly very pleased with himself this evening. He sat down in an armchair and rubbed his hands together and addressed his son in a loud voice. "Well, my boy," he said, "your father's had a most successful day. He is a lot richer tonight than he was this morning. He has sold no less than five cars, each one at a tidy profit. Sawdust in the gear-boxes, the electric-drill on the speedometer cables, a splash of paint here and there and a few other clever little tricks and the idiots were all falling over themselves to buy."

He fished a bit of paper from his pocket and studied it. "Listen boy," he said, addressing the son and ignoring Matilda, "seeing as you'll be going into this business with me one day, you've got to know how to add up the profits you make at the end of each day. Go and get yourself a pad and a pencil and let's see how clever you are."

The son obediently left the room and returned with the writing materials.

"Write down these figures," the father said, reading from his bit of paper. "Car number one was bought by me for two hundred and seventy-eight pounds and sold for one thousand four hundred and twenty-five. Got that?"

The ten-year-old boy wrote the two separate amounts down slowly and carefully.

"Car number two", the father went on, "cost me one hundred and eighteen pounds and sold for seven hundred and sixty. Got it?"

"Yes, dad," the son said. "I've got that."

"Car number three cost one hundred and eleven pounds and sold for nine hundred and ninety-nine pounds and fifty pence."

"Say that again," the son said. "How much did it sell for?"

"Nine hundred and ninety-nine pounds and fifty pence," the father said. "And that, by the way, is another of my nifty little tricks to diddle the customer. Never ask for a big round figure. Always go just below it. Never say one thousand pounds. Always say nine hundred and ninety-nine fifty. It sounds much less but it isn't. Clever, isn't it?"

"Very," the son said. "You're brilliant, dad."

"Car number four cost eighty-six pounds – a real wreck that was – and sold for six hundred and ninety-nine pounds fifty."

"Not too fast," the son said, writing the numbers down. "Right. I've got it."

"Car number five cost six hundred and thirty-seven pounds and sold for sixteen hundred and forty-nine fifty. You got all those figures written down, son?"

"Yes, daddy," the boy said, crouching over his pad and carefully writing.

"Very well," the father said. "Now work out the profit I made on each of the five cars and add up the total. Then you'll be able to tell me how much money your rather brilliant father made altogether today."

"That's a lot of sums," the boy said.

"Of course it's a lot of sums," the father answered. "But when you're in big business like I am, you've got to be hot stuff at arithmetic. I've practically got a computer inside my head. It took me less than ten minutes to work the whole thing out."

"You mean you did it in your head, dad?" the son asked, goggling.

"Well, not exactly," the father said. "Nobody could do that. But it didn't take me long. When you're finished, tell me what you think my profit was for the day. I've got the final total written down here and I'll tell you if you're right."

Matilda said quietly, "Dad, you made exactly four thousand three hundred and three pounds and fifty pence altogether."

"Don't butt in," the father said. "Your brother and I are busy with high finance."

"But dad . . ."

"Shut up," the father said. "Stop guessing and trying to be clever."

"Look at your answer, dad," Matilda said gently. "If you've done it right it ought to be four thousand three hundred and three pounds and fifty pence. Is that what you've got, dad?"

The father glanced down at the paper in his hand. He seemed to stiffen. He became very quiet. There was a silence. Then he said, "Say that again."

"Four thousand three hundred and three pounds fifty," Matilda said.

There was another silence. The father's face was beginning to go dark red.

"I'm sure it's right," Matilda said.

"You . . . you little cheat!" the father suddenly shouted, pointing at her with his finger. "You looked at my bit of paper! You read it off from what I've got written here!"

278

"Daddy, I'm the other side of the room," Matilda said. "How could I possibly see it?"

"Don't give me that rubbish!" the father shouted. "Of course you looked! You must have looked! No one in the world could give the right answer just like that, especially a girl! You're a little cheat, madam, that's what you are! A cheat and a liar!"

At that point, the mother came in carrying a large tray on which were the four suppers. This time it was fish and chips which Mrs Wormwood had picked up in the fish and chip shop on her way home from bingo. It seemed that bingo afternoons left her so exhausted both physically and emotionally that she never had enough energy left to cook an evening meal. So if it wasn't TV dinners it had to be fish and chips. "What are you looking so red in the face about, Harry?" she said as she put the tray down on the coffee-table.

"Your daughter's a cheat and a liar," the father said, taking his plate of fish and placing it on his knees. "Turn the telly on and let's not have any more talk."

The Platinum-Blond Man

There was no doubt in Matilda's mind that this latest display of foulness by her father deserved severe punishment, and as she sat eating her awful fried fish and fried chips and ignoring the television, her brain went to work on various possibilities. By the time she went up to bed her mind was made up.

The next morning she got up early and went into the bathroom and locked the door. As we already know, Mrs Wormwood's hair was dyed a brilliant platinum blonde, very much the same glistening silvery colour as a female tightrope-walker's tights in a circus. The big dyeing job was done twice a year at the hairdresser's, but every month or so in between, Mrs Wormwood used to freshen it up by giving it a rinse in the washbasin with something called PLATINUM BLONDE HAIR-DYE EXTRA STRONG. This also served to dye the nasty brown hairs that kept growing from the roots underneath. The bottle of PLATINUM BLONDE HAIR-DYE EXTRA STRONG was kept in the cupboard in the bathroom, and underneath the title on the label were written the words *Caution, this is peroxide. Keep away from children*. Matilda had read it many times with fascination.

Matilda's father had a fine crop of black hair

which he parted in the middle and of which he was exceedingly proud. "Good strong hair," he was fond of saying, "means there's a good strong brain underneath."

"Like Shakespeare," Matilda had once said to him.

"Like who?"

"Shakespeare, daddy."

"Was he brainy?"

"Very, daddy."

"He had masses of hair, did he?"

"He was bald, daddy."

To which the father had snapped, "If you can't talk sense then shut up."

281

Anyway, Mr Wormwood kept his hair looking
bright and strong, or so he thought, by rubbing into
it every morning large quantities of a lotion called
OIL OF VIOLETS HAIR TONIC. A bottle of this smelly
purple mixture always stood on the shelf above the
sink in the bathroom alongside all the tooth-
brushes, and a very vigorous scalp massage with
OIL OF VIOLETS took place daily after shaving was
completed. This hair and scalp massage was always
accompanied by loud masculine grunts and heavy

breathing and gasps of "Ahhh, that's better! That's the stuff! Rub it right into the roots!" which could be clearly heard by Matilda in her bedroom across the corridor.

Now, in the early morning privacy of the bathroom, Matilda unscrewed the cap of her father's OIL OF VIOLETS and tipped three-quarters of the contents down the drain. Then she filled the bottle up with her mother's PLATINUM BLONDE HAIR-DYE EXTRA STRONG. She carefully left enough of her father's original hair tonic in the bottle so that when she gave it a good shake the whole thing still looked reasonably purple. She then replaced the bottle on the shelf above the sink, taking care to put her mother's bottle back in the cupboard. So far so good.

At breakfast time Matilda sat quietly at the dining-room table eating her cornflakes. Her brother sat opposite her with his back to the door devouring hunks of bread smothered with a mixture of peanut-butter and strawberry jam. The mother was just out of sight around the corner in the kitchen making Mr Wormwood's breakfast which always had to be two fried eggs on fried bread with three pork sausages and three strips of bacon and some fried tomatoes.

At this point Mr Wormwood came noisily into the room. He was incapable of entering any room quietly, especially at breakfast time. He always had to make his appearance felt immediately by creating a lot of noise and clatter. One could almost hear him saying, "It's me! Here I come, the great man himself, the master of the house, the wage-earner, the one who makes it possible for all the rest of you to live so well! Notice me and pay your respects!"

On this occasion he strode in and slapped his son on the back and shouted, "Well my boy, your father feels he's in for another great money-making day today at the garage! I've got a few little beauties I'm going to flog to the idiots this morning. Where's my breakfast?"

"It's coming, treasure," Mrs Wormwood called from the kitchen.

Matilda kept her face bent low over her corn-flakes. She didn't dare look up. In the first place she wasn't at all sure what she was going to see. And secondly, if she did see what she thought she was going to see, she wouldn't trust herself to keep a straight face. The son was looking directly ahead out of the window stuffing himself with bread and peanut-butter and strawberry jam.

The father was just moving round to sit at the head of the table when the mother came sweeping out from the kitchen carrying a huge plate piled high with eggs and sausages and bacon and tom-atoes. She looked up. She caught sight of her hus-band. She stopped dead. Then she let out a scream that seemed to lift her right up into the air and she dropped the plate with a crash and a splash on to the floor. Everyone jumped, including Mr Wormwood.

"What the heck's the matter with you, woman?" he shouted. "Look at the mess you've made on the carpet!"

"Your *hair*!" the mother was shrieking, pointing a quivering finger at her husband. "Look at your *hair*! What've you done to your *hair*?"

"What's wrong with my hair for heaven's sake?" he said.

"Oh my gawd dad, what've you done to your hair?" the son shouted.

A splendid noisy scene was building up nicely in the breakfast room.

Matilda said nothing. She simply sat there admiring the wonderful effect of her own handiwork. Mr Wormwood's fine crop of black hair was now a dirty silver, the colour this time of a tightrope-walker's tights that had not been washed for the entire circus season.

"You've . . . you've . . . you've *dyed* it!" shrieked the mother. "Why did you do it, you fool! It looks absolutely frightful! It looks horrendous! You look like a freak!"

"What the blazes are you all talking about?" the father yelled, putting both hands to his hair. "I most certainly have not dyed it! What d'you mean I've dyed it? What's happened to it? Or is this some sort of a stupid joke?" His face was turning pale green, the colour of sour apples.

"You *must* have dyed it, dad," the son said. "It's the same colour as mum's only much dirtier looking."

"Of course he's dyed it!" the mother cried. "It can't change colour all by itself! What on earth were you trying to do, make yourself look handsome or something? You look like someone's grandmother gone wrong!"

"Get me a mirror!" the father yelled. "Don't just stand there shrieking at me! Get me a mirror!"

The mother's handbag lay on a chair at the other end of the table. She opened the bag and got out a powder compact that had a small round mirror on the inside of the lid. She opened the compact and handed it to her husband. He grabbed it and held it before his face and in doing so spilled most of

286

the powder all over the front of his fancy tweed jacket.

"Be *careful*!" shrieked the mother. "Now look what you've done! That's my best Elizabeth Arden face powder!"

"Oh my gawd!" yelled the father, staring into the little mirror. "What's happened to me! I look terrible! I look just like *you* gone wrong! I can't go down to the garage and sell cars like this! How did it happen?" He stared round the room, first at the mother, then at the son, then at Matilda. "How *could* it have happened?" he yelled.

"I imagine, daddy," Matilda said quietly, "that you weren't looking very hard and you simply took mummy's bottle of hair stuff off the shelf instead of your own."

"*Of course* that's what happened!" the mother cried. "Well really Harry, how stupid can you get? Why didn't you read the label before you started splashing the stuff all over you! Mine's *terribly* strong. I'm only meant to use one tablespoon of it in a whole basin of water and you've gone and put it all over your head neat! It'll probably take all your hair off in the end! Is your scalp beginning to burn, dear?"

"You mean I'm going to lose all my hair?" the husband yelled.

"I think you will," the mother said. "Peroxide is a very powerful chemical. It's what they put down the lavatory to disinfect the pan only they give it another name."

"What are you saying!" the husband cried. "I'm not a lavatory pan! I don't want to be disinfected!"

"Even diluted like I use it," the mother told him, "it makes a good deal of *my* hair fall out, so goodness knows what's going to happen to you. I'm surprised it didn't take the whole of the top of your head off!"

"What shall I do?" wailed the father. "Tell me quick what to do before it starts falling out!"

Matilda said, "I'd give it a good wash, dad, if I were you, with soap and water. But you'll have to hurry."

"Will that change the colour back?" the father asked anxiously.

"Of course it won't, you twit," the mother said.

"Then what do I do? I can't go around looking like this for ever?"

"You'll have to have it dyed black," the mother said. "But wash it first or there won't be any there to dye."

"Right!" the father shouted, springing into action. "Get me an appointment with your hairdresser this instant for a hair-dyeing job! Tell them it's an emergency! They've got to boot someone else off their list! I'm going upstairs to wash it now!" With that the man dashed out of the room and Mrs Wormwood, sighing deeply, went to the telephone to call the beauty parlour.

"He does do some pretty silly things now and again, doesn't he, mummy?" Matilda said.

The mother, dialling the number on the phone, said, "I'm afraid men are not always quite as clever as they think they are. You will learn that when you get a bit older, my girl."

Miss Honey

Matilda was a little late in starting school. Most children begin Primary School at five or even just before, but Matilda's parents, who weren't very concerned one way or the other about their daughter's education, had forgotten to make the proper arrangements in advance. She was five and a half when she entered school for the first time.

The village school for younger children was a bleak brick building called Crunchem Hall Primary School. It had about two hundred and fifty pupils aged from five to just under twelve years old. The head teacher, the boss, the supreme commander of this establishment was a formidable middle-aged lady whose name was Miss Trunchbull.

Naturally Matilda was put in the bottom class, where there were eighteen other small boys and girls about the same age as her. Their teacher was called Miss Honey, and she could not have been more than twenty-three or twenty-four. She had a lovely pale oval madonna face with blue eyes and her hair was light-brown. Her body was so slim and fragile one got the feeling that if she fell over she would smash into a thousand pieces, like a porcelain figure.

Miss Jennifer Honey was a mild and quiet person who never raised her voice and was seldom seen to smile, but there is no doubt she possessed that rare gift for being adored by every small child under her care. She seemed to understand totally the bewilderment and fear that so often overwhelms young children who for the first time in their lives are herded into a classroom and told to obey orders. Some curious warmth that was almost tangible shone out of Miss Honey's face when she spoke to a confused and homesick newcomer to the class.

Miss Trunchbull, the Headmistress, was something else altogether. She was a gigantic holy terror, a fierce tyrannical monster who frightened the life out of the pupils and teachers alike. There was an aura of menace about her even at a distance, and when she came up close you could almost feel the dangerous heat radiating from her as from a red-hot rod of metal. When she marched – Miss Trunchbull never walked, she always marched like a storm-trooper with long strides and arms aswinging – when she marched along a corridor you could actually hear her snorting as she went, and if a group of children happened to be in her path, she ploughed right on through them like a tank, with small people bouncing off her to left and right. Thank goodness we don't meet many people like her in this world, although they do exist and all of us are likely to come across at least one of them in a lifetime. If you ever do, you should behave as you would if you met an enraged rhinoceros out in the bush – climb up the nearest tree and stay there until it has gone away. This woman, in all her eccentricities and in her appearance, is almost im-

possible to describe, but I shall make some attempt to do so a little later on. Let us leave her for the moment and go back to Matilda and her first day in Miss Honey's class.

After the usual business of going through all the names of the children, Miss Honey handed out a brand-new exercise-book to each pupil.

"You have all brought your own pencils, I hope," she said.

"Yes, Miss Honey," they chanted.

"Good. Now this is the very first day of school for each one of you. It is the beginning of at least eleven long years of schooling that all of you are going to have to go through. And six of those years will be spent right here at Crunchem Hall where, as you know, your Headmistress is Miss Trunchbull. Let me for your own good tell you something about Miss Trunchbull. She insists upon strict discipline throughout the school, and if you take my advice you will do your very best to behave yourselves in her presence. Never argue with her. Never answer her back. Always do as she says. If you get on the wrong side of Miss Trunchbull she can liquidise you like a carrot in a kitchen blender. It's nothing to laugh about, Lavender. Take that grin off your face. All of you will be wise to remember that Miss Trunchbull deals very very severely with anyone who gets out of line in this school. Have you got the message?"

"Yes, Miss Honey," chirruped eighteen eager little voices.

"I myself", Miss Honey went on, "want to help you to learn as much as possible while you are in this class. That is because I know it will make things easier for you later on. For example, by the end of this week I shall expect every one of you to know the two-times table by heart. And in a year's time I hope you will know all the multiplication tables up to twelve. It will help you enormously if you do. Now then, do any of you happen to have learnt the two-times table already?"

Matilda put up her hand. She was the only one.

Miss Honey looked carefully at the tiny girl with dark hair and a round serious face sitting in the second row. "Wonderful," she said. "Please stand up and recite as much of it as you can."

Matilda stood up and began to say the two-times table. When she got to twice twelve is twenty-four she didn't stop. She went right on with twice thirteen is twenty-six, twice fourteen is twenty-eight, twice fifteen is thirty, twice sixteen is . . ."

"Stop!" Miss Honey said. She had been listening slightly spellbound to this smooth recital, and now she said, "How far can you go?"

"How far?" Matilda said. "Well, I don't really

know, Miss Honey. For quite a long way, I think."

Miss Honey took a few moments to let this curious statement sink in. "You mean", she said, "that you could tell me what two times twenty-eight is?"

"Yes, Miss Honey."

"What is it?"

"Fifty-six, Miss Honey."

"What about something much harder, like two times four hundred and eighty-seven? Could you tell me that?"

"I think so, yes," Matilda said.

"Are you sure?"

"Why yes, Miss Honey, I'm fairly sure."

295

"What is it then, two times four hundred and eighty-seven?"

"Nine hundred and seventy-four," Matilda said immediately. She spoke quietly and politely and without any sign of showing off.

Miss Honey gazed at Matilda with absolute amazement, but when next she spoke she kept her voice level. "That is really splendid," she said. "But of course multiplying by two is a lot easier than some of the bigger numbers. What about the other multiplication tables? Do you know any of those?"

"I think so, Miss Honey. I think I do."

"Which ones, Matilda? How far have you got?"

"I . . . I don't quite know," Matilda said. "I don't know what you mean."

"What I mean is do you for instance know the three-times table?"

"Yes, Miss Honey."

"And the four-times?"

"Yes, Miss Honey."

"Well, how many *do* you know, Matilda? Do you know all the way up to the twelve-times table?"

"Yes, Miss Honey."

"What are twelve sevens?"

"Eighty-four," Matilda said.

Miss Honey paused and leaned back in her chair behind the plain table that stood in the middle of the floor in front of the class. She was considerably shaken by this exchange but took care not to show it. She had never come across a five-year-old before, or indeed a ten-year-old, who could multiply with such facility.

"I hope the rest of you are listening to this," she said to the class. "Matilda is a very lucky girl. She has wonderful parents who have already taught her to multiply lots of numbers. Was it your mother, Matilda, who taught you?"

"No, Miss Honey, it wasn't."

"You must have a great father then. He must be a brilliant teacher."

"No, Miss Honey," Matilda said quietly. "My father did not teach me."

"You mean you taught yourself?"

"I don't quite know," Matilda said truthfully. "It's just that I don't find it very difficult to multiply one number by another."

Miss Honey took a deep breath and let it out slowly. She looked again at the small girl with bright eyes standing beside her desk so sensible and solemn. "You say you don't find it difficult to multiply one number by another," Miss Honey said. "Could you try to explain that a little bit."

297

"Oh dear," Matilda said. "I'm not really sure."

Miss Honey waited. The class was silent, all listening.

"For instance," Miss Honey said, "if I asked you to multiply fourteen by nineteen . . . No, that's too difficult . . . "

"It's two hundred and sixty-six," Matilda said softly.

Miss Honey stared at her. Then she picked up a pencil and quickly worked out the sum on a piece of paper. "What did you say it was?" she said, looking up.

"Two hundred and sixty-six," Matilda said.

Miss Honey put down her pencil and removed her spectacles and began to polish the lenses with a piece of tissue. The class remained quiet, watching her and waiting for what was coming next. Matilda was still standing up beside her desk.

"Now tell me, Matilda," Miss Honey said, still polishing, "try to tell me exactly what goes on inside your head when you get a multiplication like that to do. You obviously have to work it out in some way, but you seem able to arrive at the answer almost instantly. Take the one you've just done, fourteen multiplied by nineteen."

"I . . . I . . . I simply put the fourteen down in my head and multiply it by nineteen," Matilda said. "I'm afraid I don't know how else to explain it. I've always said to myself that if a little pocket calculator can do it why shouldn't I?"

"Why not indeed," Miss Honey said. "The human brain is an amazing thing."

"I think it's a lot better than a lump of metal," Matilda said. "That's all a calculator is."

"How right you are," Miss Honey said. "Pocket calculators are not allowed in this school anyway." Miss Honey was feeling quite quivery. There was no doubt in her mind that she had met a truly extraordinary mathematical brain, and words like child-genius and prodigy went flitting through her head. She knew that these sort of wonders do pop up in the world from time to time, but only once or twice in a hundred years. After all, Mozart was only five when he started composing for the piano and look what happened to him.

"It's not fair," Lavender said. "How can she do it and we can't?"

"Don't worry, Lavender, you'll soon catch up," Miss Honey said, lying through her teeth.

At this point Miss Honey could not resist the temptation of exploring still further the mind of this astonishing child. She knew that she ought to be paying some attention to the rest of the class but she was altogether too excited to let the matter rest.

"Well," she said, pretending to address the whole class, "let us leave sums for the moment and see if any of you have begun to learn to spell. Hands up anyone who can spell cat."

Three hands went up. They belonged to Lavender, a small boy called Nigel and to Matilda.

"Spell cat, Nigel."

Nigel spelled it.

Miss Honey now decided to ask a question that normally she would not have dreamed of asking the class on its first day. "I wonder", she said, "whether any of you three who know how to spell cat have learned how to read a whole group of words when they are strung together in a sentence?"

"I have," Nigel said.

"So have I," Lavender said.

Miss Honey went to the blackboard and wrote with her white chalk the sentence, *I have already begun to learn how to read long sentences*. She had purposely made it difficult and she knew that there were precious few five-year-olds around who would be able to manage it.

"Can you tell me what that says, Nigel?" she asked.

"That's too hard," Nigel said.

"Lavender?"

"The first word is I," Lavender said.

"Can any of you read the whole sentence?" Miss Honey asked, waiting for the "yes" that she felt certain was going to come from Matilda.

"Yes," Matilda said.

"Go ahead," Miss Honey said.

Matilda read the sentence without any hesitation at all.

"That really is very good indeed," Miss Honey said, making the understatement of her life. "How much *can* you read, Matilda?"

"I think I can read most things, Miss Honey," Matilda said, "although I'm afraid I can't always understand the meanings."

Miss Honey got to her feet and walked smartly out of the room, but was back in thirty seconds carrying a thick book. She opened it at random and placed it on Matilda's desk. "This is a book of humorous poetry," she said. "See if you can read that one aloud."

Smoothly, without a pause and at a nice speed, Matilda began to read:

> "An epicure dining at Crewe
> Found a rather large mouse in his stew.
> Cried the waiter, "Don't shout
> And wave it about
> Or the rest will be wanting one too."

Several children saw the funny side of the rhyme

and laughed. Miss Honey said, "Do you know what an epicure is, Matilda?"

"It is someone who is dainty with his eating," Matilda said.

"That is correct," Miss Honey said. "And do you happen to know what that particular type of poetry is called?"

"It's called a limerick," Matilda said. "That's a lovely one. It's so funny."

"It's a famous one," Miss Honey said, picking up the book and returning to her table in front of the class. "A witty limerick is very hard to write," she added. "They look easy but they most certainly are not."

"I know," Matilda said. "I've tried quite a few times but mine are never any good."

"You have, have you?" Miss Honey said, more startled than ever. "Well Matilda, I would very much like to hear one of these limericks you say you have written. Could you try to remember one for us?"

"Well," Matilda said, hesitating. "I've actually been trying to make up one about you, Miss Honey, while we've been sitting here."

"About *me!*" Miss Honey cried. "Well, we've certainly got to hear that one, haven't we?"

"I don't think I want to say it, Miss Honey."

"Please tell it," Miss Honey said. "I promise I won't mind."

"I think you will, Miss Honey, because I have to use your first name to make things rhyme and that's why I don't want to say it."

"How do you know my first name?" Miss Honey asked.

"I heard another teacher calling you by it just before we came in," Matilda said. "She called you Jenny."

"I insist upon hearing this limerick," Miss Honey said, smiling one of her rare smiles. "Stand up and recite it."

Reluctantly Matilda stood up and very slowly, very nervously, she recited her limerick:

"The thing we all ask about Jenny
Is, 'Surely there cannot be many
Young girls in the place
With so lovely a face?'
The answer to that is, '*Not any!*'"

The whole of Miss Honey's pale and pleasant face blushed a brilliant scarlet. Then once again she smiled. It was a much broader one this time, a smile of pure pleasure.

"Why, thank you, Matilda," she said, still smiling. "Although it is not true, it is really a very good limerick. Oh dear, oh dear, I must try to remember that one."

From the third row of desks, Lavender said, "It's good. I like it."

"It's true as well," a small boy called Rupert said.

"Of course it's true," Nigel said.

Already the whole class had begun to warm towards Miss Honey, although as yet she had hardly taken any notice of any of them except Matilda.

"Who taught you to read, Matilda?" Miss Honey asked.

"I just sort of taught myself, Miss Honey."

"And have you read any books all by yourself, any children's books, I mean?"

"I've read all the ones that are in the public library in the High Street, Miss Honey."

"And did you like them?"

"I liked some of them very much indeed," Matilda said, "but I thought others were fairly dull."

"Tell me one that you liked."

"I liked *The Lion, the Witch and the Wardrobe*," Matilda said. "I think Mr C. S. Lewis is a very good writer. But he has one failing. There are no funny bits in his books."

"You are right there," Miss Honey said.

"There aren't many funny bits in Mr Tolkien either," Matilda said.

"Do you think that all children's books ought to have funny bits in them?" Miss Honey asked.

"I do," Matilda said. "Children are not so serious as grown-ups and they love to laugh."

Miss Honey was astounded by the wisdom of this tiny girl. She said, "And what are you going to do now that you've read all the children's books?"

"I am reading other books," Matilda said. "I borrow them from the library. Mrs Phelps is very kind to me. She helps me to choose them."

Miss Honey was leaning far forward over her work-table and gazing in wonder at the child. She had completely forgotten now about the rest of the class. "What other books?" she murmured.

"I am very fond of Charles Dickens," Matilda said. "He makes me laugh a lot. Especially Mr Pickwick."

At that moment the bell in the corridor sounded for the end of class.

The Trunchbull

In the interval, Miss Honey left the classroom and headed straight for the Headmistress's study. She felt wildly excited. She had just met a small girl who possessed, or so it seemed to her, quite extraordinary qualities of brilliance. There had not been time yet to find out exactly how brilliant the child was, but Miss Honey had learned enough to realise that something had to be done about it as soon as possible. It would be ridiculous to leave a child like that stuck in the bottom form.

Normally Miss Honey was terrified of the Headmistress and kept well away from her, but at this moment she felt ready to take on anybody. She knocked on the door of the dreaded private study. "Enter!" boomed the deep and dangerous voice of Miss Trunchbull. Miss Honey went in.

Now most head teachers are chosen because they possess a number of fine qualities. They understand children and they have the children's best interests at heart. They are sympathetic. They are fair and they are deeply interested in education. Miss Trunchbull possessed none of these qualities and how she ever got her present job was a mystery.

She was above all a most formidable female. She had once been a famous athlete, and even now the muscles were still clearly in evidence. You could see them in the bull-neck, in the big shoulders, in the thick arms, in the sinewy wrists and in the powerful legs. Looking at her, you got the feeling that this was someone who could bend iron bars and tear telephone directories in half. Her face, I'm afraid, was neither a thing of beauty nor a joy for ever. She had an obstinate chin, a cruel mouth and small arrogant eyes. And as for her clothes . . . they were, to say the least, extremely odd. She always had on a brown cotton smock which was pinched in around the waist with a wide leather belt. The belt was fastened in front with an enormous silver buckle. The massive thighs which emerged from out of the smock were encased in a pair of extraordinary breeches, bottle-green in colour and made of coarse twill. These breeches reached to just below the knees and from there on down she sported green stockings with turn-up tops, which displayed her calf muscles to perfection. On her feet she wore flat-heeled brown brogues with leather flaps. She looked, in short, more like a rather eccentric and bloodthirsty follower of the stag-hounds than the headmistress of a nice school for children.

When Miss Honey entered the study, Miss Trunchbull was standing beside her huge desk with a look of scowling impatience on her face. "Yes, Miss Honey," she said. "What is it you want? You're looking very flushed and flustered this morning. What's the matter with you? Have those little stinkers been flicking spitballs at you?"

"No, Headmistress. Nothing like that."

"Well, what is it then? Get on with it. I'm a busy

307

woman." As she spoke, she reached out and poured herself a glass of water from a jug that was always on her desk.

"There is a little girl in my class called Matilda Wormwood . . ." Miss Honey began.

"That's the daughter of the man who owns Wormwood Motors in the village," Miss Trunch-bull barked. She hardly ever spoke in a normal voice. She either barked or shouted. "An excellent person, Wormwood," she went on. "I was in there only yesterday. He sold me a car. Almost new. Only done ten thousand miles. Previous owner was an old lady who took it out once a year at the most. A terrific bargain. Yes, I liked Wormwood. A real pillar of our society. He told me the daughter was a bad lot though. He said to watch her. He said if anything bad ever happened in the school, it was certain to be his daughter who did it. I haven't met the little brat yet, but she'll know about it when I do. Her father said she's a real wart."

"Oh no, Headmistress, that can't be right!" Miss Honey cried.

"Oh yes, Miss Honey, it darn well is right! In fact, now I come to think of it, I'll bet it was she who put that stink-bomb under my desk here first thing this morning. The place stank like a sewer! Of course it was her! I shall have her for that, you see if I don't! What's she look like? Nasty little worm, I'll be bound. I have discovered, Miss Honey, during my long career as a teacher that a bad girl is a far more dangerous creature than a bad boy. What's more, they're much harder to squash.

Squashing a bad girl is like trying to squash a bluebottle. You bang down on it and the darn thing isn't there. Nasty dirty things, little girls are. Glad I never was one."

"Oh, but you must have been a little girl once, Headmistress. Surely you were."

"Not for long anyway," Miss Trunchbull barked, grinning. "I became a woman very quickly."

She's completely off her rocker, Miss Honey told herself. She's barmy as a bedbug. Miss Honey stood resolutely before the Headmistress. For once she was not going to be browbeaten. "I must tell you, Headmistress," she said, "that you are completely mistaken about Matilda putting a stink-bomb under your desk."

"I am never mistaken, Miss Honey!"

"But Headmistress, the child only arrived in school this morning and came straight to the classroom . . ."

"Don't argue with me, for heaven's sake, woman! This little brute Matilda or whatever her name is has stink-bombed my study! There's no doubt about it! Thank you for suggesting it."

"But I didn't suggest it, Headmistress."

"Of course you did! Now what is it you want, Miss Honey? Why are you wasting my time?"

"I came to you to talk about Matilda, Headmistress. I have extraordinary things to report about the child. May I please tell you what happened in class just now?"

"I suppose she set fire to your skirt and scorched your knickers!" Miss Trunchbull snorted.

"No, no!" Miss Honey cried out. "Matilda is a genius."

At the mention of this word, Miss Trunchbull's face turned purple and her whole body seemed to swell up like a bullfrog's. "A *genius*!" she shouted. "What piffle is this you are talking, madam? You must be out of your mind! I have her father's word for it that the child is a gangster!"

"Her father is wrong, Headmistress."

"Don't be a twerp, Miss Honey! You have met the little beast for only half an hour and her father has known her all her life!"

But Miss Honey was determined to have her say and she now began to describe some of the amazing things Matilda had done with arithmetic.

"So she's learnt a few tables by heart, has she?" Miss Trunchbull barked. "My dear woman, that doesn't make her a genius! It makes her a parrot!"

"But Headmistress she can *read*."

"So can I," Miss Trunchbull snapped.

"It is my opinion", Miss Honey said, "that Matilda should be taken out of my form and placed immediately in the top form with the eleven-year-olds."

"Ha!" snorted Miss Trunchbull. "So you want to get rid of her, do you? So you can't handle her? So now you want to unload her on to the wretched Miss Plimsoll in the top form where she will cause even more chaos?"

"No, no!" cried Miss Honey. "That is not my reason at all!"

"Oh, yes it is!" shouted Miss Trunchbull. "I can see right through your little plot, madam! And my answer is no! Matilda stays where she is and it is up to you to see that she behaves herself."

"But Headmistress, please . . ."

"Not another word!" shouted Miss Trunchbull. "And in any case, I have a rule in this school that all children remain in their own age groups regardless of ability. Great Scott, I'm not having a little five-year-old brigand sitting with the senior girls and boys in the top form. Whoever heard of such a thing!"

Miss Honey stood there helpless before this great red-necked giant. There was a lot more she would like to have said but she knew it was useless. She said softly, "Very well, then. It's up to you, Headmistress."

"You're darn right it's up to me!" Miss Trunchbull bellowed. "And don't forget, madam, that we are dealing here with a little viper who put a stink-bomb under my desk . . . "

"She did *not* do that, Headmistress!"

"Of course she did it," Miss Trunchbull boomed. "And I'll tell you what. I wish to heavens I was still allowed to use the birch and belt as I did in the good old days! I'd have roasted Matilda's bottom for her so she couldn't sit down for a month!"

Miss Honey turned and walked out of the study feeling depressed but by no means defeated. I am going to do something about this child, she told herself. I don't know what it will be, but I shall find a way to help her in the end.

The Parents

When Miss Honey emerged from the Head-mistress's study, most of the children were outside in the playground. Her first move was to go round to the various teachers who taught the senior class and borrow from them a number of text-books, books on algebra, geometry, French, English Literature and the like. Then she sought out Matilda and called her into the classroom.

"There is no point", she said, "in you sitting in class doing nothing while I am teaching the rest of the form the two-times table and how to spell cat and rat and mouse. So during each lesson I shall give you one of these text-books to study. At the end of the lesson you can come up to me with your questions if you have any and I shall try to help you. How does that sound?"

"Thank you, Miss Honey," Matilda said. "That sounds fine."

"I am sure," Miss Honey said, "that we'll be able to get you moved into a much higher form later on, but for the moment the Headmistress wishes you to stay where you are."

"Very well, Miss Honey," Matilda said. "Thank you so much for getting those books for me."

What a nice child she is, Miss Honey thought. I don't care what her father said about her, she seems very quiet and gentle to me. And not a bit stuck up in spite of her brilliance. In fact she hardly seems aware of it.

So when the class reassembled, Matilda went to her desk and began to study a text-book on geometry which Miss Honey had given her. The teacher kept half an eye on her all the time and noticed that the child very soon became deeply absorbed in the book. She never glanced up once during the entire lesson.

Miss Honey, meanwhile, was making another decision. She was deciding that she would go herself and have a secret talk with Matilda's mother and father as soon as possible. She simply refused to let the matter rest where it was. The whole thing was ridiculous. She couldn't believe that the parents were totally unaware of their daughter's remarkable talents. After all, Mr Wormwood was a successful motor-car dealer so she presumed that he was a fairly intelligent man himself. In any event, parents never *underestimated* the abilities of their own children. Quite the reverse. Sometimes it was well nigh impossible for a teacher to convince the proud father or mother that their beloved offspring was a complete nitwit. Miss Honey felt confident that she would have no difficulty in convincing Mr and Mrs Wormwood that Matilda was something very special indeed. The trouble was going to be to stop them from getting over-enthusiastic.

And now Miss Honey's hopes began to expand even further. She started wondering whether permission might not be sought from the parents for her to give private tuition to Matilda after school. The prospect of coaching a child as bright as this appealed enormously to her professional instinct as a teacher. And suddenly she decided that she would go and call on Mr and Mrs Wormwood that very evening. She would go fairly late, between nine and ten o'clock, when Matilda was sure to be in bed.

And that is precisely what she did. Having got the address from the school records, Miss Honey set out to walk from her own home to the Wormwood's house shortly after nine. She found the house in a pleasant street where each smallish building was separated from its neighbours by a bit of garden. It was a modern brick house that could not have been cheap to buy and the name on the gate said COSY NOOK. Nosey cook might have been better, Miss Honey thought. She was given to playing with words in that way. She walked up the path and rang the bell, and while she stood waiting she could hear the television blaring inside.

The door was opened by a small ratty-looking man with a thin ratty moustache who was wearing a sports-coat that had an orange and red stripe in the material. "Yes?" he said, peering out at Miss Honey. "If you're selling raffle tickets I don't want any."

"I'm not," Miss Honey said. "And please forgive me for butting in on you like this. I am Matilda's teacher at school and it is important I have a word with you and your wife."

"Got into trouble already, has she?" Mr Wormwood said, blocking the doorway. "Well, she's your
responsibility from now on. You'll have to deal
with her."

"She is in no trouble at all," Miss Honey said. "I have come with good news about her. Quite startling news, Mr Wormwood. Do you think I might come in for a few minutes and talk to you about Matilda?"

"We are right in the middle of watching one of our favourite programmes," Mr Wormwood said. "This is most inconvenient. Why don't you come back some other time."

Miss Honey began to lose patience. "Mr Wormwood," she said, "if you think some rotten TV programme is more important than your daughter's future, then you ought not to be a parent! Why don't you switch the darn thing off and listen to me!"

That shook Mr Wormwood. He was not used to being spoken to in this way. He peered carefully at the slim frail woman who stood so resolutely out on the porch. "Oh very well then," he snapped. "Come on in and let's get it over with." Miss Honey stepped briskly inside.

"Mrs Wormwood isn't going to thank you for this," the man said as he led her into the sitting-room where a large platinum-blonde woman was gazing rapturously at the TV screen.

"Who is it?" the woman said, not looking round.

"Some school teacher," Mr Wormwood said. "She says she's got to talk to us about Matilda." He crossed to the TV set and turned down the sound but left the picture on the screen.

"Don't do that, Harry!" Mrs Wormwood cried out. "Willard is just about to propose to Angelica!"

"You can still watch it while we're talking," Mr Wormwood said. "This is Matilda's teacher. She says she's got some sort of news to give us."

"My name is Jennifer Honey," Miss Honey said. "How do you do, Mrs Wormwood."

Mrs Wormwood glared at her and said, "What's the trouble then?"

Nobody invited Miss Honey to sit down so she chose a chair and sat down anyway. "This", she said, "was your daughter's first day at school."

"We know that," Mrs Wormwood said, ratty about missing her programme. "Is that all you came to tell us?"

Miss Honey stared hard into the other woman's wet grey eyes, and she allowed the silence to hang in the air until Mrs Wormwood became uncomfortable. "Do you wish me to explain why I came?" she said.

"Get on with it then," Mrs Wormwood said.

"I'm sure you know", Miss Honey said, "that children in the bottom class at school are not expected to be able to read or spell or juggle with numbers when they first arrive. Five-year-olds cannot do that. But Matilda can do it all. And if I am to believe her . . ."

"I wouldn't," Mrs Wormwood said. She was still ratty at losing the sound on the TV.

"Was she lying, then," Miss Honey said, "when she told me that nobody taught her to multiply or to read? Did either of you teach her?"

"Teach her what?" Mr Wormwood said.

"To read. To read books," Miss Honey said. "Perhaps you *did* teach her. Perhaps she *was* lying. Perhaps you have shelves full of books all over the house. I wouldn't know. Perhaps you are both great readers."

"Of course we read," Mr Wormwood said. "Don't be so daft. I read the *Autocar* and the *Motor* from cover to cover every week."

"This child has already read an astonishing number of books," Miss Honey said. "I was simply trying to find out if she came from a family that loved good literature."

"We don't hold with book-reading," Mr Wormwood said. "You can't make a living from sitting

on your fanny and reading story-books. We don't
keep them in the house."

"I see," Miss Honey said. "Well, all I came to
tell you was that Matilda has a brilliant mind. But
I expect you knew that already."

"Of course I knew she could read," the mother
said. "She spends her life up in her room buried in
some silly book."

"But does it not intrigue you", Miss Honey said,
"that a little five-year-old child is reading long
adult novels by Dickens and Hemingway? Doesn't
that make you jump up and down with excitement?"

"Not particularly," the mother said. "I'm not in
favour of blue-stocking girls. A girl should think
about making herself look attractive so she can get
a good husband later on. Looks is more important
than books, Miss Hunky . . ."

"The name is Honey," Miss Honey said.

"Now look at *me*," Mrs Wormwood said. "Then look at *you*. You chose books. I chose looks."

Miss Honey looked at the plain plump person with the smug suet-pudding face who was sitting across the room. "What did you say?" she asked.

"I said you chose books and I chose looks," Mrs Wormwood said. "And who's finished up the better off? Me, of course. I'm sitting pretty in a nice house with a successful businessman and you're left slaving away teaching a lot of nasty little children the ABC."

"Quite right, sugar-plum," Mr Wormwood said, casting a look of such simpering sloppiness at his wife it would have made a cat sick.

Miss Honey decided that if she was going to get anywhere with these people she must not lose her temper. "I haven't told you all of it yet," she said. "Matilda, so far as I can gather at this early stage, is also a kind of mathematical genius. She can multiply complicated figures in her head like lightning."

"What's the point of that when you can buy a calculator?" Mr Wormwood said.

"A girl doesn't get a man by being brainy," Mrs Wormwood said. "Look at that film-star for instance," she added, pointing at the silent TV screen where a bosomy female was being embraced by a craggy actor in the moonlight. "You don't think she got him to do that by multiplying figures at him, do you? Not likely. And now he's going to marry her, you see if he doesn't, and she's going to live in a mansion with a butler and lots of maids."

Miss Honey could hardly believe what she was hearing. She had heard that parents like this existed all over the place and that their children turned out to be delinquents and drop-outs, but it was still a shock to meet a pair of them in the flesh.

"Matilda's trouble", she said, trying once again, "is that she is so far ahead of everyone else around her that it might be worth thinking about some extra kind of private tuition. I seriously believe that she could be brought up to university standard in two or three years with the proper coaching."

"University?" Mr Wormwood shouted, bouncing up in his chair. "Who wants to go to university for heaven's sake! All they learn there is bad habits!"

"That is not true," Miss Honey said. "If you had a heart attack this minute and had to call a doctor, that doctor would be a university graduate. If you got sued for selling someone a rotten second-hand car, you'd have to get a lawyer and he'd be a university graduate, too. Do not despise clever people, Mr Wormwood. But I can see we're not going to agree. I'm sorry I burst in on you like this." Miss Honey rose from her chair and walked out of the room.

Mr Wormwood followed her to the front-door and said, "Good of you to come, Miss Hawkes, or is it Miss Harris?"

"It's neither," Miss Honey said, "but let it go." And away she went.

Throwing the Hammer

The nice thing about Matilda was that if you had met her casually and talked to her you would have thought she was a perfectly normal five-and-a-half-year-old child. She displayed almost no outward signs of her brilliance and she never showed off. "This is a very sensible and quiet little girl," you would have said to yourself. And unless for some reason you had started a discussion with her about literature or mathematics, you would never have known the extent of her brain-power.

It was therefore easy for Matilda to make friends with other children. All those in her class liked her. They knew of course that she was "clever" because they had heard her being questioned by Miss Honey on the first day of term. And they knew also that she was allowed to sit quietly with a book during lessons and not pay attention to the teacher. But children of their age do not search deeply for reasons. They are far too wrapped up in their own small struggles to worry overmuch about what others are doing and why.

Among Matilda's new-found friends was the girl called Lavender. Right from the first day of term the two of them started wandering round together during the morning-break and in the lunch-hour. Lavender was exceptionally small for her age, a skinny little nymph with deep-brown eyes and with dark hair that was cut in a fringe across her forehead. Matilda liked her because she was gutsy and adventurous. She liked Matilda for exactly the same reasons.

Before the first week of term was up, awesome tales about the Headmistress, Miss Trunchbull, began to filter through to the newcomers. Matilda and Lavender, standing in a corner of the playground during morning-break on the third day, were approached by a rugged ten-year-old with a boil on her nose, called Hortensia. "New scum, I suppose," Hortensia said to them, looking down from her great height. She was eating from an extra large bag of potato crisps and digging the stuff out in handfuls. "Welcome to borstal," she added, spraying bits of crisp out of her mouth like snowflakes.

The two tiny ones, confronted by this giant, kept a watchful silence.

"Have you met the Trunchbull yet?" Hortensia asked.

"We've seen her at prayers," Lavender said, "but we haven't met her."

"You've got a treat coming to you," Hortensia said. "She hates very small children. She therefore loathes the bottom class and everyone in it. She thinks five-year-olds are grubs that haven't yet hatched out." In went another fistful of crisps and when she spoke again, out sprayed the crumbs. "If you survive your first year you may just manage to live through the rest of your time here. But many

don't survive. They get carried out on stretchers screaming. I've seen it often." Hortensia paused to observe the effect these remarks were having on the two titchy ones. Not very much. They seemed pretty cool. So the large one decided to regale them with further information.

"I suppose you know the Trunchbull has a lock-up cupboard in her private quarters called The Chokey? Have you heard about The Chokey?"

Matilda and Lavender shook their heads and continued to gaze up at the giant. Being very small, they were inclined to mistrust any creature that was larger than they were, especially senior girls.

"The Chokey", Hortensia went on, "is a very tall but very narrow cupboard. The floor is only ten inches square so you can't sit down or squat in it. You have to stand. And three of the walls are made of cement with bits of broken glass sticking out all over, so you can't lean against them. You have to stand more or less at attention all the time when you get locked up in there. It's terrible."

"Can't you lean against the door?" Matilda asked.

"Don't be daft," Hortensia said. "The door's got thousands of sharp spikey nails sticking out of it. They've been hammered through from the outside, probably by the Trunchbull herself."

"Have you ever been in there?" Lavender asked.

"My first term I was in there six times," Hortensia said. "Twice for a whole day and the other times for two hours each. But two hours is quite bad enough. It's pitch dark and you have to stand up dead straight and if you wobble at all you get spiked either by the glass on the walls or the nails on the door.

"Why were you put in?" Matilda asked. "What had you done?"

"The first time", Hortensia said, "I poured half a tin of Golden Syrup on to the seat of the chair the Trunchbull was going to sit on at prayers. It was wonderful. When she lowered herself into the chair, there was a loud squelching noise similar to that made by a hippopotamus when lowering its foot into the mud on the banks of the Limpopo River. But you're too small and stupid to have read the *Just So Stories*, aren't you?"

"I've read them," Matilda said.

"You're a liar," Hortensia said amiably. "You can't even read yet. But no matter. So when the Trunchbull sat down on the Golden Syrup, the squelch was beautiful. And when she jumped up again, the chair sort of stuck to the seat of those awful green breeches she wears and came up with her for a few seconds until the thick syrup slowly came unstuck. Then she clasped her hands to the seat of her breeches and both hands got covered in the muck. You should have heard her bellow."

"But how did she know it was you?" Lavender asked.

"A little squirt called Ollie Bogwhistle sneaked on me," Hortensia said. "I knocked his front teeth out."

"And the Trunchbull put you in The Chokey for a whole day?" Matilda asked, gulping.

"All day long," Hortensia said. "I was off my rocker when she let me out. I was babbling like an idiot."

"What were the other things you did to get put in The Chokey?" Lavender asked.

"Oh I can't remember them all now," Hortensia said. She spoke with the air of an old warrior who has been in so many battles that bravery has become commonplace. "It's all so long ago," she added, stuffing more crisps into her mouth. "Ah yes, I can remember one. Here's what happened. I chose a time when I knew the Trunchbull was out of the way teaching the sixth-formers, and I put up my hand and asked to go to the bogs. But instead of going *there*, I sneaked into the Trunchbull's

330

room. And after a speedy search I found the drawer
where she kept all her gym knickers."

"Go on," Matilda said, spellbound. "What happened next?"

"I had sent away by post, you see, for this very
powerful itching-powder," Hortensia said. "It cost
50p a packet and was called The Skin-Scorcher.
The label said it was made from the powdered teeth
of deadly snakes, and it was guaranteed to raise
welts the size of walnuts on your skin. So I
sprinkled this stuff inside every pair of knickers
in the drawer and then folded them all up again
carefully." Hortensia paused to cram more crisps
into her mouth.

"Did it work?" Lavender asked.

331

"Well," Hortensia said, "a few days later, during prayers, the Trunchbull suddenly started scratching herself like mad down below. A-ha, I said to myself. Here we go. She's changed for gym already. It was pretty wonderful to be sitting there watching it all and knowing that I was the only person in the whole school who realised exactly what was going on inside the Trunchbull's pants. And I felt safe, too. I knew I couldn't be caught. Then the scratching got worse. She couldn't stop. She must have thought she had a wasp's nest down there. And then, right in the middle of the Lord's Prayer, she leapt up and grabbed her bottom and rushed out of the room."

Both Matilda and Lavender were enthralled. It was quite clear to them that they were at this moment standing in the presence of a master. Here was somebody who had brought the art of skulduggery to the highest point of perfection, somebody, moreover, who was willing to risk life and limb in pursuit of her calling. They gazed in wonder at this goddess, and suddenly even the boil on her nose was no longer a blemish but a badge of courage.

"But how *did* she catch you that time?" Lavender asked, breathless with wonder.

"She didn't," Hortensia said. "But I got a day in The Chokey just the same."

"Why?" they both asked.

"The Trunchbull", Hortensia said, "has a nasty habit of guessing. When she doesn't know who the culprit is, she makes a guess at it, and the trouble is she's often right. I was the prime suspect this time because of the Golden Syrup job, and although I knew she didn't have any proof, nothing I said made any difference. I kept shouting, 'How could I have done it, Miss Trunchbull? I didn't even know you kept any spare knickers at school! I don't even know what itching-powder is! I've never heard of it!' But the lying didn't help me in spite of the great performance I put on. The Trunchbull simply grabbed me by one ear and rushed me to The Chokey at the double and threw me inside and locked the door. That was my second all-day stretch. It was absolute torture. I was spiked and cut all over when I came out."

"It's like a war," Matilda said, overawed.

"You're darn right it's like a war," Hortensia cried. "And the casualties are terrific. *We* are the crusaders, the gallant army fighting for our lives with hardly any weapons at all and the Trunchbull is the Prince of Darkness, the Foul Serpent, the Fiery Dragon with all the weapons at her command. It's a tough life. We all try to support each other."

"You can rely on us," Lavender said, making her height of three feet two inches stretch as tall as possible.

"No, I can't," Hortensia said. "You're only shrimps. But you never know. We may find a use for you one day in some undercover job."

"Tell us just a little bit more about what she does," Matilda said. "Please do."

"I mustn't frighten you before you've been here a week," Hortensia said.

"You won't," Lavender said. "We may be small but we're quite tough."

"Listen to this then," Hortensia said. "Only yesterday the Trunchbull caught a boy called Julius Rottwinkle eating Liquorice Allsorts during the scripture lesson and she simply picked him up by one arm and flung him clear out of the open classroom window. Our classroom is one floor up and we saw Julius Rottwinkle go sailing out over the garden like a Frisbee and landing with a thump in the middle of the lettuces. Then the Trunchbull turned to us and said, "From now on, anybody caught eating in class goes straight out the window.""

"Did this Julius Rottwinkle break any bones?" Lavender asked.

"Only a few," Hortensia said. "You've got to remember that the Trunchbull once threw the hammer for Britain in the Olympics so she's very proud of her right arm."

"What's throwing the hammer?" Lavender asked.

"The hammer", Hortensia said, "is actually a ruddy great cannon-ball on the end of a long bit of wire, and the thrower whisks it round and round his or her head faster and faster and then lets it go. You have to be terrifically strong. The Trunchbull will throw anything around just to keep her arm in, especially children."

"Good heavens," Lavender said.

"I once heard her say", Hortensia went on, "that a large boy is about the same weight as an Olympic

hammer and therefore he's very useful for practising with."

At that point something strange happened. The playground, which up to then had been filled with shrieks and the shouting of children at play, all at once became silent as the grave. "Watch out," Hortensia whispered. Matilda and Lavender glanced round and saw the gigantic figure of Miss Trunchbull advancing through the crowd of boys and girls with menacing strides. The children drew back hastily to let her through and her progress across the asphalt was like that of Moses going through the Red Sea when the waters parted. A formidable figure she was too, in her belted smock and green breeches. Below the knees her calf muscles stood out like grapefruits inside her stockings. "Amanda Thripp!" she was shouting. "You, Amanda Thripp, come here!"

"Hold your hats," Hortensia whispered.

"What's going to happen?" Lavender whispered back.

"That idiot Amanda", Hortensia said, "has let her long hair grow even longer during the hols and her mother has plaited it into pigtails. Silly thing to do."

"Why silly?" Matilda asked.

"If there's one thing the Trunchbull can't stand it's pigtails," Hortensia said.

Matilda and Lavender saw the giant in green breeches advancing upon a girl of about ten who had a pair of plaited golden pigtails hanging over her shoulders. Each pigtail had a blue satin bow at

the end of it and it all looked very pretty. The girl
wearing the pigtails, Amanda Thripp, stood quite
still, watching the advancing giant, and the expression on her face was one that you might find
on the face of a person who is trapped in a small

field with an enraged bull which is charging flat-out towards her. The girl was glued to the spot, terror-struck, pop-eyed, quivering, knowing for certain that the Day of Judgment had come for her at last.

Miss Trunchbull had now reached the victim and stood towering over her. "I want those filthy pigtails off before you come back to school tomorrow!" she barked. "Chop 'em off and throw 'em in the dustbin, you understand?"

Amanda, paralysed with fright, managed to stutter, "My m-m-mummy likes them. She p-p-plaits them for me every morning."

"Your mummy's a twit!" the Trunchbull bellowed. She pointed a finger the size of a salami at the child's head and shouted, "You look like a rat with a tail coming out of its head!"

"My m-m-mummy thinks I look lovely, Miss T-T-Trunchbull," Amanda stuttered, shaking like a blancmange.

"I don't give a tinker's toot what your mummy thinks!" the Trunchbull yelled, and with that she lunged forward and grabbed hold of Amanda's pigtails in her right fist and lifted the girl clear off the ground. Then she started swinging her round and round her head, faster and faster and Amanda was screaming blue murder and the Trunchbull was yelling, "I'll give you pigtails, you little rat!"

"Shades of the Olympics," Hortensia murmured. "She's getting up speed now just like she does with the hammer. Ten to one she's going to throw her."

And now the Trunchbull was leaning back against the weight of the whirling girl and

338

pivoting expertly on her toes, spinning round and round, and soon Amanda Thripp was travelling so fast she became a blur, and suddenly, with a mighty grunt, the Trunchbull let go of the pigtails and Amanda went sailing like a rocket right over the wire fence of the playground and high up into the sky.

"Well thrown, sir!" someone shouted from across the playground, and Matilda, who was mesmerised by the whole crazy affair, saw Amanda Thripp descending in a long graceful parabola on to the playing-field beyond. She landed on the grass and bounced three times and finally came to rest. Then, amazingly, she sat up. She looked a trifle dazed and who could blame her, but after a minute or so she was on her feet again and tottering back towards the playground.

The Trunchbull stood in the playground dusting off her hands. "Not bad," she said, "considering I'm not in strict training. Not bad at all." Then she strode away.

"She's mad," Hortensia said.

"But don't the parents complain?" Matilda asked.

"Would yours?" Hortensia asked. "I know mine wouldn't. She treats the mothers and fathers just the same as the children and they're all scared to death of her. I'll be seeing you some time, you two." And with that she sauntered away.

Bruce Bogtrotter
and the Cake

"How can she get *away* with it?" Lavender said to Matilda. "Surely the children go home and tell their mothers and fathers. I know my father would raise a terrific stink if I told him the Headmistress had grabbed me by the hair and slung me over the playground fence."

"No, he wouldn't," Matilda said, "and I'll tell you why. He simply wouldn't believe you."

"Of course he would."

"He wouldn't," Matilda said. "And the reason is obvious. Your story would sound too ridiculous to be believed. And that is the Trunchbull's great secret."

"What is?" Lavender asked.

Matilda said, "Never do anything by halves if you want to get away with it. Be outrageous. Go the whole hog. Make sure everything you do is so completely crazy it's unbelievable. No parent is going to believe this pigtail story, not in a million years. Mine wouldn't. They'd call me a liar."

"In that case", Lavender said, "Amanda's mother isn't going to cut her pigtails off."

"No, she isn't," Matilda said. "Amanda will do it herself. You see if she doesn't."

"Do you think she's mad?" Lavender asked.

"Who?"

"The Trunchbull."

"No, I don't think she's mad," Matilda said. "But she's very dangerous. Being in this school is like being in a cage with a cobra. You have to be very fast on your feet."

They got another example of how dangerous the Headmistress could be on the very next day. During lunch an announcement was made that the whole school should go into the Assembly Hall and be seated as soon as the meal was over.

When all the two hundred and fifty or so boys and girls were settled down in Assembly, the Trunchbull marched on to the platform. None of the other teachers came in with her. She was carrying a riding-crop in her right hand. She stood up there on centre stage in her green breeches with legs apart and riding-crop in hand, glaring at the sea of upturned faces before her.

"What's going to happen?" Lavender whispered.

"I don't know," Matilda whispered back.

The whole school waited for what was coming next.

"Bruce Bogtrotter!" the Trunchbull barked suddenly. "Where is Bruce Bogtrotter?"

A hand shot up among the seated children.

"Come up here!" the Trunchbull shouted. "And look smart about it!"

An eleven-year-old boy who was decidedly large and round stood up and waddled briskly forward. He climbed up on to the platform.

"Stand over there!" the Trunchbull ordered, pointing. The boy stood to one side. He looked

342

nervous. He knew very well he wasn't up there to be presented with a prize. He was watching the Headmistress with an exceedingly wary eye and he kept edging farther and farther away from her with little shuffles of his feet, rather as a rat might edge away from a terrier that is watching it from across the room. His plump flabby face had turned grey with fearful apprehension. His stockings hung about his ankles.

"This *clot*," boomed the Headmistress, pointing the riding-crop at him like a rapier, "this *blackhead*, this *foul carbuncle*, this *poisonous pustule* that you see before you is none other than a disgusting criminal, a denizen of the underworld, a member of the Mafia!"

"Who, me?" Bruce Bogtrotter said, looking genuinely puzzled.

"A thief!" the Trunchbull screamed. "A crook! A pirate! A brigand! A rustler!"

"Steady on," the boy said. "I mean, dash it all, Headmistress."

"Do you deny it, you miserable little gumboil? Do you plead not guilty?"

"I don't know what you're talking about," the boy said, more puzzled than ever.

"I'll tell you what I'm talking about, you suppurating little blister!" the Trunchbull shouted. "Yesterday morning, during break, you sneaked like a serpent into the kitchen and stole a slice of my private chocolate cake from my tea-tray! That tray had just been prepared for me personally by the cook! It was my morning snack! And as for the cake, it was my own private stock! That was not boy's cake! You don't think for one minute I'm going to eat the filth I give to you? That cake was made from real butter and real cream! And he, that

344

robber-bandit, that safe-cracker, that highwayman standing over there with his socks around his ankles stole it and ate it!''

"I never did," the boy exclaimed, turning from grey to white.

"Don't lie to me, Bogtrotter!" barked the Trunchbull. "The cook saw you! What's more, she saw you eating it!"

The Trunchbull paused to wipe a fleck of froth from her lips.

When she spoke again her voice was suddenly softer, quieter, more friendly, and she leaned towards the boy, smiling. "You like my special chocolate cake, don't you, Bogtrotter? It's rich and delicious, isn't it, Bogtrotter?"

"Very good," the boy mumbled. The words were out before he could stop himself.

"You're right," the Trunchbull said. "It *is* very

346

good. Therefore I think you should congratulate the cook. When a gentleman has had a particularly good meal, Bogtrotter, he always sends his compliments to the chef. You didn't know that, did you, Bogtrotter? But those who inhabit the criminal underworld are not noted for their good manners."

The boy remained silent.

"Cook!" the Trunchbull shouted, turning her head towards the door. "Come here, cook! Bogtrotter wishes to tell you how good your chocolate cake is!"

The cook, a tall shrivelled female who looked as though all of her body-juices had been dried out of her long ago in a hot oven, walked on to the platform wearing a dirty white apron. Her entrance had clearly been arranged beforehand by the Headmistress.

"Now then, Bogtrotter," the Trunchbull boomed. "Tell cook what you think of her chocolate cake."

"Very good," the boy mumbled. You could see he was now beginning to wonder what all this was leading up to. The only thing he knew for certain was that the law forbade the Trunchbull to hit him with the riding-crop that she kept smacking against her thigh. That was some comfort, but not much because the Trunchbull was totally unpredictable. One never knew what she was going to do next.

"There you are, cook," the Trunchbull cried. "Bogtrotter likes your cake. He adores your cake. Do you have any more of your cake you could give him?"

347

"I do indeed," the cook said. She seemed to have learnt her lines by heart.

"Then go and get it. And bring a knife to cut it with."

The cook disappeared. Almost at once she was back again staggering under the weight of an enormous round chocolate cake on a china platter. The cake was fully eighteen inches in diameter and it was covered with dark-brown chocolate icing. "Put it on the table," the Trunchbull said.

There was a small table centre stage with a chair behind it. The cook placed the cake carefully on the table. "Sit down, Bogtrotter," the Trunchbull said. "Sit there."

The boy moved cautiously to the table and sat down. He stared at the gigantic cake.

"There you are, Bogtrotter," the Trunchbull said, and once again her voice became soft, persuasive, even gentle. "It's all for you, every bit of it. As you enjoyed that slice you had yesterday so very much, I ordered cook to bake you an extra large one all for yourself."

"Well, thank you," the boy said, totally bemused.

"Thank cook, not me," the Trunchbull said.

"Thank you, cook," the boy said.

The cook stood there like a shrivelled bootlace, tight-lipped, implacable, disapproving. She looked as though her mouth was full of lemon juice.

"Come on then," the Trunchbull said. "Why don't you cut yourself a nice thick slice and try it?"

"What? Now?" the boy said, cautious. He knew

348

there was a catch in this somewhere, but he wasn't
sure where. "Can't I take it home instead?" he
asked.

"That would be impolite," the Trunchbull said,
with a crafty grin. "You must show cookie here how
grateful you are for all the trouble she's taken."

The boy didn't move.

"Go on, get on with it," the Trunchbull said.
"Cut a slice and taste it. We haven't got all day."

The boy picked up the knife and was about to cut into the cake when he stopped. He stared at the cake. Then he looked up at the Trunchbull, then at the tall stringy cook with her lemon-juice mouth. All the children in the hall were watching tensely, waiting for something to happen. They felt certain it must. The Trunchbull was not a person who would give someone a whole chocolate cake to eat just out of kindness. Many were guessing that it had been filled with pepper or castor-oil or some other foul-tasting substance that would make the boy violently sick. It might even be arsenic and he would be dead in ten seconds flat. Or perhaps it was a booby-trapped cake and the whole thing would blow up the moment it was cut, taking Bruce Bogtrotter with it. No one in the school put it past the Trunchbull to do any of these things.

"I don't want to eat it," the boy said.

"Taste it, you little brat," the Trunchbull said. "You're insulting the cook."

Very gingerly the boy began to cut a thin slice of the vast cake. Then he levered the slice out. Then he put down the knife and took the sticky thing in his fingers and started very slowly to eat it.

"It's good, isn't it?" the Trunchbull asked.

"Very good," the boy said, chewing and swallowing. He finished the slice.

"Have another," the Trunchbull said.

"That's enough, thank you," the boy murmured.

"I said have another," the Trunchbull said, and now there was an altogether sharper edge to her voice. "Eat another slice! Do as you are told!"

"I don't want another slice," the boy said.

Suddenly the Trunchbull exploded. "Eat!" she shouted, banging her thigh with the riding-crop. "If I tell you to eat, you will eat! You wanted cake! You stole cake! And now you've got cake! What's more, you're going to eat it! You do not leave this platform and nobody leaves this hall until you have eaten the entire cake that is sitting there in front of you! Do I make myself clear, Bogtrotter? Do you get my meaning?"

The boy looked at the Trunchbull. Then he looked down at the enormous cake.

"Eat! Eat! Eat!" the Trunchbull was yelling.

Very slowly the boy cut himself another slice and began to eat it.

Matilda was fascinated. "Do you think he can do it?" she whispered to Lavender.

"No," Lavender whispered back. "It's impossible. He'd be sick before he was halfway through."

The boy kept going. When he had finished the second slice, he looked at the Trunchbull, hesitating.

"Eat!" she shouted. "Greedy little thieves who like to eat cake must have cake! Eat faster boy! Eat faster! We don't want to be here all day! And don't stop like you're doing now! Next time you stop before it's all finished you'll go straight into The Chokey and I shall lock the door and throw the key down the well!"

The boy cut a third slice and started to eat it. He finished this one quicker than the other two and when that was done he immediately picked up the knife and cut the next slice. In some peculiar way he seemed to be getting into his stride.

Matilda, watching closely, saw no signs of distress in the boy yet. If anything, he seemed to be gathering confidence as he went along. "He's doing well," she whispered to Lavender.

"He'll be sick soon," Lavender whispered back. "It's going to be horrid."

When Bruce Bogtrotter had eaten his way through half of the entire enormous cake, he paused for just a couple of seconds and took several deep breaths.

The Trunchbull stood with hands on hips, glaring at him. "Get on with it!" she shouted. "Eat it up!"

Suddenly the boy let out a gigantic belch which rolled around the Assembly Hall like thunder. Many of the audience began to giggle.

"Silence!" shouted the Trunchbull.

The boy cut himself another thick slice and started eating it fast. There were still no signs of flagging or giving up. He certainly did not look as though he was about to stop and cry out, "I can't, I can't eat any more! I'm going to be sick!" He was still in there running.

And now a subtle change was coming over the two hundred and fifty watching children in the audience. Earlier on, they had sensed impending disaster. They had prepared themselves for an unpleasant scene in which the wretched boy, stuffed to the gills with chocolate cake, would have to surrender and beg for mercy and then they would have watched the triumphant Trunchbull forcing more and still more cake into the mouth of the gasping boy.

Not a bit of it. Bruce Bogtrotter was three-quarters of the way through and still going strong. One sensed that he was almost beginning to enjoy himself. He had a mountain to climb and he was jolly well going to reach the top or die in the attempt. What is more, he had now become very conscious of his audience and of how they were all silently rooting for him. This was nothing less than a battle between him and the mighty Trunchbull.

Suddenly someone shouted, "Come on Brucie! You can make it!"

The Trunchbull wheeled round and yelled, "Silence!" The audience watched intently. They were thoroughly caught up in the contest. They were longing to start cheering but they didn't dare.

"I think he's going to make it," Matilda whispered.

"I think so too," Lavender whispered back. "I wouldn't have believed anyone in the world could eat the whole of a cake that size."

"The Trunchbull doesn't believe it either," Matilda whispered. "Look at her. She's turning redder and redder. She's going to kill him if he wins."

The boy was slowing down now. There was no

doubt about that. But he kept pushing the stuff into his mouth with the dogged perseverance of a long-distance runner who has sighted the finishing-line and knows he must keep going. As the very last mouthful disappeared, a tremendous cheer rose up from the audience and children were leaping on to their chairs and yelling and clapping and shouting, "Well done, Brucie! Good for you, Brucie! You've won a gold medal, Brucie!"

The Trunchbull stood motionless on the platform. Her great horsy face had turned the colour of molten lava and her eyes were glittering with fury. She glared at Bruce Bogtrotter who was sitting on his chair like some huge overstuffed grub, replete, comatose, unable to move or to speak. A fine sweat was beading his forehead but there was a grin of triumph on his face.

Suddenly the Trunchbull lunged forward and grabbed the large empty china platter on which the cake had rested. She raised it high in the air and brought it down with a crash right on the top of the wretched Bruce Bogtrotter's head and pieces flew all over the platform.

The boy was by now so full of cake he was like a sackful of wet cement and you couldn't have hurt him with a sledge-hammer. He simply shook his head a few times and went on grinning.

"Go to blazes!" screamed the Trunchbull and she marched off the platform followed closely by the cook.

Lavender

In the middle of the first week of Matilda's first term, Miss Honey said to the class, "I have some important news for you, so listen carefully. You too, Matilda. Put that book down for a moment and pay attention."

Small eager faces looked up and listened.

"It is the Headmistress's custom", Miss Honey went on, "to take over the class for one period each week. She does this with every class in the school and each class has a fixed day and a fixed time. Ours is always two o'clock on Thursday afternoons, immediately after lunch. So tomorrow at two o'clock Miss Trunchbull will be taking over from me for one lesson. I shall be here as well, of course, but only as a silent witness. Is that understood?"

"Yes, Miss Honey," they chirruped.

"A word of warning to you all," Miss Honey said. "The Headmistress is very strict about everything. Make sure your clothes are clean, your faces are clean and your hands are clean. Speak only when spoken to. When she asks you a question, stand up at once before you answer it. Never argue with her. Never answer back. Never try to be funny. If you do, you will make her angry, and when the Headmistress gets angry you had better watch out."

358

"You can say that again," Lavender murmured.

"I am quite sure", Miss Honey said, "that she will be testing you on what you are meant to have learnt this week, which is your two-times table. So I strongly advise you to swot it up when you get home tonight. Get your mother or father to hear you on it."

"What else will she test us on?" someone asked.

"Spelling," Miss Honey said. "Try to remember everything you have learned these last few days. And one more thing. A jug of water and a glass must always be on the table here when the Headmistress comes in. She never takes a lesson without that. Now who will be responsible for seeing that it's there?"

"I will," Lavender said at once.

"Very well, Lavender," Miss Honey said. "It will be your job to go to the kitchen and get the jug and fill it with water and put it on the table here with a clean empty glass just before the lesson starts."

"What if the jug's not in the kitchen?" Lavender asked.

"There are a dozen Headmistress's jugs and glasses in the kitchen," Miss Honey said. "They are used all over the school."

"I won't forget," Lavender said. "I promise I won't."

Already Lavender's scheming mind was going over the possibilities that this water-jug job had opened up for her. She longed to do something truly heroic. She admired the older girl Hortensia to distraction for the daring deeds she had performed in the school. She also admired Matilda who had sworn her to secrecy about the parrot job she had brought off at home, and also the great hair-oil switch which had bleached her father's hair. It was *her* turn now to become a heroine if only she could come up with a brilliant plot.

On the way home from school that afternoon

360

she began to mull over the various possibilities, and when at last the germ of a brilliant idea hit her, she began to expand on it and lay her plans with the same kind of care the Duke of Wellington had done before the Battle of Waterloo. Admittedly the enemy on this occasion was not Napoleon. But you would never have got anyone at Crunchem Hall to admit that the Headmistress was a less formidable foe than the famous Frenchman. Great skill would have to be exercised, Lavender told herself, and great secrecy observed if she was to come out of this exploit alive.

There was a muddy pond at the bottom of Lavender's garden and this was the home of a colony of newts. The newt, although fairly common in English ponds, is not often seen by ordinary people because it is a shy and murky creature. It is an incredibly ugly gruesome-looking animal, rather like a baby crocodile but with a shorter head. It is quite harmless but doesn't look it. It is about six inches long and very slimy, with a greenish-grey skin on top and an orange-coloured belly underneath. It is, in fact, an amphibian, which can live in or out of water.

That evening Lavender went to the bottom of the garden determined to catch a newt. They are swiftly-moving animals and not easy to get hold of. She lay on the bank for a long time waiting patiently until she spotted a whopper. Then, using her school hat as a net, she swooped and caught it. She had lined her pencil-box with pond-weed ready to receive the creature, but she discovered that it

361

was not easy to get the newt out of the hat and into the pencil-box. It wriggled and squirmed like quicksilver and, apart from that, the box was only just long enough to take it. When she did get it in at last, she had to be careful not to trap its tail in the lid when she slid it closed. A boy next door called Rupert Entwistle had told her that if you chopped off a newt's tail, the tail stayed alive and grew into another newt ten times bigger than the first one. It could be the size of an alligator. Lavender didn't quite believe that, but she was not prepared to risk it happening.

Eventually she managed to slide the lid of the pencil-box right home and the newt was hers. Then, on second thoughts, she opened the lid just the tiniest fraction so that the creature could breathe.

The next day she carried her secret weapon to school in her satchel. She was tingling with excitement. She was longing to tell Matilda about her plan of battle. In fact, she wanted to tell the whole class. But she finally decided to tell nobody. It was better that way because then no one, even when put under the most severe torture, would be able to name her as the culprit.

Lunchtime came. Today it was sausages and baked beans, Lavender's favourite, but she couldn't eat it.

"Are you feeling all right, Lavender?" Miss Honey asked from the head of the table.

"I had such a huge breakfast", Lavender said, "I really couldn't eat a thing."

363

Immediately after lunch, she dashed off to the kitchen and found one of the Trunchbull's famous jugs. It was a large bulging thing made of blue-glazed pottery. Lavender filled it half-full of water and carried it, together with a glass, into the class-room and set it on the teacher's table. The class-room was still empty. Quick as a flash, Lavender got her pencil-box from her satchel and slid open the lid just a tiny bit. The newt was lying quite -still. With great care, she held the box over the neck of the jug and pulled the lid fully open and tipped the newt in. There was a plop as it landed in the water, then it thrashed around wildly for a few seconds before settling down. And now, to make the newt feel more at home, Lavender de-cided to give it all the pond-weed from the pencil-box as well.

The deed was done. All was ready. Lavender put her pencils back into the rather damp pencil-box and returned it to its correct place on her own desk. Then she went out and joined the others in the playground until it was time for the lesson to begin.

The Weekly Test

At two o'clock sharp the class assembled, including Miss Honey who noted that the jug of water and the glass were in the proper place. Then she took up a position standing right at the back. Everyone waited. Suddenly in marched the gigantic figure of the Headmistress in her belted smock and green breeches.

"Good afternoon, children," she barked.

"Good afternoon, Miss Trunchbull," they chirruped.

The Headmistress stood before the class, legs apart, hands on hips, glaring at the small boys and girls who sat nervously at their desks in front of her.

"*Not* a very pretty sight," she said. Her expression was one of utter distaste, as though she were looking at something a dog had done in the middle of the floor. "What a bunch of nauseating little warts you are."

Everyone had the sense to stay silent.

"It makes me vomit", she went on, "to think that I am going to have to put up with a load of garbage like you in my school for the next six years. I can see that I'm going to have to expel as many of you as possible as soon as possible to save myself from going round the bend." She paused and snorted several times. It was a curious noise. You can hear the same sort of thing if you walk through a riding-stable when the horses are being fed. "I suppose", she went on, "your mothers and fathers tell you you're wonderful. Well, I am here to tell you the opposite, and you'd better believe me. Stand up everybody!"

They all got quickly to their feet.

"Now put your hands out in front of you. And as I walk past I want you to turn them over so I can see if they are clean on both sides."

The Trunchbull began a slow march along the rows of desks inspecting the hands. All went well until she came to a small boy in the second row. "What's your name?" she barked.

"Nigel," the boy said.

"Nigel what?"

"Nigel Hicks," the boy said.

"Nigel Hicks what?" the Trunchbull bellowed. She bellowed so loud she nearly blew the little chap out of the window.

"That's it," Nigel said. "Unless you want my middle names as well." He was a brave little fellow and one could see that he was trying not to be scared by the Gorgon who towered above him.

"I do *not* want your middle names, you blister!" the Gorgon bellowed. "What is *my* name?"

"Miss Trunchbull," Nigel said.

"Then use it when you address me! Now then, let's try again. What is your name?"

"Nigel Hicks, Miss Trunchbull," Nigel said.

"That's better," the Trunchbull said. "Your

hands are filthy, Nigel! When did you last wash them?"

"Well, let me think," Nigel said. "That's rather difficult to remember exactly. It could have been yesterday or it could have been the day before."

The Trunchbull's whole body and face seemed to swell up as though she were being inflated by a bicycle-pump.

"I knew it!" she bellowed. "I knew as soon as I saw you that you were nothing but a piece of filth! What is your father's job, a sewage-worker?"

"He's a doctor," Nigel said. "And a jolly good one. He says we're all so covered with bugs anyway that a bit of extra dirt never hurts anyone."

"I'm glad he's not *my* doctor," the Trunchbull said. "And why, might I ask, is there a baked bean on the front of your shirt?"

"We had them for lunch, Miss Trunchbull."

"And do you usually put your lunch on the front of your shirt, Nigel? Is that what this famous doctor father of yours has taught you to do?"

"Baked beans are hard to eat, Miss Trunchbull. They keep falling off my fork."

"You are disgusting!" the Trunchbull bellowed. "You are a walking germ-factory! I don't wish to see any more of you today! Go and stand in the corner on one leg with your face to the wall!"

"But Miss Trunchbull . . . "

"Don't argue with me, boy, or I'll make you stand on your head! Now do as you're told!"

Nigel went.

"Now stay where you are, boy, while I test you on your spelling to see if you've learnt anything at all this past week. And don't turn round when you talk to me. Keep your nasty little face to the wall. Now then, spell 'write'."

"Which one?" Nigel asked. "The thing you do

with a pen or the one that means the opposite of wrong?" He happened to be an unusually bright child and his mother had worked hard with him at home on spelling and reading.

"The one with the pen, you little fool."

Nigel spelled it correctly which surprised the Trunchbull. She thought she had given him a very tricky word, one that he wouldn't yet have learned, and she was peeved that he had succeeded.

Then Nigel said, still balancing on one leg and facing the wall, "Miss Honey taught us how to spell a new very long word yesterday."

"And what word was that?" the Trunchbull asked softly. The softer her voice became, the greater the danger, but Nigel wasn't to know this.

"'Difficulty'," Nigel said. "Everyone in the class can spell 'difficulty' now."

"What nonsense," the Trunchbull said. "You are not supposed to learn long words like that until you are at least eight or nine. And don't try to tell me *everybody* in the class can spell that word. You are lying to me, Nigel."

"Test someone," Nigel said, taking an awful chance. "Test anyone you like."

The Trunchbull's dangerous glittering eyes roved around the class-room. "You," she said, pointing at a tiny and rather daft little girl called Prudence, "Spell 'difficulty'."

Amazingly, Prudence spelled it correctly and without a moment's hesitation.

The Trunchbull was properly taken aback. "Humph!" she snorted. "And I suppose Miss Honey wasted the whole of one lesson teaching you to spell that one single word?"

"Oh no, she didn't," piped Nigel. "Miss Honey taught it to us in three minutes so we'll never

370

forget it. She teaches us lots of words in three minutes."

"And what exactly is this magic method, Miss Honey?" asked the Headmistress.

"I'll show you," piped up the brave Nigel again, coming to Miss Honey's rescue. "Can I put my other foot down and turn round, please, while I show you?"

"You may do neither!" snapped the Trunchbull. "Stay as you are and show me just the same!"

"All right," said Nigel, wobbling crazily on his one leg. "Miss Honey gives us a little song about each word and we all sing it together and we learn to spell it in no time. Would you like to hear the song about 'difficulty'?"

"I should be fascinated," the Trunchbull said in a voice dripping with sarcasm.

"Here it is," Nigel said.

"Mrs D, Mrs I, Mrs FFI
Mrs C, Mrs U, Mrs LTY.

That spells difficulty."

"How perfectly ridiculous!" snorted the Trunchbull. "Why are all these women married? And anyway you're not meant to teach poetry when you're teaching spelling. Cut it out in future, Miss Honey."

"But it does teach them some of the harder words wonderfully well," Miss Honey murmured.

"Don't argue with me, Miss Honey!" the Headmistress thundered. "Just do as you're told! I shall now test the class on the multiplication tables to see if Miss Honey has taught you anything at all in that direction." The Trunchbull had returned to her place in front of the class, and her diabolical gaze was moving slowly along the rows of tiny pupils. "You!" she barked, pointing at a small boy called Rupert in the front row. "What is two sevens?"

"Sixteen," Rupert answered with foolish abandon.

The Trunchbull started advancing slow and soft-footed upon Rupert in the manner of a tigress stalking a small deer. Rupert suddenly became aware of the danger signals and quickly tried again. "It's eighteen!" he cried. "Two sevens are eighteen, not sixteen!"

"You ignorant little slug!" the Trunchbull bellowed. "You witless weed! You empty-headed hamster! You stupid glob of glue!" She had now stationed herself directly behind Rupert, and suddenly she extended a hand the size of a tennis racquet and grabbed all the hair on Rupert's head in her fist. Rupert had a lot of golden-coloured hair. His mother thought it was beautiful to behold and took a delight in allowing it to grow extra long. The Trunchbull had as great a dislike for long hair on boys as she had for plaits and pigtails on girls and she was about to show it. She took a firm grip on Rupert's long golden tresses with her giant hand and then, by raising her muscular right arm, she lifted the helpless boy clean out of his chair and held him aloft.

Rupert yelled. He twisted and squirmed and
kicked the air and went on yelling like a stuck pig,
and Miss Trunchbull bellowed, "Two sevens are

fourteen! Two sevens are fourteen! I am not letting you go till you say it!''

From the back of the class, Miss Honey cried out, ''Miss Trunchbull! Please let him down! You're hurting him! All his hair might come out!''

''And well it might if he doesn't stop wriggling!'' snorted the Trunchbull. ''Keep still, you squirming worm!''

It really was a quite extraordinary sight to see this giant Headmistress dangling the small boy high in the air and the boy spinning and twisting like something on the end of a string and shrieking his head off.

''Say it!'' bellowed the Trunchbull. ''Say two sevens are fourteen! Hurry up or I'll start jerking you up and down and then your hair really will come out and we'll have enough of it to stuff a sofa! Get on with it boy! Say two sevens are fourteen and I'll let you go!''

''T-t-two s-sevens are f-f-fourteen,'' gasped Rupert, whereupon the Trunchbull, true to her word, opened her hand and quite literally let him go. He was a long way off the ground when she released him and he plummeted to earth and hit the floor and bounced like a football.

''Get up and stop whimpering,'' the Trunchbull barked.

Rupert got up and went back to his desk massaging his scalp with both hands. The Trunchbull returned to the front of the class. The children sat there hypnotised. None of them had seen anything quite like this before. It was splendid entertainment. It was better than a pantomime, but with one big difference. In this room there was an enormous human bomb in front of them which was liable to explode and blow someone to bits any moment. The children's eyes were riveted on the Headmistress. "I don't like small people," she was saying. "Small people should never be seen by anybody. They should be kept out of sight in boxes like hairpins and buttons. I cannot for the life of me see why children have to take so long to grow up. I think they do it on purpose."

Another extremely brave little boy in the front row spoke up and said, "But surely *you* were a small person once, Miss Trunchbull, weren't you?"

"I was *never* a small person," she snapped. "I have been large all my life and I don't see why others can't be the same way."

"But you must have started out as a baby," the boy said.

"*Me!* A baby!" shouted the Trunchbull. "How dare you suggest such a thing! What cheek! What infernal insolence! What's your name, boy? And stand up when you speak to me!"

The boy stood up. "My name is Eric Ink, Miss Trunchbull," he said.

"Eric *what*?" the Trunchbull shouted.

"Ink," the boy said.

"Don't be an ass, boy! There's no such name!"

"Look in the phone book," Eric said. "You'll see my father there under Ink."

"Very well, then," the Trunchbull said, "You may be Ink, young man, but let me tell you something. You're not indelible. I'll very soon rub you out if you try getting clever with me. Spell what."

"I don't understand," Eric said. "What do you want me to spell?"

"Spell what, you idiot! Spell the word 'what'!"

"W ... O ... T," Eric said, answering too quickly.

There was a nasty silence.

"I'll give you one more chance," the Trunchbull said, not moving.

"Ah yes, I know," Eric said. "It's got an H in it. W ... H ... O ... T. It's easy."

In two large strides the Trunchbull was behind Eric's desk, and there she stood, a pillar of doom towering over the helpless boy. Eric glanced fearfully back over his shoulder at the monster. "I *was* right, wasn't I?" he murmured nervously.

"You were *wrong*!" the Trunchbull barked. "In fact you strike me as the sort of poisonous little pockmark that will *always* be wrong! You sit wrong! You look wrong! You speak wrong! You are wrong all round! I will give you one more chance to be right! Spell 'what'!"

Eric hesitated. Then he said very slowly, "It's not W ... O ... T, and it's not W ... H ... O ... T. Ah, I know. It must be W ... H ... O ... T ... T."

Standing behind Eric, the Trunchbull reached out and took hold of the boy's two ears, one with each hand, pinching them between forefinger and thumb.

"Ow!" Eric cried. "Ow! You're hurting me!"

"I haven't started yet," the Trunchbull said briskly. And now, taking a firm grip on his two ears, she lifted him bodily out of his seat and held him aloft.

Like Rupert before him, Eric squealed the house down.

From the back of the class-room Miss Honey cried out, "Miss Trunchbull! Don't! Please let him go! His ears might come off!"

"They'll never come off," the Trunchbull

shouted back. "I have discovered through long experience, Miss Honey, that the ears of small boys are stuck very firmly to their heads."

"Let him go, Miss Trunchbull, please," begged Miss Honey. "You could damage him, you really could! You could wrench them right off!"

"Ears never come off!" the Trunchbull shouted. "They stretch most marvellously, like these are doing now, but I can assure you they never come off!"

Eric was squealing louder than ever and pedalling the air with his legs.

Matilda had never before seen a boy, or anyone else for that matter, held aloft by his ears alone. Like Miss Honey, she felt sure both ears were going to come off at any moment with all the weight that was on them.

The Trunchbull was shouting, "The word 'what' is spelled W...H...A...T. Now spell it, you little wart!"

Eric didn't hesitate. He had learned from watching Rupert a few minutes before that the quicker you answered the quicker you were released. "W...H...A...T", he squealed, "spells what!"

Still holding him by the ears, the Trunchbull lowered him back into his chair behind his desk. Then she marched back to the front of the class, dusting off her hands one against the other like someone who has been handling something rather grimy.

"That's the way to make them learn, Miss Honey," she said. "You take it from me, it's no good just *telling* them. You've got to *hammer* it into them. There's nothing like a little twisting and twiddling to encourage them to remember things. It concentrates their minds wonderfully."

"You could do them permanent damage, Miss Trunchbull," Miss Honey cried out.

"Oh, I have, I'm quite sure I have," the Trunchbull answered, grinning. "Eric's ears will have stretched quite considerably in the last couple of minutes! They'll be much longer now than they were before. There's nothing wrong with that, Miss Honey. It'll give him an interesting pixie look for the rest of his life."

"But Miss Trunchbull..."

"Oh, do shut up, Miss Honey! You're as wet as any of them. If you can't cope in here then you can go and find a job in some cotton-wool private school for rich brats. When you have been teaching for as long as I have you'll realise that it's no good at all being kind to children. Read *Nicholas Nickleby*, Miss Honey, by Mr Dickens. Read about Mr Wackford Squeers, the admirable headmaster of Dotheboys Hall. *He* knew how to handle the little brutes, didn't he! He knew how to use the birch, didn't he! He kept their backsides so warm you could have fried eggs and bacon on them! A fine book, that. But I don't suppose this bunch of morons we've got here will ever read it because by the look of them they are never going to learn to read any thing!"

"I've read it," Matilda said quietly.

The Trunchbull flicked her head round and looked carefully at the small girl with dark hair and deep brown eyes sitting in the second row. "What did you say?" she asked sharply.

"I said I've read it, Miss Trunchbull."

"Read what?"

"*Nicholas Nickleby*, Miss Trunchbull."

"You are lying to me, madam!" the Trunchbull shouted, glaring at Matilda. "I doubt there is a single child in the entire school who has read that book, and here you are, an unhatched shrimp sitting in the lowest form there is, trying to tell me a whopping great lie like that! Why do you do it? You must take me for a fool! Do you take me for a fool, child?"

"Well . . ." Matilda said, then she hesitated. She would like to have said, "Yes, I jolly well do," but that would have been suicide. "Well . . . " she said

again, still hesitating, still refusing to say "No".

The Trunchbull sensed what the child was thinking and she didn't like it. "Stand up when you speak to me!" she snapped. "What is your name?"

Matilda stood up and said, "My name is Matilda Wormwood, Miss Trunchbull."

"Wormwood, is it?" the Trunchbull said. "In

that case you must be the daughter of that man who owns Wormwood Motors?"

"Yes, Miss Trunchbull."

"He's a crook!" the Trunchbull shouted. "A week ago he sold me a second-hand car that he said was almost new. I thought he was a splendid fellow then. But this morning, while I was driving that car through the village, the entire engine fell out on to the road! The whole thing was filled with sawdust! The man's a thief and a robber! I'll have his skin for sausages, you see if I don't!"

"He's clever at his business," Matilda said.

"Clever my foot!" the Trunchbull shouted. "Miss Honey tells me that *you* are meant to be clever, too! Well madam, I don't like clever people! They are all crooked! *You* are most certainly crooked! Before I fell out with your father, he told me some very nasty stories about the way you behaved at home! But you'd better not try anything in this school, young lady. I shall be keeping a very careful eye on you from now on. Sit down and keep quiet."

The First Miracle

Matilda sat down again at her desk. The Trunch-bull seated herself behind the teacher's table. It was the first time she had sat down during the lesson. Then she reached out a hand and took hold of her water-jug. Still holding the jug by the handle but not lifting it yet, she said, "I have never been able to understand why small children are so disgusting. They are the bane of my life. They are like insects. They should be got rid of as early as possible. We get rid of flies with fly-spray and by hanging up fly-paper. I have often thought of inventing a spray for getting rid of small children. How splendid it would be to walk into this classroom with a gigantic spray-gun in my hands and start pumping it. Or better still, some huge strips of sticky paper. I would hang them all round the school and you'd all get stuck to them and that would be the end of it. Wouldn't that be a good idea, Miss Honey?"

"If it's meant to be a joke, Headmistress, I don't think it's a very funny one," Miss Honey said from the back of the class.

"You wouldn't, would you, Miss Honey," the Trunchbull said. "And it's *not* meant to be a joke. My idea of a perfect school, Miss Honey, is one that has no children in it at all. One of these days

383

I shall start up a school like that. I think it will be very successful."

The woman's mad, Miss Honey was telling herself. She's round the twist. She's the one who ought to be got rid of.

The Trunchbull now lifted the large blue porcelain water-jug and poured some water into her glass. And suddenly, with the water, out came the long slimy newt straight into the glass, *plop*!

The Trunchbull let out a yell and leapt off her chair as though a firecracker had gone off underneath her. And now the children also saw the long thin slimy yellow-bellied lizard-like creature twisting and turning in the glass, and they squirmed and jumped about as well, shouting, "What is it? Oh, it's disgusting! It's a snake! It's a baby crocodile! It's an alligator!"

"Look out, Miss Trunchbull!" cried Lavender. "I'll bet it bites!"

The Trunchbull, this mighty female giant, stood there in her green breeches, quivering like a blancmange. She was especially furious that someone had succeeded in making her jump and yell like that because she prided herself on her toughness. She stared at the creature twisting and wriggling in the glass. Curiously enough, she had never seen a newt before. Natural history was not her strong point. She hadn't the faintest idea what this thing was. It certainly looked extremely unpleasant. Slowly she sat down again in her chair. She looked at this moment more terrifying than ever before. The fires of fury and hatred were smouldering in her small black eyes.

"Matilda!" she barked. "Stand up!"

"Who, me?" Matilda said. "What have *I* done?"

"Stand up, you disgusting little cockroach!"

"I haven't done anything, Miss Trunchbull, honestly I haven't. I've never seen that slimy thing before!"

"Stand up at once, you filthy little maggot!"

Reluctantly, Matilda got to her feet. She was in

385

the second row. Lavender was in the row behind her, feeling a bit guilty. She hadn't intended to get her friend into trouble. On the other hand, she was certainly not about to own up.

"You are a vile, repulsive, repellent, malicious little brute!" the Trunchbull was shouting. "You are not fit to be in this school! You ought to be behind bars, that's where you ought to be! I shall have you drummed out of this establishment in utter disgrace! I shall have the prefects chase you down the corridor and out of the front-door with hockey-sticks! I shall have the staff escort you home under armed guard! And then I shall make absolutely sure you are sent to a reformatory for delinquent girls for the minimum of forty years!"

The Trunchbull was in such a rage that her face had taken on a boiled colour and little flecks of froth were gathering at the corners of her mouth. But she was not the only one who was losing her cool. Matilda was also beginning to see red. She didn't in the least mind being accused of having done something she had actually done. She could see the justice of that. It was, however, a totally new experience for her to be accused of a crime that she definitely had not committed. She had had absolutely nothing to do with that beastly creature in the glass. By golly, she thought, that rotten Trunchbull isn't going to pin this one on me!

"*I did not do it!*" she screamed.

"Oh yes, you did!" the Trunchbull roared back. "Nobody else could have thought up a trick like that! Your father was right to warn me about you!" The woman seemed to have lost control of herself completely. She was ranting like a maniac. "You are finished in this school, young lady!" she shouted. "You are finished everywhere. I shall personally see to it that you are put away in a place where not even the crows can land their droppings on you! You will probably never see the light of day again!"

"*I'm telling you I did not do it!*" Matilda screamed. "I've never even seen a creature like that in my life!"

"You have put a . . . a . . . a crocodile in my drinking water!" the Trunchbull yelled back. "There is no worse crime in the world against a Headmistress! Now sit down and don't say a word! Go on, sit down at once!"

"But I'm telling you . . ." Matilda shouted, refusing to sit down.

"I am telling you to shut up!" the Trunchbull roared. "If you don't shut up at once and sit down I shall remove my belt and let you have it with the end that has the buckle!"

Slowly Matilda sat down. Oh, the rottenness of it all! The unfairness! How dare they expel her for something she hadn't done!

Matilda felt herself getting angrier . . . and angrier . . . and angrier . . . so unbearably angry that something was bound to explode inside her very soon.

The newt was still squirming in the tall glass of water. It looked horribly uncomfortable. The glass was not big enough for it. Matilda glared at the Trunchbull. How she hated her. She glared at the glass with the newt in it. She longed to march up and grab the glass and tip the contents, newt and all, over the Trunchbull's head. She trembled to think what the Trunchbull would do to her if she did that.

The Trunchbull was sitting behind the teacher's table staring with a mixture of horror and fascination at the newt wriggling in the glass. Matilda's eyes were also riveted on the glass. And now, quite slowly, there began to creep over Matilda a most extraordinary and peculiar feeling. The feeling was mostly in the eyes. A kind of electricity seemed to be gathering inside them. A sense of power was brewing in those eyes of hers, a feeling of great strength was settling itself deep inside her eyes. But there was also another feeling which was something else altogether, and which she could not understand. It was like flashes of lightning. Little waves of lightning seemed to be flashing out of her eyes. Her eyeballs were beginning to get hot, as though vast energy was building up somewhere inside them. It was an amazing sensation. She kept her eyes steadily on the glass, and now the power was concentrating itself in one small part of each eye and growing stronger and stronger and it felt as though millions of tiny little invisible arms with hands on them were shooting out of her eyes towards the glass she was staring at.

"Tip it!" Matilda whispered. *"Tip it over!"*

She saw the glass wobble. It actually tilted backwards a fraction of an inch, then righted itself again. She kept pushing at it with all those millions of invisible little arms and hands that were reaching out from her eyes, feeling the power that was flashing straight from the two little black dots in the very centres of her eyeballs.

"Tip it!" she whispered again. *"Tip it over!"*

Once more the glass wobbled. She pushed harder still, willing her eyes to shoot out more power. And then, very very slowly, so slowly she could hardly see it happening, the glass began to lean backwards, farther and farther and farther backwards until it was balancing on just one edge of its base. And there it teetered for a few seconds before finally toppling over and falling with a sharp tinkle on to the desk-top. The water in it and the squirming newt splashed out all over Miss Trunchbull's enormous bosom. The headmistress let out a yell that must have rattled every window-pane in the building and for the second time in the last five minutes she shot out of her chair like a rocket. The newt clutched desperately at the cotton smock where it covered the great chest and there it clung with its little claw-like feet. The Trunchbull looked down and saw it and she bellowed even louder and with a swipe of her hand she sent the creature flying across the class-room. It landed on the floor beside Lavender's desk and very quickly she ducked down and picked it up and put it into her pencil-box for another time. A newt, she decided, was a useful thing to have around.

The Trunchbull, her face more like a boiled ham than ever, was standing before the class quivering with fury. Her massive bosom was heaving in and out and the splash of water down the front of it

made a dark wet patch that had probably soaked
right through to her skin.

"*Who did it?*" she roared. "*Come on! Own up!
Step forward! You won't escape this time! Who is
responsible for this dirty job? Who pushed over
this glass?*"

Nobody answered. The whole room remained
silent as a tomb.

"Matilda!" she roared. "It was you! I know it was you!"

Matilda, in the second row, sat very still and said nothing. A strange feeling of serenity and confidence was sweeping over her and all of a sudden she found that she was frightened by nobody in the world. With the power of her eyes alone she had compelled a glass of water to tip and spill its contents over the horrible Headmistress, and anybody who could do that could do anything.

"Speak up, you clotted carbuncle!" roared the Trunchbull. "Admit that you did it!"

Matilda looked right back into the flashing eyes of this infuriated female giant and said with total calmness, "I have not moved away from my desk, Miss Trunchbull, since the lesson began. I can say no more."

Suddenly the entire class seemed to rise up against the Headmistress. "She didn't move!" they cried out. "Matilda didn't move! Nobody moved! You must have knocked it over yourself!"

"I most certainly did not knock it over myself!" roared the Trunchbull. "How dare you suggest a thing like that! Speak up, Miss Honey! You must have seen everything! Who knocked over my glass?"

"None of the children did, Miss Trunchbull," Miss Honey answered. "I can vouch for it that nobody has moved from his or her desk all the time you've been here, except for Nigel and he has not moved from his corner."

Miss Trunchbull glared at Miss Honey. Miss Honey met her gaze without flinching. "I am telling you the truth, Headmistress," she said. "You must have knocked it over without knowing it. That sort of thing is easy to do."

"I am fed up with you useless bunch of midgets!" roared the Trunchbull. "I refuse to waste any more of my precious time in here!" And with that she marched out of the class-room, slamming the door behind her.

In the stunned silence that followed, Miss Honey walked up to the front of the class and stood behind her table. "Phew!" she said. "I think we've had enough school for one day, don't you? The class is dismissed. You may all go out into the playground and wait for your parents to come and take you home."

The Second Miracle

Matilda did not join the rush to get out of the classroom. After the other children had all disappeared, she remained at her desk, quiet and thoughtful. She knew she had to tell somebody about what had happened with the glass. She couldn't possibly keep a gigantic secret like that bottled up inside her. What she needed was just one person, one wise and sympathetic grown-up who could help her to understand the meaning of this extraordinary happening.

Neither her mother nor her father would be of any use at all. If they believed her story, and it was doubtful they would, they almost certainly would fail to realise what an astounding event it was that had taken place in the classroom that afternoon. On the spur of the moment, Matilda decided that the one person she would like to confide in was Miss Honey.

Matilda and Miss Honey were now the only two left in the class-room. Miss Honey had seated herself at her table and was riffling through some papers. She looked up and said, "Well, Matilda, aren't you going outside with the others?"

Matilda said, "Please may I talk to you for a moment?"

"Of course you may. What's troubling you?"

"Something very peculiar has happened to me, Miss Honey."

Miss Honey became instantly alert. Ever since the two disastrous meetings she had had recently about Matilda, the first with the Headmistress and the second with the dreadful Mr and Mrs Wormwood, Miss Honey had been thinking a great deal about this child and wondering how she could help her. And now, here was Matilda sitting in the classroom with a curiously exalted look on her face and asking if she could have a private talk. Miss Honey had never seen her looking so wide-eyed and peculiar before.

"Yes, Matilda," she said. "Tell me what has happened to you that is so peculiar."

"Miss Trunchbull isn't going to expel me, is she?" Matilda asked. "Because it wasn't me who put that creature in her jug of water. I promise you it wasn't."

"I know it wasn't," Miss Honey said.

"Am I going to be expelled?"

"I think not," Miss Honey said. "The Headmistress simply got a little over-excited, that's all."

"Good," Matilda said. "But that isn't what I want to talk to you about."

"What do you want to talk to me about, Matilda?"

"I want to talk to you about the glass of water with the creature in it," Matilda said. "You saw it spilling all over Miss Trunchbull, didn't you?"

"I did indeed."

395

"Well, Miss Honey, I didn't touch it. I never went near it."

"I know you didn't," Miss Honey said. "You heard me telling the Headmistress that it couldn't possibly have been you."

"Ah, but it *was* me, Miss Honey," Matilda said. "That's exactly what I want to talk to you about."

Miss Honey paused and looked carefully at the child. "I don't think I quite follow you," she said.

"I got so angry at being accused of something I hadn't done that I made it happen."

"You made what happen, Matilda?"

"I made the glass tip over."

"I still don't quite understand what you mean," Miss Honey said gently.

"I did it with my eyes," Matilda said. "I was staring at it and wishing it to tip and then my eyes went all hot and funny and some sort of power came out of them and the glass just toppled over."

Miss Honey continued to look steadily at Matilda through her steel-rimmed spectacles and Matilda looked back at her just as steadily.

"I am still not following you," Miss Honey said. "Do you mean you actually willed the glass to tip over?"

"Yes," Matilda said. "With my eyes."

Miss Honey was silent for a moment. She did not think Matilda was meaning to tell a lie. It was more likely that she was simply allowing her vivid imagination to run away with her. "You mean you were sitting where you are now and you told the glass to topple over and it did?"

"Something like that, Miss Honey, yes."

"If you did that, then it is just about the greatest miracle a person has ever performed since the time of Jesus."

"I did it, Miss Honey."

It is extraordinary, thought Miss Honey, how often small children have flights of fancy like this. She decided to put an end to it as gently as possible. "Could you do it again?" she asked, not unkindly.

"I don't know," Matilda said, "but I think I might be able to."

Miss Honey moved the now empty glass to the middle of the table. "Should I put water in it?" she asked, smiling a little.

"I don't think it matters," Matilda said.

"Very well, then. Go ahead and tip it over."

"It may take some time."

"Take all the time you want," Miss Honey said. "I'm in no hurry."

Matilda, sitting in the second row about ten feet
away from Miss Honey, put her elbows on the desk
and cupped her face in her hands, and this time she
gave the order right at the beginning. *"Tip glass,
tip!"* she ordered, but her lips didn't move and she
made no sound. She simply shouted the words
inside her head. And now she concentrated the
whole of her mind and her brain and her will up
into her eyes and once again but much more
quickly than before she felt the electricity gathering and the power was beginning to surge and the
hotness was coming into the eyeballs, and then the
millions of tiny invisible arms with hands on them
were shooting out towards the glass, and without
making any sound at all she kept on shouting
inside her head for the glass to go over. She saw it
wobble, then it tilted, then it toppled right over
and fell with a tinkle on to the table-top not twelve
inches from Miss Honey's folded arms.

Miss Honey's mouth dropped open and her eyes stretched so wide you could see the whites all round. She didn't say a word. She couldn't. The shock of seeing the miracle performed had struck her dumb. She gaped at the glass, leaning well away from it now as though it might be a dangerous thing. Then slowly she lifted head and looked at Matilda. She saw the child white in the face, as white as paper, trembling all over, the eyes glazed, staring straight ahead and seeing nothing. The whole face was transfigured, the eyes round and bright and she was sitting there speechless, quite beautiful in a blaze of silence.

Miss Honey waited, trembling a little herself and watching the child as she slowly stirred herself back into consciousness. And then suddenly, *click* went her face into a look of almost seraphic calm. "I'm all right," she said and smiled. "I'm quite all right, Miss Honey, so don't be alarmed."

"You seemed so far away," Miss Honey whispered, awestruck.

"Oh, I was. I was flying past the stars on silver wings," Matilda said. "It was wonderful."

Miss Honey was still gazing at the child in absolute wonderment, as though she were The Creation, The Beginning Of The World, The First Morning.

"It went much quicker this time," Matilda said quietly.

"It's not possible!" Miss Honey was gasping. "I don't believe it! I simply don't believe it!" She closed her eyes and kept them closed for quite a while, and when she opened them again it seemed as though she had gathered herself together. "Would you like to come back and have tea at my cottage?" she asked.

"Oh, I'd love to," Matilda said.

"Good. Gather up your things and I'll meet you outside in a couple of minutes."

"You won't tell anyone about this . . . this thing that I did, will you, Miss Honey?"

"I wouldn't dream of it," Miss Honey said.

Miss Honey's Cottage

Miss Honey joined Matilda outside the school gates and the two of them walked in silence through the village High Street. They passed the greengrocer with his window full of apples and oranges, and the butcher with bloody lumps of meat on display and naked chickens hanging up, and the small bank, and the grocery store and the electrical shop, and then they came out at the other side of the village on to the narrow country road where there were no people any more and very few motor-cars.

And now that they were alone, Matilda all of a sudden became wildly animated. It seemed as though a valve had burst inside her and a great gush of energy was being released. She trotted beside Miss Honey with wild little hops and her fingers flew as if she would scatter them to the four winds and her words went off like fireworks, with terrific speed. It was Miss Honey this and Miss Honey that and Miss Honey I do honestly feel I could move almost anything in the world, not just tipping over glasses and little things like that . . . I feel I could topple tables and chairs, Miss Honey . . . Even when people are sitting in the chairs I think I could push them over, and bigger things too, much bigger things than chairs and tables . . . I only have to take a moment to get my eyes strong and then I can push it out, this strongness, at anything at all so long as I am staring at it hard enough ... I have to stare at it very hard, Miss Honey, very very hard, and then I can feel it all happening behind my eyes, and my eyes get hot just as though they were burning but I don't mind that in the least, and Miss Honey ...

"Calm yourself down, child, calm yourself down," Miss Honey said. "Let us not get ourselves too worked up so early in the proceedings."

"But you do think it is *interesting*, don't you, Miss Honey?"

"Oh, it is *interesting* all right," Miss Honey said. "It is *more* than interesting. But we must tread very carefully from now on, Matilda."

"Why must we tread carefully, Miss Honey?"

"Because we are playing with mysterious forces, my child, that we know nothing about. I do not think they are evil. They may be good. They may even be divine. But whether they are or not, let us handle them carefully."

These were wise words from a wise old bird, but Matilda was too steamed up to see it that way. "I don't see why we have to be so careful?" she said, still hopping about.

"I am trying to explain to you," Miss Honey said patiently, "that we are dealing with the unknown. It is an unexplainable thing. The right word for it is a phenomenon. It is a phenomenon."

"Am I a phenomenon?" Matilda asked.

"It is quite possible that you are," Miss Honey said. "But I'd rather you didn't think about yourself as anything in particular at the moment. What I thought we might do is to explore this phenomenon a little further, just the two of us together, but making sure we take things very carefully all the time."

"You want me to do some more of it then, Miss Honey?"

"That is what I am tempted to suggest," Miss Honey said cautiously.

"Goody-good," Matilda said.

"I myself," Miss Honey said, "am probably far more bowled over by what you did than you are, and I am trying to find some reasonable explanation."

"Such as what?" Matilda asked.

"Such as whether or not it's got something to do with the fact that you are quite exceptionally precocious."

"What exactly does that word mean?" Matilda said.

"A precocious child", Miss Honey said, "is one that shows amazing intelligence early on. You are an unbelievably precocious child."

"Am I really?" Matilda asked.

"Of course you are. You must be aware of that. Look at your reading. Look at your mathematics."

"I suppose you're right," Matilda said.

Miss Honey marvelled at the child's lack of conceit and self-consciousness.

"I can't help wondering", she said, "whether this sudden ability that has come to you, of being able to move an object without touching it, whether it might not have something to do with your brainpower."

"You mean there might not be room in my head for all those brains so something has to push out?"

"That's not quite what I mean," Miss Honey said, smiling. "But whatever happens, and I say it again, we must tread carefully from now on. I have not forgotten that strange and distant glimmer on

404

your face after you tipped over the last glass."

"Do you think doing it could actually hurt me? Is that what you're thinking, Miss Honey?"

"It made you feel pretty peculiar, didn't it?"

"It made me feel lovely," Matilda said. "For a moment or two I was flying past the stars on silver wings. I told you that. And shall I tell you something else, Miss Honey? It was easier the second time, much much easier. I think it's like anything else, the more you practise it, the easier it gets."

Miss Honey was walking slowly so that the small child could keep up with her without trotting too fast, and it was very peaceful out there on the narrow road now that the village was behind them. It was one of those golden autumn afternoons and there were blackberries and splashes of old man's beard in the hedges, and the hawthorn berries were ripening scarlet for the birds when the cold winter came along. There were tall trees here and there on either side, oak and sycamore and ash and occasionally a sweet chestnut. Miss Honey, wishing to change the subject for the moment, gave the names of all these to Matilda and taught her how to recognise them by the shape of their leaves and the pattern of the bark on their trunks. Matilda took all this in and stored the knowledge away carefully in her mind.

They came finally to a gap in the hedge on the left-hand side of the road where there was a five-barred gate. "This way," Miss Honey said, and she opened the gate and led Matilda through and closed it again. They were now walking along a narrow lane that was no more than a rutted cart-track. There was a high hedge of hazel on either side and you could see clusters of ripe brown nuts in their green jackets. The squirrels would be collecting them all very soon, Miss Honey said, and storing them away carefully for the bleak months ahead.

"You mean you *live* down here?" Matilda asked.

"I do," Miss Honey replied, but she said no more.

Matilda had never once stopped to think about where Miss Honey might be living. She had always regarded her purely as a teacher, a person who turned up out of nowhere and taught at school and then went away again. Do any of us children, she wondered, ever stop to ask ourselves where our teachers go when school is over for the day? Do we wonder if they live alone, or if there is a mother at home or a sister or a husband? "Do you

live all by yourself, Miss Honey?" she asked.

"Yes," Miss Honey said. "Very much so."

They were walking over the deep sun-baked mud-tracks of the lane and you had to watch where you put your feet if you didn't want to twist your ankle. There were a few small birds around in the hazel branches but that was all.

"It's just a farm-labourer's cottage," Miss Honey said. "You mustn't expect too much of it. We're nearly there."

They came to a small green gate half-buried in the hedge on the right and almost hidden by the overhanging hazel branches. Miss Honey paused with one hand on the gate and said, "There it is. That's where I live."

Matilda saw a narrow dirt-path leading to a tiny

red-brick cottage. The cottage was so small it looked more like a doll's house than a human dwelling. The bricks it was built of were old and crumbly and very pale red. It had a grey slate roof and one small chimney, and there were two little windows at the front. Each window was no larger than a sheet of tabloid newspaper and there was clearly no upstairs to the place. On either side of the path there was a wilderness of nettles and blackberry thorns and long brown grass. An enormous oak tree stood overshadowing the cottage. Its massive spreading branches seemed to be enfolding and embracing the tiny building, and perhaps hiding it as well from the rest of the world.

Miss Honey, with one hand on the gate which she had not yet opened, turned to Matilda and said, "A poet called Dylan Thomas once wrote some lines that I think of every time I walk up this path."

Matilda waited, and Miss Honey, in a rather wonderful slow voice, began reciting the poem:

"Never and never, my girl riding far and near
In the land of the hearthstone tales, and spelled
    asleep,
Fear or believe that the wolf in the sheepwhite
    hood
Loping and bleating roughly and blithely shall
    leap, my dear, my dear,
Out of a lair in the flocked leaves in the dew
    dipped year
To eat your heart in the house in the rosy
    wood."

There was a moment of silence, and Matilda, who had never before heard great romantic poetry spoken aloud, was profoundly moved. "It's like music," she whispered.

"It is music," Miss Honey said. And then, as though embarrassed at having revealed such a secret part of herself, she quickly pushed open the gate and walked up the path. Matilda hung back. She was a bit frightened of this place now. It seemed so unreal and remote and fantastic and so totally away from this earth. It was like an illustration in Grimm or Hans Andersen. It was the house where the poor woodcutter lived with Hansel and Gretel and where Red Riding Hood's grandmother lived and it was also the house of The Seven Dwarfs and The Three Bears and all the rest of them. It was straight out of a fairy-tale.

"Come along, my dear," Miss Honey called back, and Matilda followed her up the path.

The front-door was covered with flaky green paint and there was no keyhole. Miss Honey simply lifted the latch and pushed open the door and went in. Although she was not a tall woman, she had to stoop low to get through the doorway. Matilda went after her and found herself in what seemed to be a dark narrow tunnel.

"You can come through to the kitchen and help me make the tea," Miss Honey said, and she led the way along the tunnel into the kitchen – that is if you could call it a kitchen. It was not much bigger than a good-sized clothes cupboard and there was one small window in the back wall with a sink under the window, but there were no taps over the sink. Against another wall there was a shelf, presumably for preparing food, and there was a single cupboard above the shelf. On the shelf itself

there stood a Primus stove, a saucepan and a half-full bottle of milk. A Primus is a little camping-stove that you fill with paraffin and you light it at the top and then you pump it to get pressure for the flame.

"You can get me some water while I light the Primus," Miss Honey said. "The well is out at the back. Take the bucket. Here it is. You'll find a rope in the well. Just hook the bucket on to the end

411

of the rope and lower it down, but don't fall in yourself." Matilda, more bemused than ever now, took the bucket and carried it out into the back garden. The well had a little wooden roof over it and a simple winding device and there was the rope dangling down into a dark bottomless hole. Matilda pulled up the rope and hooked the handle of the bucket on to the end of it. Then she lowered it until she heard a splash and the rope went slack. She pulled it up again and lo and behold, there was water in the bucket.

"Is this enough?" she asked, carrying it in.

"Just about," Miss Honey said. "I don't suppose you've ever done that before?"

"Never," Matilda said. "It's fun. How do you get enough water for your bath?"

"I don't take a bath," Miss Honey said. "I wash standing up. I get a bucketful of water and I heat it on this little stove and I strip and wash myself all over."

"Do you honestly do that?" Matilda asked.

"Of course I do," Miss Honey said. "Every poor person in England used to wash that way until not so very long ago. And *they* didn't have a Primus. They had to heat the water over the fire in the hearth."

"Are *you* poor, Miss Honey?"

"Yes," Miss Honey said. "Very. It's a good little stove, isn't it?" The Primus was roaring away with a powerful blue flame and already the water in the saucepan was beginning to bubble. Miss Honey got a teapot from the cupboard and put some tea leaves into it. She also found half a small loaf of brown bread. She cut two thin slices and then, from a plastic container, she took some margarine and spread it on the bread.

Margarine, Matilda thought. She really must be poor.

Miss Honey found a tray and on it she put two mugs, the teapot, the half bottle of milk and a plate with the two slices of bread. "I'm afraid I don't have any sugar," she said. "I never use it."

"That's all right," Matilda said. In her wisdom she seemed to be aware of the delicacy of the situation and she was taking great care not to say anything to embarrass her companion.

413

"Let's have it in the sitting-room," Miss Honey said, picking up the tray and leading the way out of the kitchen and down the dark little tunnel into the room at the front. Matilda followed her, but just inside the doorway of the so-called sitting-room she stopped and stared around her in absolute amazement. The room was as small and square and bare as a prison cell. The pale daylight that entered came from a single tiny window in the front wall, but there were no curtains. The only objects in the entire room were two upturned wooden boxes to serve as chairs and a third box between them for a table. That was all. There were no pictures on the walls, no carpet on the floor, only rough unpolished wooden planks, and there were gaps between the planks where dust and bits of grime had gathered. The ceiling was so low that with a jump Matilda could nearly touch it with her finger-tips. The walls were white but the whiteness didn't look like paint. Matilda rubbed her palm against it and a white powder came off on to her skin. It was whitewash, the cheap stuff that is used in cowsheds and stables and hen-houses.

Matilda was appalled. Was this really where her neat and trimly-dressed school teacher lived? Was this all she had to come back to after a day's work? It was unbelievable. And what was the reason for it? There was something very strange going on around here, surely.

Miss Honey put the tray on one of the upturned boxes. "Sit down, my dear, sit down," she said, "and we'll have a nice hot cup of tea. Help yourself to bread. Both slices are for you. I never eat anything when I get home. I have a good old tuck-in at the school lunch and that keeps me going until the next morning."

Matilda perched herself carefully on an upturned box and more out of politeness than anything else she took a slice of bread and margarine and started to eat it. At home she would have been having buttered toast and strawberry jam and probably a piece of sponge-cake to round it off. And yet this was somehow far more fun. There was a mystery here in this house, a great mystery, there was no doubt about that, and Matilda was longing to find out what it was.

Miss Honey poured the tea and added a little milk to both cups. She appeared to be not in the least ill at ease sitting on an upturned box in a bare room and drinking tea out of a mug that she balanced on her knee.

"You know," she said, "I've been thinking very hard about what you did with that glass. It is a great power you have been given, my child, you know that."

"Yes, Miss Honey, I do," Matilda said, chewing her bread and margarine.

"So far as I know," Miss Honey went on, "nobody else in the history of the world has been able to compel an object to move without touching it or blowing on it or using any outside help at all."

Matilda nodded but said nothing.

"The fascinating thing", Miss Honey said, "would be to find out the real limit of this power of yours. Oh, I know you think you can move just about anything there is, but I have my doubts about that."

"I'd love to try something really huge," Matilda said.

"What about distance?" Miss Honey asked. "Would you always have to be close to the thing you were pushing?"

"I simply don't know," Matilda said. "But it would be fun to find out."

Miss Honey's Story

"We mustn't hurry this," Miss Honey said, "so let's have another cup of tea. And do eat that other slice of bread. You must be hungry."

Matilda took the second slice and started eating it slowly. The margarine wasn't at all bad. She doubted whether she could have told the difference if she hadn't known. "Miss Honey," she said suddenly, "do they pay you very badly at our school?"

Miss Honey looked up sharply. "Not too badly," she said. "I get about the same as the others."

"But it must still be very little if you are so dreadfully poor," Matilda said. "Do all the teachers live like this, with no furniture and no kitchen stove and no bathroom?"

"No, they don't," Miss Honey said rather stiffly. "I just happen to be the exception."

"I expect you just happen to like living in a very simple way," Matilda said, probing a little further. "It must make house cleaning an awful lot easier and you don't have furniture to polish or any of those silly little ornaments lying around that have to be dusted every day. And I suppose if you don't have a fridge you don't have to go out and buy all sorts of junky things like eggs and mayonnaise and ice-cream to fill it up with. It must save a terrific lot of shopping."

417

At this point Matilda noticed that Miss Honey's face had gone all tight and peculiar-looking. Her whole body had become rigid. Her shoulders were hunched up high and her lips were pressed together tight and she sat there gripping her mug of tea in both hands and staring down into it as though searching for a way to answer these not-quite-so-innocent questions.

There followed a rather long and embarrassing silence. In the space of thirty seconds the atmosphere in the tiny room had changed completely and now it was vibrating with awkwardness and secrets. Matilda said, "I am very sorry I asked you

those questions, Miss Honey. It is not any of my business."

At this, Miss Honey seemed to rouse herself. She gave a shake of her shoulders and then very carefully she placed her mug on the tray.

"Why shouldn't you ask?" she said. "You were bound to ask in the end. You are much too bright not to have wondered. Perhaps I even *wanted* you to ask. Maybe that is why I invited you here after all. As a matter of fact you are the first visitor to come to the cottage since I moved in two years ago."

Matilda said nothing. She could feel the tension growing and growing in the room.

"You are so much wiser than your years, my dear," Miss Honey went on, "that it quite staggers me. Although you look like a child, you are not really a child at all because your mind and your powers of reasoning seem to be fully grown-up. So I suppose we might call you a grown-up child, if you see what I mean."

Matilda still did not say anything. She was waiting for what was coming next.

"Up to now", Miss Honey went on, "I have found it impossible to talk to anyone about my problems. I couldn't face the embarrassment, and anyway I lack the courage. Any courage I had was knocked out of me when I was young. But now, all of a sudden I have a sort of desperate wish to tell everything to somebody. I know you are only a tiny little girl, but there is some kind of magic in you somewhere. I've seen it with my own eyes."

Matilda became very alert. The voice she was hearing was surely crying out for help. It must be. It had to be.

Then the voice spoke again. "Have some more tea," it said. "I think there's still a drop left."

Matilda nodded.

Miss Honey poured tea into both mugs and added milk. Again she cupped her own mug in both hands and sat there sipping.

There was quite a long silence before she said, "May I tell you a story?"

"Of course," Matilda said.

"I am twenty-three years old," Miss Honey said, "and when I was born my father was a doctor in this village. We had a nice old house, quite large, red-brick. It's tucked away in the woods behind the hills. I don't think you'd know it."

Matilda kept silent.

"I was born there," Miss Honey said. "And then came the first tragedy. My mother died when I was two. My father, a busy doctor, had to have someone to run the house and to look after me. So he invited my mother's unmarried sister, my aunt, to come and live with us. She agreed and she came."

Matilda was listening intently. "How old was the aunt when she moved in?" she asked.

"Not very old," Miss Honey said. "I should say about thirty. But I hated her right from the start. I missed my mother terribly. And the aunt was not a kind person. My father didn't know that because he was hardly every around but when he did put in an appearance, the aunt behaved differently."

Miss Honey paused and sipped her tea. "I can't think why I am telling you all this," she said, embarrassed.

"Go on," Matilda said. "Please."

"Well," Miss Honey said, "then came the second tragedy. When I was five, my father died very suddenly. One day he was there and the next day he was gone. And so I was left to live alone with my aunt. She became my legal guardian. She had all the powers of a parent over me. And in some way or another, she became the actual owner of the house."

"How did your father die?" Matilda asked.

"It is interesting you should ask that," Miss Honey said. "I myself was much too young to question it at the time, but I found out later that there was a good deal of mystery surrounding his death."

"Didn't they know how he died?" Matilda asked.

"Well, not exactly," Miss Honey said, hesitating, "You see, no one could believe that he would ever have done it. He was such a very sane and sensible man."

"Done what?" Matilda asked.

"*Killed* himself."

Matilda was stunned.
"Did he?" she
gasped.

421

"That's what it *looked* like," Miss Honey said. "But who knows?" She shrugged and turned away and stared out of the tiny window.

"I know what you're thinking," Matilda said. "You're thinking that the aunt killed him and made it look as though he'd done it himself."

"I am not thinking anything," Miss Honey said. "One must never think things like that without proof."

The little room became quiet. Matilda noticed that the hands clasping the mug were trembling slightly. "What happened after that?" she asked. "What happened when you were left all alone with the aunt? Wasn't she nice to you?"

"Nice?" Miss Honey said. "She was a demon. As soon as my father was out of the way she became a holy terror. My life was a nightmare."

"What did she do to you?" Matilda asked.

"I don't want to talk about it," Miss Honey said. "It's too horrible. But in the end I became so frightened of her I used to start shaking when she came into the room. You must understand I was never a strong character like you. I was always shy and retiring."

"Didn't you have any other relations?" Matilda asked. "Any uncles or aunts or grannies who would come and see you?"

"None that I knew about," Miss Honey said. "They were all either dead or they'd gone to Australia. And that's still the way it is now, I'm afraid."

"So you grew up in that house alone with your

aunt," Matilda said. "But you must have gone to school."

"Of course," Miss Honey said. "I went to the same school you're going to now. But I lived at home." Miss Honey paused and stared down into her empty tea-mug. "I think what I am trying to explain to you," she said, "is that over the years I became so completely cowed and dominated by this monster of an aunt that when she gave me an order, no matter what it was, I obeyed it instantly. That can happen, you know. And by the time I was ten, I had become her slave. I did all the housework. I made her bed. I washed and ironed for her. I did all the cooking. I learned how to do everything."

"But surely you could have complained to *somebody*?" Matilda said.

"To whom?" Miss Honey said. "And anyway, I was far too terrified to complain. I told you, I was her slave."

"Did she beat you?"

"Let's not go into details," Miss Honey said.

"How simply *awful*," Matilda said. "Did you cry nearly all the time?"

"Only when I was alone," Miss Honey said. "I wasn't allowed to cry in front of her. But I lived in fear."

"What happened when you left school?" Matilda asked.

"I was a bright pupil," Miss Honey said. "I could easily have got into university. But there was no question of that."

"Why not, Miss Honey?"

423

"Because I was needed at home to do the work."

"Then how did you become a teacher?" Matilda asked.

"There is a Teacher's Training College in Reading," Miss Honey said. "That's only forty minutes' bus-ride away from here. I was allowed to go there on condition I came straight home again every afternoon to do the washing and ironing and to clean the house and cook the supper."

"How old were you then?" Matilda asked.

"When I went into Teacher's Training I was eighteen," Miss Honey said.

"You could have just packed up and walked away," Matilda said.

"Not until I got a job," Miss Honey said. "And don't forget, I was by then dominated by my aunt to such an extent that I wouldn't have dared. You can't imagine what it's like to be completely controlled like that by a very strong personality. It turns you to jelly. So that's it. That's the sad story of my life. Now I've talked enough."

"Please don't stop," Matilda said. "You haven't finished yet. How did you manage to get away from her in the end and come and live in this funny little house?"

"Ah, that was something," Miss Honey said. "I was proud of that."

"Tell me," Matilda said.

"Well," Miss Honey said, "when I got my teacher's job, the aunt told me I owed her a lot of money. I asked her why. She said, 'Because I've been feeding you for all these years and buying

424

your shoes and your clothes!' She told me it added up to thousands and I had to pay her back by giving her my salary for the next ten years. 'I'll give you one pound a week pocket-money,' she said. 'But that's all you're going to get.' She even arranged with the school authorities to have my salary paid directly into her own bank. She made me sign the paper."

"You shouldn't have done that," Matilda said. "Your salary was your chance of freedom."

"I know, I know," Miss Honey said. "But by then I had been her slave nearly all my life and I hadn't the courage or the guts to say no. I was still petrified of her. She could still hurt me badly."

"So how did you manage to escape?" Matilda asked.

"Ah," Miss Honey said, smiling for the first time, "that was two years ago. It was my greatest triumph."

"Please tell me," Matilda said.

"I used to get up very early and go for walks while my aunt was still asleep," Miss Honey said. "And one day I came across this tiny cottage. It was empty. I found out who owned it. It was a farmer. I went to see him. Farmers also get up very early. He was milking his cows. I asked him if I could rent his cottage. 'You can't live there!' he cried. 'It's got no conveniences, no running water, no nothing!'"

"'I want to live there,' I said. 'I'm a romantic. I've fallen in love with it. Please rent it to me.'

"'You're mad,' he said. 'But if you insist, you're welcome to it. The rent will be ten pence a week.'

"'Here's one month's rent in advance,' I said, giving him 40p. 'And thank you so much!'"

"How super!" Matilda cried. "So suddenly you had a house all of your own! But how did you pluck up the courage to tell the aunt?"

"That was tough," Miss Honey said. "But I steeled myself to do it. One night, after I had cooked her supper, I went upstairs and packed the few things I possessed in a cardboard box and came downstairs and announced I was leaving. 'I've rented a house,' I said.

"My aunt exploded. 'Rented a house!' she shouted. 'How can you rent a house when you have only one pound a week in the world?'

"'I've done it,' I said.

"'And how are you going to buy food for yourself?'

"'I'll manage,' I mumbled and rushed out of the front door."

"Oh, well done you!" Matilda cried. "So you were free at last!"

"I was free at last," Miss Honey said. "I can't tell you how wonderful it was."

"But have you really managed to live here on one pound a week for two years?" Matilda asked.

"I most certainly have," Miss Honey said. "I pay ten pence rent, and the rest just about buys me paraffin for my stove and for my lamp, and a little milk and tea and bread and margarine. That's all I need really. As I told you, I have a jolly good tuck-in at the school lunch."

Matilda stared at her. What a marvellously brave thing Miss Honey had done. Suddenly she was a heroine in Matilda's eyes. "Isn't it awfully cold in the winter?" she asked.

"I've got my little paraffin stove," Miss Honey said. "You'd be surprised how snug I can make it in here."

"Do you have a bed, Miss Honey?"

"Well not exactly," Miss Honey said, smiling again. "But they say it's very healthy to sleep on a hard surface."

All at once Matilda was able to see the whole situation with absolute clarity. Miss Honey needed help. There was no way she could go on existing like this indefinitely. "You would be a lot better off, Miss Honey," she said, "if you gave up your job and drew unemployment money."

"I would never do that," Miss Honey said. "I love teaching."

"This awful aunt," Matilda said, "I suppose she is still living in your lovely old house?"

"Very much so," Miss Honey said. "She's still only about fifty. She'll be around for a long time yet."

"And do you think your father really meant her to own the house for ever?"

"I'm quite sure he didn't," Miss Honey said. "Parents will often give a guardian the right to occupy the house for a certain length of time, but it is nearly always left in trust for the child. It then becomes the child's property when he or she grows up."

"Then surely it is your house?" Matilda said.

"My father's will was never found," Miss Honey said. "It looks as though somebody destroyed it."

"No prizes for guessing who," Matilda said.

428

"No prizes," Miss Honey said.

"But if there is no will, Miss Honey, then surely the house goes automatically to you. You are the next of kin."

"I know I am," Miss Honey said. "But my aunt produced a piece of paper supposedly written by my father saying that he leaves the house to his sister-in-law in return for her kindness in looking after me. I am certain it's a forgery. But no one can prove it."

"Couldn't you try?" Matilda said. "Couldn't you hire a good lawyer and make a fight of it."

"I don't have the money to do that," Miss Honey said. "And you must remember that this aunt of mine is a much respected figure in the community. She has a lot of influence."

"Who is she?" Matilda asked.

Miss Honey hesitated a moment. Then she said softly, "Miss Trunchbull."

The Names

"Miss Trunchbull!" Matilda cried, jumping about a foot in the air. "You mean *she* is your aunt? *She* brought you up?"

"Yes," Miss Honey said.

"No *wonder* you were terrified!" Matilda cried. "The other day we saw her grab a girl by the pigtails and throw her over the playground fence!"

"You haven't seen anything," Miss Honey said. "After my father died, when I was five and a half, she used to make me bath myself all alone. And if she came up and thought I hadn't washed properly she would push my head under the water and hold it there. But don't get me started on what she used to do. That won't help us at all."

"No," Matilda said, "it won't."

"We came here", Miss Honey said," to talk about *you* and I've been talking about nothing but myself the whole time. I feel like a fool. I am much more interested in just how much you can do with those amazing eyes of yours."

"I can move things," Matilda said. "I know I can. I can push things over."

"How would you like it", Miss Honey said, "if we made some very cautious experiments to see just how much you can move and push?"

Quite surprisingly, Matilda said, "If you don't

mind, Miss Honey, I think I would rather not. I want to go home now and think and think about all the things I've heard this afternoon."

Miss Honey stood up at once. "Of course," she said. "I have kept you here far too long. Your mother will be starting to worry."

"She never does that," Matilda said, smiling. "But I would like to go home now please, if you don't mind."

"Come along then," Miss Honey said. "I'm sorry I gave you such a rotten tea."

"You didn't at all," Matilda said. "I loved it."

The two of them walked all the way to Matilda's house in complete silence. Miss Honey sensed that Matilda wanted it that way. The child seemed so lost in thought she hardly looked where she was walking, and when they reached the gate of Matilda's home, Miss Honey said, "You had better forget everything I told you this afternoon."

"I won't promise to do that," Matilda said, "but I will promise not to talk about it to anyone any more, not even to you."

"I think that would be wise," Miss Honey said.

"I won't promise to stop thinking about it, though, Miss Honey," Matilda said. "I've been thinking about it all the way back from your cottage and I believe I've got just a tiny little bit of an idea."

"You mustn't," Miss Honey said. "Please forget it."

"I would like to ask you three last things before

I stop talking about it," Matilda said. "Please will you answer them, Miss Honey?"

Miss Honey smiled. It was extraordinary, she told herself, how this little snippet of a girl seemed suddenly to be taking charge of her problems, and with such authority, too. "Well," she said, "that depends on what the questions are."

"The first thing is this," Matilda said. "What did Miss Trunchbull call *your father* when they were around the house at home?"

"I'm sure she called him Magnus," Miss Honey said. "That was his first name."

"And what did your father call Miss Trunchbull?"

"Her name is Agatha," Miss Honey said. "That's what he would have called her."

"And lastly," Matilda said, "what did your father and Miss Trunchbull call *you* around the house?"

"They called me Jenny," Miss Honey said.

Matilda pondered these answers very carefully. "Let me make sure I've got them right," she said. "In the house at home, your father was Magnus, Miss Trunchbull was Agatha and you were Jenny. Am I right?"

"That is correct," Miss Honey said.

"Thank you," Matilda said. "And now I won't mention the subject any more."

Miss Honey wondered what on earth was going on in the mind of this child. "Don't do anything silly," she said.

Matilda laughed and turned away and ran up the path to her front-door, calling out as she went, "Good-bye, Miss Honey! Thank you so much for the tea."

The Practice

Matilda found the house empty as usual. Her father was not yet back from work, her mother was not yet back from bingo and her brother might be anywhere. She went straight into the living-room and opened the drawer of the sideboard where she knew her father kept a box of cigars. She took one out and carried it up to her bedroom and shut herself in.

Now for the practice, she told herself. It's going to be tough but I'm determined to do it.

Her plan for helping Miss Honey was beginning to form beautifully in her mind. She had it now in almost every detail, but in the end it all depended upon her being able to do one very special thing with her eye-power. She knew she wouldn't manage it right away, but she felt fairly confident that with a great deal of practice and effort, she would succeed in the end. The cigar was essential. It was perhaps a bit thicker than she would have liked, but the weight was about right. It would be fine for practising with.

There was a small dressing-table in Matilda's bedroom with her hairbrush and comb on it and two library books. She cleared these things to one side and laid the cigar down in the middle of the dressing-table. Then she walked away and sat on

the end of her bed. She was now about ten feet
from the cigar.

She settled herself and began to concentrate,
and very quickly this time she felt the electricity
beginning to flow inside her head, gathering itself
behind the eyes, and the eyes became hot and
millions of tiny invisible hands began pushing out
like sparks towards the cigar. "Move!" she whispered, and to her intense surprise, almost at once,
the cigar with its little red and gold paper band
around its middle rolled away across the top of the
dressing-table and fell on to the carpet.

Matilda had enjoyed that. It was lovely doing it. It had felt as though sparks were going round and round inside her head and flashing out of her eyes. It had given her a sense of power that was almost ethereal. And how quick it had been this time! How simple!

She crossed the bedroom and picked up the cigar and put it back on the table.

Now for the difficult one, she thought. But if I have the power to *push*, then surely I also have the power to *lift*? It is *vital* I learn how to lift it. I *must* learn how to lift it right up into the air and keep it there. It is not a very heavy thing, a cigar.

She sat on the end of the bed and started again. It was easy now to summon up the power behind her eyes. It was like pushing a trigger in the brain. "*Lift!*" she whispered. "*Lift! Lift!*"

436

At first the cigar started to roll away. But then, with Matilda concentrating fiercely, one end of it slowly lifted up about an inch off the table-top.

With a colossal effort, she managed to hold it there for about ten seconds. Then it fell back again.

"Phew!" she gasped. "I'm getting it! I'm starting to do it!"

For the next hour, Matilda kept practising, and in the end she had managed, by the sheer power of her eyes, to lift the whole cigar clear off the table

about six inches into the air and hold it there for about a minute. Then suddenly she was so exhausted she fell back on the bed and went to sleep.

That was how her mother found her later in the evening.

"What's the matter with you?" the mother said, waking her up. "Are you ill?"

"Oh gosh," Matilda said, sitting up and looking around. "No. I'm all right. I was a bit tired, that's all."

From then on, every day after school, Matilda shut herself in her room and practised with the cigar. And soon it all began to come together in the most wonderful way. Six days later, by the following Wednesday evening, she was able not only to lift the cigar up into the air but also to move it around exactly as she wished. It was beautiful. "I can do it!" she cried. "I can really do it! I can pick the cigar up just with my eye-power and push it and pull it in the air any way I want!"

All she had to do now was to put her great plan into action.

The Third Miracle

The next day was Thursday, and that, as the whole of Miss Honey's class knew, was the day on which the Headmistress would take charge of the first lesson after lunch.

In the morning Miss Honey said to them, "One or two of you did not particularly enjoy the last occasion when the Headmistress took the class, so let us all try to be especially careful and clever today. How are your ears, Eric, after your last encounter with Miss Trunchbull?"

"She stretched them," Eric said. "My mother said she's positive they are bigger than they were."

"And Rupert," Miss Honey said, "I am glad to see you didn't lose any of your hair after last Thursday."

"My head was jolly sore afterwards," Rupert said.

"And you, Nigel," Miss Honey said, "do please try not to be smart-aleck with the Headmistress today. You were really quite cheeky to her last week."

"I hate her," Nigel said.

"Try not to make it so obvious," Miss Honey said. "It doesn't pay. She's a very strong woman. She has muscles like steel ropes."

"I wish I was grown up," Nigel said. "I'd knock her flat."

"I doubt you would," Miss Honey said. "No one has ever got the better of her yet."

"What will she be testing us on this afternoon?" a small girl asked.

"Almost certainly the three-times table," Miss Honey said. "That's what you are all meant to have learnt this past week. Make sure you know it."

Lunch came and went.

After lunch, the class reassembled. Miss Honey stood at one side of the room. They all sat silent, apprehensive, waiting. And then, like some giant of doom, the enormous Trunchbull strode into the room in her green breeches and cotton smock. She went straight to her jug of water and lifted it up by the handle and peered inside.

"I am glad to see", she said, "that there are no slimy creatures in my drinking-water this time. If there had been, then something exceptionally unpleasant would have happened to every single member of this class. And that includes you, Miss Honey."

The class remained silent and very tense. They had learnt a bit about this tigress by now and nobody was about to take any chances.

"Very well," boomed the Trunchbull. "Let us see how well you know your three-times table. Or to put it another way, let us see how badly Miss Honey has taught you the three-times table." The Trunchbull was standing in front of the class, legs apart, hands on hips, scowling at Miss Honey who stood silent to one side.

Matilda, sitting motionless at her desk in the

440

second row, was watching things very closely.

"You!" the Trunchbull shouted, pointing a finger the size of a rolling-pin at a boy called Wilfred. Wilfred was on the extreme right of the front row. "Stand up, you!" she shouted at him.

Wilfred stood up.

"Recite the three-times table backwards!" the Trunchbull barked.

"Backwards?" stammered Wilfred. "But I haven't learnt it backwards."

"There you are!" cried the Trunchbull, triumphant. "She's taught you nothing! Miss Honey, why have you taught them absolutely nothing at all in the last week?"

"That is not true, Headmistress," Miss Honey said. "They have all learnt their three-times table. But I see no point in teaching it to them backwards. There is little point in teaching anything backwards. The whole object of life, Headmistress, is to go forwards. I venture to ask whether even you, for example, can spell a simple word like *wrong* backwards straight away. I very much doubt it."

"Don't you get impertinent with me, Miss Honey!" the Trunchbull snapped, then she turned back to the unfortunate Wilfred. "Very well, boy," she said. "Answer me this. I have seven apples, seven oranges and seven bananas. How many pieces of fruit do I have altogether? Hurry up! Get on with it! Give me the answer!"

"That's *adding up*!" Wilfred cried. "That isn't the three-times table!"

"You blithering idiot!" shouted the Trunchbull.

"You festering gumboil! You fleabitten fungus! That *is* the three-times table! You have three separate lots of fruit and each lot has seven pieces. Three sevens are twenty-one. Can't you see that, you stagnant cesspool! I'll give you one more chance. I have eight coconuts, eight monkey-nuts and eight nutty little idiots like you. How many nuts do I have altogether? Answer me quickly."

Poor Wilfred was properly flustered. "Wait!" he cried. "Please wait! I've got to add up eight coconuts and eight monkey-nuts . . . " He started counting on his fingers.

"You bursting blister!" yelled the Trunchbull. "You moth-eaten maggot! This is *not* adding up! This is multiplication! The answer is three eights! Or is it eight threes? What is the difference between three eights and eight threes? Tell me that, you mangled little wurzel and look sharp about it!"

By now Wilfred was far too frightened and bewildered even to speak.

In two strides the Trunchbull was beside him, and by some amazing gymnastic trick, it may have been judo or karate, she flipped the back of Wilfred's legs with one of her feet so that the boy shot up off the ground and turned a somersault in the air. But halfway through the somersault she caught him by an ankle and held him dangling upside-down like a plucked chicken in a shop-window.

"Eight threes," the Trunchbull shouted, swinging Wilfred from side to side by his ankle, "eight

threes is the same as three eights and three eights
are twenty-four! Repeat that!"

At exactly that moment Nigel, at the other end
of the room, jumped to his feet and started pointing
excitedly at the blackboard and screaming, "The
chalk! The chalk! Look at the chalk! It's moving
all on its own!"

So hysterical and shrill was Nigel's scream that everyone in the place, including the Trunchbull, looked up at the blackboard. And there, sure enough, a brand-new piece of chalk was hovering near the grey-black writing surface of the blackboard.

"*It's writing something!*" screamed Nigel. "*The chalk is writing something!*"

And indeed it was.

"*What the blazes is this?*" yelled the Trunchbull. It had shaken her to see her own first name being written like that by an invisible hand. She dropped Wilfred on to the floor. Then she yelled at nobody in particular, "Who's *doing* this? Who's *writing* it?"

444

The chalk continued to write.

Agatha, this is Magnus
This is Magnus

Everyone in the place heard the gasp that came from the Trunchbull's throat. "No!" she cried, "It can't be! It can't be Magnus!"

It is Magnus
And you'd better
believe it

Miss Honey, at the side of the room glanced swiftly at Matilda. The child was sitting very straight at her desk, the head held high, the mouth compressed, the eyes glittering like two stars.

Agatha, give my Jenny back her house

For some reason everyone now looked at the Trunchbull. The woman's face had turned white as snow and her mouth was opening and shutting like a halibut out of water and giving out a series of strangled gasps.

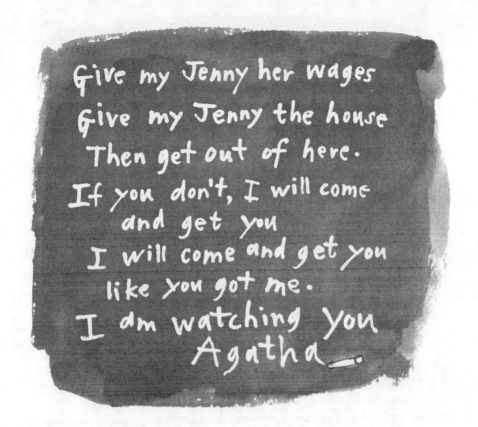

Give my Jenny her wages
Give my Jenny the house
Then get out of here.
If you don't, I will come
    and get you
I will come and get you
like you got me.
I am watching you
        Agatha

The chalk stopped writing. It hovered for a few moments, then suddenly it dropped to the floor with a tinkle and broke in two.

Wilfred, who had managed to resume his seat in the front row, screamed, "Miss Trunchbull has fallen down! Miss Trunchbull is on the floor!"

This was the most sensational bit of news of all and the entire class jumped up out of their seats to have a really good look. And there she was, the huge figure of the Headmistress, stretched full-length on her back across the floor, out for the count.

Miss Honey ran forward and knelt beside the prostrate giant. "She's fainted!" she cried. "She's out cold! Someone go and fetch the matron at once." Three children ran out of the room.

Nigel, always ready for action, leapt up and seized the big jug of water. "My father says cold water is the best way to wake up someone who's fainted," he said, and with that he tipped the entire contents of the jug over the Trunchbull's head. No one, not even Miss Honey, protested.

As for Matilda, she continued to sit motionless at her desk. She was feeling curiously elated. She felt as though she had touched something that was not quite of this world, the highest point of the heavens, the farthest star. She had felt most wonderfully the power surging up behind her eyes, gushing like a warm fluid inside her skull, and her eyes had become scorching hot, hotter than ever before, and things had come bursting out of her eye-sockets and then the piece of chalk had lifted itself up and had begun to write. It seemed as though she had hardly done anything, it had all been so simple.

The school matron, followed by five teachers, three women and two men, came rushing into the room.

"By golly, somebody's floored her at last!" cried one of the men, grinning. "Congratulations, Miss Honey!"

"Who threw the water over her?" asked the matron.

"I did," said Nigel proudly.

"Good for you," another teacher said. "Shall we get some more?"

"Stop that," the matron said. "We must carry her up to the sick-room."

It took all five teachers and the matron to lift the enormous woman and stagger with her out of the room.

Miss Honey said to the class, "I think you'd all better go out to the playground and amuse yourselves until the next lesson." Then she turned and walked over to the blackboard and carefully wiped out all the chalk writing.

The children began filing out of the classroom. Matilda started to go with them, but as she passed Miss Honey she paused and her twinkling eyes met the teacher's eyes and Miss Honey ran forward and gave the tiny child a great big hug and a kiss.

A New Home

Later that day, the news began to spread that the Headmistress had recovered from her fainting-fit and had then marched out of the school building tight-lipped and white in the face.

The next morning she did not turn up at school. At lunchtime, Mr Trilby, the Deputy Head, telephoned her house to enquire if she was feeling unwell. There was no answer to the phone.

When school was over, Mr Trilby decided to investigate further, so he walked to the house where Miss Trunchbull lived on the edge of the village, the lovely small red-brick Georgian building known as The Red House, tucked away in the woods behind the hills.

He rang the bell. No answer.

He knocked loudly. No answer.

He called out, "Is anybody at home?" No answer.

He tried the door and to his surprise found it unlocked. He went in.

The house was silent and there was no one in it, and yet all the furniture was still in place. Mr Trilby went upstairs to the main bedroom. Here also everything seemed to be normal until he started opening drawers and looking into cupboards. There were no clothes or underclothes or shoes anywhere. They had all gone.

451

She's done a bunk, Mr Trilby said to himself and he went away to inform the School Governors that the Headmistress had apparently vanished.

On the second morning, Miss Honey received by registered post a letter from a firm of local solicitors informing her that the last will and testament of her late father, Dr Honey, had suddenly and mysteriously turned up. This document revealed that ever since her father's death, Miss Honey had in fact been the rightful owner of a property on the edge of the village known as The Red House, which until recently had been occupied by a Miss Agatha Trunchbull. The will also showed that her father's lifetime savings, which fortunately were still safely in the bank, had also been left to her. The solicitor's letter added that if Miss Honey would kindly call in to the office as soon as possible, then the property and the money could be transferred into her name very rapidly.

Miss Honey did just that, and within a couple of weeks she had moved into The Red House, the very place in which she had been brought up and where luckily all the family furniture and pictures were still around. From then on, Matilda was a welcome visitor to The Red House every single evening after school, and a very close friendship began to develop between the teacher and the small child.

Back at school, great changes were also taking place. As soon as it became clear that Miss Trunchbull had completely disappeared from the scene, the excellent Mr Trilby was appointed Head Teacher in her place. And very soon after that,

Matilda was moved up into the top form where Miss Plimsoll quickly discovered that this amazing child was every bit as bright as Miss Honey had said.

One evening a few weeks later, Matilda was having tea with Miss Honey in the kitchen of The Red House after school as they always did, when Matilda said suddenly, "Something strange has happened to me, Miss Honey."

"Tell me about it," Miss Honey said.

"This morning," Matilda said, "just for fun I tried to push something over with my eyes and I couldn't do it. Nothing moved. I didn't even feel the hotness building up behind my eyeballs. The power had gone. I think I've lost it completely."

Miss Honey carefully buttered a slice of brown bread and put a little strawberry jam on it. "I've been expecting something like that to happen," she said.

"You have? Why?" Matilda asked.

"Well," Miss Honey said, "it's only a guess, but here's what I think. While you were in my class you had nothing to do, nothing to make you struggle. Your fairly enormous brain was going crazy with frustration. It was bubbling and boiling away like mad inside your head. There was tremendous energy bottled up in there with nowhere to go, and somehow or other you were able to shoot that energy out through your eyes and make objects move. But now things are different. You are in the top form competing against children more than twice your age and all that mental energy is being

used up in class. Your brain is for the first time having to struggle and strive and keep really busy, which is great. That's only a theory, mind you, and it may be a silly one, but I don't think it's far off the mark."

"I'm glad it's happened," Matilda said. "I wouldn't want to go through life as a miracle-worker."

"You've done enough," Miss Honey said. "I can still hardly believe you made all this happen for me."

Matilda, who was perched on a tall stool at the kitchen table, ate her bread and jam slowly. She did so love these afternoons with Miss Honey. She felt completely comfortable in her presence, and the two of them talked to each other more or less as equals.

"Did you know", Matilda said suddenly, "that the heart of a mouse beats at the rate of *six hundred and fifty times a second*?"

"I did not," Miss Honey said smiling. "How absolutely fascinating. Where did you read that?"

"In a book from the library," Matilda said. "And that means it goes so fast you can't even hear the separate beats. It must sound just like a buzz."

"It must," Miss Honey said.

"And how fast do you think a hedgehog's heart beats?" Matilda asked.

"Tell me," Miss Honey said, smiling again.

"It's not as fast as a mouse," Matilda said. "It's three hundred times a minute. But even so, you wouldn't have thought it went as fast as that in a creature that moves so slowly, would you, Miss Honey?"

"I certainly wouldn't," Miss Honey said. "Tell me one more."

"A horse," Matilda said. "That's really slow. It's only forty times a minute."

This child, Miss Honey told herself, seems to be interested in everything. When one is with her it is impossible to be bored. I love it.

The two of them stayed sitting and talking in the kitchen for an hour or so longer, and then, at about six o'clock, Matilda said goodnight and set out to walk home to her parent's house, which was about an eight-minute journey away. When she arrived at her own gate, she saw a large black

Mercedes motor-car parked outside. She didn't take too much notice of that. There were often strange cars parked outside her father's place. But when she entered the house, she was confronted by a scene of utter chaos. Her mother and father were both in the hall frantically stuffing clothing and various objects into suitcases.

"What on earth's going on?" she cried. "What's happening, daddy?"

"We're off," Mr Wormwood said, not looking up. "We're leaving for the airport in half an hour so you'd better get packed. Your brother's upstairs all ready to go. Get a move on, girl! Get going!"

"Off?" Matilda cried out. "Where to?"

"Spain," the father said. "It's a better climate than this lousy country."

"Spain!" Matilda cried. "I don't want to go to Spain! I love it here and I love my school!"

"Just do as you're told and stop arguing," the father snapped. "I've got enough troubles without messing about with you!"

"But daddy . . ." Matilda began.

"Shut up!" the father shouted. "We're leaving in thirty minutes! I'm not missing that plane!"

"But how long for, daddy?" Matilda cried. "When are we coming back?"

"We aren't," the father said. "Now beat it! I'm busy!"

Matilda turned away from him and walked out through the open front-door. As soon as she was on the road she began to run. She headed straight back towards Miss Honey's house and she reached it in less than four minutes. She flew up the drive and suddenly she saw Miss Honey in the front garden, standing in the middle of a bed of roses doing something with a pair of clippers. Miss Honey had heard the sound of Matilda's feet racing

over the gravel and now she straightened up and turned and stepped out of the rose-bed as the child came running up.

"My, my!" she said. "What in the world is the matter?"

Matilda stood before her, panting, out of breath, her small face flushed crimson all over.

"They're *leaving*!" she cried. "They've all gone mad and they're filling their suitcases and they're leaving for Spain in about thirty minutes!"

"Who is?" Miss Honey asked quietly.

"Mummy and daddy and my brother Mike and they say I've got to go with them!"

"You mean for a holiday?" Miss Honey asked.

"For *ever*!" Matilda cried. "Daddy said we were *never* coming back!"

There was a brief silence, then Miss Honey said, "Actually I'm not very surprised."

"You mean you *knew* they were going?" Matilda cried. "Why didn't you tell me?"

"No, darling," Miss Honey said. "I did not know they were going. But the news still doesn't surprise me."

"Why?" Matilda cried. "Please tell me why." She was still out of breath from the running and from the shock of it all.

"Because your father", Miss Honey said, "is in with a bunch of crooks. Everyone in the village knows that. My guess is that he is a receiver of stolen cars from all over the country. He's in it deep."

Matilda stared at her open-mouthed.

459

Miss Honey went on, "People brought stolen cars to your father's workshop where he changed the number-plates and resprayed the bodies a different colour and all the rest of it. And now somebody's probably tipped him off that the police are on to him and he's doing what they all do, running off to Spain where they can't get him. He'll have been sending his money out there for years, all ready and waiting for him to arrive."

They were standing on the lawn in front of the lovely red-brick house with its weathered old red tiles and its tall chimneys, and Miss Honey still had the pair of garden clippers in one hand. It was a warm golden evening and a blackbird was singing somewhere near by.

"I don't want to go with them!" Matilda shouted suddenly. "I won't go with them."

"I'm afraid you must," Miss Honey said.

"I want to live here with you," Matilda cried out. "Please let me live here with you!"

"I only wish you could," Miss Honey said. "But I'm afraid it's not possible. You cannot leave your parents just because you want to. They have a right to take you with them."

"But what if they agreed?" Matilda cried eagerly. "What if they said yes, I can stay with you? Would you let me stay with you then?"

Miss Honey said softly, "Yes, that would be heaven."

"Well, I think they might!" Matilda cried. "I honestly think they might! They don't actually care tuppence about me!"

"Not so fast," Miss Honey said.

"We've got to be fast!" Matilda cried. "They're leaving any moment! Come on!" she shouted, grasping Miss Honey's hand. "Please come with me and ask them! But we'll have to hurry! We'll have to run!"

The next moment the two of them were running down the drive together and then out on to the road, and Matilda was ahead, pulling Miss Honey after her by her wrist, and it was a wild and wonderful dash they made along the country lane and through the village to the house where Matilda's parents lived. The big black Mercedes was still outside and now its boot and all its doors were open and Mr and Mrs Wormwood and the brother were scurrying around it like ants, piling in the suitcases, as Matilda and Miss Honey came dashing up.

"Daddy and mummy!" Matilda burst out, gasping for breath. "I don't want to go with you! I want to stay here and live with Miss Honey and she says that I can but only if you give me permission! Please say yes! Go on, daddy, say yes! Say yes, mummy!"

The father turned and looked at Miss Honey. "You're that teacher woman who once came here

to see me, aren't you?" he said. Then he went back
to stowing the suitcases into the car.

His wife said to him, "This one'll have to go on
the back seat. There's no more room in the boot."

"I would love to have Matilda," Miss Honey
said. "I would look after her with loving care, Mr
Wormwood, and I would pay for everything. She
wouldn't cost you a penny. But it was not my idea.
It was Matilda's. And I will not agree to take her
without your full and willing consent."

"Come on, Harry," the mother said, pushing a
suitcase into the back seat. "Why don't we let her
go if that's what she wants. It'll be one less to look
after."

"I'm in a hurry," the father said. "I've got a plane

to catch. If she wants to stay, let her stay. It's fine
with me."

Matilda leapt into Miss Honey's arms and
hugged her, and Miss Honey hugged her back, and
then the mother and father and brother were inside
the car and the car was pulling away with the tyres
screaming. The brother gave a wave through the
rear window, but the other two didn't even look
back. Miss Honey was still hugging the tiny girl in
her arms and neither of them said a word as they
stood there watching the big black car tearing
round the corner at the end of the road and disappearing for ever into the distance.

Roald Dahl
GEORGE'S MARVELLOUS MEDICINE

Illustrated by Quentin Blake

This book is
for doctors everywhere

Contents

Grandma

"I'm going shopping in the village," George's mother said to George on Saturday morning. "So be a good boy and don't get up to mischief."

This was a silly thing to say to a small boy at any time. It immediately made him wonder what sort of mischief he might get up to.

"And don't forget to give Grandma her medicine at eleven o'clock," the mother said. Then out she went, closing the back door behind her.

Grandma, who was dozing in her chair by the window, opened one wicked little eye and said, "Now you heard what your mother said, George. Don't forget my medicine."

"No, Grandma," George said.

"And just try to behave yourself for once while she's away."

"Yes, Grandma," George said.

George was bored to tears. He didn't have a brother or a sister. His father was a farmer and the farm they lived on was miles away from anywhere, so there were never any children to play with. He was tired of staring at pigs and hens and cows and sheep. He was especially tired of having to live in the same house as that grizzly old grunion of a Grandma. Looking after her all by himself was hardly the most exciting way to spend a Saturday morning.

"You can make me a nice cup of tea for a start," Grandma said to George. "That'll keep you out of mischief for a few minutes."

"Yes, Grandma," George said.

George couldn't help disliking Grandma. She was a selfish grumpy old woman. She had pale brown teeth and a small puckered up mouth like a dog's bottom.

"How much sugar in your tea today, Grandma?" George asked her.

"One spoon,' she said. "And no milk."

Most grandmothers are lovely, kind, helpful old ladies, but not this one. She spent all day and every day sitting in her chair by the window, and she was always complaining, grousing, grouching, grumbling, griping about something or other. Never once, even on her best days, had she smiled at George and said, "Well, how are you this morning, George?" or "Why don't you and I have a game of Snakes and Ladders?" or "How was school today?" She didn't seem to care about other people, only about herself. She was a miserable old grouch.

George went into the kitchen and made Grandma a cup of tea with a teabag. He put one spoon of sugar in it and no milk. He stirred the sugar well and carried the cup into the living-room.

Grandma sipped the tea. "It's not sweet enough," she said. "Put more sugar in."

George took the cup back to the kitchen and added another spoonful of sugar. He stirred it again and carried it carefully in to Grandma.

"Where's the saucer?" she said. "I won't have a cup without a saucer."

George fetched her a saucer.

"And what about a teaspoon, if you please?"

"I've stirred it for you, Grandma. I stirred it well."

"I'll stir my own tea, thank you very much," she said. "Fetch me a teaspoon."

George fetched her a teaspoon.

When George's mother or father were home, Grandma never ordered George about like this. It was only when she had him on her own that she began treating him badly.

"You know what's the matter with you?" the old woman said, staring at George over the rim of the teacup with those bright wicked little eyes. "You're *growing* too fast. Boys who grow too fast become stupid and lazy."

"But I can't help it if I'm growing fast, Grandma," George said.

"Of course you can," she snapped. "Growing's a nasty childish habit."

"But we *have* to grow, Grandma. If we didn't grow, we'd never be grown-ups."

"Rubbish, boy, rubbish," she said. "Look at me. Am I growing? Certainly not."

"But you did once, Grandma."

"Only *very little*," the old woman answered. "I gave up growing when I was extremely small, along with all the other nasty childish habits like laziness and disobedience and greed and sloppiness and untidiness and stupidity. You haven't given up any of these things, have you?"

"I'm still only a little boy, Grandma."

"You're eight years old," she snorted. "That's old enough to know better. If you don't stop growing soon, it'll be too late."

"Too late for what, Grandma?"

"It's ridiculous," she went on. "You're nearly as tall as me already."

George took a good look a Grandma. She certainly was a *very tiny* person. Her legs were so short she had to have a footstool to put her feet on, and her head only came half-way up the back of the armchair.

"Daddy says it's fine for a man to be tall," George said.

"Don't listen to your daddy," Grandma said. "Listen to me."

"But how do I stop myself growing?" George asked her.

"Eat less chocolate," Grandma said.

"Does chocolate make you grow?"

"It makes you grow the *wrong way*," she snapped. "Up instead of down."

472

Grandma sipped some tea but never took her eyes from the little boy who stood before her. "Never grow up," she said. "Always down."

"Yes, Grandma."

"And stop eating chocolate. Eat cabbage instead."

"Cabbage! Oh no, I don't like cabbage," George said.

"It's not what you like or what you don't like," Grandma snapped. "It's what's good for you that counts. From now on, you must eat cabbage three times a day. Mountains of cabbage! And if it's got caterpillars in it, so much the better!"

"Owch," George said.

"Caterpillars give you brains," the old woman said.

"Mummy washes them down the sink," George said.

"Mummy's as stupid as you are," Grandma said.

"Cabbage doesn't taste of anything without a few boiled caterpillars in it. Slugs, too."

"Not *slugs*!" George cried out. "I couldn't eat slugs!"

"Whenever I see a live slug on a piece of lettuce," Grandma said, "I gobble it up quick before it crawls away. Delicious." She squeezed her lips together tight so that her mouth became a tiny wrinkled hole. "Delicious," she said again. "Worms and slugs and beetley bugs. You don't know what's good for you."

"You're joking, Grandma."

"I never joke," she said. "Beetles are perhaps best of all. They go *crunch*!"

"Grandma! That's beastly!"

The old hag grinned, showing those pale brown teeth. "Sometimes, if you're lucky," she said, "you get a beetle inside the stem of a stick of celery. That's what I like."

"Grandma! How *could* you?"

"You find all sorts of nice things in sticks of raw celery," the old woman went on. "Sometimes it's earwigs."

"I don't want to hear about it!" cried George.

"A big fat earwig is very tasty," Grandma said, licking her lips. "But you've got to be very quick, my dear, when you put one of those in your mouth. It has a pair of sharp nippers on its back end and if it grabs your tongue with those, it never lets go. So you've got to bite the earwig first, *chop chop*, before it bites you."

George started edging towards the door. He wanted to get as far away as possible from this filthy old woman.

"You're trying to get away from me, aren't you," she said, pointing a finger straight at George's face. "You're trying to get away from Grandma."

Little George stood by the door staring at the old hag in the chair. She stared back at him.

Could it be, George wondered, that she was a witch? He had always thought witches were only in fairy tales, but now he was not so sure.

"Come closer to me, little boy," she said, beckoning to him with a horny finger. "Come closer to me and I will tell you *secrets*."

George didn't move.

Grandma didn't move either.

"I know a great many secrets," she said, and suddenly she smiled. It was a thin icy smile, the kind a snake might make just before it bites you. "Come over here to Grandma and she'll whisper secrets to you."

George took a step backwards, edging closer to the door.

475

"You mustn't be frightened of your old Grandma," she said, smiling that icy smile.

George took another step backwards.

"Some of us," she said, and all at once she was leaning forward in her chair and whispering in a throaty sort of voice George had never heard her use before. "Some of us," she said, "have magic powers that can twist the creatures of this earth into wondrous shapes . . ."

A tingle of electricity flashed down the length of George's spine. He began to feel frightened.

"Some of us," the old woman went on, "have fire on our tongues and sparks in our bellies and wizardry in the tips of our fingers . . .

"Some of us know secrets that would make your hair stand up on end and your eyes pop out of their sockets . . ."

George wanted to run away, but his feet seemed stuck to the floor.

"We know how to make your nails drop off and teeth grow out of your fingers instead."

George began to tremble. It was her face that frightened him most of all, the frosty smile, the brilliant unblinking eyes.

"We know how to have you wake up in the morning with a long tail coming out from behind you."

"Grandma!" he cried out. "Stop!"

"We know secrets, my dear, about dark places where dark things live and squirm and slither all over each other . . ."

George made a dive for the door.

"It doesn't matter how far you run," he heard her saying, "you won't ever get away . . ."

George ran into the kitchen, slamming the door behind him.

The Marvellous Plan

George sat himself down at the table in the kitchen. He was shaking a little. Oh, how he hated Grandma! He really *hated* that horrid old witchy woman. And all of a sudden he had a tremendous urge to *do something* about her. Something *whopping*. Something *absolutely terrific*. A *real shocker*. A sort of explosion. He wanted to blow away the witchy smell that hung about her in the next room. He may have been only eight years old but he was a brave little boy. He was ready to take this old woman on.

"I'm not going to be frightened by *her*," he said softly to himself. But he *was* frightened. And that's why he wanted suddenly to explode her away.

Well . . . not quite away. But he did want to shake the old woman up a bit.

Very well, then. What should it be, this whopping terrific exploding shocker for Grandma?

He would have liked to put a firework banger under her chair but he didn't have one.

He would have liked to put a long green snake down the back of her dress but he didn't have a long green snake.

He would have liked to put six big black rats in the room with her and lock the door but he didn't have six big black rats.

As George sat there pondering this interesting problem, his eye fell upon the bottle of Grandma's brown medicine standing on the sideboard. Rotten stuff it seemed to be. Four times a day a large spoonful of it

was shovelled into her mouth and it didn't do her the slightest bit of good. She was always just as horrid after she'd had it as she'd been before. The whole point of medicine, surely, was to make a person better. If it didn't do that, then it was quite useless.

So-ho! thought George suddenly. *Ah-ha*! *Ho-hum*! I know exactly what I'll do. I shall make her a *new* medicine, one that is so strong and so fierce and so fantastic it will either cure her completely or blow off the top of her head. I'll make her a *magic medicine*, a medicine no doctor in the world has ever made before.

George looked at the kitchen clock. It said five past ten. There was nearly an hour left before Grandma's next dose was due at eleven.

"Here we go, then!" cried George, jumping up from the table. "A magic medicine it shall be!"

"So give me a bug and a jumping flea,
Give me two snails and lizards three,
And a slimy squiggler from the sea,
And the poisonous sting of a bumblebee,
And the juice from the fruit of the ju-jube tree,
And the powdered bone of a wombat's knee.
And one hundred other things as well
Each with a rather nasty smell.
I'll stir them up, I'll boil them long,
A mixture tough, a mixture strong.
And then, heigh-ho, and down it goes,
A nice big spoonful (hold your nose)
Just gulp it down and have no fear.
'How do you like it, Granny dear?'
Will she go pop? Will she explode?
Will she go flying down the road?

Will she go poof in a puff of smoke?
Start fizzing like a can of Coke?
Who knows? Not I. Let's wait and see.
(I'm glad it's neither you nor me.)
Oh Grandma, if you only knew
What I have got in store for you!''

George Begins to Make the Medicine

George took an enormous saucepan out of the cup-board and placed it on the kitchen table.

"George!" came the shrill voice from the next room. "What are you doing?"

"Nothing Grandma," he called out.

"You needn't think I can't hear you just because you closed the door! You're rattling the saucepans!"

"I'm just tidying the kitchen, Grandma."

Then there was silence.

George had absolutely no doubts whatsoever about how he was going to make his famous medicine. He wasn't going to fool about wondering whether to put in a little bit of this or a little bit of that. Quite simply, he was going to put in EVERYTHING he could find. There would be no messing about, no hesitating, no wondering whether a particular thing would knock the old girl sideways or not. The rule would be this: whatever he saw, if it was runny or powdery or gooey, in it went.

Nobody had ever made a medicine like that before. If it didn't actually cure Grandma, then it would anyway cause some exciting results. It would be worth watching.

George decided to work his way round the various rooms one at a time and see what they had to offer.

He would go first to the bathroom. There are always lots of funny things in the bathroom. So upstairs he went, carrying the enormous two-handled saucepan before him.

In the bathroom, he gazed longingly at the famous and dreaded medicine cupboard. But he didn't go near it. It was the only thing in the entire house he was forbidden to touch. He had made solemn promises to his parents about this and he wasn't going to break them. There were things in there, they had told him, that could actually kill a person, and although he was out to give Grandma a pretty fiery mouthful, he didn't really want a dead body on his hands. George put the saucepan on the floor and went to work.

Number one was a bottle labelled GOLDENGLOSS

483

HAIR SHAMPOO. He emptied it into the pan. "That ought to wash her tummy nice and clean," he said.

He took a full tube of TOOTHPASTE and squeezed out the whole lot of it in one long worm. "Maybe that will brighten up those horrid brown teeth of hers," he said.

There was an aerosol can of SUPERFOAM SHAVING SOAP belonging to his father. George loved playing

medicine from the sideboard. He took out the cork
and tipped it all down the sink. He then filled the
bottle with his own magic mixture by dipping a small
jug into the saucepan and using it as a pourer. He
replaced the cork.

Had it cooled down enough yet? Not quite. He held
the bottle under the cold tap for a couple of minutes.
The label came off in the wet but that didn't matter.
He dried the bottle with a dishcloth.

All was now ready!

This was it!

The great moment had arrived!

"Medicine time, Grandma!" he called out.

"I should hope so, too," came the grumpy reply.

The silver tablespoon in which the medicine was
always given lay ready on the kitchen sideboard.
George picked it up.

Holding the spoon in one hand and the bottle in the
other, he advanced into the living-room.

with aerosols. He pressed the button and kept his finger on it until there was nothing left. A wonderful mountain of white foam built up in the giant saucepan.

With his fingers, he scooped out the contents of a jar of VITAMIN ENRICHED FACE CREAM.

In went a small bottle of scarlet NAIL VARNISH. "If the toothpaste doesn't clean her teeth," George said, "then this will paint them as red as roses."

He found another jar of creamy stuff labelled HAIR REMOVER. SMEAR IT ON YOUR LEGS, it said, AND ALLOW TO REMAIN FOR FIVE MINUTES. George tipped it all into the saucepan.

There was a bottle with yellow stuff inside it called DISHWORTH'S FAMOUS DANDRUFF CURE. In it went.

There was something called BRILLIDENT FOR CLEANING FALSE TEETH. It was a white powder. In that went, too.

He found another aerosol can, NEVERMORE PONKING DEODRANT SPRAY, GUARANTEED, it said, TO KEEP AWAY UNPLEASANT BODY SMELLS FOR A WHOLE DAY. "She could use plenty of that," George said as he sprayed the entire canful into the saucepan.

LIQUID PARAFFIN, the next one was called. It was a big bottle. He hadn't the faintest idea what it did to you, but he poured it in anyway.

That, he thought, looking around him, was about all from the bathroom.

On his mother's dressing-table in the bedroom, George found yet another lovely aerosol can. It was called HELGA'S HAIRSET. HOLD TWELVE INCHES AWAY FROM THE HAIR AND SPRAY LIGHTLY. He squirted the whole lot into the saucepan. He *did* enjoy squirting these aerosols.

There was a bottle of perfume called FLOWERS OF TURNIPS. It smelled of old cheese. In it went.

And in, too, went a large round pox of POWDER. It was called PINK PLASTER. There was a powder-puff on top and he threw that in as well for luck.

He found a couple of LIPSTICKS. He pulled the greasy red things out of their little cases and added them to the mixture.

The bedroom had nothing more to offer, so George carried the enormous saucepan downstairs again and trotted into the laundry-room where the shelves were full of all kinds of household items.

The first one he took down was a large box of SUPER-WHITE FOR AUTOMATIC WASHING-MACHINES. DIRT, it said, WILL DISAPPEAR LIKE MAGIC. George didn't know whether Grandma was automatic or not, but she was certainly a dirty old woman. "So she'd better have it all," he said, tipping in the whole boxful.

Then there was a big tin of WAXWELL FLOOR POLISH.
IT REMOVES FILTH AND FOUL MESSES FROM YOUR FLOOR
AND LEAVES EVERYTHING SHINY BRIGHT, it said. George
scooped the orange-coloured waxy stuff out of the tin
and plonked it into the pan.

487

There was a round cardboard carton labelled FLEA POWDER FOR DOGS. KEEP WELL AWAY FROM THE DOG'S FOOD, it said, BECAUSE THIS POWDER, IF EATEN, WILL MAKE THE DOG EXPLODE. "Good," said George, pouring it all into the saucepan.

He found a box of CANARY SEED on the shelf. "Perhaps it'll make the old bird sing," he said, and in it went.

Next, George explored the box with shoe-cleaning materials – brushes and tins and dusters. Well now, he thought, Grandma's medicine is brown, so *my* medicine must also be brown or she'll smell a rat. The way to colour it, he decided, would be with BROWN SHOE POLISH. The large tin he chose was labelled DARK TAN. Splendid. He scooped it all out with an old spoon and plopped it into the pan. He would stir it up later.

On his way back to the kitchen, George saw a bottle

of GIN standing on the sideboard. Grandma was very fond of gin. She was allowed to have a small nip of it every evening. Now he would give her a treat. He would pour in the whole bottle. He did.

Back in the kitchen, George put the huge saucepan on the table and went over to the cupboard that served as a larder. The shelves were bulging with bottles and jars of every sort. He chose the following and emptied them one by one into the saucepan:

A TIN OF CURRY POWDER

A TIN OF MUSTARD POWDER

A BOTTLE OF "EXTRA HOT" CHILLI SAUCE

A TIN OF BLACK PEPPERCORNS

A BOTTLE OF HORSERADISH SAUCE

"There!" he said aloud. "That should do it!"

"George!" came the screechy voice from the next room. "Who are you talking to in there? What are you up to?"

"Nothing, Grandma, absolutely nothing," he called back.

"Is it time for my medicine yet?"

"No, Grandma, not for about half an hour."

"Well, just see you don't forget it."

"I won't, Grandma," George answered. "I promise I won't."

Animal Pills

At this point, George suddenly had an extra good wheeze. Although the medicine cupboard in the house was forbidden ground, what about the medicines his father kept on the shelf in the shed next to the hen-house? The animal medicines?

What about *those*?

Nobody had ever told him he mustn't touch *them*.

Let's face it, George said to himself, hairspray and shaving-cream and shoe polish are all very well and they will no doubt cause some splendid explosions inside the old geezer, but what the magic mixture now needs is a touch of the real stuff, real pills and real tonics, to give it punch and muscle.

George picked up the heavy three-quarters full saucepan and carried it out of the back door. He crossed the farmyard and headed straight for the shed alongside the henhouse. He knew his father wouldn't be there. He was out haymaking in one of the meadows.

George entered the dusty old shed and put the sauce-pan on the bench. Then he looked up at the medicine shelf. There were five big bottles there. Two were full of pills, two were full of runny stuff and one was full of powder.

"I'll use them all," George said. "Grandma needs them. Boy, does she need them!"

The first bottle he took down contained an orange-coloured powder. The label said, FOR CHICKENS WITH FOUL PEST, HEN GRIPE, SORE BEAKS, GAMMY LEGS,

COCKERELITIS, EGG TROUBLE, BROODINESS OR LOSS OF FEATHERS. MIX ONE SPOONFUL ONLY WITH EACH BUCKET OF FEED.

"Well," George said aloud to himself as he tipped in the whole bottleful, "the old bird won't be losing any feathers after she's had a dose of this."

The next bottle he took down had about five

hundred gigantic purple pills in it. FOR HORSES WITH HOARSE THROATS, it said on the label. THE HOARSE-THROATED HORSE SHOULD SUCK ONE PILL TWICE A DAY.

"Grandma may not have a hoarse throat," George said, "but she's certainly got a sharp tongue. Maybe they'll cure that instead." Into the saucepan went the five hundred gigantic purple pills.

Then there was a bottle of thick yellowish liquid. FOR COWS, BULLS AND BULLOCKS, the label said. WILL CURE COW POX, COW MANGE, CRUMPLED HORNS, BAD BREATH IN BULLS, EARACHE, TOOTHACHE, HEADACHE, HOOFACHE, TAILACHE AND SORE UDDERS.

"That grumpy old cow in the living-room has every one of those rotten illnesses," George said. "She'll need it all." With a slop and a gurgle, the yellow liquid splashed into the now nearly full saucepan.

The next bottle contained a brilliant red liquid. SHEEPDIP, it said on the label. FOR SHEEP WITH SHEEP ROT AND FOR GETTING RID OF TICKS AND FLEAS. MIX

ONE SPOONFUL IN ONE GALLON OF WATER AND SLOSH IT OVER THE SHEEP. CAUTION, DO NOT MAKE THE MIXTURE ANY STRONGER OR THE WOOL WILL FALL OUT AND THE ANIMAL WILL BE NAKED.

"By gum," said George, "how I'd love to walk in and slosh it all over old Grandma and watch the ticks and fleas go jumping off her. But I can't. I mustn't. So she'll have to drink it instead." He poured the bright red medicine into the saucepan.

The last bottle on the shelf was full of pale green pills. PIG PILLS, the label announced. FOR PIGS WITH PORK PRICKLES, TENDER TROTTERS, BRISTLE BLIGHT AND SWINE SICKNESS. GIVE ONE PILL PER DAY. IN SEVERE CASES TWO PILLS MAY BE GIVEN, BUT MORE THAN THAT WILL MAKE THE PIG ROCK AND ROLL.

"Just the stuff", said George, "for that miserable old pig back there in the house. She'll need a very big dose." He tipped all the green pills, hundreds and hundreds of them, into the saucepan.

There was an old stick lying on the bench that had been used for stirring paint. George picked it up and started to stir his marvellous concoction. The mixture was as thick as cream, and as he stirred and stirred, many wonderful colours rose up from the depths and blended together, pinks, blues, greens, yellows and browns.

George went on stirring until it was all well mixed, but even so there were still hundreds of pills lying on the bottom that hadn't melted. And there was his mother's splended powder-puff floating on the surface. "I shall have to boil it all up," George said. "One good quick boil on the stove is all it needs." And with that he staggered back towards the house with the enormous heavy saucepan.

On the way, he passed the garage, so he went in to
see if he could find any other interesting things. He
added the following:

Half a pint of ENGINE OIL — to keep Grandma's
engine going smoothly.

Some ANTI-FREEZE — to keep her radiator from freezing up in winter.

A handful of GREASE — to grease her creaking joints.

Then back to the kitchen.

The Cook-up

In the kitchen, George put the saucepan on the stove and turned up the gas flame underneath it as high as it would go.

"George!" came the awful voice from the next room. "It's time for my medicine!"

"Not yet, Grandma," George called back. "There's still twenty minutes before eleven o'clock."

"What mischief are you up to in there now?" Granny screeched. "I hear noises."

George thought it best not to answer this one. He found a long wooden spoon in a kitchen drawer and began stirring hard. The stuff in the pot got hotter and hotter.

Soon the marvellous mixture began to froth and foam. A rich blue smoke, the colour of peacocks, rose from the surface of the liquid, and a fiery fearsome smell filled the kitchen. It made George choke and splutter. It was a smell unlike any he had smelled before. It was a brutal and bewitching smell, spicy and staggering, fierce and frenzied, full of wizardry and

magic. Whenever he got a whiff of it up his nose, firecrackers went off in his skull and electric prickles ran along the backs of his legs. It was wonderful to stand there stirring this amazing mixture and to watch it smoking blue and bubbling and frothing and foaming as though it were alive. At one point, he could have sworn he saw bright sparks flashing in the swirling foam.

And suddenly, George found himself dancing around the steaming pot, chanting strange words that came into his head out of nowhere:

> "Fiery broth and witch's brew
> Foamy froth and riches blue
> Fume and spume and spoondrift spray
> Fizzle swizzle shout hooray
> Watch it sloshing, swashing, sploshing
> Hear it hissing, squishing, spissing
> Grandma better start to pray."

Brown Paint

George turned off the heat under the saucepan. He must leave plenty of time for it to cool down.

When all the steam and froth had gone away, he peered into the giant pan to see what colour the great medicine now was. It was a deep and brilliant blue.

"It needs more brown in it," George said. "It simply must be brown or she'll get suspicious."

George ran outside and dashed into his father's tool-shed where all the paints were kept. There was a row of cans on the shelf, all colours, black, green, red, pink, white and brown. He reached for the can of brown. The label said simply DARK BROWN GLOSS PAINT ONE QUART. He took a screwdriver and prised off the lid. The can was three-quarters full. He rushed it back to the kitchen. He poured the whole lot into the saucepan. The saucepan was now full to the brim. Very gently, George stirred the paint into the mixture with the long wooden spoon. Ah-ha! It was all turning brown! A lovely rich creamy brown!

"Where's that medicine of mine, boy?!" came the voice from the living-room. "You're forgetting me! You're doing it on purpose! I shall tell your mother!"

"I'm not forgetting you, Grandma," George called back. "I'm thinking of you all the time. But there are still ten minutes to go."

"You're a nasty little maggot!" the voice screeched back. "You're a lazy and disobedient little worm, and you're growing too fast."

George fetched the bottle of Grandma's real

Grandma Gets the Medicine

Grandma sat hunched in her chair by the window. The wicked little eyes followed George closely as he crossed the room towards her.

"You're late," she snapped.

"I don't think I am, Grandma."

"Don't interrupt me in the middle of a sentence!" she shouted.

"But you'd finished your sentence, Grandma."

"There you go again!" she cried. "Always interrupting and arguing. You really are a tiresome little boy. What's the time?"

"It's exactly eleven o'clock, Grandma."

"You're lying as usual. Stop talking so much and give me my medicine. Shake the bottle first. Then pour it into the spoon and make sure it's a whole spoonful."

"Are you going to gulp it all down in one go?" George asked her. "Or will you sip it?"

"What I do is none of your business," the old woman said. "Fill the spoon."

As George removed the cork and began very slowly to pour the thick brown stuff into the spoon, he couldn't help thinking back upon all the mad and marvellous things that had gone into the making of this crazy stuff – the shaving soap, the hair remover, the dandruff cure, the automatic washing-machine powder, the flea powder for dogs, the shoe polish, the black pepper, the horseradish sauce and all the rest of them, not to mention the powerful animal pills and powders and liquids . . . and the brown paint.

"Open your mouth wide, Grandma," he said, "and I'll pop it in."

The old hag opened her small wrinkled mouth, showing disgusting pale brown teeth.

"Here we go!" George cried out. "Swallow it down!" He pushed the spoon well into her mouth and tipped the mixture down her throat. Then he stepped back to watch the result.

It was worth watching.

Grandma yelled *"Oweeeee!"* and her whole body shot up *whoosh* into the air. It was exactly as though someone had pushed an electric wire through the underneath of her chair and switched on the current. Up she went like a jack-in-the-box . . . and she didn't come down . . . she stayed there . . . suspended in mid air . . . about two feet up . . . still in a sitting position . . . but rigid now . . . frozen . . . quivering . . . the eyes bulging . . . the hair standing straight up on end.

"Is something wrong, Grandma?" George asked her politely. "Are you all right?"

Suspended up there in space, the old girl was beyond speaking.

The shock that George's marvellous mixture had given her must have been tremendous.

You'd have thought she'd swallowed a red-hot poker the way she took off from that chair.

Then down she came again with a *plop*, back into her seat.

"Call the fire brigade!" she shouted suddenly. "My stomach's on fire!"

"It's just the medicine, Grandma," George said. "It's good strong stuff."

"Fire!" the old woman yelled. "Fire in the base-

ment! Get a bucket! Man the hoses! Do something quick!"

"Cool it, Grandma," George said. But he got a bit of a shock when he saw the smoke coming out of her mouth and out of her nostrils. Clouds of black smoke were coming out of her nose and blowing around the room.

"By golly, you really are on fire," George said.

"Of course I'm on fire!" she yelled. "I'll be burned

to a crisp! I'll be fried to a frizzle! I'll be boiled like a beetroot!"

George ran into the kitchen and came back with a jug of water. "Open your mouth, Grandma!" he cried. He could hardly see her for the smoke, but he managed to pour half a jugful down her throat. A sizzling sound, the kind you get if you hold a hot frying-pan under a cold tap, came up from deep down in Grandma's stomach. The old hag bucked and shied and snorted. She gasped and gurgled. Spouts of water came shooting out of her. And the smoke cleared away.

"The fire's out," George announced proudly. "You'll be all right now, Grandma."

"*All right?*" she yelled. "Who's *all right?* There's jacky-jumpers in my tummy! There's squigglers in my belly! There's bangers in my bottom!" She began bouncing up and down in the chair. Quite obviously she was not very comfortable.

"You'll find it's doing you a lot of good, that medicine, Grandma," George said.

"*Good?*" she screamed. "Doing me *good?* It's *killing* me!"

Then she began to bulge.

She was swelling!

She was puffing up all over!

Someone was pumping her up, that's how it looked!

Was she going to explode?

Her face was turning from purple to green!

But wait! She had a puncture somewhere! George could hear the hiss of escaping air. She stopped swelling. She was going down. She was slowly getting thinner again, shrinking back and back slowly to her shrivelly old self.

"How's things, Grandma?" George said.

No answer.

Then a funny thing happened. Grandma's body gave a sudden sharp twist and a sudden sharp jerk and she flipped herself clear out of the chair and landed neatly on her two feet on the carpet.

"That's terrific, Grandma!" George cried. "You haven't stood up like that for years! Look at you! You're standing up all on your own and you're not even using a stick!"

Grandma didn't even hear him. The frozen pop-eyed look was back with her again now. She was miles away in another world.

Marvellous medicine, George told himself. He found it fascinating to stand there watching what it was doing to the old hag. What next? he wondered.

He soon found it.

Suddenly she began to grow.

It was quite slow at first ... just a very gradual inching upwards ... up, up, up ... inch by inch ... getting taller and taller ... about an inch every few seconds ... and in the beginning George didn't notice it.

But when she had passed the five foot six mark and was going on up towards being six feet tall, George gave a jump and shouted, "Hey, Grandma! You're *growing*! You're *going up*! Hang on, Grandma! You'd better stop now or you'll be hitting the ceiling!"

But Grandma didn't stop.

It was a truly fantastic sight, this ancient scrawny old woman getting taller and taller, longer and longer, thinner and thinner, as though she were a piece of elastic being pulled upwards by invisible hands.

When the top of her head actually touched the ceiling, George thought she was bound to stop.

But she didn't.

There was a sort of scrunching noise, and bits of plaster and cement came raining down.

"Hadn't you better stop now, Grandma?" George said. "Daddy's just had this whole room repainted."

But there was no stopping her now.

Soon, her head and shoulders had completely disappeared through the ceiling and she was still going.

George dashed upstairs to his own bedroom and there she was coming up through the floor like a mushroom.

"Whoopee!" she shouted, finding her voice at last. "Hallelujah, here I come!"

"Steady on, Grandma," George said.

"With a heigh-nonny-no and up we go!" she shouted. "Just watch me grow!"

"This is *my* room," George said. "Look at the mess you're making."

"Terrific medicine!" she cried. "Give me some more!"

She's dotty as a doughnut, George thought.

"Come on, boy! Give me some more!" she yelled. "Dish it out! I'm slowing down!"

George was still clutching the medicine bottle in

one hand and the spoon in the other. Oh well, he thought, why not? He poured out a second dose and popped it into her mouth.

"*Oweee!*" she screamed and up she went again. Her feet were still on the floor downstairs in the living-room but her head was moving quickly towards the ceiling of the bedroom.

"I'm on my way now, boy!" she called down to George. "Just watch me go!"

"That's the attic above you, Grandma!" George called out. "I'd keep out of there! It's full of bugs and bogles!"

Crash! The old girl's head went through the ceiling as though it were butter.

George stood in his bedroom gazing at the shambles. There was a big hole in the floor and another in the ceiling, and sticking up like a post between the two was the middle part of Grandma. Her legs were in the room below, her head in the attic.

"I'm still going!" came the old screechy voice from up above. "Give me another dose, my boy, and let's go through the roof!"

"No, Grandma, no!" George called back. "You're busting up the whole house!"

"To heck with the house!" she shouted. "I want some fresh air! I haven't been outside for twenty years!"

"By golly, she *is* going through the roof!" George told himself. He ran downstairs. He rushed out of the back door into the yard. It would be simply awful, he thought, if she bashed up the roof as well. His father would be furious. And he, George, would get the blame. *He* had made the medicine. *He* had given her too much. "Don't come through the roof, Grandma," he prayed. "Please don't."

The Brown Hen

George stood in the farmyard looking up at the roof. The old farmhouse had a fine roof of pale red tiles and tall chimneys.

There was no sign of Grandma. There was only a song-thrush sitting on one of the chimney-pots, singing a song. The old wurzel's got stuck in the attic, George thought. Thank goodness for that.

Suddenly a tile came clattering down from the roof and fell into the yard. The song-thrush took off fast and flew away.

Then another tile came down.

Then half a dozen more.

And then, very slowly, like some weird monster rising up from the deep, Grandma's head came through the roof . . .

Then her scrawny neck . . .

And the tops of her shoulders . . .

"How'm I doing, boy!" she shouted. "How's that for a bash up?"

"Don't you think you'd better stop now, Grandma?" George called out . . .

"I have stopped!" she answered. "I feel terrific! Didn't I tell you I had magic powers! Didn't I warn you I had wizardry in the tips of my fingers! But you wouldn't listen to me, would you? You wouldn't listen to your old Grandma!"

"*You* didn't do it, Grandma," George shouted back to her. "*I* did it! I made you a new medicine!"

"A *new medicine*? *You*? What rubbish!" she yelled.

"I did! I did!" George shouted.

"You're lying as usual!" Grandma yelled. "You're always lying!"

"I'm not lying, Grandma. I swear I'm not."

The wrinkled old face high up on the roof stared down suspiciously at George. "Are you telling me you actually made a new medicine all by yourself?" she shouted.

"Yes, Grandma, all by myself."

"I don't believe you," she answered. "But I'm very comfortable up here. Fetch me a cup of tea."

A brown hen was pecking about in the yard close to where George was standing. The hen gave him an idea. Quickly, he uncorked the medicine bottle and poured some of the brown stuff into the spoon. "Watch this, Grandma!" he shouted. He crouched down, holding out the spoon to the hen.

"Chicken," he said. "Chick-chick-chicken. Come here. Have some of this."

Chickens are stupid birds, and very greedy. They think everything is food. This one thought the spoon was full of corn. It hopped over. It put its head on one side and looked at the spoon. "Come on, chicken," George said. "Good chicken. Chick-chick-chick."

The brown hen stretched out its neck towards the spoon and went *peck*. It got a beakful of medicine.

The effect was electric.

511

"*Oweee!*" shrieked the hen and it shot straight up into the air like a rocket. It went as high as the house.

Then down it came again into the yard, *splosh*. And there it sat with its feathers all sticking straight out from its body. There was a look of amazement on its silly face. George stood watching it. Grandma up on the roof was watching it, too.

The hen got to its feet. It was rather shaky. It was making funny gurgling noises in its throat. Its beak was opening and shutting. It seemed like a pretty sick hen.

"You've done it in, you stupid boy!" Grandma shouted. "That hen's going to die! Your father'll be after you now! He'll give you socks and serve you right!"

All of a sudden, black smoke started pouring out of the hen's beak.

"It's on fire!" Grandma yelled. "The hen's on fire!"

George ran to the water-trough to get a bucket of water.

"That hen'll be roasted and ready for eating any moment!" Grandma shouted.

George sloshed the bucket of water over the hen. There was a sizzling sound and the smoke went away.

"Old hen's laid its last egg!" Grandma shouted. "Hens don't do any laying after they've been on fire!"

Now that the fire was out, the hen seemed better. It stood up properly. It flapped its wings. Then it crouched down low to the ground, as though getting ready to jump. It did jump. It jumped high in the air and turned a complete somersault, then landed back on its feet.

"It's a circus hen!" Grandma shouted from the rooftop. "It's a flipping acrobat!"

Now the hen began to grow.

George had been waiting for this to happen. "It's growing!" he yelled. "It's growing, Grandma! Look, it's growing!"

Bigger and bigger . . . taller and taller it grew. Soon the hen was four or five times its normal size.

"Can you see it, Grandma?!" George shouted.

"I can see it, boy!" the old girl shouted back. "I'm watching it!"

George was hopping about from one foot to the other with excitement, pointing at the enormous hen and shouting, "It's had the magic medicine, Grandma, and it's growing just like you did!"

But there was a difference between the way the hen was growing and the way Grandma grew. When Grandma grew taller and taller, she got thinner and thinner. The hen didn't. It stayed nice and plump all along.

Soon it was taller than George, but it didn't stop there. It went right on growing until it was about as big as a horse. Then it stopped.

"Doesn't it look marvellous, Grandma!" George shouted.

"It's not as tall as me!" Grandma sang out. "Compared with me, that hen is titchy small! I am the tallest of them all!"

515

The Pig, the Bullocks, the Sheep, the Pony and the Nanny-goat

At that moment, George's mother came back from shopping in the village. She drove her car into the yard and got out. She was carrying a bottle of milk in one hand and a bag of groceries in the other.

The first thing she saw was the gigantic brown hen towering over little George. She dropped the bottle of milk.

Then Grandma started shouting at her from the rooftop, and when she looked up and saw Grandma's head sticking up through the tiles, she dropped the bag of groceries.

"How about that then, eh Mary?" Grandma shouted. "I'll bet you've never seen a hen as big as that! That's George's giant hen, that is!"

"But ... but ... but ..." stammered George's mother.

"It's George's magic medicine!" Grandma shouted. "We've both of us had it, the hen and I!"

"But how in the world did you get up on the roof?" cried the mother.

"I didn't!" cackled the old woman. "My feet are still standing on the floor in the living-room!"

This was too much for George's mother to understand. She just goggled and gaped. She looked as though she was going to faint.

A second later, George's father appeared. His name

was Mr Killy Kranky. Mr Kranky was a small man with bandy legs and a huge head. He was a kind father to George, but he was not an easy person to live with because even the smallest things got him all worked up and excited. The hen standing in the yard was certainly not a small thing, and when Mr Kranky saw it he started jumping about as though something was burning his feet. "Great heavens!" he cried, waving his arms. "What's this? What's happened? Where did it come from? It's a giant hen! Who did it?"

"I did," George said.

"Look at *me*!" Grandma shouted from the rooftop. "Never mind about the hen! What about *me*!"

Mr Kranky looked up and saw Grandma. "Shut up, Grandma," he said. It didn't seem to surprise him that the old girl was sticking up through the roof. It was the hen that excited him. He had never seen anything like it. But then who had?

"It's fantastic!" Mr Kranky shouted, dancing round and round. "It's colossal! It's gigantic! It's tremendous! It's a miracle! How did you do it, George?"

George started telling his father about the magic medicine. While he was doing this, the big brown hen sat down in the middle of the yard and went *cluck-cluck-cluck . . . cluck-cluck-cluck-cluck-cluck*.

Everyone stared at it.

When it stood up again, there was a brown egg lying there. The egg was the size of a football.

"That egg would make scrambled eggs for twenty people!" Mrs Kranky said.

"George!" Mr Kranky shouted. "How much of this medicine have you got?"

"Lots," George said. "There's a big saucepanful in the kitchen, and this bottle here's nearly full."

"Come with me!" Mr Kranky yelled, grabbing George by the arm. "Bring the medicine! For years and years I've been trying to breed bigger and bigger animals. Bigger bulls for beef. Bigger pigs for pork. Bigger sheep for mutton . . ."

They went to the pigsty first.

George gave a spoonful of medicine to the pig.

The pig blew smoke from its nose and jumped about all over the place. Then it grew and grew.

In the end, it looked like this . . .

They went to the herd of fine black bullocks that
Mr Kranky was trying to fatten for the market.

George gave each of them some medicine, and this is what happened.

Then the sheep . . .

He gave some to his grey pony, Jack Frost . . .

And finally, just for fun, he gave some to Alma, the nanny-goat . . .

A Crane for Grandma

Grandma, from high up on the rooftop, could see every-thing that was going on and she didn't like what she saw. She wanted to be the centre of attention and nobody was taking the slightest notice of her. George and Mr Kranky were running round and getting excited about the enormous animals. Mrs Kranky was washing up in the kitchen, and Grandma was all alone on the rooftop.

"Hey you!" she yelled. "George! Get me a cup of tea this minute, you idle little beast!"

"Don't listen to the old goat," Mr Kranky said. "She's stuck where she is and a good thing, too."

"But we can't leave her up there, dad," George said. "What if it rains?"

"George!" Grandma yelled. "Oh, you horrible little boy! You disgusting little worm! Fetch me a cup of tea at once and a slice of currant cake!"

"We'll have to get her out, dad," George said. "She won't give us any peace if we don't."

Mrs Kranky came outside and she agreed with George. "She's my own mother," she said.

"She's a pain in the neck," Mr Kranky said.

"I don't care," Mrs Kranky said. "I'm not leaving my own mother sticking up through the roof for the rest of her life."

So in the end, Mr Kranky telephoned the Crane Company and asked them to send their biggest crane out to the house at once.

The crane arrived one hour later. It was on wheels

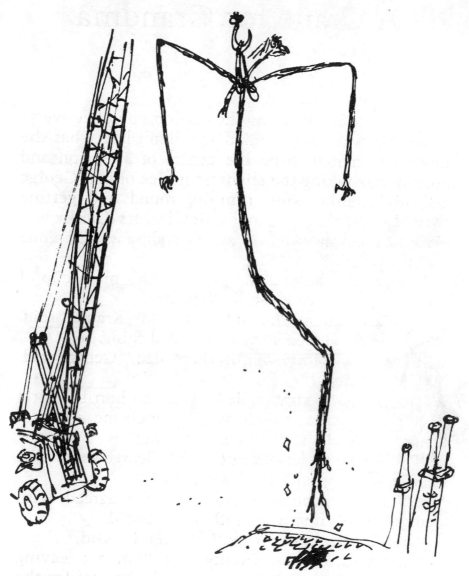

and there were two men inside it. The crane men climbed up on to the roof and put ropes under Grand-ma's arms. Then she was lifted right up through the roof . . .

In a way, the medicine had done Grandma good. It had not made her any less grumpy or bad-

tempered, but it seemed to have cured all her aches and pains, and she was suddenly as frisky as a ferret. As soon as the crane had lowered her to the ground, she ran over to George's huge pony, Jack Frost, and jumped on to his back. This ancient old hag, who was

528

now as tall as a house, then galloped about the farm
on the gigantic pony, jumping over trees and sheds
and shouting, "Out of my way! Clear the decks! Stand
back all you miserable midgets or I'll trample you to
death!" and other silly things like that.

But because Grandma was now much too tall to get back into the house, she had to sleep that night in the hay-barn with the mice and the rats.

Mr Kranky's Great Idea

The next day, George's father came down to breakfast in a state of greater excitement than ever. "I've been awake all night thinking about it!" he cried.

"About what, dad?" George asked him.

"About your marvellous medicine, of course! We can't stop now, my boy! We must start making more of it at once! More and more and more!"

The giant saucepan had been completely emptied the day before because there had been so many sheep and pigs and cows and bullocks to be dosed.

"But why do we need more, dad?" George asked. "We've done all our own animals and we've made Grandma feel as frisky as a ferret even though she does have to sleep in the barn."

"My dear boy," cried Mr Killy Kranky, "we need barrels and barrels of it! Tons and tons! Then we will sell it to every farmer in the world so that all of them can have giant animals! We will build a Marvellous Medicine Factory and sell the stuff in bottles at five pounds a time. We will become rich and you will become famous!"

"But wait a minute, dad," George said.

"There's no waiting!" cried Mr Kranky, working himself up so much that he put butter in his coffee and milk on his toast. "Don't you understand what this tremendous invention of yours is going to do to the world! Nobody will ever go hungry again!"

"Why won't they?" asked George.

"Because one giant cow will give fifty buckets of

milk a day!" cried Mr Kranky, waving his arms. "One giant chicken will make a hundred fried chicken dinners, and one giant pig will give you a thousand pork chops! It's tremendous, my dear boy! It's fantastic! It'll change the world."

"But wait a minute, dad," George said again.

"Don't keep saying wait a minute!" shouted Mr Kranky. "There isn't a minute to *wait*! We must get cracking at once!"

"Do calm down, my dear," Mrs Kranky said from the other end of the table. "And stop putting marmalade on your cornflakes."

"The heck with my cornflakes!" cried Mr Kranky, leaping up from his chair. "Come on, George! Let's get going! And the first thing we'll do is to make one more saucepanful as a tester."

"But dad," said little George. "The trouble is . . ."

"There won't be any trouble, my boy!" cried Mr Kranky. "How can there possibly be any trouble? All you've got to do is put the same stuff into the saucepan as you did yesterday. And while you're doing it, I'll write down each and every item. That's how we'll get the magic recipe!"

"But dad," George said. "Please listen to me."

"Why don't you listen to him," Mrs Kranky said. "The boy's trying to tell you something."

But Mr Kranky was too excited to listen to anyone except himself. "And then," he cried, "when the new mixture is ready, we'll test it out on an old hen just to make absolutely sure we've got it right, and after that we'll all shout hooray and build the giant factory!"

"But dad . . ."

"Come on then, what is it you want to say?"

"I can't possibly remember all the hundreds of things I put into the saucepan to make the medicine," George said.

"Of course you can, my dear boy," cried Mr Kranky. "I'll help you! I'll jog your memory! You'll get it in the end, you see if you don't! Now then, what was the very first thing you put in?"

"I went up to the bathroom first," George said. "I used a lot of things in the bathroom and on mummy's dressing-table."

"Come on, then!" cried Mr Killy Kranky. "Up we go to the bathroom!"

When they got there, they found, of course, a whole lot of empty tubes and empty aerosols and empty bottles. "That's great," said Mr Kranky. "That tells us exactly what you used. If anything is empty, it means you used it."

533

So Mr Kranky started making a list of everything
that was empty in the bathroom. Then they went to
Mrs Kranky's dressing-table. "A box of powder," said
Mr Kranky, writing it down. "Helga's Hairset. Flowers
of Turnips perfume. Terrific. This is going to be easy.
Where did you go next?"

"To the laundry-room," George said. "But are you
sure you haven't missed anything out up here, dad?"

"That's up to you, my boy," Mr Kranky said.
"Have I?"

"I don't think so," George said. So down they went
to the laundry-room and once again Mr Kranky wrote
down the names of all the empty bottles and cans.

"My goodness me, what a mass of stuff you used!"
he cried. "No wonder it did magic things! Is that
the lot?"

"No, dad, it's not," George said, and he led his father out to the shed where the animal medicines were kept and showed him the five big empty bottles up on the shelf. Mr Kranky wrote down all their names.

"Anything else?" Mr Kranky asked.

Little George scratched his head and thought and thought but he couldn't remember having put anything else in.

Mr Killy Kranky leapt into his car and drove down to the village and bought new bottles and tubes and cans of everything on his list. He then went to the vet and got a fresh supply of all the animal medicines George had used.

"Now show me how you did it, George," he said. "Come along. Show me exactly how you mixed them all together."

Marvellous Medicine
Number Two

They were in the kitchen now and the big saucepan was on the stove. All the things Mr Kranky had bought were lined up near the sink.

"Come along, my boy!" cried Mr Killy Kranky. "Which one did you put in first?"

"This one," George said. "Goldengloss Hair Shampoo." He emptied the bottle into the pan.

"Now the toothpaste," George went on . . . "And the shaving soap . . . and the face cream . . . and the nail varnish . . ."

"Keep at it, my boy!" cried Mr Kranky, dancing round the kitchen. "Keep putting them in! Don't stop! Don't pause! Don't hesitate! It's a pleasure, my dear fellow, to watch you work!"

One by one, George poured and squeezed the things into the saucepan. With everything so close at hand, the whole job didn't take him more than ten minutes. But when it was all done, the saucepan didn't somehow seem to be quite as full as it had been the first time.

"*Now* what did you do?" cried Mr Kranky. "Did you stir it?"

"I boiled it," George said. "But not for long. And I stirred it as well."

So Mr Kranky lit the gas under the saucepan and George stirred the mixture with the same long wooden spoon he had used before. "It's not brown enough," George said. "Wait a minute! I know what I've forgotten!"

"What?" cried Mr Kranky. "Tell me, quick! Because if we've forgotten even one tiny thing, then it won't work! At least not in the same way."

"A quart of brown gloss paint," George said. "That's what I've forgotten."

Mr Killy Kranky shot out of the house and into his car like a rocket. He sped down to the village and bought the paint and rushed back again. He opened the can in the kitchen and handed it to George. George poured the paint into the saucepan.

"Ah-ha, that's better," George said. "That's more like the right colour."

"It's boiling!" cried Mr Kranky. "It's boiling and bubbling, George! Is it ready yet?"

"It's ready," George said. "At least I hope it is."

"Right!" shouted Mr Kranky, hopping out. "Let's test it! Let's give some to a chicken!"

"My heavens alive, why don't you calm down a bit?" Mrs Kranky said, coming into the kitchen.

"*Calm down?*" cried Mr Kranky. "You expect me to *calm down* and here we are mixing up the greatest medicine ever discovered in the history of the world! Come along, George! Dip a cupful out of the saucepan and get a spoon and we'll give some to a chicken just to make absolutely certain we've got the correct mixture."

Outside in the yard, there were several chickens that hadn't had any of George's Marvellous Medicine Number One. They were pecking about in the dirt in that silly way chickens do.

George crouched down, holding out a spoonful of Marvellous Medicine Number Two.

"Come on, chicken," he said. "Good chicken. Chick-chick-chick."

A white chicken with black specks on its feathers looked up at George. It walked over to the spoon and went *peck*.

The effect that Medicine Number Two had on this chicken was not quite the same as the effect produced by Medicine Number One, but it was very interesting. *"Whooosh!"* shrieked the chicken and it shot six feet up in the air and came down again. Then *sparks* came flying out of its beak, bright yellow sparks of fire, as though someone was sharpening a knife on a grindstone inside its tummy. Then its legs began to grow longer. Its body stayed the same size but the two thin yellow legs got longer and longer and longer . . . and longer still . . .

"What's happening to it?" cried Mr Killy Kranky.

"Something's wrong," George said.

The legs went on growing and the more they grew, the higher up into the air went the chicken's body. When the legs were about fifteen feet long, they stopped growing. The chicken looked perfectly absurd with its long long legs and its ordinary little body perched high up on top. It was like a chicken on stilts.

"Oh my sainted aunts!" cried Mr Killy Kranky. "We've got it wrong! This chicken's no good to anybody! It's all legs! No one wants chicken's legs!"

"I must have left something out," George said.

"I *know* you left something out!" cried Mr Kranky. "Think, boy, think! What was it you left out?"

"I've got it!" said George.

"What was it, quick?"

"Flea powder for dogs," George said.

"You mean you put *flea* powder in the first one?"

"Yes, dad, I did. A whole carton of it."

"Then that's the answer!"

"Wait a minute," said George. "Did we have brown shoe polish on our list?"

"We did not," said Mr Kranky.

"I used that, too," said George.

"Well, no *wonder* it went wrong," said Mr Kranky. He was already running to his car, and soon he was heading down the village to buy more flea powder and more shoe polish.

Marvellous Medicine
Number Three

"Here it is!" cried Mr Killy Kranky, rushing into the kitchen. "One carton of flea powder for dogs and one tin of brown shoe polish!"

George poured the flea powder into the giant saucepan. Then he scooped the shoe polish out of its tin and added that as well.

"Stir it up, George!" shouted Mr Kranky. "Give it another boil! We've got it this time! I'll bet we've got it!"

After Marvellous Medicine Number Three had been boiled and stirred, George took a cupful of it out into the yard to try it on another chicken. Mr Kranky ran after him, flapping his arms and hopping with excitement. "Come and watch this one!" he called out to Mrs Kranky. "Come and watch us turning an ordinary chicken into a lovely great big one that lays eggs as large as footballs!"

"I hope you do better than last time," said Mrs Kranky, following them out.

"Come on, chicken," said George, holding out a spoonful of Medicine Number Three. "Good chicken. Chick-chick-chick-chick-chick. Have some of this lovely medicine."

A magnificent black cockerel with a scarlet comb came stepping over. The cockerel looked at the spoon and it went *peck*.

"*Cock-a-doodle-do!*" squawked the cockerel, shooting up into the air and coming down again.

"Watch him now!" cried Mr Kranky. "Watch him

grow! Any moment he's going to start getting bigger and bigger!"

Mr Killy Kranky, Mrs Kranky and little George stood in the yard staring at the black cockerel. The cockerel stood quite still. It looked as though it had a headache.

"What's happening to its neck?" Mrs Kranky said.
"It's getting longer," George said.
"I'll say it's getting longer," Mrs Kranky said.
Mr Kranky, for once, said nothing.

"Last time it was the legs," Mrs Kranky said. "Now it's the neck. Who wants a chicken with a long neck? You can't eat a chicken's neck."

It was an extraordinary sight. The cockerel's body hadn't grown at all. But the neck was now about six feet long.

"All right, George," Mr Kranky said. "What else have you forgotten?"

"I don't know," George said.

"Oh yes you do," Mr Kranky said. "Come along, boy, *think*. There's probably just one vital thing missing and you've got to remember it."

"I put in some engine oil from the garage," George said. "Did you have that on your list?"

"Eureka!" cried Mr Kranky. "That's the answer! How much did you put in?"

"Half a pint," George said.

Mr Kranky ran to the garage and found another half pint of oil. "And some anti-freeze," George called after him. "I sloshed in a bit of anti-freeze."

Marvellous Medicine
Number Four

Back in the kitchen once again, George, with Mr Kranky watching him anxiously, tipped half a pint of engine oil and some anti-freeze into the giant saucepan.

"Boil it up again!" cried Mr Kranky. "Boil it and stir it!"

George boiled it and stirred it.

"You'll never get it right," said Mrs Kranky. "Don't forget you don't just have to have the same things but you've got to have exactly the same *amounts* of those things. And how can you possibly do that?"

"You keep out of this!" cried Mr Kranky. "We're doing fine! We've got it this time, you see if we haven't!"

This was George's Marvellous Medicine Number Four, and when it had boiled for a couple of minutes, George once again carried a cupful of it out into the yard. Mr Kranky ran after him. Mrs Kranky followed more slowly. "You're going to have some mighty queer chickens around here if you go on like this," she said.

"Dish it out, George!" cried Mr Kranky. "Give a spoonful to that one over there!" He pointed to a brown hen.

George knelt down and held out the spoon with the new medicine in it. "Chick-chick," he said. "Try some of this."

The brown hen walked over and looked at the spoon. Then it went *peck*.

"*Owch!*" it said. Then a funny whistling noise came out of its beak.

"Watch it grow!" shouted Mr Kranky.

"Don't be too sure," said Mrs Kranky. "Why is it whistling like that?"

"Keep quiet, woman!" cried Mr Kranky. "Give it a chance!"

They stood there staring at the brown hen.

"It's getting smaller," George said. "Look at it, dad. It's shrinking."

And indeed it was. In less than a minute, the hen had shrunk so much it was no bigger than a new-hatched chick. It looked ridiculous.

Goodbye Grandma

"There's still something you've left out," Mr Kranky said.

"I can't think what it could be," George said.

"Give it up," Mrs Kranky said. "Pack it in. You'll never get it right."

Mr Kranky looked very forlorn.

George looked pretty fed up, too. He was still kneeling on the ground with the spoon in one hand and the cup full of medicine in the other. The ridiculous tiny brown hen was walking slowly away.

At that point, Grandma came striding into the yard. From her enormous height, she glared down at the three people below her and she shouted, "What's going on around here? Why hasn't anyone brought me my morning cup of tea? It's bad enough having to sleep in the yard with the rats and mice but I'll be blowed if I'm going to starve as well! No tea! No eggs and bacon! No buttered toast!"

"I'm sorry, mother," Mrs Kranky said. "We've been terribly busy. I'll get you something right away."

"Let George get it, the lazy little brute!" Grandma shouted.

Just then, the old woman spotted the cup in George's hand. She bent down and peered into it. She saw that it was full of brown liquid. It looked very much like tea. "Ho-ho!" she cried. "Ha-ha! So that's your little game, is it! You look after yourself all right, don't you! You make quite sure *you've* got a nice cup of morning tea! But you didn't think to bring one to your poor old Grandma! I always knew you were a selfish pig!"

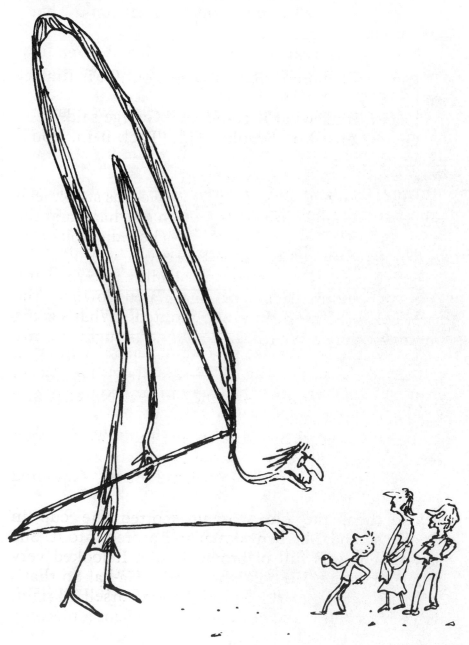

"No, Grandma," George said. "This isn't . . ."

"Don't lie to me, boy!" the enormous old hag shouted. "Pass it up here this minute!"

"No!" cried Mrs Kranky. "No, mother, don't! That's not for you!"

"Now *you're* against me, too!" shouted Grandma. "My own daughter trying to stop me having my breakfast! Trying to starve me out!"

Mr Kranky looked up at the horrid old woman and he smiled sweetly. "Of course it's for you, Grandma," he said. "You take it and drink it while it's nice and hot."

"Don't think I won't," Grandma said, bending down from her great height and reaching out a huge horny hand for the cup. "Hand it over, George."

"No, no, Grandma!" George cried out, pulling the cup away. "You mustn't! You're not to have it!"

"Give it to me, boy!" yelled Grandma.

"Don't!" cried Mrs Kranky. "That's George's Marvellous . . ."

"Everything's George's round here!" shouted Grandma. "George's this, George's that! I'm fed up with it!" She snatched the cup out of little George's hand and carried it high up out of reach.

"Drink it up, Grandma," Mr Kranky said, grinning hugely. "Lovely tea."

"No!" the other two cried. "No, no, no!"

But it was too late. The ancient beanpole had already put the cup to her lips, and in one gulp she swallowed everything that was in it.

"Mother!" wailed Mrs Kranky. "You've just drunk fifty doses of George's Marvellous Medicine Number Four and look what one tiny spoonful did to that little old brown hen!"

But Grandma didn't even hear her. Great clouds of
steam were already pouring out of her mouth and she
was beginning to whistle.

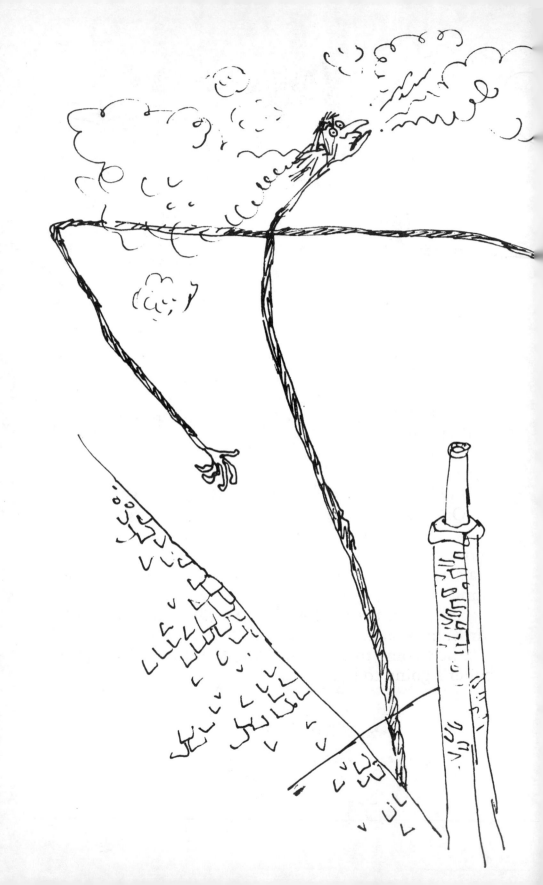

"This is going to be interesting," Mr Kranky said, still grinning.

"Now you've done it!" cried Mrs Kranky, glaring at her husband. "You've cooked the old girl's goose!"

"I didn't do anything," Mr Kranky said.

"Oh, yes you did! You told her to drink it!"

A tremendous hissing sound was coming from above their heads. Steam was shooting out of Grandma's mouth and nose and ears and whistling as it came.

"She'll feel better after she's let off a bit of steam," Mr Kranky said.

"She's going to blow up!" Mrs Kranky wailed. "Her boiler's going to burst!"

"Stand clear," Mr Kranky said.

George was quite alarmed. He stood up and ran back a few paces. The jets of white steam kept squirting out of the skinny old hag's head, and the whistling was so high and shrill it hurt the ears.

"Call the fire brigade!" cried Mrs Kranky. "Call the police! Man the hose-pipes!"

"Too late," said Mr Kranky, looking pleased.

"Grandma!" shrieked Mrs Kranky. "Mother! Run to the drinking-trough and put your head under the water!"

But even as she spoke, the whistling suddenly stopped and the steam disappeared. That was when Grandma began to get smaller. She had started off with her head as high as the roof of the house, but now she was coming down fast.

"Watch this, George!" Mr Kranky shouted, hopping around the yard and flapping his arms. "Watch what happens when someone's had fifty spoonfuls instead of one!"

Very soon, Grandma was back to normal height. "Stop!" cried Mrs Kranky. "That's just right."

But she didn't stop. Smaller and smaller she got . . . down and down she went. In another half minute she was no bigger than a bottle of lemonade.

"How d'you feel, mother?" asked Mrs Kranky anxiously.

Grandma's tiny face still bore the same foul and furious expression it had always had. Her eyes, no bigger now than little keyholes, were blazing with anger. "How do I *feel*?" she yelled. "How d'you *think* I feel? How would *you* feel if you'd been a glorious giant a minute ago and suddenly you're a miserable midget?"

"She's still going!" shouted Mr Kranky gleefully. "She's still getting smaller!"

And by golly, she was.

When she was no bigger than a cigarette, Mrs Kranky made a grab for her. She held her in her hands and she cried, "How do I stop her getting smaller still?"

"You can't," said Mr Kranky. "She's had fifty times the right amount."

"I *must* stop her!" Mrs Kranky wailed. "I can hardly see her as it is!"

"Catch hold of each end and pull," Mr Kranky said.

By then, Grandma was the size of a matchstick and still shrinking fast.

A moment later, she was no bigger than a pin . . .

Then a pumpkin seed . . .

Then . . .

Then . . .

"Where is she?" cried Mrs Kranky. "I've lost her!"

"Hooray," said Mr Kranky.

"She's gone! She's disappeared completely!" cried Mrs Kranky.

"That's what happens to you if you're grumpy and bad-tempered," said Mr Kranky. "Great medicine of yours, George."

George didn't know what to think.

For a few minutes, Mrs Kranky kept wandering round with a puzzled look on her face, saying, "Mother, where are you? Where've you gone? Where've you got to? How can I find you?" But she calmed down quite quickly. And by lunchtime, she was saying, "Ah well, I suppose it's all for the best, really. She was a bit of a nuisance around the house, wasn't she?"

"Yes," Mr Kranky said. "She most certainly was."

George didn't say a word. He felt quite trembly. He knew something tremendous had taken place that morning. For a few brief moments he had touched with the very tips of his fingers the edge of a magic world.